LEGENDS

A KALIYA SAHNI NOVEL: BOOK FIVE

K.N. BANET

KNBanet.com

1

CHAPTER ONE

MARCH 13TH, 2020

I was sitting alone on my back porch when she walked out and gracefully sat down in the chair beside me. The security system had let me know she was coming, but it was early. She had only texted me ten minutes before, letting me know she wanted to do something tonight. It was a Friday. Everyone partied on Friday, even married or mated women, she had said over text.

"Sorcha, I told you I'm not up for a party. I leave on Monday for India, and I really need to focus on that," I said, not bothering to turn in her direction. I closed my eyes and leaned my head back, the setting sun warming my face. She was my best friend, but that didn't mean I had to jump when she asked. Fae noble and arms dealer or not, I had better things to do than get drunk tonight. "Plus, Raphael will be over in a couple hours. He gets weekends. That's the deal." Normally, he came home with me on Fridays, but since we were leaving on Monday, he was making sure the cambions would be on their best behavior for Cassius and Sorcha.

"He can share for one evening," she said, chuckling as she crossed her long, perfect legs and got more comfortable in the patio chair next to mine. "He and the cambions get you every day. Work-life balance is important."

"Yup. Which is why I'm here, relaxing. I've got a lot on my mind."

"Like what?"

Oh, where do I begin? The hours-long conversation I had with Adhar last night, finalizing our trip details? My long list of responsibilities?

I'll just go with the easy one.

"Planning how I'm going to quit my job and trying to think about all the consequences."

"Which job?" she asked with a laugh. "We both know Raphael won't let you quit."

"Executioner." I narrowed my eyes on her. "Not that I need Raphael's permission to quit working for him. If I didn't want to, I wouldn't, and he knows that."

"You tell yourself that," she teased. "Why are you thinking of leaving the Tribunal? Being an Executioner is a massive part of your life, reputation, and identity."

"I've been on hiatus for over a year, and I don't really want to go back. I need to make it permanent so I can dedicate my time to the people who matter. Raphael needs me. His cambions need me. My people need me. I can't keep running around, trying to die for someone else's cause. I have enough causes of my own. I can't keep leaving the Tribunal hanging, so I should quit."

"You're probably right," she agreed. "Seems like bad timing right now, though. You leave in three days."

"Yeah. I'm going to do it when I get back. Keeping the position for the trip is extra security."

She nodded, then checked her phone casually, smiling as she typed something.

"Cassius know you're here?" I asked nonchalantly.

"He does, not that I need his permission to visit one of my only friends." She gave me a mock glare as she threw my words back at me.

"What's he doing? Normally, you two are inseparable. It's cute." They weren't a codependent couple that smothered each other or couldn't function without each other, but they were rarely apart. It was a healthy partnership, stronger together than apart. They were the best example of a good relationship I had in my life. Seeing one without the other wasn't frequent and made me curious. Sorcha was my best friend, but I had only met her through Cassius, my ex-lover and coworker.

"He's dealing with something before we have to watch over the demon spawn," she explained, using her new pet name for the cambions to make sure I knew she was annoyed with the babysitting job. "Making sure all of his estates can do without him for a month."

"What about your estates?"

"What's his is mine, and what's mine is his. He's doing all of them. He's better at it. As a child, I wasn't educated about managing those things. I'm good with finances, balancing the books, but he's so much better with the people."

"You're not bad with people," I argued, shaking my head. "Don't lie. You can have people eating out of the palm of your hand in minutes. You can manipulate them to do and say things they would rather not. You can back them into verbal corners so effectively, they don't even realize it."

"He's better as a ruler—a king, a prince, a lord, a noble—whatever title you want to use. He's good at that. He was born and raised to be someone's leader. I wasn't. I flew solo for a long time, which is how I developed my skills. I am good at winning a crowd and being the center of attention, but he's better at managing someone's needs and wants, making sure they're happy. That sort of thing."

I hummed in agreement, just wanting to relax. In a few days, I would have too much on my plate. If Sorcha wanted to relax in silence with me, I was cool with that. We sat there, watching the sunset until Sorcha finally broke, as I figured she would. I cracked an eye open.

"You never talked to me about it," she said, leaning over to put her elbows on her knees. It was a surprisingly common position for her. Sorcha wasn't the type to slouch, but she was giving me an intense stare.

"About what?" I asked, frowning. "I thought we talked about what happened last summer. I am sorry for losing my temper with you. Hasn't happened since, and it won't happen again." I was trying. It was fucking hard, but for five months, I didn't lash out at anyone for anything. I didn't keep secrets, not that I had any more to keep.

I'll be a better person, damn it.

"Not about that," she said, clearly frustrated. "Though, in your shoes, I would have snapped at me, too. I meddled in your love life and nearly got both you and Raphael killed. I wasn't a very good friend. I should have listened more, but I thought I was helping."

"We would have gotten to that point eventually without your help, and honestly...it really had nothing to do with you. I lashed out," I said, shrugging. This wasn't the first time we had talked about it, which made me confused why we were again. It was water under the bridge.

"I am incredibly grateful to you for giving me another chance, but that's not what I want to talk about," Sorcha said, huffing indignantly. She leaned back in the chair, waving a hand at me. "We never really talked about *you.*" A shiver ran down my spine as I caught her meaning, and she was right. We had never talked about *it.* "Cassius told me what you told him, but you never bring it up...and I wanted to ask how it might change your trip to India. It's been on my mind. I'm worried...concerned might be a better word. If you don't want to talk to me about it, I would completely understand, but with your trip so close..."

Ah, damn.

"Those are very similar words...worried and concerned," I mumbled, sitting up with a sigh. I wasn't avoiding it, but it wasn't easy to discuss. Raphael and I barely mentioned it. Adhar was the only person I talked to at length about it, but there was little to talk about. "What do you want to know?"

"How...What..." For the first time since I had met, Sorcha was at a loss for words. I chuckled as she grew thoughtful, knowing she was going to hit me with a heavy question right off the bat. I wondered if my willingness to talk about it surprised her.

Likely. Normally, when I don't mention something, it's because I don't want it mentioned at all.

"I read the legend," she whispered, looking at the sunset again. It wasn't the direction I expected her to go.

"Yeah, figured you would. It's readily available in over a dozen languages." Once Cassius knew the whole story, I knew he would have told Sorcha, and Leith was never far. The cambions started digging into everything about my kind whenever they had a spare moment. There wasn't a single one of them who didn't have the story of Kaliya memorized. That it took Sorcha months to bring it up was surprising. "It's...mostly true, though it's written from a human perspective, not a naga's. I try to correct little details, but it's not always enough. The specifics of the magics and stuff, human legend problems."

"Of course. And you..."

"Are his reincarnation. Yup. Named after him because my mother knew." *Thanks for that, Mom.*

"I'm just..." Sorcha shook her head. "Fae don't reincarnate. When we die, our bodies are returned to the fae realms, where the last remnant of our magic is absorbed back into the source of the power. Our bodies become part of the land. We don't rot...we fade. No bodies left behind. We're definitely not reborn. I think I want to understand that part a little more before I voice my thoughts."

I didn't really know what to say to her, but the basics were simple enough, so I started there.

"Every naga after the first generation is a reincarnation of a previously living naga. That's just the way our species works. Originally, a thousand of us were born, and those are the only naga souls in existence. Every new life is given a blank slate to try again at this whole thing called life." I glanced at her, making sure she was following. "There can only be one thousand living nagas because there's really no way to create new ones. Back in the day, if one died, a mated couple would quickly get pregnant and bring that soul back into the world. It worked for a time...until we started dying too fast, and we lost track of who was reincarnated from whom. I am the first reincarnation of the original Kaliya. My soul has lived no other lives, not that I remember or that anyone knows."

"But not every naga knows things like you, right? Cassius said this wasn't normal."

"We're not supposed to remember our past lives, and nobody ever has before me. Hearing the stories or knowing the people...that's different. Learn from the past and all that." I closed my eyes and let memories that weren't truly mine, fly by. When I opened them again, Sorcha was staring at me. "I remember because of witchcraft done by my mother and the witch, Devika," I reminded her, knowing Cassius would have passed that along; he told his wife literally everything. She nodded, clearly following. "Then I forgot, also thanks to witchcraft. My mom bit off more than she could chew, so she had the witch block the memories from me. Mating Raphael started breaking down the spell, which caused blackouts.

"The moment I couldn't fight the truth anymore, it all came back, and I was scared my previous life would swallow this one, but...he died. I'm here, proof of that.

They're just memories. I feel the ghost of feelings, but it doesn't always feel real." I tilted my head to the side, looking into my desert. "It's as though I've memorized every moment of a movie, but with a little something extra. I'll take it over blacking out, though. I don't lose time anymore. Does that help?"

"Very much so. Thank you," she said, nodding. "You seem to handle it rather well, but how will your people react?"

"Adhar is taking it well, but he's the only one who knows," I answered. "He'll be the only one who knows for a while. My past life doesn't have the best reputation, even among the nagas. Wasted potential and tragedy. Tried to outsmart Garuda and got killed by Krishna, making the nagas a new enemy. A depressing failure." I snorted. "Sound like anyone you know?" She gave me what I could only describe as a ghost of a smile, making me realize something was bugging her, and it wasn't the mechanics of reincarnation and how it played out for me. "Sorcha, what are you thinking about?"

"Your current situation reminds me of me, actually. Only a handful of fae know about my origins. You and Raphael are the only two who know who aren't fae. Do you know why?"

"You can't trust the fae..." I answered, furrowing my brows as I tried to work through the confusion she was creating.

"Because you're something *other* like I am." She quickly waved her hands as I raised my brows. "Let me explain. I was handpicked by Oberon and Titania to be altered from a human baby into the fae I am. That might make some people think I'm...more special than they are, especially considering Oberon and Titania are generally absentee parents. They don't interact with their children much, not even their direct ones. It's something King Brion and I spoke about when he finally figured me out, well before he abdicated the throne.

"There are some who would kill me for being even slightly closer to Oberon and Titania than they are. Hell, his own brother tolerates my existence and keeps my secret because it would threaten his power if he didn't. That doesn't mean he likes me. He's the second-born son, and his parents didn't tell him what they had done. Brion went through a similar wave of emotions when I met him. Jealousy is a huge factor in my situation. And...I'm a freak in terms of the fae, being born as a pure human baby. Something *other*." She leaned closer, but I was already beginning to really see what she was trying to say.

"You have the memories of a past life, something nagas aren't supposed to have." She reached out and took my hand, rubbing it with a thumb. "You are also reincarnated from a controversial character from your people's past. You, my friend, are already a very controversial person. You have very little connection to the people you came from. You have powers that were lost, and tell me if I'm wrong, your memories reveal something new about your people, something that was lost to time. The first Kaliya also had a cambion mate, which was what made him so powerful. *You* are vastly more powerful than them. You are something different from them, Kaliya. I want to know if you've really thought about that."

"I hadn't really considered it that way yet." Her words made it a problem, which would bother me now. "I've been more focused on...just going back at all, really." Just planning the trip was a time-consuming task that took months. The rest of my time was considering the implications of the trip and how they would react to seeing me again. The only real distraction I had was training with the cambions or when Raphael didn't let me think at all.

She must have noticed my shift in confidence and humor because her expression turned sad. Letting go of my hand, she covered her face.

"I'm sorry. Don't feel like I'm trying to make you an outcast or something. It's just been on my mind, and I know the dangers of shaking the status quo, even if you don't have a choice in the matter. I just want you to keep that in mind when you see them again...for your safety."

I nodded, then rested my chin on my hands.

"It's not that," I murmured, staring at the land that had been mine for years. I was pensive, thanks to this conversation, though the thoughtful mood had been coming since I sat down. There was so much to think about. "I'm already an outcast. You just made me realize there're layers I hadn't thought about. Don't feel bad. It's good that someone pointed it out to me." When she looked up, I chuckled. "Every naga lives in India, hidden from the rest of the world and never gets seen by the general public. I live as if I'm going to die tomorrow, spouting crazy conspiracy theories, and sound like an

American. Did you think I was a well-respected and loved ruler of my people?"

"Well, no..." she said, a small smile returning.

"See? So, no worries." I shrugged. "I'll deal with them. They'll be freaked out by Raphael, and they don't know me. I don't know them, either. It'll be a learning experience."

"I guess it will be," she agreed. Her smile grew bolder, and a troublemaking glint appeared in her eyes. "If they give you a hard time, tell them your best friend is worse and maybe more powerful than you."

I laughed. "Maybe?"

"Do you want to find out?"

"No, not really," I conceded. I didn't know all of her powers, but I knew enough. This woman was a founder of the Market, the sidhe who could safely wield iron and had the ability to make incredibly powerful magical objects. I didn't *want* to know the full scope of her power. "What a pair we make. The poor men in our lives."

"Poor?" Sorcha gave me a disgusted look. "You mean lucky."

"She does," Raphael interjected. "I am a very lucky man."

2

CHAPTER TWO

I turned quickly to see him standing behind us. I couldn't even guess how he had snuck up on me.

"You're early," I said lamely as he walked up to us, crossing his arms as he surveyed us as though we were committing a crime.

"You seem surprised, which means you weren't paying attention to your security system or our mate bond," he pointed out as he smiled down at me as though he was teasing me, but that didn't mean he wasn't serious. He was lightly reprimanding me for not paying enough attention. "Sorcha, good to see you. Please don't distract her. Her safety means a lot to me."

Down, boy.

"Good to see you, too," Sorcha replied, doing her best impression of a chastised child, but I could see her smirk. "Do you mind if I hang out for a little while longer?"

"He doesn't really get a say," I said darkly, glaring at her. "Stay as long as you like."

"Good," she said, jumping up.

"Wait a minute," Raphael started, but Sorcha put a hand in front of his mouth, earning herself a deep growl from the cambion.

"I told Cassius to bring dinner here," she explained. "He's already on his way."

I couldn't stop a groan as she pranced inside and left us on the back patio.

"Looks like we're entertaining Cassius and Sorcha tonight," I said as I stood up and smiled at my mate. His dark expression wasn't because he didn't like them. Friday night was the first of only three nights we had together every week, and he liked to keep them between us. I was trying to keep my head down, so I allowed it. Besides, I liked having him to myself, pretending as if the outside world didn't exist. "Don't look like that," I teased, reaching up to touch his cheek. "We're leaving for a month and won't have much contact with them. At least Cassius is handling dinner, so we don't have to cook."

His grumbling, incoherent reply only made me grin.

"Consider this revenge," I said lightly as I followed her inside.

"For what?" he asked, moving to keep up with me.

"Being a little overprotective while I'm in my own house. I didn't need to be chastised. I wasn't paying attention, so I missed you coming home, but it was only you. I knew the moment Sorcha got here. I wouldn't have missed an unauthorized visitor to my property. It's a good thing. It means I've learned to let the mate bond go to the back of my mind instead of being the only thing I think about."

Before I could reach the door, he wrapped an arm

around my waist and pulled me against him. It was a cool day in March, making the heat radiating from him perfect. I leaned back into his hold.

"I *want* to be the only thing you think about," he murmured huskily in my ear. The heat between us turned up several degrees, and I knew he was trying to woo me into sending Sorcha away instead of letting her stay and wait for Cassius. Raphael had an insatiable appetite for anything that involved us partially or fully naked. It was the only thing we did when he came over for the weekends.

"How am I supposed to stay safe if I'm only thinking about seeing you and taking your clothes off?" I asked patiently. Now that he was here, it wasn't a good idea if I just ignored that Sorcha was in my house or Cassius was already on his way over.

No. We can entertain friends for one night. All we ever do now is have sex, damn it, and we're leaving in only a handful of days.

"Point made." He chuckled, nodding as he let me go. "What were you and Sorcha talking about? I only caught part of it. Something about who was more powerful."

"Oh..." I let my shoulders slump. "About me and *that*. She wanted to talk to me about it, about how my people may react. I can see where she's coming from. She brought up some solid points about continuing to keep it a secret from the other nagas. I was already planning to, but..." I looked over my shoulder at him and watched his full lips open, then close again. His brows furrowed as he considered what he wanted to say, and I nearly laughed as he repeated the process two more times.

"Just spit it out," I ordered.

"I was going to accuse you of overthinking everything," he said cautiously, rubbing the back of his neck. "But I know better than to say that because you always overthink, yet you're almost always the one with the correct solution. You see pieces of the puzzle I don't, and you know more. So, I've learned to trust your instincts. Sorcha is who-knows-how-old, and I'm not stupid enough to say she overthinks things, either, which means you two must have thought of something important if you agree. There's really nothing to say, I guess. They're your people, but all the cambions know..."

"Do you trust them?" I asked, crossing my arms. "Your cambions?"

"With everything...my life, yours, our secrets."

"Then I do. Plus, you can always give them a gag order, or I can find a witch powerful enough to do a geas. Hopefully, the magic would work on them. Maybe we can test it on someone. I don't want that, though. I trust them." It was a work in progress, but I was putting my money where my mouth was. I was going to trust them until they proved otherwise. Then I would go with more extreme measures. There was another piece of the puzzle as well. "Besides, this can't be permanent. Eventually, my people will need to know. Then it won't matter who knows because most supernaturals on the planet really won't care if I'm some legendary figure reborn. Some of them probably are themselves. Really, the secrecy is just for me. It's...a lot."

"I know," he said gently, reaching to touch my white hair, and stared intently at it. "We can postpone this trip."

"No," I said, shaking my head. "Someone will have to die in the next three days to keep us from getting on that plane. Beyond the fact it took three months to plan everything, I have to do this. After what happened last year, I've put it off for too long." Most of the trip was formalities. The other nagas needed to know who Raphael was, and he needed to know them. They were tied together now for as long as I lived. Also, it was unfair to my people that I was busy helping rule someone else. I needed to show my face.

"Are the rakshasas giving them trouble?"

Then there's that. I was hoping we wouldn't get to that until we got on the plane.

"Adhar says he's heard some complaints through the grapevines." I almost didn't continue, but in the interest of trying to be a better person and worthy of this mate of mine, I explained more. "He's expecting an official letter any day to ask me to show my face to the new rulers as they scramble to replace the royal family. The only reason we've had the time we've had was thanks to the chaos. It's settling, and any good ruler will get justice for the previous ruling family. I'm enemy number one right now, and if the nagas don't want an all-out war, they'll hand me over for some sort of trial...or maybe an execution, but Adhar wouldn't agree to those terms. He would agree to a trial if he knew it would go in our favor. He'll probably get a formal request the moment they confirm I've entered India."

Raphael's eyes narrowed as he leaned very close to my face.

"When did he tell you that?"

"Last night during a three-hour phone call. I was planning to tell you, but we've had a bit of a busy day, and we try to focus on training when I'm at the compound. So, I was waiting for dinner...or when we were already on the plane."

"Kaliya—"

"Look, I'm telling you now because I know you deserve to know. They will *not* execute me. My case is solid, and if I have to kill a few more of them to deal with it, I will. Trial by combat will be the choice made, considering the circumstances of my crimes, and one rakshasa can't beat me. I have to do this, or I leave the other nagas vulnerable." I reached up and patted his cheeks gently. "I'll be fine. We'll be fine. Everything will be fine. This is politics. Messy politics, but they tried to kill me, so I killed them. Self-defense doesn't work as an airtight defense since they're not a species with the Tribunal, but it will count in my favor. I'll have to do this the hard way, but the self-defense claim gets me a chance to fight my way out of it. I won't lose."

"I guess I should be grateful you've thought it out."

"I won't go *that* far," I mumbled, shrugging. "But it would be nice to be recognized for my intelligence and—"

He leaned in and kissed me, leaving me breathless and speechless.

"Does that work?" he asked as he released me and walked inside. It took me a moment to realize what happened. He'd caught me off guard and run.

Laughing, I walked after him in no rush. Sorcha was playing on my television, and Raphael quickly jumped to her side to help pick a movie. Ignoring them, I opted to shower and put on fresh clothes. I had come home and gone straight to sit out back. That neither of them pointed out my sweatiness was a testament to our friendship.

"Please don't pick anything so sweet and romantic, I need to see a dentist," I called out as I headed to the back of my house. I had to work to reach my room, moving through the growing pile of suitcases. Raphael and I each packed three for the month-long trip, and it still wasn't enough. At some point, I would have to do laundry while we were on the damn trip. I tried not to think about that as I dumped my dirty clothes on the floor and showered. The trip was three days away, and there were a hundred things I still needed to do before we left. I had no reason to fret over the chores I would have to do while in another country.

Feeling safe, I didn't rush to finish when I heard Cassius arrive. When I was clean, dressed, and presentable, I headed out to see them already sitting at the table. No one was eating, as Sorcha and Cassius had manners that dictated they wait for me. Raphael was eyeing the food as they talked, but he was patient and cunning. I smiled as he moved the dishes he liked closer to his section of the table, rearranging everything to fit his needs. The smell in the air told me that Cassius had hit up a local Hawaiian barbeque place I loved. It was an affordable way to buy a lot of food, which was always helpful when Raphael was at the table.

For a moment, I just watched.

I was hit with a pang of sadness that for the next

month, I wouldn't see all of us together. Even with all the shit the four of us had gone through, the mistakes we all made, it was nice to know they were my friends.

"It's good to see you," Cassius said, looking over his shoulder at me. "Are you going to sit down? I brought some of your favorites."

Well, all the mistakes Raphael, Sorcha, and I have made. Mister Perfect has never screwed up. Now he's bribing me with food for some reason.

"I see that," I said as I approached the table. "Why are you trying to butter me up? Is this when you finally break and give Sorcha what she wants? Are we all going to become swingers now or something?" I was expecting a blush, but he laughed.

"Oberon, no," he answered. "Sit down and eat something. We just wanted to spend the evening with you two. You'll both be busy all weekend, won't you?"

"Raphael will be. Everything I need to do is done except some stuff around the house," I said with a smile. Raphael groaned. "You should have finished today if you didn't want to go back this weekend."

"I won't be the only one busy," he grumbled. "Cassius, you'll be meeting me there tomorrow, right?"

"Yes, which is why I'll be staying here for the night," he said.

I only laughed at my mate's expression.

3

CHAPTER THREE

After dinner, I went back outside, bringing a drink with me to stare at the stars. There wasn't too much light pollution, which allowed a beautiful view of the stars whenever the cloud cover was nonexistent, which was most nights. I was still thoughtful, even after dinner and the movie. It seemed like the perfect night to stare at the stars.

I wasn't alone for more than five minutes before Cassius came out. For a moment, he just stood next to me, nursing a glass of water.

"Ready for that trip of yours?" he asked blandly as if I went back to my homeland often, and there was nothing special about the trip.

"Sure," I answered, trying not to dwell on it. "I would be more ready if it was already time to leave, and I didn't have to think about it. Weeks of planning have made it seem like a much bigger deal than it probably is."

"You realize every criminal in the world has already heard about it, right?"

That made me frown as I turned to him. "Excuse me?"

"The private plane you're taking for the trip. One of them leaked you'll be flying to India. They didn't leak the plane, the date, or any other details, only the destination. Everyone knows Kaliya Sahni is going home. I was told this morning through a friend in Atlanta who monitors the company you're using and their associates." He put his drink down on the small patio table and sighed. "There's been no threats against you. You'll have a safe trip. That's been handled."

"You weren't managing your estates today, were you?"

"It wasn't me," he countered with a small smile. "My wife still has her contacts, and she put the word out for them to ignore your trip unless they wanted a fight they couldn't win. It'll keep you safe until you step foot in India. We can't do much once you're there. Our political power doesn't reach that far."

"Well, damn," I mumbled, downing the rest of my whiskey. "Is that her way of continuing to apologize for last year? You can tell her it's—"

"No. It's because you and Raphael are our only friends," he said, his smile refusing to budge as he turned back to the stars. "Part of her is amazed you even speak to her. When I picked you up that day and heard what you had been through, I wouldn't have been surprised if you shut the world out and never spoke to anyone again."

"I would never cut her out for what happened last year. She meddled, but she was trying to give me something no one else ever had. She wanted her friend to be happy and loved."

"Sorcha chases a normalcy we'll never have," he said, a sad expression flying over his face. "She wants it more than anything else. She wants to have friends and normal problems...She and I argued about it, with me saying as a friend, she should respect your wishes. She thought a good friend would help you find happiness in a world that was often cruel. We were both right, but she refused to acknowledge any of your concerns because she was chasing some sort of normalcy she can't have. It wasn't all about you."

"That's why I forgave her. I was angry, but I really understand why she meddled, and it doesn't erase the problems, but her friendship means a lot to me." I closed my eyes. "Looking back, I think the best thing she's ever said to me was that she didn't like that I think of myself as broken. That meant something, even though I fought it. She had faith in me finding happiness I never had for myself. That's why her friendship means more to me than her mistakes."

"I know that, and you know that, but they don't," he said, pointing over his shoulder to the two inside. "They haven't known you long enough to know you're chasing something you can have, and you run from it because it's safer for them."

"Yeah," I whispered.

I didn't know what those two were up to, and normally, when they got together, it was trouble for someone. Everyone thought Sorcha and I were the deadly duo, but truthfully, it was Sorcha and Raphael.

Trouble for Cassius and me to clean up.

"If I cut anyone out of my life, it would have been

him," I said, shaking my head in dismay. "He was the one who called me paranoid and ignored my feelings, thinking he could just...handle it all. Like none of it was serious or dangerous or...you know." Part of me was still aching over those words, his admission of his dismissal and how it all played out. It still hurt when I thought about it too long.

"Yes, of course." Something shifted, and his expression changed, the smile fading to a somber look I knew all too well. "Look, I haven't wanted to pry, but how are you two? I know the system you have right now is working for you, but this is an entire month out of the country. It's going to be a huge test on your mating, your partnership. I know you've lived together for some time, but that was before...everything. His memories coming back, the mating..."

I took my time trying to find the right thing to say. Raphael and I had a complicated situation, and if I said anything wrong, Cassius would worry.

"We're good when we ignore what happened last October. I see him at the cambion compound. Training is going really well. He's watchful and attentive, and it's easy to work with him. When we're here, we just...live in each other. I have to milk my venom once a week if I don't want to be uncomfortable, so that takes most of the weekend. That's one reason we don't see you and Sorcha as often right now. We're...busy. Sex and work don't make a relationship, does it?"

"No, it doesn't."

We were both thinking about the relationship we had once had. Sex, alcohol, and work was what Cassius and I had shared. It had brought us close as people, but it was also a toxic disaster. We were both angry and depressed people, self-destructing our only option. He'd been the smart one, getting out before it got to that point. It forced me to clean up my act a little, which only meant I quit drinking so much and threw myself back into work and hunting bounties.

Which was how I found Raphael.

"We flirt and we're good in each other's company. It feels easy, but we haven't..." I changed course, not finding the right words to continue that train of thought. "Part of me doesn't really believe it's real, you know? We don't live together full time. In five months, we've turned into a casual sex relationship. We don't have the time or energy to go on dates. It feels easy, but it doesn't feel...complete. Something is off, and I can't put my finger on it. A month out of the country might make it worse, but it might help us. Or we'll stay the same, only this time, I'll be busy ruling, and he'll be stuck on the sidelines, waiting for me to have time for him." I kicked a rock off my patio, staring at the desert as I continued. "He's apologized for all of it, but..."

"You're not moving past it," he whispered.

"Not completely," I confirmed. "Cassius, he hurt me so much. Hearing him dismiss me, calling me paranoid... it burned. Of all the people, my mate dismissed me."

"Has he done it since?"

"No." Something I was grateful for. "I love him. That must count for something, right?"

"I like to think it does. He's most certainly in love with you."

"I know." There was no denying the love there. I would die for him, and he would die for me. I would fight to keep him by my side for eternity, and he wasn't letting me go any time soon, not that he could if he wanted to.

It was everything else that was the problem. Maybe it was just me.

It could very well just be me. I've never done this long-term committed thing before.

"While you're gone, I'll oversee the final wave of construction in the compound." Cassius shuffled about as if he was suddenly uncomfortable. "The mansion will be done before you get back. That means you'll be moving in with him and the cambions full time, right?"

"He and I haven't talked about that."

"You helped design the thing, and you haven't talked with him about moving into it?" He sounded incredulous, which wasn't surprising.

"When he and I mated, it was already an uncomfortable topic. It was moving really fast for me, when I've gotten used to living alone in my own space, without people trying to manage me all the time. Hell, compound lifestyle is one of the things I ran away from in India. I helped design the mansion, but we never talked about move-in dates. I've...been avoiding it. I think he has been too. Maybe it's too close of a conversation about how this all happened. We had to arrange this whole thing, and some cambions weren't happy with me, but they're happy for Raphael. Sammy still doesn't talk to me outside of training because I lied to her. So, no, we haven't talked about it. We designed the mansion, sent the plans to that stupid fucking werewolf, then promptly never brought it up again." Frustrated, I ran a hand through my hair. "Look, it's complicated. I don't know what else you want me to say."

"I want to know if you're happy." There was an earnest note in his words that made me close my eyes.

That's a hell of a question, Cassius.

"Honestly? I've had so much on my mind, I don't know," I whispered. "We have good moments. We have nothing moments, moments where we just exist. There are no really bad—"

"But you don't know if you're happy."

"Cassius, there's just been a lot. I know it's been five months, but...happy hasn't been the objective recently. Work, this trip, the cambion home..."

"If you've been trying to ease my worries, you have done so poorly," he said softly, the breeze almost overpowering his words.

"It was the goal, but I think I gave up on it five minutes ago," I countered, smiling a little. "He's not a bad man, but the last five months have flown by. I don't think we've found our footing, not really. We survive and make each other smile when we see each other, but I don't know if I'm happy, not with the way things are right now. It might not even be him. It could be a combination of everything, and he just happens to be the closest thing. It's not like I'm *unhappy*. I just don't know if this is what I want in my life because I haven't had the time to think about it. I haven't had a real chance to process fucking anything."

"You haven't talked to him about any of this, have you?"

"Not at all."

Cassius let the silence stretch out. I would have worried about Sorcha or Raphael hearing me, but I knew Raphael wasn't in the living room anymore. He was in our bathroom, I assume taking a shower before turning in for the night. Sorcha was cleaning up my living room, and her hearing wasn't supernatural.

"Why not?" Cassius demanded.

"Because it terrifies me. Because telling him I'm not sure if I'm happy would really hurt him. It's such a big thing to talk about when we have ten million other things going on. We're about to go to India for a month. The compound is continuing to grow, and training with the cambions has gotten intense. They're advancing faster than I thought they would. I've got the Tribunal on my mind as well. Do you really think now is the time?"

"It's the relationship you're in for the rest of your life. The timing of an important conversation doesn't really matter. It just needs to happen."

"I'll get to it," I promised softly, groaning. "Look, why don't you go kiss your wife goodbye and get some sleep? Actually...why isn't she staying the night, too?"

"Because of my pureblood and my need to maintain a connection to the fae lands, I won't be able to stay at the compound every night. She will be. She deserves a few more nights in her own bed, and I didn't want to make an early morning drive out here.

"Also, if you quit working for the Tribunal, make sure you give me a heads-up beforehand. I want to be at that meeting, and I'll need to clear my schedule." He gave me a smile then headed inside, leaving me chuckling. It would be a hell of a meeting. There would be more than one of the Tribunal members glad to see me leave.

Once I was certain Cassius was heading to bed and Sorcha was gone, I went inside and headed for my bedroom. Raphael was already in bed, playing on his phone as he waited on me. He never went to sleep before I got in bed, something I found both endearing and a bit over the top.

"Do you want to milk your venom this weekend?" he asked clinically. He didn't seem excited, which told me something was off.

"No. I want to be ready for anything on this trip. If the arrival goes smoothly, I'll milk when we're secure in India." I tried to sound professional, as though his new attitude didn't bother me.

"Okay."

I got into bed with a yawn, resisting the urge to curl into him. He wasn't having any of that, putting his phone down and rolling to wrap his arms around me.

"Sorcha told me what Cassius said he was going to talk to you about," he said, burying his face in my hair.

Well, that explains everything.

"About the leak?"

"Yeah, I don't like it. I think we should cancel or postpone. I don't like criminals knowing what we're doing or where we're going. It's going to bug me."

"We can't," I reminded him. "I think you're more worried about meeting my people than you are about a little danger. This is the second time today and the ninth time this week you've tried to find a reason to move this trip." I moved to kiss his jaw and sighed. "The days when you could move in the world as an unknown ended a long time ago, Raphael. People have known what you're doing and where you're going since you first got Mygi's attention, the day you met the Tribunal, or the day you introduced the cambions to them. There's always going to be someone monitoring where you go and what you do. If I made a few calls, I could get you the schedule for Wagner for the next week. That's our life. We have to go now because if we cancel, they're going to think we're scared. That's the last thing we want."

He groaned but didn't argue.

I cozied up to him, nuzzling his chest and weaving my legs with his. His hand ran down my back and over the curve of my ass.

4

CHAPTER FOUR

The day came too fast. I woke up early Monday, getting out of bed before Raphael realized what was happening. Today, we were getting on a plane. I had stayed home all weekend, checking our bags, packing extra weapons, and finally, the pieces of my people. I was finishing up my check of those when Raphael appeared in the living room. Everything had to be packed perfectly. I would not risk anything breaking during the flights from Phoenix to San Francisco, then to New Delhi. It was going to be a long day of travel.

And them, those pieces of my people.

"You're taking those back home?" he asked, unsurprised. He knew what this was.

"Yeah. They need to go home, too," I whispered, running my fingers over the only obscene thing I could see—a snakeskin purse made from a naga. "Maybe some of them can be identified. Most of it will be burned, but I...I've always wanted to take them home." Under the purse, there were things that would make some gag, if not throw up. Pieces of my people, finally going home just like me. "This trip is also for them. Maybe I can finally bring them justice or peace."

"If you need help, let me know," he said gently, touching my shoulder before he grabbed two of our bags and walked out. My BMW would be cramped for the drive to the airport.

I closed up the crate and followed Raphael, loading it in on the bottom so the duffel bags could sit on it. It took an hour to load the car so nothing would fall on us in the front seats. We were silent as we closed the trunk and gathered our last two bags, our small carry-ons, which would hopefully be enough to keep us occupied for the near twenty-four hours of plane rides.

As we loaded in for the last drive we'd take in Arizona for a long time, my chest grew tight, but I ignored it. I let Raphael drive, rubbing my chest without thinking as we took the fastest route to the airport possible, Raphael speeding on top of that.

Too fast. This is happening too fast.

I tried to shove the thought aside. Months of planning flew by, and now I had to do this. My palms grew clammy, and my mouth was dry.

We should turn around. I don't want to do this.

I closed my eyes and took a deep breath, trying to will myself to relax. Of all the times to get anxiety, now was a bad one.

I should have expected this. I can manage. Once we're on the plane, there won't be any turning back.

"Kaliya? Are you okay? You're breathing a little heavy, and you're sweating."

Of course he noticed.

"I have a bit of anxiety," I explained, trying to focus on slowing my heart rate and stopping the new shake in my hands.

"We can postpone."

I opened one eye to glare at him.

"It's going to be fine. Once I'm on the plane, it should go away. It's just nerves."

"Seems like a lot more than nerves," he mumbled, shaking his head. "Should just postpone until you're ready."

"You know what? We're visiting your mother next and seeing how well you deal with it," I snapped. He growled in return. For a long time, we pretended as if his human family didn't exist, but I was feeling cranky and more than a little petty about his postponing talk. He didn't want to go on this trip, and it was bugging me, but he also wouldn't let me go alone.

We'd had this roundabout conversation several times a day now...ten times. He asked ten times over the weekend to postpone or cancel the trip. I was done hearing it.

"Let's not," he snarled.

We finished the drive in silence. When we parked at the airport, I jumped out, grateful for the fresh air as I walked up to the pilot and small staff of the chartered private plane.

"We need to talk," I snapped, making sure they realized I was there for them. "I heard that part of my itinerary was leaked. Is this going to be a problem going forward, or should I hire another company right now?"

Eyes went wide as Raphael came up beside me, adding his imposing force of nature to the weight of my angry questions. If there was one thing he and I were good at, it was intimidating people. Not a single supernatural-run organization in Arizona didn't know about us and how far we would go to get what we needed. Wagner had to tell his entire pack to stop trying to step on our toes. Imani banned the vampires from going within fifty feet of the cambions. Now, I was turning it on a group of humans who ran a company that often catered to supernaturals.

We're going to have a reputation if I'm not careful, but damn I am tired of this bullshit.

"W-We f-fired the s-source of the l-leak," someone explained. He was pale and fearful as he stepped in front of the others. "Only d-destination country was r-released. The rest of y-your itinerary is secure," he continued, rubbing his hands together.

"Thank you," I said with a smile, trying to soften my expression and my voice. "Raphael, will you unload the car so they can load the plane?"

"Sure. I'm glad everything is cleared up," he said, also going to a more friendly sounding version of himself. It wasn't fake. Raphael could be overbearing and dangerous, but he was also a really nice guy, almost a gentle giant if he liked someone. I knew that wouldn't matter to the humans in front of me, but it mattered to me. Every day, that part of him disappeared a little more, overshadowed by his warlord nature and his responsibilities.

"Thank you," I said, touching his arm before he had

the chance to walk away. He gave me a smile and left me with the humans. Two followed him with nothing but strong arms, and a third pushed a cart, much like you would see at a hotel.

"Would you like a refreshment while you wait?" a woman asked me. "You're clear to load now. We prepped the plane for your arrival."

"Actually, I want to take a walk around the plane," I answered, heading for it. She followed me, hovering as I checked everything. I knew little about planes, but a short call to Hisao had given me a brush-up on how to check for tampering. It wasn't something I used to do, often flying commercial. Now, I didn't feel confident in anything that involved strangers.

I was growing more paranoid, but no one I knew was stupid enough to say that to my face. As they loaded the plane, I went over the mental checklist Hisao had taught me. I took my time, my anxiety coming back as I walked around—sweaty palms, shallow breathing, accelerated pulse.

This plane is going to fly me home.

Part of me hoped I would find something wrong, but the other part didn't because the sooner I got through the trip, the easier future trips would be. It was time for me to return. There was a long list of things I had to deal with, and I couldn't put them off any longer.

The small wish something would be wrong persisted until I finished my check of the jet, then stepped back, sighing.

"Looks good," I said finally. "Tell whoever needs to

hear it, but I'm glad you take such good care of your aircraft," I said to the woman still hovering beside me.

"We hold ourselves to higher safety standards than the commercial airlines because the safety of our clientele is important to us, Miss Sahni."

"Good," I said softly, then walked around the plane once more to get to the stairs. Raphael was waiting for me as the three humans who helped him moved away from the plane. The pilot and his co-pilot were already in the plane, with the pilot waiting for us to come up so he could properly greet us.

"Are you ready?" Raphael asked, looking over my face.

"Yeah, go on up," I said, swallowing the lump in my throat.

He gave me one last concerned look before heading up the stairs and shaking the pilot's hand.

My feet were planted to the ground, and while Raphael could have just hauled me, I wanted to face this myself.

I was leaving Phoenix, which was not an irregular occurrence. The Tribunal sent me all over the country when they had trials and didn't have time to make a door for me. I had traveled all over the world.

This trip was to India, a place that was more than just my homeland. It was the place where my parents died, the place that made me feel small. I had either been shoved away like a delicate princess or a poor orphan trying to survive. I had never had power in that place.

I looked down at myself, not seeing a scared little girl's body but the woman I had become. I was going back to my people as a new person. As Sorcha said, I was *other*.

I wasn't the girl who had run away. I wasn't even the rumors and stories they heard about my movements.

It was time for me to return.

With one last deep breath of the arid air I loved so much, I boarded the plane. I shook the pilot's hand with a smile, then walked into the luxurious passenger section. It wasn't a large plane. It had a skeleton crew and was designed for long, intimate flights for the wealthiest people in the world. There was a way to turn some of the chairs into beds, and the bathroom even had a shower. There were tables for food and activities, screens to watch movies, and a state-of-the-art mini bar ready for entertainment. I was certain they had entire meals prepped for us as well. I couldn't remember everything from the amenities section of the contract.

"Kaliya—"

"It's too late to postpone," I said as I sat across from Raphael. "How do you like the plane?"

"It's nice, and I wasn't going to say we can postpone," he said with a bite. "I was going to ask if you were okay. You've been off since you got up this morning."

I looked into his chocolate brown eyes, seeing the warmth and worry. Across from me wasn't the fuck-buddy mate I saw in recent days, but the man I had fallen in love with.

"I'm not," I admitted, crossing my legs under the table and looking out the window. "But I will be. Once I get there and confront everything I left behind, I will be." After a moment, I decided it was time to get into whatever he was thinking. "What about you? You've been against this trip. Are you okay?"

"Do...do you think they'll accept me?" he asked softly.

I blinked several times in shock as I turned back to him.

"Is that what you've been worried about?"

"Well, I see what you deal with when it comes to my people, and...yes, Kaliya, that's one of things I've been worried about."

"Oh." I went for blunt. "No, they won't accept you."

"You say that like it's inevitable," he said with a smile that told me he was trying to mask a myriad of other feelings.

"It is," I said with a shrug. "It's not because you're... what you are." I sighed. "It's because you're with me. It's how they've been my entire life. Once I didn't follow the plan they wanted me to follow. Once it was seen I wasn't the mate of another naga, I wasn't good enough anymore."

"Kaliya..."

"I'm not scared of India; I'm scared of the people in it," I admitted softly, voicing the source of my anxiety. "I'm scared of how they are very good at making me feel small. And how nothing I ever do will be enough for them because it wasn't what they wanted from me. They'll think you're powerful and strong, a wonderful new ally who couldn't possibly betray us, but you'll be at my side, and they'll hold it against you."

"If that's how it's going to be,"—Raphael leaned forward—"fuck them. I'll always pick you. I don't need their approval or acceptance."

I smiled, feeling more confident about the trip as the doors were closed and the stairs were rolled away. I took his hand, feeling a bit of hope about the trip. Maybe this was exactly what he and I needed.

"Thank you."

We were silent as an attendant gave us a quick safety briefing. We listened dutifully, then took the drinks offered as the plane moved into position. I got a water while Raphael got a beer. Since it wasn't a commercial flight, there weren't any rules about drinks. So long as we kept our hands on things, they wouldn't spill. Moments later, the plane was on the runway, and we were taking off.

I watched Arizona disappear and settled into my seat for the long trip ahead.

I'm going home.

5

CHAPTER FIVE

It was the most boring trip of my life and one of the longest, but we eventually landed in New Delhi. The only thing that saved me from being cramped and in pain were the chairs folded up and gave me space to stretch, and I had forced Raphael to join me.

"How do you feel?" I asked him as we touched down, the plane bouncing around a little as it slowed to a more manageable speed. "Any soreness?"

"No. Stretching every four hours was a pretty good idea," he said with a smile. "Plus, being able to sleep in a real bed probably didn't hurt either."

"Good. Our trip is going to be pretty dangerous until we are secured, so I wanted you—"

"You wanted me ready for anything. I know. Kaliya, this is the tenth time you've tried to brief me as if we're about to go on a mission for the military. We're visiting your family, not going to war...yet," he added, sighing and shaking his head. "Just stop treating this as though we're about to drop into a war zone, please."

I narrowed my eyes, and he threw up his hands.

"Or continue to do just that. Whatever makes you comfortable," he said, trying to sound patient and nice, but there was a tenseness in his face. He was getting frustrated with me, and he was right to. This was actually the twelfth time I tried to make sure he knew exactly what to do when we got off the plane.

"We're not going to rent a car. We've already hired a human to drive us to a location, then we have to do a little hiking, and..." I trailed off as he stared at me, bags under his eyes. We had slept, but planes were exhausting even with that. We still had one more plane ride, though thankfully, it was much shorter. "Yeah, just follow my lead."

"I will," he promised. "I won't talk to anyone, and I won't wander off with any strangers. If we see any other supernaturals, I'll pretend to ignore them unless they bother us."

"And I'm going to keep an eye out for anyone following us," I said, nodding.

I stood up as the plane rolled to a stop. The attendants waited at the door, and once the stairs were connected, I took my carry-on from Raphael and walked off the plane, waving to the staff as I went. They had been really nice for the long journey. They were also my way home. Playing nice would only help me in the end.

As a few men took our luggage off the plane, I saw the ride I hired. I had gone through the same company Adhar used to get Nakul and the witch who helped in that situation. He trusted the company, and since he lived in the country, I trusted the company. The driver jumped out and helped load our suitcases and the crate into the back, frowning at how much there was. I nearly said something, but really, the only thing I could think about was how humid it was compared to Arizona. While I took in the fact that I was back in my homeland, Raphael was talking to the plane's staff and the driver.

"Thank you so much for the smooth flight." Then he turned to the driver. "Is there enough space for everything?"

"Yes, yes," the driver said quickly in English with a thick accent that brought tears to my eyes. It wasn't like Adhar's, bringing back different memories. The nagas had a slightly different accent, probably developed over the years of isolation. There was something distinct about the accent of those from New Delhi. "Come. It's not safe to stay in the open." Hearing the accent of the locals sent me back to the time I fended for myself after witnessing my family murdered. I had been running for my life, and it had been the first time I interacted with humans.

I sighed, turning to look at the driver. I hadn't expected to be dumbstruck the moment I got off the plane, but I wasn't surprised.

The cry of an eagle overhead made me shiver, but I ignored it. Birds of prey were always a source of instinctual fear for my kind. Even in Arizona, I was a little weird about the natural birds of prey, especially since my memories of my previous life had returned. He had never tried to desensitize to the sound, and his fear came through, along with my own. Now, I was jumpier about the noise and had to restrain myself.

"You're right," I said, walking to them. "Let's go." My English was more American, but only because I had trained myself to sound like that. Like an actor that could play roles, I long figured out how to erase most of the evidence that I had come from this country or from any specific place. If I wanted to, I could sound as if I was born and raised in London, Spain, or France. I couldn't erase the physical appearance I inherited, but I could erase the accent of my homeland, so I had.

We loaded into the van, and he raced off. The city was barely recognizable. I had seen photos over the years, but being on the streets of New Delhi differed from pictures. The last time I had been on the streets, cars hadn't filled the lanes. The wealthiest of people probably had one, but they had been exceptionally rare. Part of me felt as if I had time traveled. This wasn't the city where I had once run in the streets, a dirty orphan child trying to stay alive. I had jumped forward a hundred years, and nothing was recognizable. New Delhi had just become the capital, thanks to the British.

Shit, I am an Indian from the colonial period. Fucking weird.

I huffed at the changes the last century had brought as our driver took us out of the city. He was rambling on about something, and I knew Raphael was listening, but I was staring out my window, watchful of anything and everything.

"Kaliya, do you want to see the Taj Mahal?" Raphael asked.

"No," I answered simply. "Not today, at least. We'll be

back in the city before our trip is over, and I'll make sure we see it, but not right now."

"It's a date," he said, turning back to the driver. "Thanks for the recommendation. I did some research and knew it was here, but I hadn't really thought about going."

"Why come to India if not to see the sights?" our driver asked.

"He's meeting his in-laws," I answered with a sharp smile. "I'm bringing an American home. He should be focused on that."

The driver laughed. "Adhar says you haven't been in India since you were young. They can't be too surprised. You even sound like an American."

"I've been away a long time," I confirmed in Hindi with perfect pronunciation, the language of my birth. One of my parents forced me to learn English very young, thanks to the language's growing dominance over the world. I could also speak passable Punjabi and Urdu, thanks to their prevalence in the region. I'd had to learn if I wanted to survive on the streets. I saw his shock in the rearview mirror, then he gave me an appreciative nod.

"What did you say?" Raphael whispered. "You don't have to tell me, but..."

"I'll have to teach you Hindi," I said with a chuckle. He gave a sharp nod. I had been joking, but he was serious, which touched me. "I was telling him I had been away a long time."

"We could have postponed, so I had time to learn."

"It would take years, and we don't have years to postpone this trip," I said, patting his thigh. "Everyone in my family speaks English, so don't worry too much. There won't be a language barrier unless they're talking behind your back. If that happens, I'll be there to call them on it. I won't let them be snide or rude to you."

"I can speak passable Spanish," he offered, frowning. "Do any of them know that?"

"Not at all," I said, shrugging. "Only me and only enough to get by." Thinking about it, I realized the list of languages I could converse in was getting long—English, Hindi, Punjabi, Urdu, Japanese, and Spanish. "They've never had a reason to learn it. It's not a language spoken here."

"Yeah..." Raphael sighed. "Why didn't I think of this problem earlier?"

"You and I have been really busy. When were you supposed to learn Hindi? While you stayed up all night, looking over contracts and financial reports or during our weekends?"

"Fair." He leaned back, trying to stretch his legs in the cramped van. "How many languages are spoken here?"

"A lot. Hindi, Punjabi, English, and Urdu are the top four. There are at least half a dozen more as well. Many people speak Hinglish and Punglish, mixes of Hindi or Punjabi with English, using words from each to create something more people can understand."

"Like Spanglish?" Raphael laughed, shaking his head in disbelief. "Wow."

"Yeah, exactly like Spanglish."

"Are you sure there are no sights you want to see before I take you to the drop-off point?" the driver asked.

"Positive," I said. "We really need to get settled before we sightsee."

Raphael asked questions about the city and the surrounding area as we drove. Nothing looked familiar to me anymore, but I tried to teach him.

As the van slowed to our destination, Raphael groaned. I knew he wasn't looking forward to the next part of the trip. While my parents had lived relatively close to New Delhi, which was why I was so familiar with it, the other nagas recently moved onto their properties in Assam, a decently long trip from New Delhi. Since I was afraid of tails, I had to be careful about flying directly into the country too close to their location. That made our trip more arduous than it needed to be and why it took so much planning to achieve.

"Do you need any help?" our driver asked, looking through the seats at us.

"You can go," I said with a smile. "We've got it from here."

Jumping out, we unloaded. I waved the driver to leave and sat down on a suitcase.

"You said there was a bit of a hike here, and I'm strong, but I don't think I can get all of this to wherever we need to be next." Raphael crossed his arms, sighing at the suitcases. "The crate, while important, is actually the hardest part. I don't know what to do. Are we making multiple trips?"

"No," I answered, checking a small watch I put on just for this. "Just wait twenty minutes with me. Stretch your legs. We've been cramped for too long."

He did as I asked, casting wary glances around us. We were well and truly alone, but it wouldn't be for long.

Time ticked by. I joined Raphael and stretched. He snuck in a kiss, making me smile as we listened to the noises of the world around us. I wrapped my arms around his waist and closed my eyes, letting the moment seem more perfect than it really was.

A twig snapped. Raphael tensed in my arms, but I stayed relaxed as I pulled away and checked my watch again.

"You're quiet, but you're not that quiet," I called out softly, the peace of the moment broken. "The only way to sneak up on a snake is to be a snake, and you are no great serpent."

"Ah, I am not, but I have had many more years of practice at it than you have," Adhar answered, revealing himself, walking to us casually. Behind him, Nakul followed with a smile. Raphael visibly relaxed, but I noticed there was still a tenseness to him. He was trying to pull off the ready-but-not-ready act, I was very good at. I ignored it and went to the two nagas. "It's good to see you two. The trip has been long."

"I'm glad we could meet you," Adhar said. We didn't shake hands. There were a few ways to greet him that would have been proper, so I chose the simplest and most common. I brought my hands together in front of my heart and bowed my head. Adhar and Nakul returned the gesture. Then I looked back at Raphael, and he obliged with grace, as I had taught him.

Adhar looked around us and frowned at our suitcases. "Maybe I should have brought another pair of hands."

"Sorry. I was thinking about how to prep for a month-long trip to a possibly hostile country, and,"—I waved my hand at everything—"this happened. I normally travel light. I can carry two or three, and our smaller bags can be shoved into two of the big ones. The crate..." I trailed off with the sudden realization I never told Adhar about what the crate held. He certainly knew I went after those things, but I hadn't mentioned I was bringing them home. "The crate needs gentle handling. I think three of us can get everything, and Raphael can carry the crate."

"You can put a bag on my back, too. If I don't trip, it should be fine," Raphael said quickly.

Adhar looked at my mate, Nakul leaning over his shoulder to do the same thing.

"I told you he was a big one," Nakul said dryly with a hint of jealousy. "We don't make them that big here."

"No, we don't," Adhar agreed. "But I do like that idea, Mister Alvarez. Kaliya, does that work for you?"

"Definitely, but...he can get bigger," I said, clearing my throat after as I looked away from them. Raphael laughed, and his scent changed. When he passed me to grab the biggest duffel, he was over seven feet tall in his cambion form. I gave an amused smile to my fellow nagas.

"You were right." Adhar crossed his arms beside me. "He was perfectly human, then he...wasn't."

"Yeah."

Loading up, we walked away from the dirt road where Raphael and I had been dumped. We walked for an hour until we found a small airport, not on any map and didn't service commercial airlines. It was for bush planes, and my people owned one for emergencies.

As we loaded the plane, Nakul powered up the engines. I knew he could fly, and it was the part of the trip that scared me the most. Cassius and I had chased him for a long time, and it was one way he got around the world killing people. He would take small flights in planes much like this one to cover his tracks, leaving no tickets behind. We only heard stories about the Indian man who bribed his way onto privately owned planes. On one occasion, when we had nearly had him, he had stolen the plane, revealing he was a pilot.

The flight wasn't terrible, but it had me holding on to a safety bar with white knuckles at a couple of points. Raphael seemed less worried but still tense. Adhar and Nakul talked in front, Adhar playing copilot, even though he couldn't fly the plane. I knew what he was doing, keeping Nakul in line and present in the current world. Nakul was supposed to be under house arrest, and he was mentally fragile. A bout of serial killing insanity because your mate and son were murdered, then being mentally violated with magic and ordered to kill your niece tended to leave people unstable.

He'd nearly done it. I was definitely going to die if it hadn't been for Raphael's quick thinking. Or Leith's.

When we landed, we loaded into Adhar's truck and headed for his home, which would be mine for the rest of our stay.

"Do you know how to fly?" Nakul asked me from the passenger's seat in the front.

"No."

"I'll take you wherever you want to go while you're here," he said with a smile. "You ask, and I'll get you there. I know you have a meeting with the rakshasa at some point. You'll want more warriors for that."

"I'm sure we can work out something," I said with a tight smile, not wanting to turn him down but definitely not wanting to be his passenger more than I had to be. I would learn to fly the plane myself if I had to. It couldn't be *that* hard.

We drove deep into the jungle, going off-road for parts. Assam had a beautiful jungle. For a short period, Adhar had kept me at the very compound estate where we were headed. I had always wanted to play in the jungle but never could. My life and world had been the walls of the estate, just as it had been with my parents. Growing up, I had only had the smallest urge to leave, like any child, but with Adhar, I had been angry, confused, and heartbroken. It had been hard on me, but I had been given a taste of freedom, and I had craved another.

Looking back, it was even less surprising I had run away.

6

CHAPTER SIX

Adhar drove through the open gates, and I could smell the magic in the air through the open windows. The security system was magic, but not witch magic...or fae for that matter. It had no register I could identify, but something had certainly been guarding the border, telling certain things they couldn't come in.

"Who does the security for us now?"

"Runes of power," Adhar answered. "Everything is engraved with runes of power, which are blended in with the detailed wood and stonework, so they're not noticeable."

"Of course," I whispered. It was one of the things I had forgotten, a lesson from my parents when I was young. My mother and father had walked me around the compound, pointing them out and telling me some nagas knew how to draw them perfectly, and they made sure every home was as safe as possible. Neither of my parents could, saying their work with it wasn't smooth enough. "I should have remembered that. Who's trained in it now?"

"Nakul and I, though I have been training Vikrant to do them for the last few decades. He's the one who lives nearby with his mate, in case you forgot." Adhar pulled his truck into a fairly modern garage. Instead of torches, there were light bulbs. Instead of dirt, it was paved or gravel. As we got out of the truck, I didn't head inside the house or help with the suitcases, my feet taking me somewhere, following this train of thought. I saw a battery in the garage that held power, with wiring leading up. I saw the automatic garage door opener, something I had just seen in action. He had not one but two cars, the truck and a black SUV. I went back outside and looked up, seeing the signs of solar panels on the roof and small lawn lights lined the pathways.

My heart raced, and I wasn't sure why. I was dumbstruck I hadn't been transported back in time to what I had left. Everything had changed.

Adhar walked with deliberation to make sure I knew he was there. I knew it was Adhar and not Nakul or Raphael because I could taste his particular scent on the air, taking it in like any snake would. My thermal senses read him as well, like a pit viper, giving me a strong silhouette of him in my mind. Nakul was taller, and Raphael was blazing hot in comparison to a naga.

"I know things have changed," he said gently, walking to stand beside me.

"You've modernized."

"Most of India has. Well, as much as it's capable of in these more rural areas. We have to conserve our electricity use. Lights are only on when necessary, which isn't frequent. Both my vehicles are electric, a pricey modification, but necessary since I didn't find it safe to continue getting petrol when I needed it. I only finished those modifications two years ago."

"What?" That was surprising. "Did you put a Tesla in a pickup truck?"

"Not quite, but close enough," he said with a small smile. "I can, as the young people say, get with the times."

I winced. I had told him to do just that a hundred times, probably more.

"I added electricity when solar became a private option. I had to wire the entire house myself. Other homes are still being updated, but we're getting there. I've been testing new security as well, to stop relying on only magic and add in some of the more advanced human options."

"It would be easier if you could hire contractors," I pointed out. "Everyone knows where I live, but few are stupid enough to test me or my security."

"Not many are still too many," he countered. "At least for families with babies. We have many babies now and must keep them safe. But you are deflecting. You are surprised by the changes. I wanted to make sure you were okay."

"It's just...a lot," I said, shaking my head. "New Delhi wasn't the city I remembered, either. I should have been more prepared. Obviously, everything is different. It's been a hundred years."

"A very long time, but before that, we were consistent for centuries and very little changed. The last century has been...faster than those before. Advances in technology and other conveniences have come at a rate almost no one can keep up with, at least not us older supernaturals. We're not used to a world this fast."

That I knew.

"With all the changes in my life, maybe I was hoping to come back to India and see one thing that hasn't changed," I theorized. "This place, it's part of my life, my feelings about it. Some things can't change, right? Now it's all different, and not even pictures could have prepared me. No logical amount of thinking prepared me for just how different it is."

"Well, it's not all different. As I said, we use electricity sparingly, so all our cooking is still done in the traditional way," he said, crossing his arms behind his back. "And we still maintain the property in the way you were taught as a child. No lawnmowers for us. Well, I have a push mower, but I've started making Nakul do that for exercise while I garden."

"Stop acting like an old man," I teased. He didn't look that old, certainly not gardening all day old.

"I am an old man," he retorted. "Seeing the outside world change, bringing those changes into my home has reminded me just how old I am. Take electricity, for example. Lightning in a wire, making bulbs create light. When I was a child, lightning was still a god's fury from a storm, a strike power that had to be heavenly in source. Lightning strikes were dangerous, but we had no idea how they worked. Now, we harness a very similar power and know everything there is to know about it. There are entire industries that store the power and send it to people. Now, I can make it, so the sun powers things in my home. I have seen the world evolve from knowing *nothing* to knowing things that would have been the secrets of the universe to people from my time. I *am* old, Kaliya."

"You sound tired."

"I am." There was unmistakable sadness in his statement. "Much of it is how long I've been on this earth, but some of it is you." He gave me a weary smile. "You might have the white hair, but I am the one who is feeling it. We'll talk more about it later, once you and Raphael have settled in."

"You know, I've never asked. Did anyone in my family tree go white early, too?"

"I thought you knew. Yes, there was someone else, and I was fortunate enough to know him. Your grandfather on your father's side. Your father probably never mentioned it because he didn't think you would end up with it. He and your brothers had all escaped it, and your grandfather was killed shortly after your father mated your mother."

"He was killed on his trip home," I said, nodding. His mate, my grandmother, had been killed on the same trip. My mother's parents were killed shortly after the birth of my oldest brother, also traveling home from a visit to meet their first grandchild. Traveling around India was never safe for our kind. Whether enemies from the old times or new poachers looking for an easy way to make money, we never knew peace in the traditional sense. We could only steal it when we had the chance and keep persevering.

What really struck a chord was there were no pictures of my grandparents from either side. I never saw them, could never see my grandfather's white hair. I didn't know what type of snake they looked like or the colors of their scales. Did they have intricate patterns on their hoods when they were about to strike?

Living in the open, I hadn't considered many of the challenges of my people, ones I hadn't thought about as a child. I had no pictures of my parents or brothers. There were no paintings or sketches because we didn't allow that. It would make us even more identifiable if the images were released.

I sighed.

"What is it?" Adhar asked, turning his body toward me, giving me his undivided attention.

"Pictures. I don't know what they look like because we don't allow for reproductions of our physical appearance. That's still a rule, isn't it?"

"Yes, especially in the digital age," Adhar confirmed. "Do you like taking pictures?"

"Not particularly, but it's...People have pictures of their families. They take pictures with their friends. They go on trips and take pictures of the sights. I don't have any of that from growing up. It just hit me that I have no pictures of my parents or my brothers. I don't take many myself, but..."

I pulled out my phone and was grateful to see its battery was surviving. I was trying not to use it and had location services turned off. I purposefully disconnected from the service provider, not that I would have gotten coverage in this part of the world. I pulled up pictures of Sorcha and me from a night at Jackalope, then another of Raphael and me kissing in the gym, with

Sammy in the background, glaring at us, looking like she was about to start cutting off body parts. All of them had been taken by friends and sent to me, mostly Sorcha and Gabby. Gabby thought she was being sweet. Sorcha was brutally teasing me. It didn't matter who sent me the pictures, though. I always appreciated them.

"You don't have this," I said, letting him see the life I lived. "My friends take a great deal of effort recording our lives together, and when I'm away from them, I get to see them."

"You seem to have wonderful friends," he said, leaning in closer. "Who is the silver-haired beauty? Is that the fae... Sorcha?"

"That's right, and the blonde? She's Sammy, a cambion warrior. I'm training her for Raphael. Well, I'm training all the cambions. She's been mad at me recently. I lied to her, and I deserve it."

"I see," he whispered. "I understand why you feel the way you do. The rule has not always existed. I take very good care of paintings and sketches of nagas we lost, even some of my own parents. I wasn't the ruler yet when it was created, but I agreed with it."

"But you felt the loss," I said, nodding. "There are no other nagas who understand now, are there?"

"No," he confirmed. "Aside from the occasional baby picture, none of the nagas, other than you and me, ever had our images captured. I only allowed baby pictures recently because...well, they're babies. Put thirty of them in the same room, and a stranger will have a hard time picking out the right one without help. Plus, they grow up so quickly and change so much. It's our immortal appearance that must be protected."

"Well, yours does," I said with a small smile. "I'm not in hiding."

"This is not an insult." He lifted a hand and pointed at my chest. "Look at what you've had to become to achieve the freedom you have."

"Sounds a little like an insult," I said, looking down at the finger pointed at my chest, then back up at him.

"It's not," he repeated. "You should just remember not everyone has it in them to do what you have done. Some must take other paths. One thing your journey has taught me is there is no one right answer that will fit every one of our people. You found the path for you. I must guide those that can't take that path." He lifted his hand and touched my cheek gently. "Maybe there may be some who want to take the path you have. I would hope you would guide them as I guide the others. Maybe, one day, we'll send each other pictures and commission portraits of our people and no longer miss out on such a mundane yet precious thing in life." He backed away. "Which we will discuss later. Nakul and Raphael should have been able to get everything put away in your suites by now—"

"Adhar," I said strongly, cutting him off. "What are you getting at?"

"Later," he said, looking away from me and walking toward a nearby door. "You've only just arrived, and there is much we have to go through during this visit. This is not a pressing matter." He turned back to me and gestured for me to follow, reminding me of the times he'd had to drag me back inside as a child when I was out practicing with the talwar my father had used to teach me. "As I was saying, your things should be in your suites by now. Raphael will be right across the hall from you—"

"Raphael will sleep in my room," I said with a smile. "We're mated."

"But you're not married," he said, sighing heavily. "There's been no ceremony."

"The ceremony was always only a formality," I retorted. "He doesn't need to be my husband. I need to milk my venom, and I have a perfectly able mate to help me, who I enjoy in my bed. He will stay in my suite, Adhar."

A small smile formed as I went at him with my argument, and a twinkle entered his dark brown eyes. I realized he was pulling my leg, and I glared at him, but there wasn't much heat in my anger.

"He's not your husband," Adhar repeated.

"Then I'll be a trashy American, but I'm going to sleep in the same bed as my mate, Adhar," I retorted, trying not to laugh. *He's actually fucking with me. When did Adhar get a sense of humor, or is this something I've missed all these years because I was angry? Did I never give him the chance to mess with me like this?*

"Please don't. I have never had a trashy American live with me before," he said, unable to hide his smile. "I'll let him stay in your suite if you don't embrace that stereotype. Please."

"Good deal," I said, catching up with him. As he opened the door and held it to let me in, I looked at him. "You were always going to let Raphael stay with me, right?"

"Obviously." His eyes were gentle but still danced with humor. "He's not of our culture, and he will need your help to navigate this world. You will need his support to face what you ran from. I would never separate you from your mate, formal ceremony or not."

"Thank you." Before I could get inside, he grabbed my arm.

"I've also asked Nakul not to bring up children again," he said, more seriously. "If he bothers you, please let me know." Adhar, gods bless him, blushed and released my arm. "Is there anything you and your mate need to..."

"We brought everything we need to make sure it doesn't happen," I said quickly, feeling my face heat. "Don't worry about that. You don't need to add anything to the supply run."

I never wanted Adhar to have to buy me condoms, a situation I would not allow under any circumstance. Raphael and I could go without sex if that became an issue.

With his nod, I finally went through the door he held open for me. He was right behind me, and I felt too much as I saw that much of Adhar's home here in Assam was very much how I left it. Sure, the torches and candles once used had been replaced with light bulbs, but the structure of the building was the same. The floorings were newer but the same type, and the walls were freshly painted but the same colors they'd always been. There were tile mosaics and brilliant colors on the trims, matched with beige for the majority of the wall. None of those things had changed.

I walked into the first room, a classic living room as

most westerners would consider it. Sitting or gathering room were also good descriptions. On the other side were sliding glass doors, a new addition that didn't change the effect of the space. Once, it had been open, leading to an inner courtyard. Even now, some doors were left open to let in the breeze. The courtyard was the main garden where Adhar liked to work, and it was beautiful. My mother had also taken pride in the courtyard garden, and I knew it was because that was where visitors would spend a majority of their time. It was a pride and joy thing. It was still beautiful and inviting. The fountain in the middle wasn't new and was showing its age. I walked across the living room, looking out on the courtyard, knowing Adhar was following my every step, taking in my every reaction.

"I've only done little updates," he said casually. "I've tried to keep the bones of this home the same through the years."

"It's nice," I said. "You have a lovely home. You always have."

"Thank you."

I was going to say more, but we could both hear the one thing that was disrupting the beautiful and peaceful state of the home—a not quiet conversation that sounded like it was getting heated by the second.

"We should check on Nakul and Raphael. I shouldn't have left them alone to look around," I said with a groan. I was regretting being so taken by the place, I didn't pay enough attention to the people. "Raphael only knows Nakul when he tried to kill me, and during that whole thing, Nakul threatened Raphael. They won't be on good terms." I had expected it yet stupidly let myself be sidetracked.

"They need to work through it like the adults they are." There was a thud, then Nakul's hiss. "But I think you're right. Maybe I should have monitored them and let you walk around on your own."

7

CHAPTER SEVEN

I let Adhar lead. While I could hear what was going on and knew where the two men were, it was Adhar's home, and he would lay down the rules about fighting. I tried not to think about the two men having their heated discussion in my old suite. While the rest of the house seemed unchanged, this room was *very* different from what I remembered. If I wasn't witnessing Raphael in his cambion form, holding onto Nakul's neck, I would have asked Adhar about the changes.

"Fighting is not tolerated in this house," Adhar snapped, and everyone winced, including me. Adhar, gentle, old naga, aged beyond our wildest dreams, who liked to garden, was also a ruler of his people. He wasn't afraid to throw the weight of that into his words. I had been on the receiving end of that as a child more times than I could count.

Raphael released Nakul, who hissed again as he rubbed his neck. The only good thing about the scene was Raphael was completely in control. His eyes were black and red, but the veins were small, so there was no reason to think we were about to have him in his full cambion form in the house.

Or, gods forbid, his demon form.

"Raphael, what's going on?" I asked, coming up beside Adhar.

"He was telling me I wasn't allowed to be near my niece," Nakul hissed to Adhar, pointing at my mate. "She's my niece, and I've worked hard. I am allowed to see her."

"I said I didn't want you *alone* with her," Raphael snarled. "I remember what happened last time, and it's only been just over a year. I can't trust that you don't have some lasting effects of that spell, and I am *not* going to find her bleeding out in a kitchen again."

"You don't have a say in the matter, and I am healed!" Nakul retorted, baring his fangs at Raphael.

"And I don't trust that. I'm sorry. I'm not saying you can't see her at all, but if you put her life in danger, I will fucking end you."

"Like you can," Nakul snapped.

"Try me," Raphael growled, growing several inches as the black veins raced over his skin.

I jumped in and put myself between them. Adhar grabbed Nakul's arm and yanked him toward the door.

"No. We're not going to get into these fights," I said, looking between them. "We have to live together for a month. There will be other nagas and babies in this house before the end of the week. You will both behave." I gave my full attention to Nakul. "He's right, Nakul. It hasn't been long enough to test the limits of your healing.

Anything could set you off. But you're more than welcome to sit and talk to me during meals or any other time. We just can't be alone together. Even if you were healed, we have so much history, and there's..." I sighed. Nakul was a serial killer, and nothing could change that, but he was my serial killer. He was one of my people and my responsibility, a tragic figure who created more tragedy. "We'll need to talk about it. Adhar can sit with us instead of my mate if that makes you more comfortable, but we absolutely cannot be alone together. I won't take a risk that might lead to you killing me or me having to kill you."

Nakul seemed hurt, but Adhar's grip on him never wavered. Adhar, keeping himself somewhat behind my uncle, nodded, agreeing with my judgment on the matter.

"We talked about this, Nakul," Adhar said. "I know you wish to spend time with your niece, and we will make sure that happens, but we talked about this."

Nakul gave a small hiss of dissatisfaction but lowered his head. "I will patiently await my turn."

I turned to my mate, knowing Adhar had my uncle well in hand.

"I'm not a baby who needs to be coddled, Raphael Alvarez. Don't you dare try to treat me like one," I said, narrowing my eyes. He was massive now, fully into his cambion form.

"I won't let him risk your life," he growled. Raphael didn't like to be threatened by anyone, but he was normally under better control. It had to be Nakul. That was the only explanation.

"It's handled," I snapped. "No one disagrees with you

about the terms of Nakul and I being in the same room. You could have trusted that there are two other people who would have considered this. You didn't need to pick a fight."

"I didn't pick a fight. We were talking, and I thought I would be honest with him about the safety of my mate. He's the one who made it a big fucking deal."

"And the hand around his throat?" I inquired, raising an eyebrow.

"He said..." Raphael growled, a clear sign this was what pissed him off. "He said since you weren't already pregnant, maybe I should be more worried about how I was performing than your protection."

Slowly, I turned to Nakul, who intelligently kept his head down. While it was a petty insult about a man's fertility, it pointed to a deeper problem even Adhar didn't want. We had literally just been talking about it, and it had already come up.

"Don't ever go there with my mate again. Never go there with *me*," I hissed, closing the distance between my uncle and me. "Do you understand me?"

"I was angry that he was presumptuous to think he could tell me what I could and could not do," Nakul said softly, demurely even.

"I don't care," I whispered, leaning in close. "The topic is off-limits for you, no matter what the situation is. Are we clear?"

"Yes, my niece—"

"Yes, Kaliya Sahni, ruler of the nagas, Tribunal Executioner, and mate of Warlord Raphael Alvarez," I corrected. "Being my uncle doesn't give you more leeway to mess around and poke at the way I live my life. It gives you *less* because I expect you to respect our choices. I *demand* that you respect our choices in the matter." It was harsh, but it wasn't just the question of babies or the disrespect to my mate. It was beyond the pure biology of the matter too, considering it could take some couples centuries to get pregnant with their first child.

It was also the sexism. As a woman, I was expected to pop out baby nagas as fast as possible, no matter my position or my role. No matter what my power was, I was expected to be mated, then pregnant.

It fucking pissed me off.

"We're—"

"Don't," Adhar snapped. "She's made herself known."

"I know the argument, and I don't care," I said, not backing off from my uncle. "I will not leave an orphan behind if I die fighting for our people. I won't risk the life of a hypothetical child. I have battles to fight and wars to win. Once I am satisfied with those, my mate and I will discuss a family, but until then, I expect silence on the matter." I looked at Adhar, who nodded once more, then backed away from my uncle and let Adhar pull him out of the room.

"I'll let you two settle in while I prepare something small to keep you from growing too hungry before an official meal," he said as he reached back for the door and swung it closed.

"Thank you," I called out as the door clicked closed. Another small change. We had proper doorknobs now, and mine even had a deadbolt lock.

I heard the mattress squeak behind me.

"I'm sorry," Raphael said, groaning as I watched him put his head in his hands.

"Apology accepted." He looked up again, surprised. "Do you want children?" I asked suddenly.

His face flushed, and that was the answer I needed.

"I see," I whispered, wondering why we hadn't talked about it. I had decided not to get pregnant, and he never brought it up. "Why didn't you tell me?"

"Because it's a two-person decision to have children. It's a one-person decision not to have them. We have decades. I'll fight alongside you, and one day, hopefully, you'll be ready. His comment pissed me off because..." Raphael shook his head. "What if we can't? We're not the same species. Our kind has only run into each other once before, and..." He gestured to me. "Only you know the intricacies of that. No cambion has had a child, not after our demon nature was...turned on. Activated was the word Mygi liked to use. So, I don't bring it up because I know you don't want them yet, and I don't know if we can."

I blinked, opened my mouth, then closed it.

"Did...they have children?" he asked tentatively.

"No," I whispered. "Not in my memory. Some tellings of the legend that mentioned daughters or anything similar are wrong from my memory. They never had children. Mind you, the stories also say he had two wives. My memory says otherwise to that, too."

"I'm up for a lot of things, but a second mate is not one of them," he said, his face blank and his chocolate brown eyes too hard for me to argue with. I would have tried to tease him a little bit but not with that expression.

"No second mate," I promised. "I find one hard enough to adjust to." I sat beside him. "This is a heavier conversation than I expected. I shouldn't have asked like that."

"Question...you say some legends are wrong, but you're a naga. How was the truth about Kaliya and his mate not written down by other nagas?"

"Politics and fear," I explained. "It's something I'll be talking to Adhar about if you want to sit down with us when we do that. While we've been planning this trip, he's pulled out every old scroll and written piece of information he could find that even mentions Kaliya. We're going to review all of it. I have memories of things, but I want to see how they line up. By the time I was born, there were no nagas alive who had known him. Many of our old documents have been lost to fires and time. Age plays a part, too, as Adhar can't remember literally everything he's heard over his lifetime. It's impossible. The older you get, the more information you have to store, and the more likely you are to forget some obscure fact from someone else.

"I'm rambling and getting off-topic, but the base answer to your question is politics and fear. Kaliya loved Rama with everything he had. She was the center of his world, but she wasn't human. Kaliya's closest brother knew many would be fearful of her and her family. I don't know what happened to them, but I will say...they decided it was best to tell the other nagas she was human, and she never used her power in front of them. That's why we never knew Kaliya's power was caused by something outside of naga culture. As for the second wife..." I tilted my head to the side. There was one section of his memories I tried to avoid—his time at the Yamuna River and the events leading up to his death. I didn't like having those memories, but sometimes they showed up in my dreams, especially leading up to this trip. It only took a second to conjure the face of the second woman who had been at the Yamuna River with them as if it had only been yesterday for me.

"It was Rama's mother, who looked young enough to be his wife because she was immortal, thanks to her mating with Rama's father."

"Do you know their names?"

I saw his burning curiosity. Rama and her parents were his people.

"Lalika and Sohan were Rama's mother and father, respectively. They were loving and doting, and her father was a great warrior who purposefully didn't take credit for anything. He was secretive, leaving his wife and daughter to live alone deep in the jungle, so they were safe. He knew exactly what he was but never met others like himself. He'd fallen in love with Lalika and stopped looking. That was the story he told Rama's mate, old-Kaliya, anyway. We'll never know the truth, I think."

"It's nice hearing about them, even if we don't know the full story," Raphael said, sighing. "At least a human and a cambion can mate and have families. That's something I always like when you talk about them. I'm not like Nakul. I'm not going to tell the cambions to mate and have children right now, but it's nice to hear they have the option."

"You could have asked me about it before. I'm always willing to tell you whatever I remember about them."

Raphael turned away, and I could tell the discussion was over. Whatever his reasons, he hadn't felt comfortable asking before now, or maybe it was the timing.

I got up, deciding I needed to unpack. When I stayed somewhere for a week, I didn't bother, but a month? That was too long to live out of a suitcase. It also gave me a chance to see the changes Adhar had made to the suite. This was by far the most modern, western-looking room in the house. Maybe it was my fault since most of my house was similar to it. I never did tell Adhar about my bedroom in Arizona, how traditional it was, a piece of India hidden away in my modern American home. Adhar tried to give me somewhere where I was comfortable. It was clearly intended to be my space in his compound whenever I needed it.

I ran my hand over a wooden dresser as I dropped a suitcase next to it.

He tried. It's honestly touching, if shocking. He did this for me and Raphael, and I'm grateful. It would have been weird to stay with my mate in the room I slept in as a child.

It just didn't fit the house, and that was the weirdest part about it. I started unpacking, letting Raphael think about whatever he wanted to think about.

He shuffled behind me, and I saw his shirt fly into the corner of the room, landing in the place I knew would turn into our laundry pile. Then his pants followed. It was warm, and I could smell his sweat. I had an unhealthy fascination for his sweat. Most people would look at him and think it was gross, but when I could smell it, my mind went to him working those hard muscles in the gym or in my bed, building up that sweat while we worked out in other ways.

The sound of a zipper and clothes rustling made me turn around.

"Is there a chance I can convince you to stay naked?" I asked as he went through the suitcase at his feet. I wanted something nice to look at.

He chuckled softly. "No, not right now. Adhar is going to bring food, remember? I just wanted to put on something fresh until I could find out how to take a shower in this place."

I inhaled, realizing there were a few more things I forgot to mention or even ask Adhar about.

"I don't know if there is a shower," I said, clicking my tongue on my teeth. Raphael paused, frowning as he looked up.

"How am I supposed to get clean?"

"A bath we could fill by hand or a cold stream. I forgot to ask Adhar if he has a modern bathroom."

"Toilets?" Raphael asked, a desperate expression taking over his face.

"Maybe?" I shrugged. "I'm not looking forward to roughing it, either, but I grew up like this, so it doesn't seem weird to me."

Raphael yanked on a pair of gray sweatpants—the best color—then stomped to the door. I followed him, wanting to head this off before he freaked out. I watched him make eye contact with Nakul in the courtyard, then he kept walking.

So, he's desperate but not ask Nakul desperate. Good to know.

I followed him to the kitchen, which I hadn't seen yet. Adhar was arranging small sandwiches on a plate.

"Where is the bathroom?" Raphael asked with absolutely no politeness. Adhar's eyes went wide at my mate's rudeness. The old naga wasn't used to anyone talking to him like that, other than me, and he hadn't tolerated it from me for decades.

"I forgot to ask if you updated the plumbing, then forgot to warn Raphael things are a bit...rough here," I added quickly, giving Adhar a look I hope he recognized. I needed him to ease Raphael into this.

Adhar looked at me, then back to my mate.

"Bushes," he answered, but I caught the twinkle in his eyes.

"Adhar!" I said, moving farther into the kitchen. "Come on, don't tease him." I nearly laughed at my mate's expression. I liked this Adhar a lot. He really knew how to pull someone's leg. *Maybe it's because we're in his house, or he's excited to have visitors. He's definitely loosened up.*

Adhar laughed. "We installed a well. There is running water and working bathrooms. Since they weren't a part of the original construction, everyone has to share when the estate is full. There are toilets and sinks in the house. For bathing, you'll have to visit the small bathhouse. I'll take you there once you eat."

"Bathhouse? Like a hammam?" I asked, leaning on the counter. "Is that...appropriate?"

"When I have visitors, there is a schedule for when men and women may go, giving them privacy. Mated couples may take a time slot together if they so wish, but it's not frequent. It was an easier solution than installing multiple showers and bathtubs. The toilets and sinks were hard enough to plumb. A bathhouse was the solution, but yes, it is a hammam."

Raphael, my darling mate, caught the one thing I hadn't expected.

"Why is a hammam the important part of this?"

"It's a Turkish bath," I explained. "Typically associated with Islamic culture, though they are less popular in recent years. Just an interesting choice for Adhar. India has a large Muslim culture, and Adhar, while respectful of other people, normally does nothing that isn't more traditionally Hindu. Or more traditionally naga since our lifestyle and culture is its own variant." I looked back at Adhar. "Good thinking, though. Saves a lot of trouble for the logistical issues and probably helps with cleaning."

Adhar nodded. "Yes, I thought so as well, and the nagas who have used it have enjoyed it. It's a nice place to get together for women to talk. The men are required to leave them be and if applicable, watch the children while they have some time to themselves." I nodded. Every woman needed time away from the daily struggle. "The younger men like to talk about the things young men do without the women deflating their egos. We old men are just glad to have a moment of peace or to watch the young men act like the fools they can be." Raphael chuckled. "It's been an interesting experiment I've enjoyed watching unfold. I have a bathhouse at each of my homes now."

"You've updated all of them? I bet that took time."

"Well, you've had us moving quite a bit with the arrival of Nakul and the dangers you've faced possibly exposing us. Even for this trip, the other nagas will arrive from one of their homes and return to a different one to cover their travel plans and keep our enemies guessing if we're found out. It's given me time to see each of my homes and give them the time they so deserve."

"I thought Kaliya couldn't expose you. She doesn't know where anyone lives, right?" Raphael looked between us, frowning.

"Well, I know this estate, but I don't know where any of the other nagas live due to safety precautions. It's a typical chain of information." I frowned, watching my once caretaker while I tried to piece together something that was bugging me. "I thought this one wasn't used anymore. I figured you would have let it go and built a new one."

"I almost did, but I like this one the most. The security here has never been tested, but the moment it is, I'll move on." He picked up the platter of finger food with one hand and pointed to the courtyard with another. "Let's go sit and talk. You should both eat something and...kick up your feet. That's correct, yes?"

"Yeah, Adhar, that's correct," I said with a small smile, watching how he nodded, pleased with himself.

8

CHAPTER EIGHT

Once seated in the courtyard, I pulled up an ottoman and kicked up my feet on it, slipping off my boots in the same movement. Typically, Adhar was strict about indoor and outdoor shoes, but I figured the excitement of our arrival had pushed that to the wayside. I took the chance to bring it up as he sat down, clearly wearing his indoor shoes, as was Nakul. Raphael was still in his boots, and I knew something had to be done.

"Sorry about our boots," I said with a sheepish smile, waiting for him to rap me on the knuckles. "I'll make sure we put on our indoor shoes once we've eaten something."

"I was going to give you more time to settle in. Did you bring any? I would have prepared some, but I forgot to ask for your shoe sizes."

"We brought some. I prepared for this, and it just... slipped my mind," I explained.

Raphael hurriedly took off his boots, grabbed mine, and ran them to the front door. I tried not to chuckle. I certainly hadn't cared enough to deal with it right then. He clearly had other plans.

We were silent until he was back. He handed me the black slippers I had picked out for just this and slid my feet into them, then kicked them up again. Wearing a more masculine pair, Raphael threw his feet on the same ottoman. He invaded my personal space, cozying up beside me on the outdoor couch and throwing an arm over my shoulder. With Adhar and Nakul there, I was uncomfortable with the public display but enjoyed that he wasn't scared. He didn't let the two ancient nagas intimidate him. Once Raphael settled again, Adhar pointed to the floor.

"You will mop the tracks you've gotten everywhere when you have rested," he told me.

"Less than twenty-four hours in your home, and you're giving me chores," I said, sighing heavily. "Why am I not surprised?"

"You and I both know you need structure and discipline, or you will continue to forget the rules," he retorted patiently.

He's not wrong...his judgment doesn't make me feel any less of a child. Some things certainly never changed. I'll add following all rules without needing reminders to my list of personal improvements I'm working on.

"Now that we are all seated, I think we should let Nakul know about some of the more...secretive parts of your trip," Adhar continued, looking directly at me. Nakul's eyes narrowed, flicking between his roommate and me, his niece, as he realized we were keeping big secrets from him. "He'll be here the entire time, and eventually, he'll overhear something. Keeping it from his ears for this long has been a challenge."

"You've had me clean every centimeter of this home every time you talk to her. You always tell me about the calls after they happen. I knew something was going on," Nakul said, glaring at Adhar.

"I wasn't ready for it to go further among the nagas than Adhar," I explained, also glaring at Adhar. I still wasn't ready, but Adhar used my weapon against me—logic. Logically, it was stupid to keep it a secret from Nakul now. Even as Raphael and I had talked in our room, he'd been sitting in the courtyard. It would have been all too easy for him to sneak closer to the door and overhear us, and I was lucky he didn't choose to do that.

"What's going on? Between a new mate who is not a naga and the business with the rakshasas, how much more could be going on during this trip?" Nakul's demand was reasonable. He was, by far, the most experienced warrior alive among the nagas. He and I were probably on par, matched in combat skills in multiple ways, our weaknesses and strengths balancing out. I could need him, but admitting that left a bone in my throat.

He's fucking crazy, and crazy isn't reliable.

"Don't interrupt me," I warned. "Once I start, I don't want to stop and lose my place. Leave your questions for the end, please." Nakul nodded, agreeing to my terms without a word. I took a deep breath and glanced at Adhar, who gave a tiny nod, then at Raphael, who tightened his arm around my shoulder, giving me his support. The betrayal in this story still cut deep.

“My mother and the witch, Devika, did something when I was a child, and we’re just now discovering the repercussions. They devised a spell to discover who a naga is reincarnated from.” I watched Nakul sit up and lean over, his eyes intense. “I was the test subject. They did it on me shortly after my birth, not knowing it would change...everything.”

“It worked,” Nakul whispered, interrupting me, but seeing the shock on his face, I allowed it.

“It worked,” I concurred, looking down at my hands in my lap. “My mother realized she made a mistake because the spell didn’t just reveal who I was reincarnated from, it also reawakened all the memories of that previous life. She had a baby with the memories of a life lived thousands of years before. She asked Devika to block the memories, trying to give me back the promise of reincarnation, a *new* life. Devika did, adding a trick to keep me from trying to reveal them because she *really* didn’t want me to find out. It was emotional manipulation. When I drew too close to the truth, I mentally stepped back, refusing to believe it, disregarded it. Very simple spell woven into a complicated one. Shortly after Devika did that for my mother, she reported to whoever she was working for that it had worked, and they needed to kill me and my family.” I closed my eyes. Five months and it still burned. Devika had been my friend for years, had been my mother’s friend for years.

“That was the attack,” Nakul said. I looked up to see he had turned pale.

“They had masked the attack on my family as an attack on all the nagas, trying to wipe out naginis.” I blinked back tears. "And to kill all the children of the time, as well...like your son. It was an effective attack, but it missed the target, who disappeared and wasn't found until Adhar pulled her off the streets of New Delhi. Me."

Nakul was breathing hard. I had just taken him back to the event that had caused him to snap. Adhar reached out and rubbed his back and whispered things to my uncle, I tried not to hear, and eventually, Nakul calmed down. He didn't stay seated, however, moving to stand behind the couch and leaned on it, his intense stare pinning me to stay exactly where I was.

"How did you find out?" he asked.

"Raphael and I were captured and drugged, unable to defend ourselves. The rakshasa king, Mehar, revealed he had been hunting me since the night he failed to kill me as a child. He forced us to mate when we couldn't do anything about it. He wanted to verify something." I twisted my hands together, refusing to let them shake.

I'm stronger now. No one is going to hold me like that again.

"Mating with Raphael cracked the blocking spell and revealed what my mother had done to me. It was a... process because I was also combating Devika's added twist without knowing it. I started blacking out, getting memories of my previous life at some bad times. On top of that, we learned cambions give some of their unique abilities to their mates. I had gotten those as well. I was dealing with a lot, but eventually, I had all my memories back and knew who I was in my previous life. Devika revealed the rest while she tried to hold us for someone else, whoever she was working for. That's the mystery I'm trying to solve. The rakshasa royal family was an unfortunate pawn in their king's need to hunt and kill me."

"Some rakshasa are more predatory than others, and we've never been on the best of terms with the species," Adhar added. "As you well know."

"Yes," Nakul agreed softly. "You killed the king, so his mate and his sons worked with Devika, who knew you would come for a gift your mother left you. I know that part of the story. Then you chased Devika to her home in Sri Lanka and killed her."

"Well, I didn't kill her. Her assistant did," I huffed, still disappointed I didn't have more time with the old hag to get more answers. She knew who she was working for, but I never got the chance to find out.

"You keep skimming over one part," Nakul said, his words like the steel of a blade, cutting directly through me and to the heart of the matter.

"Kaliya," I whispered.

The silence seemed to quiet even the outside world. The birds didn't chirp. The wind didn't rustle the trees. No one moved.

I looked up at Nakul and met his intense stare.

"My name was the only hint she left me. I am Kaliya, the demon serpent reborn, with all of his memories, all of his secrets,"—I turned to Raphael—"and even the same path, it seems."

"What does that mean?" Nakul demanded.

"Kaliya, our Kaliya, through the memories of her previous life, discovered why the original was so immensely powerful, and she is currently growing into that power," Adhar explained. "He was also mated to one like Raphael. Rama, who the nagas had all believed to be a human, most likely a witch in some theories, was a cambion, and he had received the cambion-mating gifts—their incredible rate of healing and their red magics. Kaliya has ascended to the power to return to our most powerful of forms."

Nakul sagged, the shock finally hitting him. I could only watch as he struggled to get back to his seat. We stared at each other for a long time.

"One reason we're here is to dig into the lessons of my past life. I'll be telling stories I can remember from his life, and Adhar will write them down and compare them to what we know. Kaliya, his mate, his brother, and her family...together, they kept some of the most dangerous secrets of our kind. Rama and her mother, Lalika, were there when he was killed by Krishna." I pulled away from Raphael and stood to pace around the courtyard. "Whoever tried to kill me wanted to verify I was like Kaliya. They knew how powerful the original had been, knew the secrets of the demon serpent and his mate, and didn't want me to get that powerful." I lifted a hand, summoning the demonic magic. "So, we need to—"

"Find Rama and her family," Raphael cut me off.

"It's been thousands of years, Raphael. They're probably dead," I countered, hating the idea as soon as it entered my ears and buried itself in my brain. "I was going to say we need to dig deeper in the old legends and hopefully find some clear information I can compare to my memories."

"Do you not know the fate of Rama and her family?" Adhar asked. "You try not to speak of them."

"No, I don't know their fate. I was *dead*," I snapped. Adhar's eyebrows went up, and I inhaled in regret, looking away from him, and ground my teeth together. "I have memories of being with a woman I have never met." I took a deep breath, trying to control an insane wave of uncomfortable anger. I really didn't like the idea of trying to find out if they were alive. "I can feel my hands on her body, and my fangs sink into her flesh in my dreams. I can feel the whispers of how much he loved her as if I'm remembering an ex. I'm not comfortable with the idea of meeting her. I know she or her parents could still be out there because they were alive when I...when *he* died on the Yamuna River, but..." I closed my eyes, trying to get them to understand. My gut screamed it was a bad idea, but my heart...something about it hit me in the chest and made me want to run.

"Meeting the ancient cambions could help mine," Raphael said softly. I looked down at him, and he was staring at the floor. "We could share information, bring them into our community, or just have allies out there who figured out how to navigate in this world. Her mother could teach us about how human mates change. Her father could teach them better than I could about finding their mates and how it feels." He looked up and met my stare.

"You and I are the anomaly. Rama was, too, but they're *real*. Her parents were a real cambion and human couple, and they could help my people. They could tell us if cambions can have families and how because they obviously did. We can't skip this. I didn't even think to consider them because we've been so wrapped up in everything about the nagas and you, but I can't pass up on the chance. They could be out there."

I tried to think about why I was against it, figuring it was because he was right. The cambions in Arizona would fucking kill for a chance to meet others of their kind who had lived through it all. Finding someone with answers was a great idea. Meeting Rama, if she was even still alive, would be brutal for me. It would cut her and me open and leave us hurting. I was her mate reborn, yet not with her, not the right sex. Would she have expectations of me? Would she take offense with Raphael? I didn't know, but those were emotional problems. My problems, which had no place keeping the cambions from vital information about themselves. No place at all.

Fuck.

"I have some vague memories about where they lived," I said, running a hand through my messy hair. I hadn't redone it since the plane ride, and it was beginning to show. "We should have considered this to be important before we planned the trip. It could take weeks, months, or even years to find them. They were off the grid for who knows how long before he found Rama, and if they're still alive, they've been off the grid since. Raphael, we searched for any clue about what you are for months and never heard of them or anything like them."

"I didn't think about this because we've been really busy with everything else. When I'm at the compound, I have to stay focused on the cambions, and whenever we talked, you just told me the trip preparations were coming together. We've barely talked about your memories of his life or Rama's family. You only told me their names today because I asked. I never wanted to pry because you were dealing with a lot, but this is a *good* idea...for both of us, Kaliya. For the nagas and the cambions. We can make the time."

"The world has changed in the last couple thousand years, Raphael. I can't even use landmarks," I pointed out. I wasn't trying to put him off the idea per se, but I was trying to find every excuse not to dive into this mystery on this trip.

"I have seen the changes happen. I can help you relate the old memories you have with the current world," Adhar suggested. "Just as I will help put together the old legends with what the original Kaliya knew about them. If he was keeping secrets in his own story, others must have as well. This would be no different, but it could lead to a source of information we could use, a living source. He is right. You should have already considered this."

I glared at him, and he met me with that patient stare I *hated*. He'd given it to me enough as a child. It was his 'you're young and don't know any better' face.

"We'll start searching," I finally promised, looking away from all of them.

"Thank you—"

"We'll start, but we're still leaving when the month is up," I continued, cutting my mate off. "We'll come back if we have to, but we can't leave Cassius and Sorcha hanging at home. I also have the Tribunal to deal with, and we're just wrapping up with the compound in Arizona. I *have* to deal with the rakshasa on this trip. There's way too much going on to run off chasing ghosts and leave everyone hanging." I groaned and threw a hand at Nakul, remembering someone in the room had only just learned about all this.

"How are you feeling? I know this has been a lot for you. If you need a few days...or weeks, or even months, to process it, don't worry. We're all in the same boat. Take all the time you need."

"I think we should start your training," he said simply, leaving everyone in silence as he got up and went into a suite across the courtyard from mine. When he came back out, he was carrying two talwar. "Training your physical body will help you deal with the emotional and mental challenges of being a ruler. You're a warrior like me. We like physical work. It comes naturally to us and clears our minds."

9

CHAPTER NINE

He was giving me an out, but not just for me. He was looking to clear his own mind. He wanted to train, but while proficient, Adhar wasn't a typical warrior. He was more of a scholar and was only skilled in the talwar through hundreds of years of practice, not because he genuinely enjoyed it.

Thinking of the two living together, I wondered if Nakul had the chance to train.

"It's not safe," Raphael said quickly, putting himself between us.

"We'll be right here in the courtyard," I said, walking past him and taking the offered sword from Nakul. "Right, Adhar?"

"Yes. I still allow training in the courtyard," Adhar said, almost sad. "Please try not to break the furniture or crush my flowers. Raphael, help me move some of the furniture, and we shall watch."

"But—"

"You work out when there's too much on your mind,"

I pointed out. "It's been a long time since I've trained with someone who might be equal to me with the sword." I tested the weight of the talwar Nakul had given me, then shook my head and put it down, ignoring the men around me as I went to get mine. Nakul probably had his hands on these weapons every day, which would give him an edge if I used a weapon I wasn't accustomed to. For safety, I needed to use my own.

I really wanted to do this, and I wanted to do it with Nakul. He was batshit crazy, but his insight and his decision to spar told me he wasn't all lost. I wanted to hold onto the belief that he was still as crazy today as he had been the day I sent him to prison so I wouldn't feel strangely conflicted every time I saw him. At the same time, I needed one warrior who could keep up and his insight into my mind, how I worked, was something only he uniquely understood.

I unzipped the long case I used to pack my weapons. My hand hovered over my katana, a precious gift from Hisao, but I went to my talwar. I was better at the katana since I'd formally trained into adulthood with it. I was good with my talwar, but it was based on training I received as a child, just beginning to learn, then years of forcing myself to get better and smarter. Nakul was a master at the talwar. I could learn something.

It would also give us both a chance to work out whatever emotions were swirling in us, thanks to the discussion we were taking a break from.

I walked back out, knowing neither of us was wearing the right clothes, but I could fight in anything. I was always on my guard, and everything I wore was made to allow for combat. I kicked off my slippers, knowing that going barefoot would be fine with Adhar. Nakul was already barefoot as he waited in the cleared courtyard. Adhar and Raphael were seated together on a couch, out of the way but watchful.

"Are you going to tell me your thoughts?" I asked as I stepped into the lowered courtyard and stood across from my uncle.

"We'll spar first," he said simply. "Don't hold back. I am in control of myself. The spell done on me while I was in prison has been broken, and it shouldn't rear its ugly head."

As far as we know.

I was playing with fire, but risking my life was just easier than dealing with the complicated feelings I had about finding Rama.

Falling into an old habit, I bowed to Nakul, who offered one in return. He was my elder and another warrior, someone who could teach me something, which let me think of him like Hisao. Hisao was also a little crazy, though he had never tried to kill me. Sparring with that werecat had also been an exercise in something dangerous.

When I rose from the bow, my senses had sharpened. The lights and shadows were clearer as I focused on my opponent.

When we finally clashed in a lightning-fast move, I realized we had both struck with the speed our natures allowed us. We were snakes, and lightning-fast strikes, barely perceptible to the human eye, were gifted to us by the gods who had brought us into existence. Nakul was the only naga I had ever faced in battle.

Quickly, I realized I had never fought him at his best and had a feeling he still wasn't. We darted around the courtyard, steel clashing at speeds I knew no other would have matched—only us. I had never worked so hard in a sparring match. I normally reserved my ability to move so quickly for desperate situations or trickery. I *never* used it on someone in a sparring match because I knew they couldn't keep up. Beyond that, the dance my uncle and I performed was just that—a dance. We were running through training patterns, something he was leading. If this was life or death, I would disengage and try another type of attack, but here, we gave each other a workout. I could see the concentration on his face and the intensity of the match in his eyes. We clashed over and over, matching each other in speed and power.

He wavered first, moving a little too slow to catch my attack. I stopped short and jumped back to keep myself from cutting him open from shoulder to hip. He was panting as he slowly sat on the ground. I was breathing hard as well as I leaned against a pillar at the edge.

"Good workout," I said, nodding appreciatively.

"You are better than you were," he said, staring at his blade in his lap. "You weren't old enough to learn some of the patterns I just ran you through."

"Instinct—"

"Muscle memory is required to get every step perfectly correct," he said, cutting me off. "Even I falter when I haven't practiced enough, but you fell right into the exercise without thinking, without those lessons. You wouldn't have learned them until you were an adult. When your parents died, they'd only taught you the basics, and I doubt anyone out there uses the exact training we nagas have for centuries."

Adhar gasped but didn't add his thoughts. I looked at him, then back at my uncle, and it clicked.

"You think I have his muscle memory."

"Muscle memory is memory," Nakul said with a one-shoulder shrug he must have picked up while he was running around the world or in prison, not something he'd done when I was a child. He'd been more proper back then.

I glanced at Raphael, who was staring at the center of the courtyard, his expression thoughtful. I remained silent, wondering if anyone wanted to continue this.

"You could have never matched me with a talwar when we fought," Nakul finally continued, running his fingers over the blade. "I never wanted to kill or hurt you, so I allowed you to capture me and send me to prison. I fought against the spell that told me to kill you, which was the only reason you had the chance to survive, with your mate's help, of course. You are better now, and you don't even realize how much better."

"I train frequently," I said stiffly. I knew coming to India would reveal things, but we hadn't even been here a day, and I felt as if I was being dissected.

"Not with that," he countered, pointing at my talwar. "You prefer the Japanese blade gifted to you by the one who made you into an assassin. When the situation grows tough, and you need to fight harder, you move to that blade, leaving the talwar behind." He gave me a sheepish smile. "I have looked into your life since coming to live here and read the reports and records Adhar has access to from the Tribunal. I did it to grow closer to you, to know you better."

"I write thorough reports," I mumbled, now regretting that.

Why, though? He's trying to learn about me, and I should be happy about that. He's my last living biological family member. He wants to know me as I am now. Maybe I've guarded my privacy a little too hard, a little too long. What he did isn't anything Adhar didn't do to keep track of me, and I never really cared about Adhar doing it.

However, it was Nakul, and my uncle had once been a serial killer.

I would like just one person in my life not to be so wrapped up in complicated bullshit.

Nakul stood when I had been silent for too long and came a little closer.

"Would you like to train more?" he asked, tilting his head with an earnest look.

"No," I answered, shaking my head. "You've pointed out something I've been missing. I should have noticed it already."

I went to put my talwar away and sighed, hating how it suddenly felt as though I had wasted five months when I had been trying my damnedest to figure everything out. Once it was neatly tucked away, I watched the men put the furniture back where it belonged and get seated. Raphael finally ate something, and my stomach growled, so I grabbed a sandwich as I sat down.

"I've been teaching someone the basics of chakram," I

explained as I stared at the sandwich. "But other than a couple of throws, I don't really try anything special. I had no proper training because of my age, just a few basics and what I learned by watching my father and brothers."

"Your father was gifted with them. He would have been the person to watch," Nakul added. "You've been playing it safe because you feel you aren't skilled."

"I don't want to hurt anyone or myself without proper training." Everyone sat quietly while I took a moment to eat my sandwich. Once it was done, they were all still waiting patiently for me to say something. "He was good at them, one of the most powerful and skilled nagas around before the events at the Yamuna River." I stared at my empty hand. "Do you think I could use them?"

"I think your mother opened up a world of possibilities for you that none of us can fathom," Nakul said, finally giving me an indication of his thoughts. "I think you could do it, but I would like to train you, so you aren't teaching your student the wrong things. I won't have my niece teach people our secrets and doing it *wrong*."

"It's one of my cambions," Raphael said, finally jumping back into the conversation. "And with Sammy, you can teach her how to do it right all you want, but she's still going to do it in the way she wants. She's the poster child for trouble. You can tell her to do something, and she'll find the worst way to get it done. You can't even get mad at her because she got it done, but you clean up the mess after."

I snorted at the dismay in his words and almost parental annoyance.

"Sounds like someone I know," Adhar said with a small smile, and Raphael chuckled as I huffed in anger at the old naga.

"They might seem the same on a surface level, but Kaliya is more level-headed, something I am *eternally* grateful for. If the problem is a knot, Kaliya will find the beginning and end and think of how to unwind it. If she gets angry or stuck, she'll step back and look at it from a different angle. She's relentless, which is what leads her to find new solutions and see problems differently than us. She'll figure it out, but it might not be in the way we think. Then she'll come back to you and tell you how to prevent the knot because she's also figured out what caused it and why it was a problem."

I smiled at Raphael's description but hid it behind a hand as I sank down into a more comfortable position on the couch. He said it with respect and a heaping helping of admiration that made my heart flutter like I was a child told my dress was pretty.

"And this Sammy?"

"If I told her to fix the knot and she can't untie it..." Raphael groaned. "She'll set it on fire and get me a new string. No knot, no problem. She won't even tell me where she got the string. She probably stole it because she couldn't bother with that step since I didn't specify anything about it."

I burst out laughing, unable to contain it. It was so *Sammy*.

"You have to be very clear with Sammy," he continued, but I heard the exasperation.

"Sounds arduous," Adhar said, shaking his head.

"Thankfully, Kaliya has been the most troublesome problem child of the nagas, and as you pointed out, she is not too much of a problem." He looked at me. "The only reason it's not your uncle is he wasn't a child when he became troublesome."

Nakul looked up from whatever he'd been staring at and nodded, but he wasn't smiling, and that caught my attention.

"What are you thinking about?" I asked softly.

"What your mother did and how we're going to deal with it," he answered as I moved to sit closer to him, switching sides with Raphael. We did so seamlessly as he realized what I was doing without me needing to say anything.

"It's been on my mind for months," I said, sighing. "Devika might have betrayed her, and all of us as the nagas, but..."

"You feel like she betrayed you, too, which is valid," Nakul said, looking across the courtyard and not making eye contact with me. "She did dangerous, unknown magic on you, then locked the knowledge away, leaving you scrambling to find out what others knew about you. Leaving you with nothing but questions. She betrayed you, but I think she did it out of her love for you." Anger flashed over his face. "You don't want to know what I'm thinking, Kaliya. It's not kind and doesn't help us."

"I've been thinking and saying a lot of not kind things recently about her," I admitted softly. Sometimes, I *hated* her and what she had done to me. Sometimes, I was heartbroken she couldn't even be bothered to tell me anything in her letter to me. Sometimes, I just wanted to disappear and pretend her mistakes weren't my problem.

"She gave you so much power, then ripped it away from you," he said softly. Then the anger came back, not just a flash but stamped on his face. It sent a chill down my spine. "She also violated the ideas of our reincarnation. Your mother was foolish to think there would be no repercussions, not just on you, but for all of us. She was so daring to trust an outsider. Look at everyone who had to pay for that mistake.

"My wife and son, dead because our enemies, whoever they may be, wanted the attempt on your life to look like a culling. I don't blame you because you were a child, but her? She should have told all of us what she had done. She was one of our *rulers*. Instead, the sun came up that morning, and so many were dead, including her. We sat in the dark for over a century because she... she brought it on us and can't even answer for it." He finally looked at me, and I felt the weight of his pain. "Do better than her. If you do anything in this life, do that."

"I'll do my best," I promised.

He softened. "Yes, I know you will." He lowered his head in his hands. "I'm sorry if it seemed like I took my anger out on you. It wasn't my intention."

"Anger is better than nothing," I said, shrugging. "Besides, I asked for it. Your feelings on this are a good warning about what will happen when Adhar and I finally tell the other nagas."

Nakul inhaled sharply, sitting up with the shocked expression I had given him more than once since this conversation started.

I took a sandwich and ate it, not continuing that line of thought. Raphael ate with me while Adhar and Nakul watched us. Once the plate was cleared, I stood.

"I think it's time Raphael and I retire for a bit. Tell me when the first of the others get here or if you hear from the rakshasas. I want to deal with them the moment we get word."

"I will," Adhar promised.

10

CHAPTER TEN

I wasn't sure how long Raphael and I hid in our room, wanting some peace and quiet. After we were done unpacking and I was certain Adhar and Nakul would be asleep, I grabbed my toiletries and went to find the bathhouse. Raphael followed me, his eyes heavy with exhaustion. I knew he was only holding on to get clean, then he would pass out, which wasn't a bad thing. He would sleep at night and wake up for the morning like any normal person. I was the one who wasn't tired at all and knew I would not sleep this first night. Even if I had stayed awake for days, there was no way I was going to sleep my first full night back in India. Once we were clean, I pushed my mate into the bed and tucked him in.

"Do you want to milk your venom?" he asked, the words slurring from how tired he was.

"Are you even awake?" I asked, pushing his dark hair from his forehead. *He needs a haircut. Why didn't we do that before we left?*

"I can be," he mumbled.

I chuckled and kissed him gently. "No, I'll be fine. We can do it on another night."

I left him there as he snored softly and went into our small toilet closet. I didn't really know how else to describe it. A half-bath would have worked, but that implied there was a full bath somewhere, and there wasn't. The bathhouse wasn't a bathroom. The concepts didn't mesh.

I leaned on the sink and sighed, looking at my reflection. Wet unmanaged hair and the wild red-orange eyes of my snake form reflected back. I was on guard even though I knew everyone in this building would be ready for a fight if we were attacked. Adhar and I had gone over the security talks for months. If no one had found us at the drop point to meet him and Nakul, no one knew we were here.

No one followed us. I didn't see any supernaturals at the airport. The driver doesn't know where we are. We landed the plane where no one would know. We were in the truck before anyone could see us, and no one followed the truck. I am safe for now. I am safe.

It had been a perfect arrival, but that didn't calm me. I left the little room and went into the courtyard, falling onto a couch and staring at the sky. It was cloudy, typical of the tropical monsoon climate of the region. It wasn't the clear night sky I was all too used to. The humidity was too high to dry off, leaving me damp and uncomfortable after only twenty minutes.

I hissed at the sky, knowing I couldn't change the

weather. Getting off the couch, I left the main building, heading out toward the bathhouse. I veered away from it and went into the guarded portion of the jungle. Everything was walled off, so I was safe until I reached one of those walls and jumped over it, which I had done once before.

My skin itched. Walls. A compound. Unseen stars. A brewing storm. Closing my eyes, I listened to the jungle and thought about the night I ran away. I had been so angry that night, my planning not finished, but it was the last time I was ever going to argue with Adhar about finding the people who killed my family. It hadn't just been Adhar, though. There had been a handful of men here for some sort of meeting, but I hadn't been allowed in. Adhar had told me to go to my room. When he finally came to see if I was asleep, we fought about my future, my inclusion, and my ideas. I had been a pissed-off teenage girl. He had been an old man at his wit's end.

He left, locking me in, so I had left through the window, with only a small bag and the clothes on my back.

I heard him coming, walking too obviously for me to miss.

"Kaliya, it's late. Aren't you tired?"

"I went this way," I said, not answering his question.

"I know." Adhar stepped up beside me. He remembered that night just as well as I did. "When I woke up, I had been ready to apologize for the harsh words we exchanged. I didn't find you at breakfast and remembered I had locked you in your room, something I still regret doing. I opened your door, and you were gone. I called every man in the house to help me find you, expecting you would be out here, like now, but we followed your trail to the wall and saw the places you had used the vines to climb. We tried tracking you further but lost you about a day from here. Did you sleep at all, or did you just keep walking?"

"I ran, and I didn't stop until my legs gave out. I couldn't tell you how long that was. I don't remember." With a heavy sigh, I turned my back on my escape route, Adhar mimicking me. "What are you doing up so early?"

"Getting ready to leave. Nakul and I will be back by dawn with Mahavir, Devesh, and Eshika. They live the closest and are the most secure to move. Mahavir also has a calming effect on Nakul, and Nakul enjoys playing house."

"That doesn't surprise me. He likes to remind everyone he's my uncle."

"Devesh is his nephew and likes being related to him. You might like Eshika as well. She's very direct and won't be easily scared of you or Raphael."

"Do you think the other mates will be?"

"Most definitely." Adhar reached out slowly and put his hand on my upper back. "While you're an adult, this is my household, and I would feel more comfortable if you went inside while I was gone. You should try to get some sleep if you can."

"I'll think about it," I said, stepping out of his reach. "But tell me...what was that conversation that night? Why were the men here?"

Adhar closed his eyes, his shoulders sagging and turned away from me.

"It didn't go anywhere," he said softly. "And I was against the idea. I refused to allow it."

"What was it?"

"They hadn't liked that you didn't mate another naga, that you were wild and opinionated... and traumatized. They knew I was having difficulties with you, something I had told one of them in confidence, but that trust had been misplaced. He spread it around that you were a problematic child who needed more discipline, and I should hand you off to a stricter family." Adhar shook his head. "You were hurt, and I was out of my depth, but we would have made it work, I think."

"Adhar?" He sounded as if he regretted every word that came out of his mouth.

"They wanted me to start a vote to strip your position from you. They wanted to stop you from becoming a ruler of the nagas." Adhar looked over his shoulder, his eyes brilliant green, his snake eyes. I felt my anger reflected at me in that gaze. Adhar would never forget what transpired that night, and he hated that.

I was angry just hearing what had been discussed. I had never been the best ruler, never attached to the role, given it by the burden of being the only one who could hold it. I was like an absent parent, but to hear my people had conspired against me? It infuriated me. All I had ever done, all I had ever wanted, was to make sure they would one day be safe, and their lost loved ones would be avenged. I had been working for that since I was a *child*, and they had been talking about stripping me of it and forcing me to live under someone's thumb.

"I refused, but I was angry they even tried. Our people had never done something like it before, and while we were desperate, I had hope for you. I left the meeting furious, telling them never to speak of it again. By the time I went to check on you, and you snapped at me, I lost my temper and made the biggest mistake of my entire tenure as ruler. I snapped back, not keeping the cool head I normally tried to manage you with. Even then, you listened to logic. You were too smart, even when you were angry."

"Neither of us was logical that night," I pointed out.

"Yes, but you were a child, and I was the adult. I expected better of myself. You deserved better from me. Then you were gone, as I deserved for treating you like I had."

"Did they try again?"

"Two of them acted as if you were dead the moment we lost your trail. They waited on the birth of a new female naga, one they could shape from birth to be the... proper ruler, in their minds. One was smart enough to come to me and ask me to do the vote in your absence. He had a feeling you would come back one day, just as you had after you lived on the streets when your family was killed. I threw him out of my home and let him figure out his way back to his own.

"The last just considered the conversation a moot point and waited, watching how everything unfolded. I don't know how he feels about you today. He was never one to tell me much about his feelings, preferring to keep them to himself. He spoke little that night at the meeting." Adhar blinked, and those green snake eyes were gone.

"Since you've come back, and I made sure it was known that your position was held, all four have kept their own counsel. I don't expect that to hold now that you're here. They'll all be here."

"Who?" I asked softly, wanting to know which ones would give me the most problem.

"Aamir, Dalar, Pavan, and Vikrant. Vikrant was, and still is, the wild card."

"Thank you." I remembered them. One had been mated to a human already. Two found their human mates after I had run away. One of the four hadn't been so lucky in finding a mate, not me or anyone else. None of them had actually wanted me as a mate for any reason except I was a nagini, which was enough for the three to be disappointed when I wasn't their mate. I had been a traumatized mess. No one liked me back then. *I* didn't like me back then.

Survivor's guilt is a hell of a thing.

"If you feel unsafe—"

"There is nothing they could do that would make me feel unsafe," I said with a smile, confident in my abilities and everything I had gone through. Emotionally, this trip was already tiring, but physically, I had never been more ready. Sparring with Nakul had only enforced that.

"Then I will let you stay out here. Remember, I'll be back right before dawn, so if you wish to greet them, be waiting in the courtyard." Adhar started walking away, but I wasn't done talking to him.

"Adhar," I called out before he left my sight. He looked back again, and I took the chance to say what needed to be said. "Thanks for believing in me and protecting my interests when I couldn't. If you can forgive me for the years of running around and the attitude I've taken with you over those years, I can forgive you for being a man not prepared to raise a difficult orphan and an old supernatural who finds change slow and hard."

"Then all is forgiven." He smiled as though I had taken a weight off his shoulders. "If you would like, I keep files on everyone in my office. You know where they are. Feel free to do some research while I'm gone. You should know more about your people before they arrive."

Listening to his truck start and the tires roll over the earth until he was gone, I went back inside. In his office, I went to a filing cabinet he kept under his desk, found the files he kept on everyone, and pulled out the four folders. None of their addresses were listed, a smart move. Adhar had them recorded somewhere, but not with everything else. He also didn't have pictures, but that was fine. I knew the faces of the adult nagas and could easily conjure them in my head.

I looked over those four files with a high level of scrutiny. Their professions and roles in the community were the most important. Dalar and Pavan were considered the naga version of unemployed. Dalar was mated in the last century, the most recent of the nagas except me, and was the father of the twin baby boys. I could accept that. He would be distracted during his time here with the babies, probably anxious about being away from home. I couldn't see him picking a fight, and I certainly wouldn't try to pick one with him, not while he and his wife managed their new family.

Pavan had no excuse for not picking up a useful skill to help other nagas. Unmated and with no responsibility? He would be easy for me to crush. If he said anything, I would destroy him. The other two were more of a problem, one because he was an unknown, and the other would be actively hostile.

Vikrant had sympathy from the other nagas on his side. His sister and her mate had been killed during the culling that left me an orphan. He was training with Adhar to learn the runes of power that helped defend our homes. He seemed to live a quiet life and never got into trouble. There was no way to plan for this one, and that bothered me. He had a mate now, but information on her was practically nonexistent. Adhar didn't keep the mates and the nagas in the same place, but I didn't feel the need to hunt down files on the mates. I wanted to meet the women without prejudging.

Aamir, that bastard, was a capable tracker. He'd been the one to help Adhar find me in New Delhi and probably tried hard to find me when I ran away. He'd rescued nagas from captivity once when they had been captured on the road to be killed later. From memory, he saved his mate from something, but I didn't know the story. He had the respect of everyone and had worked to save me more than once. He hadn't held that over my head as a child, but he would now if he still hated me.

To make matters worse, Aamir was Roshni's father and had found his mate long before I was born. I hadn't been told the names of the parents for security reasons. This was my first time really seeing it.

To think, one of these assholes was blessed with a daughter, and of all of them, it was fucking Aamir.

I read for hours, looking at the clock when I turned through the pages to keep track of the time. An hour before dawn, I put the files away and went to wake up Raphael. If I was going to be awake to meet them, I needed my mate with me.

11

CHAPTER ELEVEN

"I understand it will be a bit of a performance because we need to make a good impression, but why did I have to wear a suit?" Raphael asked, clearly amused by the way I had chosen his wardrobe for the day. "I'm sure they would have been fine if I wore more comfortable clothes."

I looked him over while adjusting the tie I picked out for him. He looked...delicious.

Maybe I should have saved this suit for a different occasion.

"We both know this suit isn't uncomfortable, and it fits you perfectly," I countered. "I packed five of your best suits for this trip just for this. After introductions, you can wear whatever you like...including those gray sweatpants," I murmured, leaning in to nip his ear with my teeth.

He growled and wrapped an arm around my waist, yanking me closer to press our bodies together.

"I'll remember that," he whispered in my ear, his hand sliding down from my lower back to my ass.

I used his jacket to hold him to me, and as his lips drifted over mine, I let myself forget about where we were, what we were doing, and why. Just for that moment, it was only us.

When it was over, we released each other and moved to stand side by side, knowing Adhar would drive up any moment. I checked the time after a few minutes. Dawn was only fifteen minutes away, and the closer it came, the more I worried about something happening.

Trust Adhar. He's moved these families around for centuries and has never planned a failed move.

Most attacks came from mistakes made by people who didn't realize just how thorough Adhar could be in the travel plans of the nagas. He'd never lost anyone coming to or leaving his house. When someone tried to do it on their own, they increased the chance of being hurt. In the one hundred years since Adhar had taken over the job, not allowing others to make plans for themselves, no one had been lost in a transition. From memory, my mother didn't have that good of a record, and she had brought guests to and from our home more often than was normal.

Now that I think about it, that's probably how Mehar and the others knew where we all lived. Our families all spent lots of time together.

Her failures didn't have to be mine or Adhar's. She'd been a good ruler, a revolutionary compared to the old minds of the nagas, and being a revolutionary was dangerous. I knew that from experience.

Five minutes before the sun glowed over the horizon, I heard a vehicle roll up the drive and go into the garage. I rubbed my palms together. Nakul and Adhar were familiar faces, but I had never met Eshika or Devesh. Mahavir, I knew, but our last conversations had been tense. I sighed heavily.

It had been the situation with Nakul that marked a noticeable turning point between Adhar and me. There had been a shift there based on the decisions I made as I grew to understand why he had done what he had. He and Mahavir had protected Nakul while he'd been running around for the same reason I sent my uncle to India after the prison incident.

Since that moment, Adhar listened and respected me more. I was calmer with him, and we had finally started working together. The respect between us deepened into a new friendship since I had mated. He was a layered and complex individual, and I had never tried to peel those layers back. He'd spent years waiting for me to act like the adult I wanted him to treat me as.

I had no idea if Mahavir and I would have the same growth. Adhar and I were required to be on speaking terms. Mahavir and I didn't have nearly the same circumstances.

I heard the door open and saw Adhar first. He gave me a smile, nodding at how Raphael and I were waiting for him. He moved to hold the door open, allowing a woman who had to be Eshika to enter. Next was a teenager in those strange colt years, a little clumsy and probably taller than he knew what to do with. He towered over his mom but was sheepish when she smiled up at him and waved for him to hurry along.

Next came Nakul and his brother. They looked so similar, near copies of each other except for their mouths. Mahavir's lips were pressed into a thin line, looking too small for the jawline he shared with his older brother. Nakul was wearing an amused smile. They carried two suitcases apiece, dropping them right inside the door.

"I'll get the others," Nakul said, walking out before Adhar could close the door.

I waited patiently as Mahavir looked over his family. Devesh was the only one who openly looked at me, his gaze curious and a little fearful. His father caught the stare and followed it to me, his eyes narrowing.

"Kaliya," he said softly. "This is my mate and wife, Eshika Kisku, and our son, Devesh Kisku." He spoke in English, so I didn't need to translate for Raphael. I waited another beat for him to continue the introduction. He looked at his wife. "This is Kaliya Sahni, the female ruler of the naga."

Eshika bowed with her palms pressed together over her heart, then slapped the back of her son's head. He copied her, his face darkening with a blush. Mahavir was last when Adhar cleared his throat to remind him of protocol.

I returned their greeting, then gestured to my mate, realizing how Raphael towered over my people. Most of us never rose over six feet. He was six and a half and could get bigger...much bigger.

"This is my mate, Raphael Alvarez. He is the Warlord of the cambions." I didn't elaborate. Adhar and I had already discussed how to introduce Raphael's kind to the other nagas. They had been given information on what Raphael was. It was only fair I passed on as much information as Raphael would allow, considering he knew so much about the nagas before meeting most of them.

Raphael, with all eyes on him, put his hands together and bowed his head. Adhar and Nakul had been pleased I taught Raphael something of our customs before we came, but Mahavir told me not everyone would feel the same.

He snorted with derision. "You could have been the mate to another naga but refused to give my son a chance. You thought a demon was a better choice. To many, rakshasas are also demons. You should have at least mated one of those, so you didn't have to train an outsider to mime our culture but not understand the meaning."

Eshika gasped, shocked by her mate's rudeness, and before Devesh could say anything, she reached out and shook her head, silencing whatever he thought he could say. Raphael stiffened and straightened up. Adhar was still holding the door open as Nakul brought in two more suitcases. Nakul gently put them down but said nothing as Adhar closed the door. The weight of their stares was heavy.

They were all waiting on me.

I moved slowly, lifting my chin and keeping my head high as I closed the distance between.

"You were unmated when I came of age. Do you remember what you said?" I whispered, leaning close to

Mahavir, making it clear my words were only for him. Out of the corner of my eye, I saw Eshika pull her son away from us, going into the courtyard and giving us the space needed to have a private conversation. Adhar and Nakul followed and helped the mother and son get comfortable. Raphael didn't move. He was the stubborn ruler of his own people and had just been disrespected as well. He had to stay and be strong under the scrutiny.

"It was a long time ago," Mahavir replied, glaring at me.

"Let me enlighten you because I don't like to forget things. Everyone was so disappointed I didn't have a naga mate, but there was one man who was relieved." I gently poked his chest. "We're not blood-related in any way. It was possible, but when it was all over, you turned to another male and said you had prayed not to be my mate because you didn't want to be burdened with a broken wife once I reached adulthood. I heard you as I walked out, unwilling to face any of you anymore."

Mahavir tried to step back, but I grabbed his shirt.

"I was hurting," Mahavir said, swallowing. "I had just lost my brother, my sister-in-law, and my nephew."

"So was I," I hissed. "Do you love your son so little, you would give him a *broken* wife? You would wish that on him when you weren't man enough to take it on yourself? Pathetic. Be happy I'm not petty or vindictive enough to tell your mate." I released him and brushed my hands together as if I was wiping off dirt. "When I was told about Devesh coming of age, I had already found Raphael. I already knew who my mate was and wasn't interested in another option. Devesh didn't have a chance. Maybe if he was already an adult, but certainly not at his age. I don't look at teenagers and children as future spouses, regardless of the biological reasons that force our species to do so. And for as long as I live, that practice won't happen." I sighed, looking at the people waiting on us then back at my mate before turning to Mahavir again.

"Say anything rude to me or my mate again, and I'll make sure you pay for it. You talk to me about respect and culture, but you've disrespected not only one of your rulers but one of another supernatural species. He's learning, and you should respect the effort he's making. If you don't want to listen to me on this matter, you can take it to Adhar and file a complaint."

"Which will be ignored," Adhar said from his place in the courtyard, standing in the middle and waiting for us to join him. "Raphael is an honored member of this community, just as Kaliya is an honored member of the cambion's community. Disrespect will not be tolerated."

Well, I wouldn't call myself an honored *member of the cambion community, but I'm certainly part of it. Not that I'm very honored as a naga among my own, either.*

Mahavir lowered his head. "My apologies, Warlord."

"Apology accepted," Raphael said in a tone I only heard when he was mad with his cambions—the stern ruler who would throw them through walls to get his point across. He'd only had to do it once and had gotten the point across.

Wrapping my arm in Raphael's, I guided him to the courtyard, directly across from Mahavir's family, and forced him to sit. I didn't sit until Mahavir joined us, looking as if he was regretting everything in his life. He looked at his son for a long time, then at me before sitting down. Once he was seated, I nodded to Adhar, and we took our seats.

"Welcome to my home," Adhar said kindly, smiling at the small family. "Once you've eaten something and we've discussed the rules of my home during this visit, we'll move your things to your rooms, and you'll be able to rest."

"Thank you, Adhar," Eshika said with a smile. "It's a lovely home. I haven't been to this one yet."

"Yes, I think the last time your family stayed with me was when Devesh was still a newborn."

"Oh yes! We still have the blanket you gave us. It's still just as soft and lovely as it was the day we took it home."

"I'm glad to hear it. Maybe one day, it can swaddle a second child."

"Oh, that would be so lovely. I hope it's another boy, so I can give him your name after everything you've done for us."

Adhar and Eshika had the relationship I had expected. From what I'd heard, the human women who found themselves as naga mates absolutely adored the old naga we called our ruler. There was a familial friendship, as though he was a doting grandfather or uncle.

"Darling sister, let's proceed with the formalities before your boy falls asleep," Nakul said with a chuckle. He kicked Devesh's foot, making the boy's head come up. The young man blinked rapidly and yawned.

"Sorry," he mumbled.

I resisted the urge to smile as Eshika sighed heavily at her son.

"We're your people, and you're falling asleep? I thought you were too excited to sleep."

"The couch is very comfortable," he mumbled.

"Isn't it?" Raphael asked, leaning back. "Got to be careful, though. You look like you're going to be tall, and couches get less comfortable the taller you get. I've learned from experience."

Devesh went from sleepy to alert. Maybe the teen thought he would be ignored, but Raphael didn't do that. He paid attention, always seeing too much. I had found the trait both annoying and attractive when we had lived together. As he grew confident in his role with the cambions, I started seeing new parts of him. I noticed it when we weren't together, but he was learning how to act to get people to like him, respect him, or fear him. He'd always been watchful, but now, he was learning how to use what he saw. He saw a teen boy and decided pointing out a friendly similarity with the young naga would get him further than ignoring him.

"He will be," Eshika said with a smile, playing with her son's hair. "Taller than his father and his uncle."

"He'll be tall like his grandfather," Mahavir added, looking at Raphael then at Nakul. "Our father was a giant."

"Yes. Mother had been a tiny thing, though." Nakul smiled, but it was pained. I knew little about Nakul and Mahavir's parents other than they had been long-lived. "Now, to the house rules. I woke very early and would like a nap before midday."

"Yes. The bathhouse is run on a schedule, which is posted in the kitchen. Couples may sign up for two-hour slots to use at the same time, but it can't overlap with other, prescheduled times. If there's nothing else scheduled, women have first use of the bathhouse, and men are barred from entry for three hours. Men can have the next three-hour period, and every evening cleaning responsibilities are for the men. I'll expect all of you to join me."

I covered my mouth, trying to hide my shit-eating grin as Eshika's eyes brightened with joy, and her smile broadened.

"I don't have to clean the bathroom?" she asked innocently.

"No, but I would like if everyone kept their private rooms cleaned and clean up after themselves in other public places, such as the courtyard. You won't be responsible, however, for cleaning up after anyone else. There will be too many of us staying here to leave the cleaning to a small number."

He didn't say it, but Adhar's intention was clear. While everyone was at his house, the women wouldn't be housemaids for their mates, children, or other nagas. His small glance at me could have meant a thousand things, and I fully intended to ask him when I had the chance.

Eshika changed as she turned to her husband. The smile turned victorious and cutting.

"You asked why I was excited to come here? This is why," she said before kissing her mate's cheek. "Teach Devesh to scrub well, so I can use him when we get home."

"Of course, darling," Mahavir said, sighing and smiling at the same time. "Did you hear that, my son?"

Devesh didn't look as if he was paying attention, staring at Raphael and me.

"Devesh, your father wants you," I said softly. That made Devesh blink.

"Yes, Father?" he asked, recovering quickly.

"Your mother wants you to learn to clean. You'll do so," Mahavir said sternly.

"I know how to clean," he said, huffing.

"Learn to clean better then. Practice makes perfect means the same thing with a mop as it does with the sword," Eshika said. "You may continue, Adhar."

"Thank you." Adhar was fighting a smile.

As Adhar continued with rules, which barely applied to me, I realized he was right. I did like her.

12

CHAPTER TWELVE

"I need to retire for a few hours," Adhar said finally. "Tonight, I'll pick up another four people. Take the day to get to know each other."

"Who's next?" I asked as we all stood.

"Aamir and his family and Pavan, who has been helping their family with security."

I frowned. That hadn't been in their files.

"Is it safe for Roshni to travel?" Mahavir asked before I had the chance to comment on Pavan's current responsibility.

"As safe as it is for any of us," Adhar said, tilting his head at Mahavir. "They will be fine. They're one of the first families coming, and they will be the first to leave."

"To catch our enemies off guard," I said, not directing at Mahavir, but my intention was clear. I was proving I was smarter. "Our enemies find our patterns, which is how they do their more coordinated strikes against us. The same way poachers find a trail and place traps. If they move before we've established a pattern, Roshni and her family will be safe. It's the last of the ones coming here and leaving who will be at the most risk."

"Which is why my pick-up points are in different locations," Adhar said, nodding at my insight, which wasn't really insight. We had talked about this for months.

"With parts of the trip to your compound being off-road, they won't know where you've gone unless they're willing to get lost in the jungle to find your trail again. They also won't know if it's us or humans. We're not the only ones hiding in the jungle."

"I've become used to making sure no one can follow me," Adhar said. "Now, let me show you to your rooms. Kaliya, Raphael, could you get their bags? I must retire, and Nakul..."

Nakul was already heading to his room, waving at us as he disappeared from view.

"Yeah, we got it." I headed for the bags. This gave me the chance to see where the nagas would stay in relation to my room. It was the paranoid part of me—know where everyone is in relation to me, so I can help them if I hear anything. I did the same thing at my home and the cambion compound. Over five months, I had memorized which cambion lived in which house and who was on what duty. Remembering those things was easy for me.

I grabbed two of the suitcases of the same color, noticing there were two in each color, and when I reached their rooms, Devesh tried to take one from me.

"Show me where to put it," I said, smiling. He nodded, silent as he ducked into the room Adhar had assigned him. He wasn't being forced to stay in the same room as his parents, which would have made me concerned about space, but Adhar's home was massive. Not only did it have a second floor, I had yet to explore, there was also a bunker basement he'd slowly dug out for years. I put the suitcase on the teen's bed.

"There you go," I said. "Is this one yours as well?"

"Yeah."

I dropped it next to the first, then left. As I walked out of Devesh's room, he followed me out.

"Yes?" I asked as I walked back to my suite, knowing he was tailing me.

"I wanted to..." He was so nervous, I almost pitied him. I hadn't gone through a socially nervous phase growing up. I had been thrust from normal to abnormal so quickly, I hadn't had the chance to be nervous. I had to survive, which meant I had to fight.

I stopped as I reached my door, looking patiently at the teen. Behind him, Raphael was walking out of Devesh's parents' suite and turned to head our way.

"Ask anything you like. I'm an open book."

Raphael shook his head at my words and gave me a mocking look as he waited behind the young man. I resisted a smile. Devesh didn't know he was blocking my mate. Youthful absentmindedness. He was so focused on me with his sight, he was ignoring his other senses. He could feel Raphael's heat just as well as I could. There was literally no way Raphael should be able to sneak up on a naga. It was biologically impossible, but this boy was proving that sometimes, the impossible happened.

"Why?" he asked softly, using Hindi instead of English. I didn't translate for Raphael immediately because this was personal to the young man. I would explain to Raphael later. "Why didn't you want to meet me?"

I had bruised him. I hadn't really considered that earlier, but there it was in his eyes. Rejection. Every naga before him, male and female, had met others of our kind as a teenager to see if their mate was there. I had robbed him of that, and while he might not be angry with me, he certainly wanted an explanation. There was sexism in the entire tradition, but that wasn't the problem with Devesh. I thought it happened too young. I would *never* meet a sixteen-year-old boy to see if he was my mate, a potential sexual partner to have children with. It would have been a formality since nothing would have been official until he was in his mid-twenties, but that changed nothing. This ancient tradition of my people left a bad taste in my modern mouth, and stopping it was a hill I was willing to die on.

"You're on the cusp of manhood, but you're not a man. You should focus on who you'll be as a man." I used Hindi, respecting the young man's choice. "What type of man will you be? What will you want in a mate, that person you will have to spend centuries with? Do you have a passion you want to chase? A hobby you want to foster into a profession?"

"My father said—"

"I wasn't asking about what your father said. I was asking about you," I said sternly, stopping that train of thought in its tracks. "I think the nagas do this tradition too young."

"If age is the problem, why not wait to see when I was old enough?" Devesh gave me a hurt look.

I wondered what he saw when he looked at me. I was wearing a simple business look, not presenting myself as a warrior, not yet. It was part of my act. I didn't want to scare people the moment they walked in. These were my people, and that would have been unfair to them and mean of me.

"Devesh..." I sighed and walked to him, grabbing his shoulders. He was taller than me. "Hypothetically, if you were twenty-five instead of sixteen, let me tell you what would have happened. I would *not* have moved back to India. I won't do that for *anyone*. You would have had to leave your home and come to mine in America, a place you've never been. I would not have been a subservient wife. I would not have stayed at home, safe from any dangers. I would have continued to live my life the way I wanted. I fought to have that right. Not even my mate can take away my hard-earned freedoms. He's strong enough to handle it and even expects it. He asked me to train his people to protect themselves. Tell me, is that the life you wanted? Did you want a mate who killed people for a living?"

His eyes went wide, and I finally realized they had not told him everything about me. Maybe they thought he was too young or that I would die before it became an issue. I didn't care about the reason. Obviously, I had to crush this boy's impression of me.

"Devesh, I'm a Tribunal Executioner," I said gently. "From about your age to my thirties, I was trained by the world's best assassin, so I could survive in a world that is hostile to us and everyone else in it. I honed my body into a weapon and developed a reputation for being one of the most dangerous people in the United States. I have killed more people in my life than you have met in yours." I felt the shiver run through him, but I held on, keeping his attention on me.

"I won't give up my warrior calling for anyone, not even my mate. Is that what you would have wanted? To live in another country, possibly by yourself, if you weren't strong enough to keep up with me? Because I don't slow down. I would train you, and if you couldn't protect yourself..." I let him think of that possibility for a moment.

"I don't live the type of life you're used to or should even want. In the last couple of years, I've had more brushes with death than even I'm comfortable with, which is saying something because my first brush with death was at the age of twelve. Did you think you would meet me, and I would be a good naga mate and wife? That possibility never existed. If you're not a warrior, that's okay, but you would never stop me from being one." I released him with one hand and pointed past him. He turned and practically jumped out of his skin at the sight of my silent, massive mate.

"But him? He's a warrior, too. He's fought as hard for his people as I have fought for you and all the nagas. He's my partner. He was made for me, and I was made for him." I smiled at my mate, then let it fade when I turned back to the teenager.

"So, Devesh, that's why I didn't leave the possibility open for when you were old enough. I found perfection for me, which is why I think nagas rush into finding mates too young. I knew what I needed in a mate, even as I fought it. You have no idea what you're looking for because you haven't even discovered who you are." I squeezed his shoulder gently, then reached out to Raphael, who took my hand.

"You should get some rest," Raphael said kindly as he walked past Devesh.

"Yes, sir," Devesh said, bowing his head quickly and running away. I waited until the teen had locked himself in his room to look at Raphael again.

"He has guts to confront me, but he didn't know the battle he was fighting," I explained vaguely before I pulled my mate into our suite. I still wasn't tired. In fact, the conversation brought even more life into me. Devesh was young and impressionable, and maybe I should have felt guilty, but I was damn grateful I had the chance to add a new viewpoint to his world. Maybe he would stop thinking about mates for a decade or two until he was more prepared to have one.

Once I was certain Raphael and I were alone, I explained to him what Devesh and I talked about. Raphael listened patiently, not threatened by the seventeen-year-old boy who had dared come to his mate and demand why he didn't have a chance.

"I think you made the right judgment," Raphael concluded. "He had an idea of who you were supposed to be, probably based on his mother and other mates."

"Every culture raises its children with its ideals. He clearly didn't know enough about me. You hit the nail on the head. He definitely built an image of me in his head based on what our culture taught him about women. It's not that we're not strong, but we're certainly not in charge. We're not warriors in comparison to the men."

"They, not we," he whispered, unbuttoning his jacket.

"What?"

"You said, 'we're not really warriors,' and I was correcting you," he said as he threw the jacket over the back of our reading chair. "The other women of your culture might not be, but you certainly are, and you should never say anything that points to otherwise. I won't allow anyone to make my mate seem like less than she is...including her." He chuckled, giving me a guilty look. "That includes me when I'm a dense ass who doesn't listen to my better angels."

"Yes, you are capable of that." It was how we ended up mated.

"Now..." He reached out, and I didn't react in time. He yanked me to him with a smolder. "Enough of them. I believe we started something earlier that we didn't get to see through to the end, and they have nothing to do with it."

"And we won't right now," I countered, putting my hands against his chest. "I want breakfast." I wasn't hungry, but the idea of getting it on right now made me want to escape the room.

He growled but lowered his head against mine.

"Breakfast sounds like a good idea. I'm fucking starving," he agreed, mumbling petulantly. I knew he would be. I hadn't fed him before Mahavir and his family arrived.

13

CHAPTER THIRTEEN

Raphael and I never made our way to the bedroom activities he wanted. I showed him around the estate as we waited for a simple breakfast to finish cooking in the woodburning oven Adhar still used, then took him on a tour around the grounds, showing him the artificial pond Adhar had built after I moved in.

"Adhar built everything here, didn't he?" Raphael asked, looking around at the many small constructions around us. If we weren't in the jungle, it would have been dangerous for Adhar to build so much on one estate, but he used the tree cover and thick underbrush to hide the sprawling estates he kept.

"Yeah. He's a scholar and ruler, but,"—I gestured around—"he has a lot of time on his hands. He lived alone for decades. Him and his homes. My mother once said Adhar found peace in it. He has the oldest homes of our people. The bones of the home we're in right now are actually from before we went into hiding. He built literally everything else here by hand, learning to do it all on his own." I went to one of the closest sheds and opened the door, finding Adhar's collection of fresh timber. "He cuts down the trees he needs and treats the wood. When he dug the pond, it was before we had things like bulldozers. He had to develop tricks for moving large amounts of dirt at once. He never asked for my help, not even to push the wheelbarrow around."

"Why did he put a pond in? Did he need to keep a water source?"

"I..." With a sigh, I closed the shed and looked at the pond, still well maintained and crystal clear. It had to have been redone since I left, possibly lined, and there was now a water feature. Somehow, Adhar got his hands on a pump. "I don't know. I have a theory, but it feels egotistical to say."

"You think he built it for you." Raphael reached out and ran a hand over my hair. "Seeing Adhar talk to Eshika, I wouldn't say it's egotistical. He seems to give his people what they need and what they want. I almost think it makes him happy to do it."

Of course he saw that.

"Yeah," I agreed softly. "He's changing, though. It wasn't always this obvious. Even in a couple of years, he's... learned to bend a bit more. Maybe it's the circumstances. We've never dealt with anything like me. Maybe he's just finally accepting I'm not going anywhere, and he can't make me bend all the way to him."

"Or maybe, after a century, you've both reached a place of understanding," he countered.

"Don't act wise with me," I warned. "I've seen you

ruling the cambions for a few months now." And it was like watching a train wreck some days..

"Tell me I'm wrong," Raphael said with a taunting grin.

"You're probably not," I said, dismissing him with a wave of my hand. "Come on. Let's go check on breakfast and make sure I didn't burn the house down."

Breakfast was safe and nearly finished when we got back. Adhar kept fresh rice for the household at all times, and I paired it with bread and baked veggies. It wasn't a typical breakfast, not even a real dish, but it would fill us up for now. I had warned Adhar, Raphael needed a lot of food to stay in shape, and I was eating more like a human now. He'd told us he would stock enough food, but we would cook for most of our meals. As we sat down, I realized I was finally living the life many nagas dealt with, having a human mate that needed more food than we did. Now I was one of those people who needed food. Nagas could go a few days without a large meal or eating at all. Snakes digest slowly and conserve energy.

"Mahavir's family will have a food day," I said as Raphael looked at his food, clearly disappointed. Not with the quality, because he wasn't foolish enough to say anything I cooked was bad, but the amount. I hadn't made enough to satisfy him because I was afraid of going too fast through Adhar's food stores for just the two of us. "I'll help Eshika with it so we can—"

"You should spend the days going to the archives," he countered with a smile. "You know your own mind. If you work on that, I'll help Eshika. She's got a bite to her, and the way she expects her son to clean, she might just accept a man in the kitchen. Plus, it would let me make sure enough food is prepared."

I chuckled, nodding. "She'll be in the kitchen all day, from the moment she wakes up to the end of the day. I hope you're ready for that."

"Sounds like my mother," he said, shrugging. "Though she threw me out of the house when she cooked unless it was holidays. Then she had to teach me everything for tradition."

"How many holidays were there?"

Raphael looked up with a small, wistful smile, staring at the courtyard but not really seeing it. "To her, nearly every day was a holiday. God had blessed her with a beautiful family, and she sent her prayers in food and love."

I didn't know how to reply, so I reached out and squeezed his hand.

You can have her again, Raphael. We can do that for you. Just ask.

Instead of saying anything else, he started eating. Eshika came out shortly after we started, looked at what we were eating, and shook her head.

"For a big man, that can't be enough," she pointed out in Hindi, looking at me. I couldn't read her expression, so I took her words as teasing instead of condemnation. I wasn't in the mood for an early morning pissing match with a human mate.

"There's no such thing as enough food for Raphael," I replied. "He doesn't speak Hindi, though, so please stay in English."

"Oh, I'm sorry," she said in English, putting a hand to

her forehead. “This might sound bad, but he looks a bit like us, doesn’t he? I didn’t even think.”

I looked at Raphael, seeing the Central and South American heritage in him. His family hailed from Mexico, but I knew there was a bit of a melting pot in his family.

No, I don’t see it...Well, actually...he has the dark hair and brown eyes, and his skin tone falls in the same range. At a glance, he could pass as Indian. Maybe. Someone would have to not be paying attention.

Which Eshika hadn’t been, so I let it slide.

“Yeah,” I agreed, shrugging. “He could hide in a crowd if he needed to.” It made Raphael chuckle.

“Everything you think about is how to use it in a stressful situation,” he said, putting down his fork. “For once, I think you’re wrong. I’m too tall. I tower over people. It makes them look at me, especially other women.”

“Oh no, I have a tall, attractive, muscle-bound mate. All the men want to be him, and the women want to be with him.” I laid it on thick, putting the back of my hand to my forehead. “What am I to do?”

Eshika laughed as she started prepping for the day. Raphael was bent over the table, his shoulders shaking.

“I know better than to ask you to hide in a crowd,” I said blandly, dropping my hand. “Please.” I pushed my plate toward Raphael. “Finish this for me, so we don’t waste food. I’m heading to the archives to do some reading.”

Raphael dragged the plate closer, possessive of the food, especially my leftovers. Even though I ate more food, I still couldn't eat what he could. He devoured all of my leftovers before they had the chance to make it to the fridge. The only time we had real leftovers was when he cooked for just the two of us. He sometimes made three times too much because his eyes were bigger than his stomach.

Which is absolutely insane. His stomach is practically bottomless.

"Eshika," he said, looking up. "Do you want help today?"

Eshika nearly dropped the pan she was holding, looking at Raphael with wide eyes, then at me, confused.

"Is he serious?" she asked. "He wants to help in the kitchen?"

"He does," I confirmed. "Enjoy and make sure he doesn't eat as you cook. He can be sneaky."

"But—"

"Have fun!" I called, walking out quickly before she could tell me it wasn't Raphael's place to do that sort of thing. Whether it was because he was a man, my mate, or a ruler, I didn't care. It would be good for both of them. He had never seen a massive naga meal, where the food never stopped for the entire day because it was our day to eat. She needed to see Raphael wasn't like the naga men she was used to. She wouldn't have to work very hard to get him to cook and clean.

Adhar had digitized the information, but I wanted to see it in person, so I headed to the archives. The air smelled of old parchment and magic, and the air felt stagnant. There were no windows in the archive, and the door closed with a seal. Everything in the room had been preserved magically, but even magic faded.

That's probably why he started digitizing it. They're going to crumble one day, so he has to save them while he can.

I frowned, wondering if I could run out of oxygen in this room if I wasn't careful, then shrugged. I would leave if I started to feel uncomfortable.

Putting on a pair of gloves, I hunted for anything from the first generation of nagas. The gloves weren't medical-grade, but they would keep my skin oil off the parchment. As a child, Adhar had shown me the archives, but I hadn't been interested. I had wanted to train with a sword, to fight and avenge my family.

I was an idiot kid. I should have realized they were one and the same. A warrior without knowledge swung blindly. A scholar with no sword couldn't act on anything they knew or defend the precious information they guarded. I had to be both. I've become both.

Now, looking at the archive, I nearly drooled. If I had spent more time in them or asked Adhar for information from them sooner, I may have learned something important. Now it was all at my fingertips, and I didn't know where to start.

I should have asked Adhar for his directory. I have no idea how he has this organized.

Randomly, I pulled things off the shelves. Three of the first five were letters between nagas, now archived for the future, which many cultures did for historical purposes. America had letters written by George Washington, and the UK had letters penned by Queen Victoria. As the nagas died out, these letters had become precious insight into our earlier generations, our grandparents, great-grandparents, and further. They were also our previous lives.

As I read them, I lost track of time, seeing glimpses into a past I remembered. There were a few events I thought were familiar, as though my previous life had heard the rumors of them. Or maybe Adhar or my mother had mentioned them to me.

Probably both.

I sat down, lost in the past, reading about nagas trying to find farmland. Some talked about humans moving closer and struggling to adjust to living near humans. One mentioned how a human caught him charming a snake and tried to mimic it. The human, thankfully, hadn't died, but the naga was certain it was because he intervened.

The older the parchment, the more stories I saw that were echoed in the human legends of our people. We had been born of Kadra and Kashyapa, who were very much real, and some even talked about their mother, though no one spoke of their father. Some talked about leaving Ramaniyaka, finally tired of their mother and looking to make their own destinies. Kadra had been a scheming woman. Once, her husband had turned her into a river. She had eventually been changed back, but. I could see why her sons wanted to go out on their own.

Reading the stories felt as though I was reading about brothers I knew, who would eventually come to Adhar's home and recognize me. There were even references to me...well, my previous life. They talked about the beautiful mate he found during a trip away from

Ramaniyaka and the great power that forced him to return to the island that held their mother. They spoke as if it was interesting gossip until they discovered his plan to fight Garuda at the Yamuna River. Then there were references about how Krishna killed him.

I couldn't find anything written by Kaliya. It shouldn't have bothered me because I had his memories, but it did.

I was sitting among probably dozens of these letters when I heard the door slide open.

"Raphael and Eshika said I would find you here," Adhar said, closing and locking the door behind him. He sat across the wooden table from me and looked at everything I had. "Have you learned anything interesting?"

"Ramaniyaka and Ramanaka are the same thing," I said, looking up. "Which I already knew, but then, why did it have two names?"

"You are probably the only person who can answer that question," he said as he grabbed a second pair of gloves. Once they were on, he gently lifted a letter, and his eyes quickly scanned it. "I've read everything here over the years, many repeatedly."

"Why is there nothing by Kaliya?" I asked, waving a hand over what I had pulled out. "Unless you've put it somewhere else, I think I've found everything from the first generation of nagas."

"It all disappeared. I don't know when because it was before I took charge of the archive. Why are you so interested?"

"Some memories are easy to recall, and some aren't. The big ones? They come to me like one of my own would. Moments with Rama are things he would have clung to until the very end, and he did. I remember the moment he knew he was going to die because he didn't listen to Krishna. It's a strong memory, and it comes to me in my dreams, just like the nightmares about my family dying or the time I was captured in China by humans. But writing letters, who would he write them to? I've forgotten emails I've written ten minutes after I sent them because they didn't really matter to me. I have all his memories, but I think my brain categorized them in the same way I do with memories I've made in this life, important and not important. The difference is...there are things I would find important he wouldn't, and I can't... recategorize those memories." I sighed. "I hate it, you know. Remembering his life, feeling how he felt. It's like there's someone else living in my skin. There are situations where he and I would react differently." I closed my eyes. "As with Rama, there are some things I can't stop his memories from coming up and experiencing his feelings. I, Kaliya Sahni, am uncomfortable meeting her. Think of the explanations I would have to give her. He makes me love her, too, and... ache to see her," I hissed and rubbed my temple.

"I thought you said you were in control. That there was no—"

"He's *not* a separate person trying to take me over. I thought like that at first, but he's not. That feeling was caused by my fear and the overwhelming sensation of remembering so much at once. He's who I used to be, and I have to be careful not to let the old emotions from his memory color what I see, feel, or do. That's the rub.

That's what made this so fucking weird for months. The life I once lived could change me." Feeling too young for a moment, I rubbed my eyes to stop a wave of sudden tears. "It's not fair that I have to live with this always haunting my steps," I whispered. "I see things that remind me of his life. I read these letters, and I feel as if I knew these nagas, as though they were my brothers. I had brothers, damn it. I wanted to be reminded of *them*, the ones I saw die for *me*."

I accepted the hand Adhar placed over mine and squeezed, grateful for his silent support. It meant so much.

"So, he is like a presence but not truly," Adhar said, his voice radiating the calm, thoughtful nature I needed at that moment. "They are not the feelings you would have, they are unnatural."

"Yet perfectly natural," I said, nodding. "It leaves me in a weird place when it happens."

"That is why you never want to look for Rama or her family, even though it could help everyone, cambion and naga alike."

"It will hurt her," I whispered lamely.

"Pain is common, and if she is still alive, she will be accustomed to the sensation. Your heart is in a good place. Let's focus on something else." He released my hand and started collecting the documents I had pulled out.

"Like what?"

"Like what changes you wish to make to our culture," he said, slowly organizing everything I had pulled off his carefully organized shelves. "I've been looking at my rule and the nagas I've kept around me. We're fighting for a version of a culture we've grown accustomed to, but it hasn't always been this way among our kind. We've changed before. It took me a long time to reflect and see I was fighting the inevitable. The most disappointing conclusion was the hypocrisy of what I was doing. I have been fighting to preserve parts of our culture that weren't even around when I was born."

Once he was done putting things away, he pulled out a few different ones.

"Read these and compare them to how we do things now. Memorize it if you want to argue with the other nagas. You might be a ruler, which gives you power, but you need to argue with them. Many of them refuse to see you as anything other than the child you were."

"Always go to war with more than one weapon," I said softly.

He nodded. "Remember, tonight I'll be leaving to get Aamir and his family. Now, I'll leave you to this and check on everyone else." He walked out, leaving me with the ammunition I needed to arm my argument.

14

CHAPTER FOURTEEN

I waited next to Raphael again early the next morning. Adhar had gone to pick up Aamir and his family, which included little Roshni. I had spent most of the day in the archives until Nakul demanded I eat something. I had found my mate sitting in the courtyard, trying to be part of a conversation. I saved him from being awkwardly ignored by Mahavir any longer by joining in and forcing the other naga to see my mate and speak to him while I ate. After that, we got some sleep. Now, I had him in another suit, standing beside me for another one of these performances.

"Eshika likes you," I said, watching the door where I expected Adhar to enter.

"Do you think so? She's snappy." I heard the humor laced in his words as if he found Eshika funny.

"She is snappy, isn't she?" I chuckled. "In that good way, though." I spent a moment thinking about her. "She's contradictory if you think about it."

"I haven't thought about it, but feel free to explain it to me."

"She accepts the place she's been put in the household—wife, mother, the live-in maid, the cook, and the assistant...the accessory. *But* there's a power to her that really shows who's in charge of that household. Mahavir may be the respected one in our culture, and to other nagas, she's his accessory, but he's not allowed to think of her like that. Look at how he responded to her about the cleaning thing. He just accepted that his son would learn exactly what she wanted him to learn. He'll make sure their son is up to her expectations."

"You're beginning to show your age, old lady," he teased. "It's a new millennium, and generally, spouses try to make each other happy. Mahavir may just want his wife happy."

"Maybe, but if you think all the nagas will be the same, all I ask is that you don't hurt anyone when you learn otherwise."

"How will others be?"

"Among the nagas, wives, specifically the human mates, are expected to be silent. The man of the house does the talking. Mothers teach daughters how to be good housekeepers and wives for their future husbands. Fathers teach their daughters self-defense, but that's *it.* They teach their sons their trade or how to be great warriors. Mothers have no place teaching sons anything because what would a human woman know about being a naga, especially a male one?"

"What about female nagas? You told me your father taught you when you were young, and it didn't sound like self-defense. Your mother was a ruler. That doesn't sound like silent. Also, Mothers teach daughters to be good wives but… they're not having human daughters."

"I mean, you just said it, I'm not human. Our culture was initially based on one thousand nagas, all male, with their *human* wives. Part of the problem is our culture wasn't built to have female nagas. Our culture wasn't built for me, a nagini. They had to make a new word for it, something other, different from the original. We weren't part of that first important generation that laid the building blocks of what we are. We didn't exist, and they had no reason to think they would start dying and being reborn as daughters instead of sons.

"Way back in the day, the first female nagas were essentially princesses. We've slowly merged into the culture and tried to find our own place, even though we've always been outnumbered. We're not reborn in a perfect fifty-fifty split. Maybe we would be, but time and death are against us." I shook my head sadly, thinking about the state of things. "We can't be treated as second-class citizens because we're reborn from the originals, but we don't have a penis." I shrugged a shoulder. "Being a nagini gives me a lot more wiggle room than Eshika has, but it never stopped other nagas, men outside my family, from trying to force me into the same place she's required to live. A lot of it comes from men who never had a nagini in their family or household, actually.."

"It's been thousands of years, and the naga people still don't know how to deal with women of their own kind?"

"We're immortal," I reminded him. "Adhar is three thousand years old. Mahavir is six hundred. I don't know exactly how old Nakul is, but it's way older than his brother. Other than the minors, I am the youngest naga. We had a bit of a dry spell, and now we're in a baby boom."

I adjusted my top, looking down at it. I hadn't picked out anything traditional for a reason. Mahavir hadn't pointed it out, but I looked like a classy businesswoman. I wanted to make a statement. I was professional, not the girl who had run away. I would not wear the traditional clothing of a culture I didn't always agree with.

"So, change comes slowly," he said, thoughtful. "Do you think they're happy?"

"The other nagas? I don't know. They just are."

"Their mates."

I thought hard about how to answer. Happiness was an elusive thing. Even when things were going well, and there was literally nothing wrong in life, happiness was elusive. Finally, I gave up trying to answer a question I tried not to think about.

"I don't know. Before this, I...I've never spoken to them for more than a few minutes, and I was a child then, before my parents died." Guilt rose. "Sorry. You're a very hands-on ruler with the cambions, but I've never been... accessible to the nagas or their mates. It was always easier that way. Safer."

"You're pretty accessible right now, but I didn't ask if they are or aren't happy. You can't read their minds. I asked you if you *think* they're happy."

"I can't even guess, Raphael. There are too many factors, and I'm biased. I hate the way they live, even if they like it or accept it. I hate the way we make women second-class and silent among the rest of us. One reason I don't know them is for security. But really? Some of these men will not be happy with me near their mates, who I might ruin by showing them things can be different." I rubbed my forehead. "So, I can't even guess. I wouldn't be happy if I was kept in a cage and asked to be quiet. I *wasn't* happy with it, and I ran. But I don't know them."

He didn't reply, and I was grateful he let the conversation die.

Then he surprised me again.

"How did you end up with a two-person ruling system with a man and woman if they don't think women are equal to men?"

"The Tribunal. We needed representatives, and all other species were doing male and female representatives. We were told to get with the program if we wanted their protection. I understand it. Different perspectives, different needs, and all that. There are some supernatural species with clear differences in male and female, based on power and ability." I thought about the Tribunal. I had enough experience to make some snap judgments.

"There are also some members of the Tribunal who would kill you for treating them as less for their sex. Take Corissa, a powerful werewolf. She doesn't have her seat because Callahan is her husband. She's a powerful Alpha of her own pack in her own right. They stay with her at all times, and she doesn't publicize where her pack is located. They're completely loyal to her, and I've only met two members because they're so secretive. I think she's making sure no one knows just how powerful she really is. Corissa has two weaknesses." I lifted two fingers. "Her husband, who is always looking for a good fight, which is how he climbed to the top, and her sometimes bleeding heart. She refuses to see women treated like less because of what is between their legs and is willing to rock the boat. Those are some of the battles she fought to get to where she is. She would have never allowed the nagas of that time to send two men and not one of our women." I waved my hand. "There are only a few exceptions, like yours, and they are rooted in similar things, hierarchy that can't be changed or a decision by every member of the species, and even numbers, like there's no one who can take the position. If there was a female cambion out there equal to you, they would expect you to let her rule beside you."

"If there is no female naga..."

"A human mate wouldn't be able to take my position. If I died right now, Roshni would be the ruler, and she hasn't even had her first birthday. Before she was born, the nagas would have had to report to the Tribunal that I died, and the next daughter would be automatically given the position." I grit my teeth, remembering the conversation with Adhar. If they had succeeded, how would the Tribunal have reacted? It never happened, so I would never know, but it was something else to think four nagas were so bold, they would snub the Tribunal's requirements.

I didn't know what they had been thinking, but I knew the Tribunal.

Fucking idiots. Corissa or Alvina would have eaten you alive just because they could.

"Kaliya? You look as if you figured something out."

"I did. I should have realized it before. They enforce it because there are women on the Tribunal, and those women wouldn't want to be treated like second to their male counterparts. So, they make every species do the same thing, equalizing it. *Genius*. They force people to see them as equal by slowly erasing the gender-based power dynamics of other species and equalizing people in their own homes. Gods, that's good and fucking insidious at the same time."

Raphael chuckled. We waited in silence until I heard the truck arrive. As the garage opened, Nakul walked out and sat in the courtyard. I thought he had gone with Adhar, but I didn't care either way.

"What are you doing here?" Raphael asked, looking back at my uncle.

"This group was too big for me to fit in the truck, especially since the baby needed a car seat," he explained, yawning. "But I want to see the little nagini when she gets here."

Suddenly, I was nervous. Another nagini. A baby, but still, something like me. I hadn't seen another female of our species since I was a kid.

Adhar came in first, holding the door for a woman bringing in a carrier. Right behind her, Aamir was exactly as I remembered. His expression was stiff, and he made no move to help his mate with the hassle of the diaper bag and carrier. She dropped the diaper bag the moment she could, then took the carrier to a side table, putting it down gently.

Aamir wasted no time, crossing the room and getting much too close to me.

I'm grown up now. He can't look down at me anymore. I'm in charge here.

I waited, feeling less patient with Aamir than I had with Mahavir. He needed to introduce his family, or we were going to get off on a bad foot.

"I didn't believe Adhar when he told me you had come," he said, his brow furrowed, making him look ten years older than the age his immortality had frozen him at. "Finally came crawling back. At least I didn't have to drag you back."

Yup, he still hates me.

"We're snakes. We don't crawl. Well, *I* certainly don't." I crossed my arms, glaring at him. "Still a nasty piece of work, aren't you?"

"I am an honorable member of our community. You're the one who went missing for decades, then refused to come home and face us."

"Face you?" I shook my head, dismissing that. "There was nothing to face. I'm a ruler of the nagas, a representative of our people to the Tribunal. Where I go and what I do is only for Adhar and the Tribunal to comment on. I've spent years keeping all of you safe by not being here and keeping a target off your backs." Behind Aamir, I saw Pavan walk in, his eyes narrowing on me. "Be a little fucking grateful at least one of our kind is still willing to risk their life for the betterment of everyone."

"You ran away because you were a selfish child who wanted to do whatever she wanted. From everything I've heard, you grew up into that woman. Your parents should have disciplined you more."

"Yet I'm not the one who walked into a house as a guest and threw out the rules. Introduce your family, Aamir. You can't hide them from me or vice versa. We're all going to be here for a little while."

He hissed, and Adhar suddenly appeared next to him.

"You will show respect in my house," the old naga said softly, his gentle way of speaking more threatening than placating. The stern expression on his face only enforced that and made Aamir back away from me.

"She needs to deserve it," Aamir said bitterly.

"I trust her as my equal, and that should be enough for you to introduce your family. You two can go back to fighting once that basic courtesy is done. If you don't, I will introduce them, and there will be consequences if I have to step in any more than I have."

Aamir hissed but waved a hand toward his mate, who was watching us fearfully. She came forward, holding a bundle that had to be Roshni.

"This is my mate, Saranya Majhi, and our daughter Roshni Ulupi Majhi."

Ulupi? Normally, if we're not named after the first generation, it's our middle name.

It was an interesting choice of middle names. I knew who Ulupi was from both my education and a memory of her face flashing in my mind. She was the daughter of Kauranya, one of the kings of the nagas. In my past life, I had known Ulupi. She had been a wife, a mother, and a *warrior*.

It was an odd choice for Aamir because I was certain

he didn't believe women could be good warriors. At least, he'd always left me with that impression. It also left Roshni with no names from the first generation, a broken tradition.

"It's a pleasure to meet you both," I greeted, ignoring Aamir. I put my hands together over my heart and bowed my head. Saranya quickly handed Roshni to Aamir and greeted me.

"It's an honor to finally meet you," she said demurely in a husky voice that probably drove every single man she met wild and brought Aamir to his knees when no one was looking. When she was done, Aamir gave his daughter back to her. Roshni started stirring, and Saranya frowned at her daughter, then at me. "Would you like to meet her?"

"I would," I said, not sure why. Roshni was a baby. We wouldn't have long discussions about being the only two like us. There would be plenty of time for me to hold the baby. I could have done it after they settled in.

I want to right now.

She stepped closer and turned the bundle to me. Roshni began to fuss as her mother moved her around, then the strangest thing happened. I leaned closer, meeting the big baby eyes as they pondered me, and she went quiet. Her mouth was open, and I knew she had all the same senses as me. She could taste me in the air, feel my fluctuating body temperature, which was cooler than her mother's. There was no way she didn't realize the same thing I did.

Her eyes went wider.

This was the first time she met someone like her, and

her instincts and senses were telling her that. Even when we were young, we had instincts, more than human babies and many other supernatural species. She recognized me, and I recognized her.

"Hi," I whispered.

She gave a little babble that made me smile.

"I think she likes you," Saranya whispered.

"She knows," I explained, bringing a hand up and poking Roshni's nose. She laughed and wiggled in her mother's arms.

"Well, here I thought she wanted to sleep, but maybe she just wanted to see you." Her mother was taking it in stride. She slowly unwrapped her daughter from the swaddle, and her chubby little arms reached for me, little fingers trying to grab me. I let her touch my face but had to watch out for her trying to poke me in the eye. I stepped back once I decided she had enough time.

"I'll let you get her settled." I gestured to Raphael, who was once again waiting on me to get on with the formalities. "This is my mate, Raphael Alvarez, Warlord of the cambions. Adhar, they're all yours."

Adhar gave me a half bow as I stepped back, putting even more distance between the family and me.

"I'll see you in the archives later, yes?"

"Yeah, I'll be there," I promised, then remembered there was one more. "Pavan, nice to see you. Thank you for doing guard duty for Aamir's family."

Pavan nodded, sinking a little lower. He'd been trying to hide since he walked in. I would deal with him later. I escaped with my mate now that we had the chance, and we went back to our suite.

"How many of these do we have to do?" he asked as he got out of the suit.

"There are only twelve living nagas, four human mates, and one cambion mate. Seventeen people and eleven of us are here." I crossed my arms. "Only one more group is coming, and it shouldn't be too eventful. They'll be too busy with the twins, and we'll get out of their way as quickly as possible. Vikrant and his mate live within hiking distance and will arrive on their own. Adhar says they know how to cover their tracks. They've been living close for years with no issues."

Do I know anything about his mate?

"Thank God," Raphael said, falling onto the bed. I sat down next to him and kissed his cheek. He pulled me over him and held me in place, claiming my mouth. As his hands roamed and my body came to life, I felt a rush of something unidentifiable. Something made my stomach twist, and I pulled away.

"Let's get on with our day," I said softly, getting off him, and went to find more comfortable clothes.

15

CHAPTER FIFTEEN

My estimation of Dalar's arrival was accurate. He and his mate looked as if they wanted to pull their hair out and hadn't slept in days. The baby boys were loud enough to hear from inside the house, and they were in the truck. The introductions were rushed, Adhar and I trying to get them into a place where they could deal with whatever the two screamers needed.

"They probably just need a nap," Dalar said, sighing. "They refused to sleep for us. Hopefully, a soft bed will get them down and in better moods when they're awake again."

I waved the poor father away, who ran to help his mate, Basanti. It wasn't until after he was gone that I realized I never got the twins' names.

Oh well. I'll ask later.

"Can we do that with Aamir?" Raphael asked Adhar, who had to turn away to cover his smile.

"No, but then, he's not one of the terror twins," Adhar answered.

"No," I answered, then waited for Adhar to finish, cracking a smile at the nickname. 'Terror twins' was going to stick with those boys for the rest of their lives. I'd make sure of it. Then I got to Aamir. "Has he even come out of his suite? Has anyone seen Saranya and Roshni since they arrived?"

"We have," Raphael said, pointing between him and Adhar. "He's definitely avoiding you. He'll check the courtyard for you before Saranya comes out."

"Wow," I said, shaking my head in disbelief. "Adhar?"

"It is disrespectful, but we should let Aamir see you for a few days and let him calm down. He's scared about moving his daughter around too much, which has added to his foul mood."

"I'll give him until the meeting. If he doesn't grow some respect by the end of the meeting, I'll just walk into his suite to check on Saranya and Roshni, and he won't be able to stop me. I'll even give the woman a sword and start training her just to piss him off." I snapped my fingers and pointed at Adhar. "That's another change I want to make. I want the human mates to be trained in self-defense, basics with the sword, firearms, all of it. I don't need them to be great warriors, ready to fight in battle, but it would be nice to know they can stick the bad guys with the pointy end if they have to."

"That's..." Adhar sighed heavily. "Two of the four mates are already on the same page, Eshika and Vikrant's mate. From what I know, Mahavir trains her alongside Devesh. Vikrant is quiet about his mate, so I don't know the status of his efforts. Aamir would never let Saranya pick up a sword. Basanti is like me, more of a scholar.

She's the only mate I can leave in the archives without worrying, the only mate who wants to go in there. I'm not sure she would be entirely thrilled, but I've also never asked her."

Frowning, I looked over the empty courtyard. Nakul was with his brother and family, Aamir was avoiding me, and Dalar was appropriately fixated on his terror twins.

"Would you like my advice?" Adhar asked, looking over the empty courtyard as well. "When Vikrant and his mate arrive, don't take time at the bathhouse with Raphael. Go during the time for the women and see all four of them in one place. They need to know you, and you need to know them. Eshika already adores both you and your mate. I'm certain Saranya would like to ask you questions about what her daughter is." He looked around me at my mate. "And Raphael needs to sit down with the men. You both need to be part of the community, even if you want to keep withdrawn from it. Change comes easier from those we know. I don't know a single person, naga, human, or otherwise, who wants to change their lives for strangers."

"I agree," I said, nodding at his wisdom. "It's just been a long few days, getting them here and being distracted with the archives."

"You have a month here, then the rakshasa will come calling for you. You may take your time." He touched my shoulder before walking away, heading toward the archives. Before he disappeared from view, he gave me a frown. "And milk your venom."

"How do you know I haven't?" I asked, crossing my arms.

"Aside from the fact I think *everyone* will know when you do, your cheeks are looking a little puffy. You are probably very good at ignoring the tension too much venom causes, but it's unhealthy. You should know better."

"I might need it."

"You will not need all that venom." Adhar's flat expression was all I needed, but he continued anyway. "A regular bite will only expends drops and be devastating to whatever you decide needs to die. You probably have enough to take down a herd of elephants and more. Don't push yourself. You know better."

In the quiet, I could hear his footsteps and the sound of the glass doors to the archive as he shut himself in. He was looking for any hints about Rama and her family, something I flat out refused to look for.

While I wouldn't stop Raphael and Adhar from trying, doing it myself was a line I couldn't bring myself to cross. As of right now, I hid behind the laundry list of obligations I already had, but I knew that wouldn't last forever. Eventually, I would have free time, and it would be brought up again.

"Let's go milk your venom," Raphael said, wrapping an arm around my waist.

"Let's wait until later tonight, so we can sleep afterward," I countered. "The last thing I want is to be caught in the throes of fucking you, and someone needs to talk to me. I don't want to miss the chance to talk to Saranya or anyone else."

"That's not a terrible idea," he agreed. "Who knows when the others might suddenly need us for something."

It also gave me time to find another way to deal with my venom issue. I didn't know why, but the idea of having sex was just...not something I wanted to do. There were a dozen reasons that played a part in it, but I was out of sorts about a lot in recent months.

"Do you have plans for the day?" I asked. "Have you considered a way to spend your free time?"

"No. What about you?"

"I was thinking about finding the best place to get into my snake form and sit in the sun. It's been a long time since I've just enjoyed the peace of not...being."

"Yeah, you have the tank in your office, but I never see you use it."

"I barely have the chance anymore."

"Go. We're together all the time." He kissed my forehead. "I brought a couple of books to read, and I'm certain Adhar will let me into the archives if I have nowhere else to be."

"You wouldn't be able to read anything in there, but he would love to teach you more about our kind." I played with his jacket, then pushed him slowly in that direction. "Go. Get some education. I've taught you a lot, but there are some things he can explain better."

He kissed me one more time but didn't head to the archives. He went to our suite. As I walked out the back, I saw him exit in more casual clothes and head that way.

The moment I got outside, I let the morning sun soak into my skin. There were some prime places Adhar kept clear for sun at different times of the day. It was a necessity if he wanted to sun in the thick jungle, and sunning was a favorite pastime of most nagas. I lived in the desert, and while I never laid outside in snake form because of birds, laying in the sun in any form was always nice.

I went to find a nice rock, touching it to see how it was warming up for the day. I shifted once I was satisfied it would heat quickly and curled up for a nap. I didn't actually sleep, staying alert, but I was using my snake instincts and senses to do all the work, feeling for the vibrations of potential prey and the signs of predators or intruders to my space.

The sun was blessedly warm but not hot like Raphael or Arizona, and I craved the heat. I readjusted, hoping to find the warmest spot before giving up on that idea. I would have to live with what I had.

Then there was the humidity. It was so humid I could choke on it. It had rained at least three times since we had arrived, and it sat in the air, ready to make someone sweat the moment they walked outside. Thanks to the courtyard and the openness of Adhar's home, it was inescapable and now ate away at my peace and serenity. Nagas were like normal snakes in that fashion, except we were different person to person instead of by species. A cobra and a rattlesnake had different needs. You couldn't set their tanks to the same settings. It would risk their health. As a naga, it wasn't so serious. I would not have health concerns from the humidity. We had our own preferences. I always liked it drier, while Adhar loved the humidity. He liked an easy warmth, and I loved blazing hot.

I tried to suffer through it, wanting some quiet. As a naga, we had some unwritten rules. We didn't bother others when they were in snake form most of the time. We used our snake form to get away from the trappings of the life we lived and to reconnect with the wildness of what we were.

As I laid there, feeling restless, it was put to the test. Aamir walked out, his wife behind him carrying little Roshni. She wasn't swaddled, her little arms flailing about as she gurgled at her mother. Aamir noticed me first as he passed. I didn't lift my head, but I kept my gaze on him. He turned away and kept walking. Saranya glanced at me, her gaze curious, but it was clear she knew the rules. It was Roshni who made the fuss.

I would have chuckled if I could. I lifted my head at her fussing, rising into the typical cobra pose, swaying to keep my balance. Aamir sighed, looking back at me, then at his daughter.

"It's bath time. We don't have time for this," he said with annoyance I felt was unwarranted.

"I think she's curious," Saranya said softly. Roshni was looking at me with wide eyes, making all sorts of noises. When her mother didn't move her closer, and her wiggling didn't get her what she wanted, her face contorted, and the wail that left her was ear piercing.

The wail broke Aamir's resolve.

"Are you okay with letting her see you?" he asked me but kept his eyes on his daughter, clearly frustrated. "I don't like you, but I know you're not a danger to her."

I tried to nod my head. Aamir took his daughter from Saranya and brought her closer, going to one knee in front of me. The baby reached out and tried to pat my head. I slithered closer so she could reach me. She cooed at the touch of my scales.

"She likes seeing you in your snake form," Saranya said, putting a hand on his shoulder. "She knows."

"She's a nagini. I wouldn't expect anything else," Aamir said stiffly. "There, you've seen another snake, Roshni. It's time for your bath."

It's only been thirty seconds, Aamir. You know she wants more than that. She should be able to see one of her own kind.

If Roshni was older, she could have joined me in snake form or tried to. Each child shifted for the first time at different ages, but there weren't many nagas who made it to their teens without shifting. If she was older, Adhar would ask me to sit down with her and talk at length about the life of a nagini. Her father would fight it, but she deserved to know someone who lived it.

I couldn't argue with Aamir over an eleventh-month-old baby, though. He lifted her away and started walking to the bathhouse as she clearly made it known she was not done seeing me. Saranya looked at me one last time, sighed, then followed her husband and child.

I lowered myself and considered trying to go back to my hunt for peace and relaxation, but there was no way I would find either of those things, so I would do something else.

Adhar said he noticed I had too much venom, and in my snake form, it was clear to me. Since mating Raphael, the need to bite him all the time subsided. He was claimed and mine, but it didn't slow down the production of venom. It was my natural defense mechanism, and now I had a mate to protect. That was why Raphael and I had sex-filled weekends. He didn't want me using a cup, especially after Mehar had milked my venom that way. He wanted to be bitten, wanted to have that piece of me. For him, and all mates, it wasn't deadly, but it was an intense aphrodisiac.

Maybe I can get a bite to eat...

The idea was distasteful and would make it clear I was having a problem with being in this house and using my mate the way he wanted to be used. Eating as a snake was reserved for the most desperate times. There was really no reason unless I was starving.

I moved through the thick grass, passing Nakul talking to his brother and nephew. I didn't stop to listen because it wasn't my business. There was also the problem that if I knew they were there, they would know I was around. I kept moving, passing them at a leisurely speed.

"Kaliya?" Nakul called softly.

"You smell her, too?" Mahavir asked.

"Yeah," Nakul answered. I kept moving, hearing one of them rustling behind me. I could have darted away but felt no need to escape their view as I headed to wherever I was going. "I see. Have a nice day," he said. It was the most he could get away with saying without being accused of treading on my request for privacy. "She's in snake form, probably looking for a place to relax."

"You know, one thing I've noticed since we got here is that she is much more standoffish than I figured she would be," Mahavir said lightly, maybe thinking I was out of earshot. Maybe he wanted me to hear.

Or maybe he just doesn't care.

"She's a complicated individual with a lot on her plate. While we don't see it, there's a lot she does for the nagas, much she carries on her shoulders without saying anything to us. And why would she say anything? What have we done in her life to show her we can be trusted?"

I moved faster and finally found a place on Adhar's estate where I figured I would be alone. I shifted back to my human form and sat on the jungle floor, staring through the trees. The cry of an eagle sent an instinctual fear through me. It was more annoying than anything, but I had never had such a strong reaction.

Maybe it's because these are the predators of my homeland. I would be more attuned to them as a natural danger.

In my hunt for peace and quiet, I realized one thing.

I would not find any…not here. There were too many people and too many memories.

I had convinced myself this trip was coming home, but sitting in the land of my birth, I'd never felt farther from it.

16

CHAPTER SIXTEEN

Adhar found me hours later to tell me Vikrant and his mate had finally arrived.

"It's so weird that they live close enough to walk," I said as we headed for the house.

"It's a day-long hike," Adhar explained. "They're willing to do it, and it's actually safer because they can keep an eye on the tracks they leave behind. From what they've told me, they often leave false trails and take different routes, just to make sure."

"Smart." As the house came into view, I realized they were the last arrival, and we had to get to work after this. First, I wanted to focus on something that had been conveniently unspoken since my arrival and long before. "I don't know anything about Vikrant's mate. Over the years, you've told me little things, and on this trip, you've told me bits about Eshika, Saranya, and Basanti, but nothing about this mate. Any reason?"

"Ah, I didn't mean to. She's not well-liked among the

nagas for reasons out of her control, which makes me wary of bringing her up to others."

"What's the problem?"

"To voice the reason gives me a bad taste in my mouth, and I strongly disagree with it. We don't have control over these things, and—"

"Adhar, just tell me. You know I won't give a damn."

He stopped and sighed, then leaned toward me.

"He met her while she was hiking too close to his home—"

"I don't need their love story. I need to know what I'm fighting against with the other nagas."

"She's British. She's white," he finally said, his nostrils flaring in anger. "It's never happened before, but I wasn't expecting other nagas to have a problem."

"No fucking way," I said, groaning as I pushed a hand through my hair. "Let me guess, he mated the enemy. She's one of the colonizers, and now she's invading our homes here."

"It is rooted in that, yes," he confirmed. "We're not human, and a mate is a mate. To be treasured and protected, brought into our society to be with us, regardless of those circumstances. This isn't the first time a naga found his mate among humans who could be perceived as the enemy. I guess living away from the human culture, I didn't think our people would feel the effects of colonization and British rule the way the humans did. I didn't think any of our people would have strong feelings about it. I was wrong, and it's been decades."

"You put your foot down, right?" I asked cautiously.

"From the moment it started. They would say nothing within earshot of me, but there's..." He shook his head sadly. "She was expected to live by our culture with traditions she didn't know."

"I see," I whispered, looking toward the house. "She wasn't Hindu, which is a good starting place for humans who end up with us. They at least have some understanding of what we are."

"She didn't know what nagas were," Adhar confirmed, nodding. "And Vikrant, bless him, refused to teach her and force her to be someone else. Everything she has learned since she mated with him is something she wanted to learn. You might like her, but please, don't cause her any more trouble than she already has. She's an outsider."

"I'm not surprised," I said with a hiss. "I wish you had told me about her sooner, but I get respecting her privacy. She's probably someone the others whisper about."

"Yes, though with you and Raphael here, she might get a break," Adhar pointed out, putting his hands behind his back. "She's old news now, I guess."

I could tolerate that. I was used to the side-eyes and anger from my people and could take on more to keep her from being treated in ways she didn't deserve.

I smiled a little as I found my way to deal with this new situation.

I can't teach some of these nagas to be better people, but I can remind them that honor, power, and sacrifice come in many forms. I can remind them those things are respected.

I followed Adhar inside and saw the couple standing at the front door. Vikrant was exactly as I remembered.

His face was stone, his expression unmoving as I walked across the space. His mate, though, looked at me curiously, as others had. While I completely understood the reason for the look, I also was feeling like an exhibit at a roadside freak show. It was emphasized by how blue her eyes were, making them impossible to miss among the sea of brown eyes.

"Welcome to my home," Adhar said. After a round of greetings, Vikrant looked at me, moving his mate to his side.

"Kaliya, this is my mate, Eleanor Clarke," he said. His stare was intense, and based on the tense way he was carrying himself, he probably expected me to freak out or say something snide like he probably got from others. It was interesting he introduced her with what I assumed was her maiden name instead of the family name he traditionally would have given her. It was insanely modern, even more modern than their mating.

"Eleanor? That's a beautiful name. It's a pleasure to finally meet you." With her, I reached out with a handshake. She was the only person I had done so with since arriving in India.

Eleanor looked at my hand, surprised by the offer, then took it, smiling.

"It's a pleasure to meet you as well," she said, hopeful. She had a strong shake. As we let go, my mate finally appeared.

"Sorry I'm late," he said, looking at me first.

"It's fine. We just started the introductions." I turned him to look at Vikrant and Eleanor and introduced him the same way I did with everyone else. I was really fucking grateful this was the last time we had to do this because it was getting tedious as fuck.

Eleanor and Raphael stared at each other a long time, taking in the fact neither of them was Indian like the rest of us. Raphael could, maybe, blend a bit more, but I didn't think that mattered to them at that moment. In a world as small as ours, finding a potential ally was hard but important, especially as a perceived outsider.

"Well, you're not what I was expecting," Eleanor finally said. "I don't know what I was expecting, but you are certainly not it. Maybe I was expecting horns. Unlike my mate, I knew what a cambion was by definition. It was nice to know something about a supernatural that he didn't."

"Eleanor," Vikrant whispered, his stony face finally cracking, giving way to loving exasperation. There was no missing his love for her as he kept his arm wrapped around her waist, clearly not wanting to let go of her, and the way he spoke, as though he expected it from her, and he loved it, even as he pleaded with her not to embarrass them.

"I'll take that as a compliment," Raphael said, taking her comment in stride. "And don't feel you've gotten it wrong. I can have horns when I want them."

"Really?" She moved forward, even as Vikrant tried to stop her. "Can you?"

"I have three forms. This one is fully human most of the time. I have what we call the cambion form, and I have a full demon form," he explained. I stepped back to give them space, waving for Vikrant to come closer to me. This was the first time any of the nagas or their mates had asked Raphael about what he was with genuine interest. I assumed it was because we had given out an information packet, but now I knew it was because he wasn't a naga, and he was mine. They wouldn't give him the time to teach them anything more.

Now, Raphael had the chance to talk to someone, and Eleanor was delighted she was meeting something new. As Raphael explained how his transformations worked, I turned to Vikrant, who was staring intently at his mate.

"He won't hurt her," I said patiently.

"I haven't seen her so excited in years," he whispered, finally looking at me again. Adhar moved closer to us, leaving the mates alone with their conversation. "She was excited about meeting our people when we got together, but since then..." He shook his head. "How are you, Kaliya?"

"Trying to ignore the condemnation I get whenever I'm around other nagas can be tiring, so I'm tired," I answered, shrugging casually. It wasn't exactly true, but it wasn't far off. Since our mates were getting along, I was testing the waters with him. Mahavir and I had too much complicated bullshit between us with Nakul to be close, even if Eshika and Raphael got along great. I didn't know Vikrant all that well. Aside from a bit of worry he once supported an effort to remove me from power, I had no real feelings about him. He hadn't been cruel.

"I see," he said, his eyes flicking toward his wife again. "Adhar doesn't say much about the life you live, but I know you're a...Tribunal Executioner. That's the title, correct?"

"It is, but I won't be for much longer. With everything

going on, after this trip, I'll be stepping down permanently."

"You mean everything going on with your mate. I read everything Adhar sent me. He's establishing a new people, and they have been through many terrible things. It would make sense that you would like to focus on something that matters so much to your mate."

"Don't put words in my mouth," I warned softly. "It's more than just the cambions. It's us, too. I've been an absent ruler for a long time, and it's time for me to change."

"Do you think you're welcome?"

I couldn't read his expression, so I didn't know if he meant he wouldn't welcome me or if he meant others. Mindreading wasn't in my wheelhouse.

"I don't need to be welcome. It's my position, and I'm going to take it. No one can tell me I can't."

"Good. You will need to hold on to that when they come for you," he said, nodding. He turned to his mate and waved for her while I was left in shocked silence. "Let's put our things away, then we'll spend more time with Kaliya and Raphael."

"Oh, yes!" she said, jumping to get her bag, leaving Raphael chuckling. As Vikrant got his suitcase, she looked at my mate with a dazzling smile. "I do hope you feel comfortable showing me how you transform while we're here. Don't feel pressured, but I would very much like to see more."

"I'm sure we can find a moment," Raphael said, his smile dazzling and beautiful. He certainly loved the attention, and Eleanor seemed innocent in her interest.

"As long as you promise not to break out the lab equipment."

She laughed, nodding. "I don't have any, so don't fret over anything like that."

Vikrant was smiling as he walked away with his mate, who was talking so fast, it was almost unintelligible. Adhar stepped closer to me, and Raphael looked at us with a grin.

"I like her," he declared. "She must be friends with Eshika, yeah? They seem like two women who probably have a great time together."

"I don't believe they've ever spent much time together." Adhar shrugged. "Eleanor rarely visits. Vikrant feels comfortable leaving her at home by herself, and she has told me she enjoys the private time when he leaves the house."

"Vikrant isn't what I expected," I said, watching them disappear. Familiar with the house, they hadn't needed anyone to show them their rooms. "And Eleanor Clarke? Any explanation for that? His family name is—"

"It's why you won't see Vikrant spend much time with the other nagas during this trip. He took her last name and has never given me an explanation why, but he is now Vikrant Clarke. He doesn't want anyone using the family name of his birth for any reason."

"Okay..." I lifted my hands. "I won't say anything about it. I'm going to get into a fight about this, aren't I?"

"Vikrant doesn't need your protection, but if you feel drawn to defend him and his choices, I will certainly not stop you." Adhar sighed heavily. "I say he doesn't need your protection because he will say the same to you at some point. He made it clear to me when I tried to defend his choices with some of the others. He will be grateful, though, if you step in for his mate. He's willing to kill for her."

"As he should be," Raphael said, nodding appreciatively.

"Who are the troublemakers in this case?" I had guesses, but I didn't want to assume. I had the undying need to know my enemies and was tired of surprises.

"Pavan is the worst. Dalar made some underhanded and unnecessary comments."

"Dalar isn't a threat right now," I said dismissively. "But Pavan…" I trailed off, thinking about the quiet and missing male naga. He showed up and shut himself away, not coming out since I arrived. I knew Aamir was alive because Roshni cried, as babies do, but Pavan did a disappearing act on me. "Where is he?"

"We're not the only strange couple." Raphael was also looking toward the suite with Vikrant and Eleanor. "There's a lot more drama among the nagas than I expected."

"What are you thinking?" I asked him, wrapping my arms around him from behind.

"There are only seventeen people in your culture, including me. There's a similar amount of cambions. For years, I figured the stupid drama between my cambions was because we were new and didn't know what was going on. We were being changed and experimented on, which left us stressed and more willing to get into fights or cause problems as a way to lash out. We're close, brought together by our shared trauma, and have become something close to a family.

"I figured the nagas would be more of a...unified force, thanks to how established you are. I was wrong. You're even more of a mess than my kind. At least our fights are in the open. We yell at each other and fight, but we don't...whisper behind each other's backs." Raphael shook his head. "It's underhanded and leaves a bad taste in my mouth that your people would treat each other like this after having to hide from the world and losing so many of your people. There are better things to do than hate someone's choice of their last name."

"Well, there's also the fact she's British and white, and we're in India. You know, one of the places Britain thought it had the right to colonize and rule without thinking about the people who already lived here." He growled in my arms. "But I agree with you," I said, sighing against his back. "We should do better. It's not like Vikrant picked a British woman, ignoring what was going on. He didn't really have a choice if he wanted to mate, and he clearly loves her."

"Some wanted him to go without a mate before settling with her," Adhar said softly. "Why don't you two have a seat, and I'll get them something small to eat."

As he walked away, I dragged Raphael into the courtyard.

17

CHAPTER SEVENTEEN

When Eleanor and Vikrant came out of their room, Adhar was putting down a large plate of finger foods. Eleanor showed no hesitation, grabbing something and eating as Vikrant thanked Adhar for the meal.

"So, where is everyone else, or am I still too British for them to bother with me? You've convinced one naga to give me a chance, so I guess I should be grateful for that," she said once she was finished with her sandwich, directing her statement at Adhar. No one else had tried to start a real conversation, but I wasn't expecting her to go from zero to sixty that quickly. She hadn't been hostile earlier. Adhar took it in stride as if he expected it.

"Um..." I blinked, looking at Adhar. "Do you know where anyone else is? I mean, no one has really come out for these introductions when people have come. It's always just Raphael and me. I think everyone meets up for a light dinner every night, yeah?"

"That's correct, not that you have attempted to participate in that."

"Yeah, well..." I shrugged one shoulder. I could see Eleanor watching us carefully. She clearly knew the deal with some of the other nagas, but she didn't know me. I didn't need the aggression coming off her or the confrontation she was clearly looking for. "I have better things to do with my time."

"Yes, I don't think I've ever seen you read as much as you have in the last three days," Adhar said with a small smile. I was trying to distract him from Eleanor's clear aggressive tactic, and Adhar was falling for it. "Have you found anything interesting?"

"Not yet," I answered with a sigh, letting my head fall back so I could stare at the sky. "Unless the occasional headache counts. We might need better lighting in there, but it's really not a big deal."

"I don't notice. I'm normally the only person there," Adhar said, almost regretfully, and I could hear the ache of old loneliness. "I'll take your suggestion under consideration and see what I can do."

"It's no rush. You don't have to change anything if you don't want to. I would rather preserve everything in the archives and deal with headaches. There's no reason to put them at risk just to make me more comfortable." I turned to Eleanor. "So, yeah, no one comes out here when someone arrives. Nothing against you."

"Not yet," Vikrant said, eyeing the sides of the courtyard.

"Not yet," I agreed. "Mahavir and Aamir both gave me an earful when they arrived and have been avoiding me since. Pavan barely said hello, and I haven't seen him since. The only nice arrival was Dalar, thanks to the terror twins screaming their heads off. So, it really wasn't all that enjoyable, even if no one gave me a cutting comment."

"You're..." Eleanor frowned. "You're a naga. Why would they give you a cutting comment?"

I looked at Vikrant, clearing my throat.

"I didn't want her to make any judgments about you before she met you," he said, not looking at me or his mate. "Eleanor, Kaliya has lived away from our community all these years for a reason. Some in the community were harsh with her when she was a child and had just lost her family, and she ran away. It's been a hundred years since any of us have seen her in person."

"Except Nakul," Raphael muttered darkly. He would never let me forget that.

"Ah yes, excuse me for the error. Nakul had also roamed the world for a while..." Vikrant was clearly uncomfortable with the direction of the conversation.

"Nakul is nice. He's been nothing but kind to me when I've seen him. Is he here for this...gathering?"

I nearly snorted but kept my mouth shut. If she didn't know he used to be a serial killer, I wouldn't tell her. If I thought he was a danger to her, I would in a heartbeat, then probably put the man out of misery, but that wasn't Nakul. Harming the nagas was the last thing he ever wanted. Being a danger to a mate went against the core of who he was.

"He is," Adhar said with a smile. "He lives with me, so

of course, he's here. I believe he's spent the day with Mahavir and his family. He is probably still with them."

"His brother," she said, her lips pursing.

"Mahavir can be an ass, but he's a reasonable ass. If you throw logic at him, he gets with the program real quick. He's hotheaded sometimes, but not stupid. You can outwit him and force him to step back and think." I certainly didn't think he would dislike her for being British. That was too petty for Mahavir.

However, her current attitude could very well turn him away from wanting to spend any time with her. I need to work on this.

"You haven't been around them for a hundred years, and you know how to handle them?" She was disbelieving and even a little haughty.

"I know Mahavir better than most because of a… situation," I answered lamely. "As for the others? I've had a few decades of experience working with difficult people. I learned to read them quickly, figure out their goals, what they need or want, then what they fear. Plus, I knew them as children, and Adhar has been helping me catch up." I pointed at her.

"You are so used to being an outsider, you're looking for a fight. Better to be the aggressor than the victim, right?" Her mouth dropped open to object, but I lifted my hand, the universal sign for 'don't talk,' and she obliged, keeping quiet. "I feel that. I've gotten lots of bullshit over the years, including from Adhar here, but you need to learn to turn it off long enough to see you're sitting among allies. Raphael and I are the last people who will hate on you because of the culture of your birth. So, tone it down. If you can't turn it off, you'll never give any of them a reason to change their opinions if that's what you want."

She flushed, nodding. "I'm sorry."

"Don't be sorry," Vikrant said quickly to his mate, then turned to glare at me. "My wife shouldn't have to change who she is for them."

"I'm not telling her to change who she is. I'm telling her to turn off the defense mechanism for a minute, so I can actually figure out who she is," I countered. "The most real thing I've seen from her is her excitement over meeting Raphael. Since then, she's been on guard, and it's obvious. She came into this conversation with hostility, and I have done nothing to deserve it, and I certainly won't take it."

Vikrant looked like I had whacked him across the side of his head with a two-by-four. Eleanor shrank a little, and I felt bad, but I didn't take shit from the other nagas, much less shit from their mates, and I had to draw that line at every opportunity I had the chance.

"You're right," she finally said, sighing. "I'm so used to getting...bullshit, as you say, I've started treating these trips like going to battle."

"Which is totally understandable. I came here ready for the same thing."

"I guess I thought you were only here because Adhar was forcing you to meet me," she said, looking down at her hands.

That made Raphael laugh, elbowing Adhar.

"You hear that? Eleanor has so much respect for you, she thinks you can force Kaliya to do anything," he said, his laughter making it hard for him to finish the sentence. "Oh, Christ. Eleanor, there's not a single person on this planet who can make Kaliya do anything she doesn't want to do unless they cheat." He put a hand over his face, his entire body shaking with laughter. "Shit, if anyone could, I would need to find them and learn their damn secrets."

Adhar laughed, leaving me to stare at them in annoyance while the couple sat in bewildered silence. Then Vikrant cracked a smile.

"I guess nothing has changed," he said, wrapping an arm around his mate.

Adhar lost his mind, leaning over to laugh and making me wonder if he was going to fall to the ground. When Adhar and Raphael finally had control over themselves, Adhar wiped his eyes.

"Forgive me. The idea Kaliya would ever blindly do as I say is just...comical," he said, breaking out into a crazy little laugh that pointed to the years of stress he had, trying to control me and learning there was no way in hell he ever could. "Raphael, I'm certain you've run into the same challenges."

"Absolutely, which I've just had to come to terms with. The cambions have to follow my orders. They don't have a choice." Raphael smiled at me, so much love in the expression that I nearly lost my breath. "But not her, and I'm grateful for that now. I've learned some hard lessons about trying to convince her to do anything she doesn't want to and not listening to her."

I took his hand and squeezed.

"I'm glad you've found someone who sees you for

who you are and appreciates it, Kaliya," Vikrant said quietly.

I held on to Raphael's hand as I studied the naga. This man had asked Adhar to take me out of power, but not even Adhar really knew his thoughts. Vikrant was very good at controlling his face, and he chose his words carefully. With people like Vikrant, there was one tactic I always tried if I didn't think it would get me killed.

Confront them head-on and force them into revealing something.

"Why did you join the other nagas to talk to Adhar about removing me from power when I was a kid?" I asked bluntly. "You haven't seemed like a supporter of that since you arrived. In fact, you've been mostly pleasant, and that's more than I can say for a lot of the others. I know you were there, and I need an explanation."

Eleanor gasped, turning on her mate with wide eyes as he lowered his head.

"They thought I was a believer to their cause, and I'm the one who convinced them to talk to Adhar. Truthfully, I was uncomfortable with their talk, and I thought the only person who could put an end to it was Adhar. I trusted Adhar to shut them down once their whispers were out in the open, and they had made fools of themselves," he explained. "And he did exactly that. What I wasn't expecting was for you to run away the same night. Did you know what had been discussed? Did you fear for your life after learning about it? Adhar would have never let anyone harm you, and I would have protected you if I had to."

"Adhar only told me when I got here. I've spent the last century not knowing what was said that night. In fact, I spent a hundred years trying not to think about it. For a long time, I treated this place and its people as something far away I would never see again. I could do my part from where I was, and there was no reason for me to come back." I let go of Raphael to turn my body toward Vikrant. "I haven't confronted the others, and I might not. It was a long time ago."

"Don't let your guard down," Vikrant warned. "I'm not saying they're a danger to your safety, but some of them will do everything they can to undermine your position. They'll use every excuse they can to rob you of influence and space among us. As long as you stayed gone, they've been quiet, but the moment this trip was in the early stages of planning and after hearing about your mate, the whispers have started again."

"Perhaps we should talk about this in a more private location," Adhar recommended, looking around, probably wondering the same thing I was—there could be a number of listening ears.

"No," I said with a smile. "I like talking about this in the open. There are few of our kind, and Raphael was right. We shouldn't have to whisper about these sorts of things in the corner. Why not bring everything into the open? That way, we can move forward and leave the past behind." I exposed my teeth. "Or they can test me and learn the hard way, I'm not someone they can toy with anymore."

"Well, I am certainly done. I am going to go read for the rest of the evening," Adhar declared, shaking his head at us. "We have a long day tomorrow. Everyone will be present for breakfast, and all nagas are required to attend a meeting after that."

"I'll clean up," Raphael promised before anyone else could offer.

"Thank you," Adhar said with a grateful bow of his head.

"You two should probably get some sleep. Adhar was telling me you had to hike," I said, standing up. "Thank you, Vikrant, for telling me the truth."

"I could have been lying to you," he said as he and his mate also stood. Eleanor stole another two sandwiches from the plate before Raphael picked up the dish.

"Yeah, you could have been. It's not like I wouldn't watch my back around you, anyway. There are less than five people in the world I don't watch my back around." I started walking toward my suite. "And none of those people are nagas." As I opened the door, I looked back at them. "It really was nice meeting you, Eleanor. I hope this trip marks the beginning of a better time among our people for you. We're in the same boat because I'm hoping it marks the same thing for me as well. We should band together and prove they've judged us wrong."

"I would like that," she said, nodding quickly.

I closed myself in my suite, knowing Raphael would be there soon. I was exhausted. Eleanor was a little rough around the edges, but to many people, so was I. Vikrant was smart and full of secrets. I was surrounded by people I barely knew, and most didn't like me. I sat on the edge of my bed and waited for Raphael to come in.

"You okay?" he asked.

I finally broke.

"Yes. No. Both," I answered. "This trip is putting some things in perspective and doing it quickly."

"Like?"

I tried my best to find the words to explain the issue I was facing.

"I'm not happy here. I'm not happy with a lot of things about my life, but I am happy with you and with our lives in Arizona. That place...it's home, and I miss it so much right now. I was out of sorts before we left, but I would take our lives there over this any day." I smiled sadly at him as he came over to me. "And I don't know if you noticed it or not, but I've been avoiding having sex with you since we got here, and..."

"That didn't cross my mind," he said, sitting next to me. He spoke dryly enough for me to catch the sarcasm, but when I dared to look at him, his expression wasn't angry or frustrated. "I didn't want to pry because...I think this is your lab, which is something you have to be ready to talk about. I can't force it. It might not have been traumatic in the same ways, but it's obviously marked who you are. So, I've been trying my best at patience. You know, the very thing I didn't have with you last October and should have. This is all on your schedule, Kaliya. I'll wait as long as you need to talk. If you don't want to right now, it won't hurt my feelings."

"My lab. That's a good way of putting it." I moved up the bed and put my head on a pillow. "So much about this place makes me feel uncomfortable about having sex with you. Those men out there? They'll be able to hear it through the walls and judge me. It'll be like putting on a damn show to the people who are always looking for something wrong with me. But that's for me to get over, and I will eventually get over it. I'm sorry you have to wait."

"I'll survive. We're mates, and that's eternity. I learned my lesson about rushing things, believe me." He laid down next to me, both of us over the blankets and fully clothed, but it felt intimate. "Why were you out of sorts at home?" he asked gently, running his knuckles over my cheek.

"We've been so busy, I hadn't stopped and smelled the roses. Cassius asked me if I was happy, and I didn't know how to answer. I hadn't tried to be happy, and I was hung up on everything that happened to us with Mehar and Devika and our mating. That's another way this trip has set me straight. I love you, Raphael. You've apologized enough for what happened, and I forgive you. You've stood beside me while I've started to navigate a role I've neglected for a century. You've taken all of this in stride for me. You..." I blinked back tears. "You mean the world to me. If I had to make any changes...I just wish we did more than have sex at home. I want to go out with you, see movies, have fancy dinners. I want what we have to be more...substantial. More than what we have right now. That's all."

"I wish you said something sooner. I am always willing to make time for you. I would like that, too. You *know* I want more time with you, to do more with you. That's all I've ever wanted."

"I feel guilty for taking your time away from the

cambions." I stared into those warm chocolate eyes as I laid my soul bare. "That hasn't changed."

"I wish you didn't, but I can't force you not to feel that way. All I can do is tell you repeatedly that it's fine, and I'm willing to do that." He smiled. "Now, you're asking for more time with me, to do more things with me, and I'm taking it as a sign it's sinking in."

"I'm a slow learner."

He snorted. "No, you're not. You logically know if you're not happy, you need to change something in your life. You know if it's with me, you need to tell me because I can't read your mind. You're a problem solver and would have known the solution to the problem instantly."

"Then what's my problem?"

"I'm wondering if you think you're a burden." That hit home, bringing tears back to my eyes. He hit the nail on the head. "But you're not. You're not stealing time away from other, more needy people. My cambions? They're survivors and can definitely take care of themselves. The danger of being with you? That's a bit more...present, as I was forced to learn, but I'd face it again for you. I would face it every day for the rest of eternity, as long as I wake up every day with you. Do you want to know why?"

I nodded, unable to say anything.

"To me, you are the most beautiful person I'll ever have the pleasure of knowing. You see yourself as damaged goods, and I understand why you see that in the mirror, but I see a woman who has fought for everything she has and still found time to help others. Someone who would throw away her own happiness to protect the life of the man who loved her. A woman who has fought a war no one else believed in because she knew it would save her people. It's not a burden to have you in my life. It's an *honor*." He kissed my forehead. "And if you need to milk your venom, but you're not ready to do anything else, I bet we can ask Adhar for something you can use. Now, get some sleep."

"Thank you," I whispered, feeling inadequate. The words felt too small, but they were all I could say. Based on his smile, it was the right thing.

"Beginning tomorrow, I'm going to stop tolerating how they talk to you," he warned me with that smile. "I will not see you fight this battle alone. I've been a good boy, making a good impression since we got here, met all of them before making any judgments or making an ass of myself. It's time they really understand how dangerous your mate is, especially if Vikrant is right, and they're going to try shit."

I had no reply except a smile. If he was willing to wait patiently for me to figure out my shit, I was willing to let him off the leash he was wearing for me.

18

CHAPTER EIGHTEEN

I woke up the next day, ready for anything. Raphael went with me for our first official breakfast with the entire cast of this tiny world I was born into. Previous days had held unofficial get-togethers between the families, catching up on their own times, but now, everyone was here. As we walked in, I took stock of the situation, seeing who was with whom, identifying cliques, and who was kept apart from the others.

Mahavir was talking to Nakul while Devesh hovered at their side, looking around, probably trying to figure out where his place was. Typical teenager thing, trying to understand how he stood in an intimidating group of adults, especially since there was no one his age. He was forced to go from child to adult with no in-between, and there was little I could do to help him.

Aamir holding his daughter in his arms, a sight that was almost endearing. I hated the man, but it was clear he loved and would put his life on the line for her. He was talking to Dalar, who juggled one of the terror twins while Pavan was holding the other.

"It doesn't get easier," Aamir said with a sigh, using English. A little surprising, but not when Adhar was walking around aimlessly, keeping an eye on everyone. He would have laid down the law about speaking in a language that everyone could understand. While many of the nagas had a whole list of reasons to dislike me, they all respected Adhar. He was too damn old and a second-generation naga. They weren't going to go against him on principle.

"Mine feed into each other. It's never-ending," Dalar said, looking exhausted. "One is asleep, the other cries, then they're both crying, and..." Dalar closed his eyes, definitely begging for someone to put him out of his misery.

"This one stinks," Pavan commented in a bone-dry voice, his face blank.

Dalar rang out several curses in Hindi, switching babies with Pavan, and ran off with the stinky twin. Beside me, Raphael must have seen and heard the same thing because his chuckles drew some eyes to him, but there wasn't a missed beat in their conversations.

Vikrant and Eleanor were standing alone in a far corner of the courtyard. They made an appearance but were totally absorbed in each other. I had a feeling their exclusion wasn't their only problem but also their need to stay with each other. They had the vibe I got from Sorcha and Cassius, with a bit of a co-dependent note to it.

I walked through them and headed into the spacious kitchen. Eshika, Saranya, and Basanti were cooking together and talking. There were laughs and smiles here, but Eshika noticed Raphael and me.

"Oh, good morning!" she greeted brightly. "Raphael, you were such a big help the other day. You don't have to, but you're welcome to help us again if that's something you would like to...what did you say? Play helper?"

"He helped in the kitchen?" Saranya's head swiveled back and forth between Eshika and my mate as if it was on a damn pole, then at me. "He helped in the kitchen?" she asked again.

I looked at Raphael, not wanting to say anything for him.

"I know my way around the kitchen," he confirmed. "I do most of the cooking between Kaliya and me."

"Because he eats so much," I said with an overdone groan. "This man tried to eat me out of house and home." That caused Basanti to giggle, and Eshika laughed.

"He does," Mahavir's spitfire mate agreed. "Devesh asked me if all Americans can eat like that."

"Not all Americans, but all cambions. We burn a lot of energy and need to eat a lot to keep up our fitness," Raphael answered.

I snorted, fighting hard not to fall into a fit of laughter.

They thought it was an American thing. I can't. I just can't.

"Today, I'm going to stay out of your way," Raphael said with a smile, bowing his head politely. "You look like you have this well in hand and have a system I don't want to disrupt."

"We'll go check on everyone else," I said, wrapping my arm with my mate's.

"Would you like to help us?" Saranya asked softly as though she was afraid of stepping on my toes. I met her gaze and sighed.

"I used to help my mother, but cooking was never a skill for me to write home about. I can still whip together a couple of her recipes, but it's been a long time since I've made any of the dishes you're making. I wouldn't be of any help."

"She also needs to be at Adhar's side," Eshika pointed out. "She's one of them, Saranya. She can't play housekeeper like the rest of us. Nakul says she's an accomplished warrior, so I don't think she spends her time cooking and cleaning."

"Oh, yes." Saranya nodded quickly. "Sorry to bother you with...playing housekeeper."

I pushed Raphael to walk out without me, wanting to nip this in the bud. He obliged, kissing my cheek before he left. I went deeper into the kitchen, entering a space I was certain most of those men would prefer I stayed in.

"There's nothing wrong with being a wife and doing these things if you enjoy them," I said, looking at the dishes they were finishing and the others baking in the stone oven. Over a cooking fire, they were heating a pan to start another dish. They intended to make food for the entire day, which would take most of the day. "There's nothing wrong with being good in the kitchen. In fact, with the quality of these dishes, I bet you three could make amazing money owning a restaurant in a different world and under different circumstances. You have the teamwork down and the endurance to cook all day." I gestured at everything they had done so far. "I don't have those things. It's not that I look down on this. The only thing I look down on is when someone isn't given a choice in the role they're to play."

They stared at me, then looked at each other.

"So, you like that Vikrant doesn't send Eleanor here," Basanti said cautiously. I wondered if she was asking for herself or just trying to compare me to others.

"If Eleanor doesn't like to cook, why should she? If she wants to read, tend a garden, or learn to use a sword, she should do those things. The same goes for you, Eshika, and Saranya. If you enjoy this, then you are more than welcome to do it. Raphael is both a warrior and a decent cook. There's nothing saying you can't have it all." I lifted my hands in a shrug.

"I am a warrior. That's all I know how to be, all I ever wanted to be, so when someone tried to force me to learn how to be a good wife, I fought back. It was against everything I wanted here." I tapped my heart. "At the end of the day, following this is the easiest way to happiness and peace. At least, in my opinion." I stepped back, letting that sink in.

"I'll get out of your way, but if any of you need anything, come to me. I'll be using the bath tomorrow during the women's hours. You're welcome to join me if you want to talk more. I would enjoy having company that doesn't have a penis." Eshika laughed, Basanti giggled with a blush, and Saranya gave me an enigmatic look.

When I walked out, Adhar was right outside the door with a small smile.

"Good job," he whispered, so none of the others

would hear. "When Raphael came out alone, I knew it had to be something like this. You handled that very well."

"I try," I said, trying not to let his praise really change anything. "I can do better."

"If you think so, I look forward to seeing you reach for the stars. They are the easy battle, though." He tilted his head toward the kitchen.

"I've fought in many battles that were much more dangerous," I countered. "And I've won wars that were ignored by others because of the seemingly insurmountable odds." I could have been accused of overconfidence, but I had to present myself as I believed I was. I was a warrior of renown. My reputation was well earned, and my skills were honed to a deadly point with the unerring accuracy necessary to stay alive in the world.

If I believed it, I showed it to them. They would have to confront it and either acknowledge it or test themselves against me. If I didn't believe it, they would never respect me.

My eyes found Raphael, who was talking to Vikrant and Eleanor.

"He made directly for them and got some dirty looks," Adhar whispered.

"He's not going to be nice anymore," I warned. "If you see him get into it with another naga, just let it play out. They need to know what they're dealing with when it comes to my cambion. Hell, you need to know. He's tired of playing nice while they make rude comments."

"So, what you're saying is this gathering might be the death of me," Adhar said with a humorless chuckle.

"Thank you for the warning, and I'll keep my eye out. Unless someone is going to die, I will allow things to play out."

I smiled at him, then headed for Nakul and Mahavir. Devesh was the one who made the most obvious move when he saw me, but I knew his father and uncle were completely aware of my movement. Nakul wasn't considered one of the best warriors in the room for no reason.

"How are you all this morning?" I asked, keeping my words friendly and light. "I just checked on breakfast, and it looks just as good as it smells."

Nakul laughed, nodding as he made an obvious display of sniffing the aromas floating in the air.

"Eshika is a genius in the kitchen," he said, sighing happily. "I always enjoy when she gets in there and starts using her magic."

"She's not a witch," Mahavir said dryly.

"It's an expression," I said, giving Mahavir a mildly annoyed look. "Come on. Sometimes, talent and skill seem like magic to other people. If she's as good as old Nakul says she is, she must be one of the best."

"She enjoys it," Mahavir said, his face morphing into one of love. "Even if Devesh and I aren't hungry, she goes into the kitchen and tries new things, forcing us to taste test. She's very excited to try new things for so many people. She's also hoping to get some of her recipes into the other households to see how the other mates enjoy making them. She likes to think of cooking as an experience that should be savored like the food is after she's done with it."

"That sounds wonderful. If she wants to write down any of those recipes for Raphael and me, we'll take them home and test them on others. We have an entire compound of cambions to feed daily. They need to add some flavor to their lives." I winked.

Nakul laughed, and Mahavir's smile grew as he relaxed.

"Are they all American?" he asked, clearly interested in these bland cambions.

"No. They come from all over the world, but they've been robbed of a normal life for a long time. Some of them were taken into captivity before we had home computers and cell phones. Others never saw the outside world." I looked around. "A couple of them have shown interest in learning more about me and where I come from, especially since I'm mated to their warlord. I want to give them something from home that's useful to them. They're always looking for ways to make enough food for all of them, and our dishes are often made in massive amounts to be eaten throughout the day. Maybe they can send back some suggestions to Eshika as well."

"I think she would very much like that," Mahavir confirmed, nodding slowly. "That's very thoughtful of you."

"We'll see how it goes, although they might throw a fit because it's spicy." I rolled my eyes and finally got Mahavir to laugh.

"For children, Eshika always makes a less spicy version of her dishes, so it's easier on their stomach. Maybe we can start them with that."

"Oh no," I said with a devious smile. "They're

immortal and *love* to act tough. They'll be fine with the authentic dishes. When they're screaming at me because it's too spicy, I'll just remind them about all the trouble they give me during training."

I miss Sammy and her trouble.

Nakul had to bend over, laughing harder than I had ever seen.

"Kaliya, please don't plot the demise of my people," Raphael said, sliding into the conversation as if he had always been there. He knew I would never do any irreparable harm to anyone who relied on him, but joking about it was free game. It let me feel like I could keep up with the demon spawn, as Sorcha took to calling them.

As the cambions got used to freedom, they were like wild college students, full of power and feeling on top of the world as others learned they weren't to be fucked with. While most teenagers and college students only thought they were immortal, the cambions actually were, and someone had to work very hard to kill one of them. It was a recipe for trouble that left most of Arizona keeping a wide berth around the cambions. Even Paden declared they couldn't go to Jackalope without Raphael there to manage them.

"I would never plot their *demise*," I said innocently. "Only some light pain and suffering they deserve sometimes."

"You sound like an exasperated mother," Nakul said as he wiped his eyes.

"Well, my cambions can be problem children," Raphael said, his face the picture of bleak hopelessness that came to many fathers at some point. "It's a phase they're going through, and this trip has been a blissful break."

"Yes, but who's watching them if you're here?" Mahavir asked.

"A couple of our friends who have enough power to handle the cambions. Unless they're ganged up on, but that's unlikely. The last thing anyone back in Arizona wants is for us to cut this trip short to go deal with them." I didn't name Cassius and Sorcha, not rubbing in their titles and their association with me. Yet. At some point, I would need to point out my powerful friends, but I needed to save that weighty bit of ammunition for a real fight.

"You said..." Devesh trailed off as we all looked at him. He wasn't used to the weight of this much adult attention, but this was the perfect training ground for him.

"Ask whatever you like," I said kindly.

"You told me earlier you train the cambions, and Uncle says you're a warrior." He looked nervous as more of the room looked at him. I heard other conversations die as they waited for him to finish. "But you also said you're an assassin."

"Ah..." I nodded, seeing what he was getting at. "To me, warrior and assassin are the same thing, something I was taught by my mentor. I'm just as effective in an all-out fight, meeting my opponent head-on as I am giving them a quick death in the dark. As for the cambions, I train them in basics, how to control their strength, so they don't go further than they intend. I teach them to protect themselves if they are caught off guard, about their strengths and weaknesses, how to account for those problems. Those were skills I had to learn because I have to be ready for anything and always remember where I stand compared to other supernaturals."

"Warrior and assassin can't mean the same thing, though," Aamir said, coming to our conversation. He still held his daughter as he joined the circle we had formed. "Warriors are honorable. Assassins are not. There's no world where they can live harmoniously, which is why they have different names."

"That depends on the circumstances. The world isn't black and white, Aamir, not even shades of gray. Its myriad of colors become a full picture and tells a story of hard decisions, good, evil, and in-between. Even the most honorable have dark moments in the tapestry of their life, places where you could judge them solely for that and claim they are unworthy." I met his gaze, putting my morality in the open and daring him to judge it, as I could and would judge his at every opportunity.

"I don't assassinate someone who deserves an honorable fight. The people I kill have proven they have no honor, often guilty of crimes and charged with death by the Tribunal. Do they have honor when they run from the judgment and face the consequences of their actions? Do they have honor when they murder innocents for their own gain? Why should I give them honor when they have proven they don't respect the ideals I uphold with others? They would only use honor against me because they don't understand its importance. Therefore, I give them none."

"You've spent a lot of time trying to justify how you have become an assassin when you know there's nothing honorable about it. Having a good argument doesn't change the facts. You claim to be a warrior, but we all know the only way you can win a fight is through underhanded tactics." Aamir gave me a look of disgust. "Yet you stand here and try to sway a young man to your ways of thinking."

"You know absolutely nothing about my mate or her tactics, so I suggest you think carefully before you bite off more than you chew," Raphael warned softly.

"And what leg do you have to stand on?" Aamir snapped. Pavan was suddenly at his side, and Aamir passed off his daughter to the other naga. "You follow her around like a lost child, unable to speak our language, helping our *women* in the kitchen. You should worry about your own people and leave me to mine. With you as their leader and Kaliya training them, I have a feeling they won't last long. Maybe you should go back to where you came from and prove me wrong."

The scents around me changed, and I smiled. I knew Raphael was changing behind me. It was slow, probably just a peek at what he was. I could envision the black eyes with their blood-red iris, the black veins growing over his face, his body growing, a little taller, a little broader, more imposing with every second.

"Your people might not be my business, but how you speak to my mate is," Raphael said, his words merging with a growl.

"Your mate is a cun—"

Raphael caught Aamir off guard, but what really worried me was Roshni in the other naga's arms. As Raphael's hand snapped out and grabbed Aamir's neck, he also finished his transformation into the cambion form that still stunned me with its size, over seven feet tall, not including his horns. His gray skin with black veins made him seem like a marble statue. His snarl echoed in the space.

"You had a warning," Raphael growled down at the naga in his clutches. "You want to pick a fight with me, which is what you'll get if Kaliya doesn't kill you first. For the sake of your daughter, keep your mouth shut and don't leave her without a father." Raphael leaned down, putting his face in Aamir's. "I'm willing to do that if I have to. I don't care if you like either of us, but you'll respect us."

Aamir hissed, fangs down. I knew Aamir could change to snake form to escape, but he didn't, which was smart. Raphael could snap the snake in half. I had to make those sorts of decisions all the time. While I respected that thinking from Aamir, I really didn't like what was going on.

I reached out, thinking about Roshni, who was getting fussy. Pavan was keeping her way too close to this for my comfort. He should have taken her across the room. She would recognize the conflict, and it could very well leave her terrified of Raphael for the rest of her life. As my hand touched Raphael's shoulder, he started shifting back but didn't remove his hand from Aamir's neck. The grip wasn't hard enough to cause lasting damage, which impressed me. It took an immense amount of control for any of the cambions to shift and keep the strength they exerted consistent.

He finally released Aamir, stepping back to get out of range of any potential bite, something I had taught him to do. He was immune to my venom, and there was a chance he could survive the venom of others, but it would be a painful experience if it was possible. I didn't need my mate downed as he tried to survive whatever Aamir's venom would do to him. Every naga had different effects, but all were based in nature. It narrowed down the possibilities, but none of them were good.

"Have I made myself clear?" Raphael asked, at my side again. He had turned on the dangerous warlord I knew he could be. The confidence that poured off him was in stark contrast to the good-natured man he could be, the man I fell in love with. Now, I loved both sides of him.

"Adhar!" Aamir turned to the other ruler, but not before I saw the fear in his eyes.

"You insulted his mate," Adhar said patiently, but I saw the fear in him, too. He hadn't seen exactly what Raphael was capable of. My mate had moved *fast*, almost naga fast, catching even me off guard. "He acted as you would have if someone insulted Saranya, or Mahavir would behave if someone viciously cut Eshika down. You know I won't hold him to a different standard than any of you." Adhar crossed his arms. "Now, everyone needs to cool their tempers. Breakfast should be out soon."

19

CHAPTER NINETEEN

Breakfast was brought out shortly after Adhar forced us to break it up. Nakul didn't stay with his brother and nephew, following me and Raphael to our own place in the courtyard, far away from Aamir, who had gone back to Pavan. Dalar finally came out, looking around fearfully. He would have heard everything. He left the twin he'd had in their suite and quickly took the other there. Aamir refused to put Roshni down or give her to anyone else, keeping her to his chest possessively. Pavan hovered, sending a glare at me before turning his back. I didn't get any food yet, letting them get theirs, so there were no unnecessary comments. I didn't want to stress Adhar out too much.

"Well, that could have gone much better," Nakul said, giving me a sympathetic look. "Few people know my... history," he admitted softly. "Adhar, my brother, and his family. Vikrant, but not his mate. No one else. If they did, they might not jump on you so quickly. My apologies."

"Why don't they know?" I asked, keeping my voice

low like his. We were far enough away from the rest to worry about anyone overhearing us, but he'd jumped into a sensitive topic that had to be handled with care. Care I was inclined not to give because it pissed me off it was kept a secret.

The delicate line of protecting my people's future and working with the Tribunal. Some of these fools will never understand the balance or what it costs me.

"Would you believe me if I said I am ashamed?" He looked around the room. "For years, I was an honored warrior, but I tarnished that in a period of insanity and darkness. I ruined myself and will spend my life trying to make up for something that I can't. Adhar has been a great help, telling me to focus on the good things I can do now. I can never tell my victims I'm sorry, but he believes I can save others one day. He has so much hope for me, but I have been scared to share my shame."

"I've never properly asked what you were thinking those years, and I don't want to...What you did was terrible, whether or not you were in your right mind." I said nothing else. Humans had similar things happen in their world. Sometimes, people lost their minds, and they hurt people...killed people. Sometimes, they could be helped, sometimes they couldn't, but in every case, what they did is unforgivable, and Nakul's crimes were immense.

"The only way to move past it is to admit your shame," Raphael said, leaning against a pillar. "Face it head-on and fight to right the wrongs you've committed."

"I can't bring people back to life," Nakul said, shaking his head.

"An *honorable* man would admit he took those lives," Raphael said, his expression dark. "And face the consequences for the rest of his life, in every situation he's met with. Since *honor* means so much to you nagas." Raphael wasn't holding back. His distaste for Nakul was clear, and his temper from Aamir was still too hot for him to attempt being nice anymore.

Nakul took it, not looking away from Raphael as my mate cut to the heart of the problem.

"You are a young man, powerful and confident," Nakul started, staring at my mate with an unreadable expression. "Normally, I would tell a young man like you, he doesn't have the wisdom to attack me, to question my decisions about my life or my honor." Nakul bowed his head. "But I think...maybe, you have called me on something Adhar has been too gentle with, thanks to our long history and his proximity to what happened to my family." He turned to the room.

"Tell the men at the meeting later," I suggested. While I disagreed about keeping it secret, I hadn't been here for years. I had neglected my duties on a personal level, so I had no leverage to chastise them for the decisions they made without my input. "It'll get to their mates. Eshika has probably kept her silence out of respect for you. If their mates or she doesn't ease them into it, I'll do it." He gave me a look, and I quickly added more. "I'll do it honestly and respectfully if it comes to that, but they deserve to know. Aside from Raphael's argument, there's more at play here than just your honor, Nakul."

"You're talking about the Tribunal," he guessed.

"I am. We're accountable to them, and they went out

on a limb, letting us bring you here instead of shoving you back into the prison. There are other species who got similar treatment after that incident, but it leaves victims justifiably angry as if justice was being subverted. Now, I haven't heard of your victims making a fuss, but that doesn't mean you get to live here and pretend none of it ever happened." I crossed my arms, trying to show him just how angry he made me with this.

"Damn it, Nakul. You're not the one who has to deal with the repercussions. I do, and it's already hard for me. You know it is. I try to be sympathetic because my job as ruler is to protect you, but you know how I feel about what you did."

Nakul nodded, taking my words as patiently as he had taken Raphael's. Nakul wasn't a fool, and he made no real excuses. He gave me the truth, then took the verbal beating he received. The fact he did was one of the few ways I knew this man in front of me wasn't the same as the one I tossed into a prison cell and tried my best to forget. He didn't argue.

"I'll speak to Adhar," he said simply. "Thank you for being truthful with me, and I'm grateful for the wisdom and patience you've brought to me. I will do my best to repay you for this chance you've given me."

He turned and started for Adhar. I sighed, heading to get breakfast. While talking to Adhar, I hadn't noticed how Basanti, Eshika, and Saranya had come out to enjoy breakfast with everyone. They would be without their mates all day, so it made perfect sense they would try to squeeze in a little time before they found themselves excluded.

"Raphael?" I was watching Saranya hover by her husband, but I knew Raphael's attention was on me.

"Yes?" he asked softly, leaning down to say it in my ear.

"Try to get to know Saranya while I'm gone with the other nagas. I want you to tell me what you think of her when I come back." I turned toward him, not wanting to stare too long. "Basanti, too, if you can. Eshika and Eleanor are pretty open, but those two are quieter. I want to know if that's just their way of things or if they're having a hard time opening up. They're both dealing with infants right now as well."

"I don't know if I'm completely comfortable spying on women," Raphael whispered.

"Then you don't have to tell me anything, but you're a mate, and you can't come to the meeting. Basanti has twins, and she'll need help. Eleanor is still an outsider. You're pretty good at easing the tension when you want to."

"So, really, this is just a request for me to be productive, and..." I saw the light bulb. "You just want me to stick close to them, no matter what I decide to do."

"I would not ask for *that* because I don't want you to get the impression something bad is going to happen," I said, a smile forming as I picked at my food. "But as a precaution, I would feel better if you stayed close to them with whatever excuse you like...I know you're just a nice guy who would help them if you saw they needed it." I took a bite to eat as he narrowed his eyes. "You're just in a bit of a mood, thanks to Aamir, and you would want a moment alone to cool down, but you might not get that chance."

"You,"—he leaned in, meeting my eyes—"know how to make a man feel needed when you want to," he said. "I'll do it...but you knew I would."

I pushed my plate toward him, but he shook his head and got his own. He'd been so foul about Aamir, he hadn't made a plate when we walked down there. As he was walking back, Eleanor and Vikrant walked with him, and I could see the dazzling curiosity in her eyes as she approached. Once he was back, she was practically shaking with the need to ask questions.

"I should have known you wouldn't miss it," I said once I was done chewing. "Oh, I'll be in the bathhouse tomorrow morning if you want to join me."

"I'll think about it," she said quickly before looking at Raphael. "All of your people can do that?"

"Yes," Raphael said with a smile. "Some look different. We have a biological caste system, and the caste we belong to seems to dictate what powers we have. Some take forms like mine. Some look different and are meant for different things."

"Caste system?" I saw the switch in her excitement to disappointment and even apprehension.

"Yeah, we don't have a choice," Raphael said, not reading Eleanor as well as I did. He hadn't yet caught her change.

"It's nothing like what exists in India or anywhere in the world," I said quickly. "The cambions..." I looked at Raphael. "They can't leave or ignore the system the way a human can. It's part of what they are, probably rooted in their demon side. They can't even fight to go higher in their caste like a werewolf can in a pack."

"Really?" Eleanor was now more attentive to the information, although some of her excitement had worn off and probably wouldn't come back.

"There's power in it," I explained while I let Raphael try to figure out why it was necessary. "Raphael is the ruler because he is the highest caste around, as far as we know, and they can't help but want him to lead them. They look to him because that's what the demonic side of their nature tells them to do. Even the most temperamental cambions, ones who like to stretch the rules or test his patience, are also driven by a need to work for the community, please Raphael, and even keep him safe from anything they perceive as a threat. He's driven to lead them and protect the weaker ones of his culture, which pushes him to do his best. If a cambion walks away from the community, they don't get a free pass. They can't convince themselves it's not their belief system anymore. If they ran into Raphael at some point, they would probably have the same feelings to follow him and let him rule."

"Oh, and there's noticeable...differences in the cambions based on this?" She nodded. "I saw in the packet there were types of cambions, but you didn't put this in it."

"Not fully," Raphael confirmed. "I'm uncomfortable putting some things down on paper for the masses, so I can protect their privacy for now. It could have been leaked, so I kept some areas sparse in terms of the other cambions because you wouldn't meet them."

He hadn't wanted to expose any weaknesses. If the wrong people knew mage and 'civilian' cambions existed, not as strong or big as him, they would be targets for exploitation. Even now, I knew he had no intention of going into detail. Explaining the caste system and saying each type of cambion was different would have to be enough.

We didn't have much time left. Nagas didn't eat much, except me. I hurried to finish my plate while Raphael gave Eleanor general information, promising over time, he would probably be willing to say more.

"There are security issues we have to worry about, and it's easier for me to treat everyone equally when I decide who to share information with," he explained.

To my knowledge, he had never told the werewolves and fae helping build the compound about the differences. Sammy and Raphael were the only cambions who had used their powers in the public eye, both with devastating effect. The few people still alive from the lab who knew were carefully guarded in prison. Raphael could talk to them at any time, but only him. Several of the people who didn't try to run had been executed.

Once my plate was clear, I took it to a growing stack I knew the mates would be forced to clean. Guilt ran through me, so I picked up the entire stack and carried it toward the kitchen. I was nearly there when Saranya caught up with me.

"You shouldn't be—"

"It's fine," I said simply, not letting her get in my way. Stepping around her was easy, but she was relentless.

"But you're a ruler, and—"

"I lived alone for a long time and did my own dishes." I put them on the counter and started the water in the sink. Adhar's house was a contradiction of old and new—woodburning oven and a kitchen fire, plumbing and light bulbs, homemade soap. "I have a free moment, and I..." I trailed off, wondering if I really wanted to admit I had the urge because I felt guilty she was expected to do it.

"You..." I looked back at her as she tried to find the right thing to say. I saw her worried glance toward the courtyard.

"Are you worried about something? You're allowed to tell me anything, and I'll keep your confidence. It's the least I can do." I washed the top plate, which was mine.

"You're not what Aamir has always made you seem," she said softly, coming to my side. She grabbed a plate, held it for a minute, then put it back down. "I've been a mate longer than anyone else here. I'm older than you, but you carry yourself with a maturity I wasn't expecting."

"I'm one hundred and nineteen years old," I said with a smile. "I had to grow up sometime. Sure, I can be mature, but I'm also known to get into fights. I'm abrasive and refuse to live the life that was expected of me. Some would call me incredibly selfish."

"Selfish isn't the impression I have since we met, though I was told to expect it," she said more strongly. "I just wanted to say that."

"Do you want to help?" I asked her, nodding to the dishes.

"I actually despise doing the dishes."

"Oh. Then go." I waved her off with a soapy hand. "I

might not finish them, but I'll do as many as I can before I go. I don't really enjoy doing them, either, but I don't have that many to do, and Raphael helps. I can suffer for a few minutes."

"Thank you so much." She ran out to spend precious time with her daughter. I was halfway done when Adhar came to find me.

"We're getting ready to head out. I agree with you and Nakul. We'll tell the others about his past to clear the air," he said, looking over my shoulder. He seemed to be in a good mood, probably thanks to the food, which had been delicious. "Still trying to win points with the mates? I think they all like you from first impressions. Now, they just need to get to know you."

"I didn't like that we were leaving them to clean up the mess," I answered, shaking my head. "It's not about points. It's about pulling my weight, doing what I can to keep the household functioning. Doing dishes is a chore, but it's not a hard one if people pull their weight." I finished the plate in my hand, rinsed my hands, then cut the water. "I don't think I should help the other women just because I'm a woman. We all sat out there and talked and had a good time...or a not-so-good time, depending on how you look at it. Either way, we did that while they were in here, busting their asses, probably before most of us were awake, to prepare all this food.

"Then we're so rushed to go off and have a meeting that we can't spend ten minutes helping clean up the mess?" I gave him a look as I dried my hands on a small towel left on the counter. "Seem fair? Seem like the logical way for a household with this many people to function efficiently? Four women, three if you don't include Eleanor, doing all the work? Raphael will help, but he needs to play beginner politics with those assholes, so they don't look down on him or me."

"I do the dishes, too," Adhar said softly in a way I knew I had just fucked up and overstepped. "And so does Nakul. He and I are the only people who live here full time. You know Mahavir and Devesh help Eshika. She's made it clear she likes when they do a good job. You know I have the men in charge of keeping the bathhouse clean. Do you think I've given no thought to this?"

I shut my mouth and schooled my face before I stepped on his toes again.

"I have to split the chores in a way they'll accept," Adhar continued. "Because you're *right*. There are fifteen people here, and it's difficult for only three to four people to manage. If you would like, we can sit down and continue talking about my house rules, but every household here has already heard them and agreed to them. Some men even grumbled about it if that makes you happy." It did, in a perverse way.

"They will sweep and mop the floors daily...starting tomorrow, after this meeting. There's a number of other things they will help with, including some upgrades and repairs to the building I need their help with. And yes, sometimes, I will send them in here for a deep cleaning to make their mates smile, just because I can. Please never forget if some men in our community don't appreciate them, I have a soft spot for the women who have given up their human lives and families to have new ones here. I will do my best without offending anyone to make sure they know *I* appreciate them."

"I'm sorry." The apology was genuine, and I hoped he could hear that.

"You're already forgiven," he said, reaching out to guide me away from the sink. "You feel passionate about things, which can make you run your mouth without thinking. You've mostly grown out of it, but I know our bad habits sometimes have the tendency to rear their ugly heads. You realized your mistake quickly, and I don't think you'll make the same mistake again."

"Too bad it took us over a hundred years to figure each other out," I said softly. "I could have used some of that wisdom and patience a long time ago."

"Yes, I know. Come, we can't keep them waiting any longer."

20

CHAPTER TWENTY

With no time wasted, Adhar and I walked through the courtyard, and the other nagas came with us. Raphael waved goodbye, standing next to Eleanor, and surprisingly, with Eshika on his other side. He had already brought two of them together while I was throwing a fit over the dishes.

We walked down a well-worn trail into the wild, deep jungle Adhar maintained within his walls. All he did was trim occasionally to keep the paths clear, and the canopy kept us well protected from any prying eyes. There were tricks to hiding buildings like the house, but I didn't know them all that well. If I had stayed in India, I would have learned, but I lived in the desert, where I could see for miles on a clear day, and my address was a matter of public record now.

He led us to a small building and opened the door. It had the smell of being recently cleaned, but not with the harsh chemicals I had become used to over the years. Adhar used homemade everything, like the soap in the kitchen. I often wondered how he had the time to maintain everything, but living alone for so long, he probably had little else to do. Nakul was welcome company and an extra set of hands, further helping him to keep his place in pristine condition.

What really struck me was that I had never gone in this building before. I looked at everything with interest. The wood was intricately carved and recently restained. Benches lined the sides of the room, with a few chairs available for anyone who couldn't fit on a bench. Along the back wall were a case and bookshelf system. There were the artifacts of our people. I hadn't thought about it, but he didn't keep any inside the house. He used to, just as my mother had, but he had moved them all out here. From weapons of the first generation to the bones of Garuda, our history in physical form sat before me.

I walked to them, looking over all of it.

"I built this as more mates came, and we needed a better space to talk," Adhar explained, pulling up two chairs. He put them down next to me and gestured to be seated. "We used to meet in my home, but it got crowded in the archive. I figured we needed a special place while the mates worked on things in the house, with us out of their hair and not needing to be silent."

"These sorts of meetings didn't start until our numbers were low, so we never had to think about it before," I said, shrugging. "I was never allowed in them while I lived here or while my family was still alive."

"We don't allow children, no matter what their position might be," Adhar said, taking his seat. I followed suit and looked around the room, seeing a division form.

It had already been noticeable, but now it was clear. Aamir, Dalar, and Pavan were a happy little band. Dalar and Pavan probably followed Aamir, thanks to his age, experience, and personality. He could be charismatic in a sort of man's man way. Devesh was squeezed between his uncle and father, and I could tell this was his first time being included in such a meeting.

I'm one hundred and nineteen years old, yet I have more in common with the seventeen-year-old than I do anyone else here. Wow, there's something wrong with that, and I don't even know whose fault it is anymore.

Vikrant was sitting on a free chair, positioned closer to Mahavir than Dalar, but he still kept himself separate.

"Yeah, you probably talked about some heavy things I wasn't ready for," I said, agreeing with Adhar's judgment. "If my mother hadn't thought I was ready to attend, there was no reason for you to think I was ready. How do we begin?"

"We open the floor with the first naga who wants to speak," Adhar explained, then looked at the other nagas. "There are some events from the last century that must be made clear before we can talk about our future. In the spirit of truthfulness among us, you will hear the complicated history of two of our most powerful. I've kept this private in the spirit of letting both souls heal before potentially reopening the wounds. Today, they're ready for this to be spoken about."

"No," Mahavir snapped as his brother stood up at the end of Adhar's small speech. "Brother—"

"This has nothing to do with you," Nakul said with a gentleness that threatened to make me regret this, but it had to be done. Not just for Nakul, but for me, and not just for the reason Nakul had apologized for.

Nakul went to the center of the room, his back to Adhar and me, but able to see the others. It wasn't a large building, but it was spacious enough to let Nakul position himself to talk to those who needed to hear him without backing up into us.

"Roughly one-hundred-seven years ago, an attack was committed against our people." I closed my eyes as Nakul spoke. "Many were lost. Warriors, women…and children."

I fought to breathe as I listened to him recount that horrendous night and the days after. Finding their bodies, the image forever burned in his brain. Desperation. Fear. I listened, but I heard no words. I only saw a flash of my experience from that night and the days after I was left reeling.

"That night, I became a man none of you would have recognized," Nakul continued after his recounting. "And Kaliya became a girl who no one could understand."

I opened my eyes, staring at the back of his head. I knew our stories were tied together. We took the paths none of the other nagas dared attempt. They took us to different places in life, but in the end, we had both reached the same point in time and found ourselves on opposite sides.

"I disappeared quickly, searching for a balm to pain I couldn't admit existed. There is nothing that can ease the pain of what I had taken from me, but I had the skills of a warrior and pain in my heart, and I could use both things, and I did." Nakul looked back at me and extended a hand cautiously. An invitation, one I didn't have to take, but I knew Nakul wanted to show the nagas something, and telling my story wouldn't hurt me, not anymore.

I didn't take the hand, but I stood.

"I was forced to go back to a life that did nothing to help me overcome my loss. I'll concede and remind everyone here I was a child and didn't actually know what I needed, only what I wanted," I said, stepping beside him and looking at the other nagas. "I was expected to get with the program others set for my life, and I felt no one understood what burned inside of me—a need to avenge my family. I thought there was no way I would ever stop hurting so bad. I grew to hate the walls that surrounded me, feeling trapped." I looked at Nakul. "I thought the people around me were stupid for grieving and trying to move on, stupid for refocusing their efforts on keeping us secret and safe. I had already seen it fail and knew it would fail again. I still believe the latter, but I should have given myself time to grieve properly."

"We took different paths, didn't we?" he asked softly.

"Very different." I waited for him to say something, but when he didn't, I continued my half of the story. "I was untrained and foolish, driven only by survival and a need to avenge my family, and it caught up to me. I was captured by humans who sold the bodies of supernaturals to high-paying customers for their own use. Not to be butchered for parts, but to be used so they could say they had something that wasn't human."

They all reacted to that. Vikrant was the easiest to look at, and his face paled. I quickly looked around, barely moving but taking in their expressions. Mahavir was horrified, and his son clearly understood my meaning as well. Even Aamir and Pavan looked a little sick. Dalar was the worst of that group, though. I was pretty certain it was going to bring him to tears.

"Being rescued was happenstance," I continued, knowing I had to finish this part of the story before Nakul would continue. "By a werecat of all things, one the werewolves call the Assassin. Hisao said he saw something in me that made him take pity on me. He carried me out, put me in his carriage, and took me from China to Japan. He gave me a choice to learn from him or take what I needed to survive on my own. I took the training. Hisao, son of Hasan, the most accomplished assassin in the history of the supernatural, trained me personally and helped me find the path I needed to be on. I didn't know his reputation at the time, but I quickly learned."

"And after you left his training, you became a Tribunal Executioner," Nakul said, nodding at me.

"That's right. Hasan was, and still is, a member of the Tribunal, so Hisao had several contacts to get me a meeting to see if I could work for them. I had the choice of being an Investigator or an Executioner. For safety reasons, I chose the job that let me kill more. As I was leaving Hisao's training, I finally contacted Adhar and let him know I was alive."

"I will never forget that day," Adhar said softly. "I broke down in tears once I knew no one was looking."

"When did you two meet again?" Aamir asked, taking Adhar's interruption as a sign he could ask questions.

"Nakul?" I stepped away from him, letting him take

the floor. I had only told my story to give context to what Nakul needed to tell them.

“Brother, please,” Mahavir pleaded.

“I grew so desperate for someone to help me, to help our people, I started…” Nakul dropped his head. “Kaliya, I shouldn’t ask, but…”

Mahavir got to his feet.

“Please don’t,” Mahavir whispered, holding his hands out to me. “He’s been through enough.”

“They need to know,” I said gently, pushing his hands down. “I know you want to protect him, but…you didn’t see, Mahavir. You didn’t see what I had to, and you didn’t hear the anger of the Tribunal or the cries of the ones left behind.”

Mahavir, defeated by those gentle but true words, sank back into his seat.

“I was asked to look at a case by one of the Investigators,” I explained. “I recognized something that no others had. I knew the positioning of the bodies, knew the sort of injuries. A woman and her son, roughly the same age as…” I said softly. “I walked into that house and saw something I had heard about in great detail.”

“I am no longer honorable,” Nakul whispered. “I gave in to the black madness of grief and anger.”

“I don’t understand,” Aamir said, looking at me.

“Nakul had become one of the most elusive and infamous serial killers the Tribunal has ever dealt with,” I answered. “He was recreating the murders of his family every time he killed.” I took a deep breath. “I had to help catch him because I was one of the few people who could.” I looked at Nakul, refusing to meet the eyes of the other nagas. I decided right then not to get into the details of the chase. Mahavir hadn't known his brother had been killing people when he visited. Adhar hadn't known either. I had told them he was a suspect. Adhar had lied to me in his effort to protect one of his own. Like me, he was also always caught between the two—respect for the power of the Tribunal and protect his people. This had been the first time those two things had come into conflict. Adhar had made his decision.

And I had made mine.

"And I did, with the help of the Investigator that took on the case, who is still a good friend of mine to this day."

"Nakul, you couldn't have..." Aamir stood, stepping around me to look directly at the warrior he had known and respected for so long. "Tell me you didn't do this." He grabbed the old warrior's shoulders, shaking them. "You..."

"I did," Nakul said softly. "Not a day goes by, I do not think about the pain I inflicted on others and the lives I cut short. Not a single day. At the beginning, I became a man none of you would have recognized. Even now, I am not the man I used to be because this tale isn't done."

"I wanted to execute him," I said as Aamir released Nakul. He stepped back from me, looking at me with disgust and fear.

"He's one of us," Aamir said. "No matter—"

"He butchered families," I retorted, snapping viciously as I grabbed hold of the rage I had felt. "Nothing about that, no matter what has happened to the nagas, is excusable. But I was overruled. Adhar went to the Tribunal, pleaded that based on our numbers, Nakul could be imprisoned. That he was mentally unwell, explaining the reason Nakul had gone mad. Nakul was shoved into a jail I live relatively close to, the only supernatural jail in the world run by the Tribunal, with handpicked wardens of three of the five ruling species." I leaned close to Aamir. "He butchered families the way mine had been butchered. The way his own had been butchered. He would have died decades ago if I had my way."

"I wanted to die," Nakul whispered softly, barely more than a breath. "I had my first moment of clarity in decades and wanted to die, but I let Adhar take me to the prison instead."

That was something I hadn't known. I looked back at Adhar and saw he also hadn't known that.

I need to wrap this up before it takes all our time.

"I left Nakul to rot in that prison. Just over a year ago, Nakul settled down to live with Adhar." I pushed a hand through my hair, deciding to keep the rest vague. "I was working on a personal case, rooted in the mysteries surrounding my mate. His enemies became mine, and they had contacts in the prison. I had a walkthrough on the schedule. There was a breakout, designed to kill me and recapture my mate because he was an incredibly valuable asset to the company he had been running from when I met him. While some prisoners were bought and bribed to kill me, some, like Nakul, were turned into sleeper agents, spelled to kill me when they had the chance."

"I would never hurt another naga or a mate," Nakul said. "Never. I can't..."

"Nakul, to his credit, tried to warn me something was coming when I walked past his cell before the initial break out. He couldn't remember being spelled, but he fought against it. Compulsion spells work best when you spell someone to do something they might have done originally. It gives them a nudge or gets rid of their reservations. Using a compulsion spell, tied in with memory manipulation spells, on someone who would never do the action, requires power and...cruelty. It's a violation akin to what I had gone through at the hands of the humans Hisao rescued me from." I tapped my chest, feeling the same pain when I learned what had been done to Nakul.

"Nakul failed us, losing himself to grief and madness. I failed him for not protecting him while he served his time. So, after it was all said and done, I talked to the Tribunal. Witches helped with the damage done to his mind as much as they could and brought him here to continue healing with Adhar. He's under house arrest and will be for the rest of his life, no matter how long it is." I turned away from them and headed for my seat. "That's it. That's the story of two nagas following the trauma that led us down different paths until we finally clashed."

"Would you kill me now if I asked you to?" Nakul asked, a soft plea tucked under the pain.

I froze, staring at my chair but unable to move. I heard someone jump so quickly, another naga yelped, and a bench fell to the ground, but I didn't look back.

"Nakul! You're doing your penance now, telling everyone what you did and facing their judgment. You faced the judgment of the Tribunal, and they allowed this. Adhar has allowed this. After everything you've gone through, brother..." Mahavir was fighting for his brother, the last person in his family.

I knew the reason Mahavir disliked me was wrapped up in the situation with Nakul. He'd pitied me as a girl, didn't want me as a burden because I would have been a broken woman and a terrible wife. I couldn't really blame him for those things, but his anger with me came from this, and now, his brother was asking for something that left me speechless.

My uncle was asking me if I would kill him.

"Kaliya?" Nakul cut through the buzz in my head. "Would you?"

I turned to look at him. The answer was easy to find, but why it was my answer was much more complicated. My first reason was easy to find, but the second...

Like a movie reel, moments of my life came to me. Watching Carter die for a battle he shouldn't have been a part of. The unsettling pain I had for Nakul when I learned about the magic done on him, so he would kill me because of a fight I brought on myself. The time I had tried to assault Sorcha, one of my few friends before Raphael could see the demon had turned into a man. The time I had ripped out the intestines of Mehar, torturing him with no real objective other than pain, making him beg for death as I buried my entire fucking hand inside his abdomen.

Some were mistakes I made. Some were temporary moments of madness fueled by vicious need. Others had made me pay for some of those moments, people justified as what was necessary, but I would always know the truth and carry the weight of them.

No one walked away from trauma without some issues. I could have easily become Nakul if it hadn't been for Hisao. To this day, I showed signs of slipping past the point of no return. Luckily, I was surrounded by friends who gave me chances to correct myself, and in return, I gave them chances.

The thought never escaped me—I could have been just like Nakul, and there was evidence pointing to that in almost every area of my life. It was an important piece of my complicated feelings for my uncle.

"No," I answered softly. "I wouldn't do it and don't think I could do it if asked." I sighed, looking down at my hands, thinking of the blood they had shed, the lives I had ended. *If anything had been different...* "For two reasons. One, you don't deserve it. You think death will absolve you, and it might, but it'll also give you peace, and that's something I don't think you deserve. You claim you want to die, but you let Adhar save you from execution, and now you have to live with that. The second reason? Just like you have to live with the guilt of what you did, I have to live with the fact that I understand you all too well. We'll both die at some point, but until then, you better live in the name of those people for the rest of your long life, Nakul. If you stray from it, then yes, I could possibly be the one who finally ends you, but until that point... You will not convince me to give you the peace of death."

I took my seat, a clear sign the conversation was over. It took time for everyone to regain their seats, Nakul staying on his feet the longest, staring at me with knowing eyes.

"We need to move on," I declared. "We need to discuss the rakshasa king, Mehar, how I killed him, what will happen when the rakshasa send word they want me to stand for what I did."

21

CHAPTER TWENTY-ONE

Nakul finally sat down, staring at Aamir across the room, who looked like we had just shaken the foundation of his world. I had known Nakul was respected, but I didn't know Aamir was so attached to who he believed Nakul was. If I had, I might have picked a different approach, though it probably wouldn't have mattered.

I turned to Adhar, who was not watching Nakul, Mahavir, Aamir, or even Devesh. He was looking at me, sadness in every line of his face. It lasted for what seemed like an eternity, wondering what he saw but not curious enough to ask. Eventually, he turned away from me and looked at the room of nagas.

"We're all that's left of our people," he said softly. "Three babies who must be kept safe while they grow. Twelve nagas out of a thousand that could be alive today if we..." Adhar shook his head. "Kaliya made some startling discoveries last year. While she traveled the world and many of you thought she neglected her duties, she has been working tirelessly to find the truth behind everything that has happened to us."

"Those close to me call it an obsession," I added.

"I once thought you were looking for answers where there were none," Adhar said guiltily. "I have been proven wrong." His voice grew stronger. "As she freed her mate's people from their captivity and revealed them to the world, Kaliya ran into someone she was certain had been involved in the murders of her family members. She requested more information on the rakshasa from me, but all I could give her was information from five hundred years ago. We haven't interacted with them in a very long time. She met one and was certain he had played a role in that terrible night. That night wasn't a simple kill of a naga who had left our protections or even an attack on a single household."

"It was an assault from an enemy hellbent on wiping out our kind. A declaration of war we still haven't admitted we're fighting." I leaned back in my seat. "I have treated it like that for years, refusing to think it was anything else. I have always thought someone had to be behind this, that it wasn't *just* random acts of violence, though they may have played a small role. Something bigger was going on." I took a deep breath. "And I was right."

"What did you learn?" Vikrant demanded, leaning forward, putting his elbows on his knees, and staring at me intensely.

"Mehar, king of the rakshasas, captured my mate and me with the intent to kill us both," I answered. "*But* he only had *permission* to kill Raphael. The person he answered to, the person who probably paid and funded his hunt for me for over a century, wanted to be the person who killed me."

"Why you?" Aamir asked.

"I'm my mother's daughter." It was a vague version of the truth. Still reeling from the revelation about Nakul, and with this new information I had to give them and the rakshasas to think about, I didn't think they were ready to learn what exactly had been done to me. I also wasn't ready to trust them with that information. If Nakul could hide he was a serial killer for over a year, I could keep my secret among the select few who knew for another couple of weeks. "I had escaped the attack when I was supposed to die, the attack where Mehar and others invaded my family home and killed everyone else, a simultaneous assault, orchestrated to happen at the same time as several others. I disappeared every time he had the chance to get close. He was still hunting in the old ways, so when I finally resurfaced—a Tribunal Executioner with extra protections and trained by the best—he couldn't come for me the way he had other nagas. With the advances in technology and my reputation and skill growing, he opted for the long and slow hunt to complete what was started that night. He had to adapt, just like I did."

"Then he finally caught up to you," Mahavir said, nodding. "I take it finding your mate played a role."

"Absolutely, especially since my mate is neither human nor naga. Cambions, as Raphael and I learned, give their mates some abilities." I pulled a dagger from my boot, making Adhar jump a little. "I'm *always* armed,

Adhar. Don't be surprised." I lifted the dagger and exposed my other palm. "Cambions have a healing rate unmatched in all other supernaturals. This was in the information packet we dispersed."

I dragged the dagger over my palm, hissing in pain. I let the blood pool there, obscuring the view as I felt the skin knit back together. It would leave a scar I would have to get removed, but I had to show them. Slowly, I tipped my hand and let the blood fall to the ground, then wiped the rest away, exposing the scar.

"That was passed on to me," I finished, showing them the new scar.

"Incredible," Nakul whispered.

"Yeah. My theory is Mehar obviously knew something about cambions and what they could pass to their mates if their demonic sides are activated, which is incredibly dangerous. When Raphael's demonic side was activated, he killed every human in the building, people he knew, his friends. If a cambion's demonic side isn't activated, you can't tell they aren't human. If they stay in human form, you can't see or smell the difference. You've all had at least a day to notice that. You probably caught the way his scent changed."

"Kaliya and I theorize if Raphael had never been a victim of this organization that captured his kind, he would have been her completely human mate," Adhar said. "There's no reason for us to believe other nagas will have cambion mates, but the cambions have a blood test they can do for any mate who wishes to see if they can become a cambion. This is completely at your mate's discretion, not yours. You will have no say in the matter."

Adhar glanced at me, and I nodded, letting him go through with this thing that he and Raphael had talked about. I hadn't been part of this discussion.

"The cambions don't have access to what their captors used to activate their demonic sides, so even if your mates are potential cambions, nothing can be done. Even if they did, Raphael has made it clear to me the risks involved would be too high and potentially devastating to both our people and his. Cambions can and do kill each other when they're out of control, and a single powerful one could kill everyone in this room if it's out of control."

"Are you certain?" Dalar asked.

"In his demon form, not the cambion form you've seen, but his full demon form, Raphael is larger than an African elephant, and could kill dozens, potentially hundreds," I answered, remembering that night. "Another cambion tried to intervene, and she was hit hard, nearly killed. He nearly killed me, and the only reason he didn't was I am his mate as much as he's mine. It was close...closer to death than I like."

"There's nothing we can do about this right now, so we'll turn our attention back to the rakshasa," Adhar said, gesturing for me to continue.

"Mygi was the organization keeping the cambions captive and secret. I saw Mehar at their lab the night my team went to take it and free those inside. He was either educating himself or verifying information he already had with the visit, and he knew Raphael was my mate." I sighed, looking at the new scar on my hand. "When he captured Raphael and me last October, I hadn't bitten Raphael. I hadn't wanted to. He had to rule his own people, and I didn't want to give him our enemies. Our mates...they're targets." I rubbed my face. "I wanted to spare him. Spare him from trips like this that take him away from his people. From...all of it, including having a broken mate. So, when I got the chance, I walked away from Raphael and tried not to be drawn back in."

"As you should," Vikrant said softly.

I dropped my hand and met his gaze. Instead of condemnation, there was respect in his gaze.

"Your mate should be the most important person to you. If you felt being with him was a danger to his safety, you did what you had to do to protect him. As you should." Vikrant nodded. "There are days I regret not walking away to keep her safe and happy, let her live out her life in peace, and hopefully find a less complicated and dangerous love. I'm very good at being secret. None of my homes have ever been tested by potential enemies. I lost my sister and brother-in-law the same night both of you lost your families, and that colored my judgment. I was lonely. I fell in love and brought her here without thinking about how this life would affect her. Sometimes, I wish I could go back and do what you talk about doing —walk away."

"It doesn't work. Take it from me. He wanted me as much as I wanted him, and he didn't...my mate didn't listen to me when I told him it was dangerous, as men often don't." I gestured at everyone around me. "We were captured, and the mate bond was forced on us. Yes, that's exactly the way it sounds. We were paralyzed using a compound I never got the chance to research, and Mehar did the mate bond for us while we were helpless. If it wasn't for the cambion powers activating in me as a cambion mate, we would have died that night. Mehar would have beheaded my mate, then handed me over to whoever wanted to kill me. It's finding that person that is important. Mehar was a hunter. He lived for it, but who he works for? Whoever they have either deep pockets, a lot of power, or both."

I watched them all nod and felt a wave of vindication. They agreed with me, which meant I had done it. I had finally earned a shred of their approval at a terrible cost.

To protect Raphael, I would have welcomed being the hated, absent ruler for eternity. Well, it's too late for that. This is what I have.

"It goes deeper, though. Devika, the witch my mother favored? She had been an agent for whoever our enemy is for as long as I've known her, probably longer. The only reason she didn't betray us sooner was she was passing fond of us for a time. When Raphael and I were betrayed by her, she tried to hold us until she could hand us over. That's how valuable he and I are to whoever this is. So, even if your mates have potential to be cambions, my recommendation is don't go further with it. It's a big ass target you don't want."

"Sounds like it," Mahavir agreed.

"We've been scouring the archives to find clues to who this enemy might be," Adhar said, keeping the poise he had this entire meeting, even as we all shifted around from sitting too long. "The attacks on Kaliya show it might be heating, and now, we have a dead rakshasa king on our hands. Kaliya killed him in self-defense, and she'll be able to use that argument when they call for her to stand before them."

"They're still going to call for her execution, even if their king attacked another ruler unprovoked," Aamir said, staring at me, not Adhar. "*Two* of their rulers. Are you capable of dealing with that?"

"I'll kill all of them if it's required," I said with a smile. "I'm more than capable of it. I killed their king, then I killed his mate and his sons when they tried to avenge him. There is nothing the rakshasas can throw at me that scares me. There's no challenge I'm not willing to face. If they call for an execution, they'll agree to meet me for trial by combat, or they'll just start dying."

"Does anyone here disagree with our planned approach with the rakshasas?" Adhar asked.

No one spoke up.

"Very well. When they send out the wish to see her, we will let her and her mate face them. We shall pray for their success and safe return, and hopefully, an end to this situation."

"Was this the last item to be discussed?" Mahavir asked.

"No," I said quickly, going for a wild card play. "For their own safety, you will all begin training your mates to defend themselves from potential attacks. It's beyond time they learned how to pick up a blade and stick the enemies with the pointy end. Get it done." I stood. "That's all. Adhar?" I'd put him in a corner, with all of his potential arguments thrown out the window because I didn't care about them.

"I see no reason to disagree," he said. "In one year, I'll

make a tour around the households and test the skills of each mate to make sure this training is being given."

"Adhar!" Aamir was furious now. Whatever approval I had received from him, I had just thrown out the window.

"With the growing problems for our people as Kaliya has performed her investigation and been targeted herself, there's a need that everyone must be able to pick up a sword. If you wish to leave Saranya to the fate of being cut down, unable to defend herself, she can live with me," Adhar continued, drawing a line I hadn't expected him to. "So will your daughter, so her mother can continue to take care of her." He stood and presented himself as a strong force at my side.

"The nagas must continue to adapt to survive. We've been stagnant for some time, and it has caused us irreparable damage. We must evolve, as we have before, and Kaliya has been the only one who has come with potentially life saving changes we can make. This is simple. It is the start of what I expect to be many changes she and I will continue to discuss." Adhar leaned down toward Aamir. "Like the fact none of your children will have a mate search ceremony until they're twenty-five, which you, Dalar, and I can discuss with Kaliya privately."

Oh shit, Adhar. Couldn't you ease them into that one when I gave you the chance? Did Aamir strike a nerve? Fuck.

"Of course, Adhar," Aamir said, nodding, his expression now schooled. "I look forward to the discussion."

"Then this meeting is over. Take some time to think about what's been talked about here. Talk to your mates, and if they have concerns or suggestions, we would like to hear those at our next meeting."

Adhar and I walked out together, leading the others.

"That was an explosive ending, Adhar," I said softly.

"After what you had just told them, there should have been no argument to training their mates. Not now. We all must finally admit we're at *war,* and we must *act* like it. That means every able hand should be able to hold a sword. I have to worry about all their lives, and if my nagas won't do right by their mates, I have to make sure those mates are protected." He side-eyed me. "I have to worry about all of them but you. You've been preparing for this since you were a child."

"Damn right I have," I said, nodding sharply.

It was strange to hear him finally call it what it was.

We were at war.

We just didn't know who we were at war with.

22

CHAPTER TWENTY-TWO

Adhar and I made it back to the main house before anyone else could catch up. I looked back, my hand on the door, ready to head in.

"What do you think has them dragging their feet?" I asked, already knowing the answer.

"Really?" Adhar looked back as well, then gave me a weird look.

"Yeah, I know. We did just tell them a lot."

"We did. They'll probably want to know more from Nakul. They, like you, have to reconcile a man they trust to hold their babies with what he did. Beyond that, I'm certain they might think about our future—"

The door was yanked from my hand and flew open to reveal Eshika.

"Shh," she hissed, a very good imitation of a naga.

"Um..." I looked at my empty hand, right where I had left it but now just hovering in the air instead of touching a door.

"The babies are all asleep," she snap-whispered. I was

certain yelling in the lowest volume was a skill only mothers had. “If they’re woken, someone will get hurt.”

I nodded slowly, not wanting to test her. Adhar pointed back down the path.

“You might want to tell them as well,” he said softly. “Before they get here and accidentally do so.” We couldn’t hear the other nagas, but it was a great distraction for the violent woman blocking our way inside.

Eshika’s eyes narrowed before she blew through us like a tornado. Adhar gestured for me to get inside, and I did, waiting for him to close the door softly behind us. I was tiptoeing toward the courtyard even though I had years of training to walk quietly without looking like an idiot. I knew Raphael was there, could feel him through the mate bond, and after the meeting, I really wanted to see him.

I froze when I saw my mate on the couch in the middle of the room, the sun pouring over his serene face. He was totally out, in a position that made me think he’d fallen asleep while sitting on the couch. His arms were stretched over the back, his legs kicked out, and his head had fallen back, letting the sun illuminate the perfect angles of his face and the scars that did nothing to detract from its perfection.

But it was more than just his sleeping face that made me stop. Someone had put a swaddle on him and put a baby in it, lying on his chest as he slept in the sun. I looked further down my mate’s body and saw two more babies, each tucked to the side of him.

As Adhar sighed happily, I started walking again, unable to contain a smile at the scene.

"I'm not asleep," Raphael murmured with not even a twitch. He didn't even open his eyes. "I know you're there."

"Do you need anything?" I asked softly.

"Ottoman. Want to prop my feet up," I looked around and found the closest one, walking gingerly to it. "Thank you."

I slid one slowly to him as he lifted his feet. We tried to be quiet, and it worked. He stretched his long legs out in a more comfortable position. I went to look for the mothers of these babies, not because I wanted my mate back, but to commend them for their idea of giving my mate all the babies. They deserved a break, and if they could get the new guy to give them one, I was going to hang out with them.

I felt a twinge of guilt, but I checked the kitchen first. Sitting out were several dishes, ready for people to eat but no mates. Adhar joined me in the search, grinning as we looked. We found two of them sitting in a parlor, whispering and drinking tea. Saranya and Basanti were looking very relaxed, enjoying themselves immensely.

"Ah, here they are," I said, walking in, Adhar staying outside. He closed the door behind me, leaving me with the mothers. I could have kept looking for Eleanor, but these were the two who had figured out my best-kept secret.

"Since the babies aren't crying, Eshika must have been able to warn you," Basanti said with a smile.

"She did, then went off to threaten the others," I confirmed, sitting down in a chair that gave me the option to talk to both of them. "I saw the babies, too."

"You don't mind, do you?" Saranya sat up straight.

"Not at all. I bet he's enjoying himself," I said with a chuckle. "How did it happen?"

Saranya sighed heavily. "Roshni woke up from her nap. She ate, we changed her, we burped her. I rocked her, and nothing was working. He asked for a chance, just to give me a chance to sit down for a minute. Eshika told me he was trustworthy, and he's your mate, and...I let him try. We were all here, and if he was a danger, he already could have tried...something..."

"It's okay to be nervous around someone new, even my mate. You're rightfully protective of your daughter." I wasn't offended that she was cautious with Raphael. In her shoes, I would have needed to be convinced. "What happened?"

"She cozied into him like...a cat," Saranya continued, giving me a shy smile. "I was stunned. He sat down once she was asleep and hasn't moved since. Basanti put the twins with him as well, wanting to test it, and they did the same thing."

"Those boys cuddled into him like they had their new favorite thing," their mother said with a shake of her head. "For months, Dalar and I have tried to find something to put them both down quickly, just so we can get some quiet. There's something about your mate."

"He's warmer than all of us," I explained. "That's the secret. Just like normal snakes, we like a good rock, heated by the sun. It's amazing, relaxing, yet energizing as it warms us up. We're not really cold-blooded, but we don't regulate our body temperatures as well as most mammals. When we get cold, we get sluggish. Finding something warm that heats us up as we relax on it." I pointed to some of the extra cups they had, not able to reach the little plate they had made for themselves. "May I have a glass of tea?"

Saranya poured one for me and handed it over. I sniffed it before I drank it. As it touched my tongue, I closed my eyes. It had a good flavor, a soft one I wasn't used to. I couldn't identify all the notes, and there was something I liked about that. It wasn't familiar, but it wasn't too different from what I was used to.

"But we're...warmer than nagas," Saranya finally pointed out.

"Yeah, but Raphael is hot in comparison. He's actually the warmest supernatural I've ever encountered," I said, smiling over my cup. I had to do a quick conversion in my head before I could continue. I had grown used to the measurements used in America in my attempt to blend in and didn't use Celsius with anyone on a daily basis anymore. "Humans are thirty-seven Celsius. Raphael is hotter than werewolves and werecats, who are both around thirty-nine. He's all the way up at forty-one Celsius on a normal day. He doesn't get much cooler than that, but he can get even warmer by a degree or so. It happens when cambions use their powers a lot."

"That's...that's so hot," Basanti said.

"Yeah, and it feels amazing to sleep next to it," I said with a grin. "Your children probably felt the heat that pours off him and decided he was the perfect choice of warm *rock*." I felt devilish, hanging out with other women. "He's hard like one too." I had to turn away when Saranya gasped, and Basanti giggled.

We laughed together until we heard a crash and a baby cry. I was at the door as two more terrified and upset children joined in. I was in the courtyard, dagger in my hand to fight off an enemy, when I saw what was going on. I took in the scene in seconds, trying to identify friend and foe so I could attack.

What I found in the courtyard told an uncomfortable and potentially dangerous story. The only thing I could be grateful for was the fact there were no intruders. This was purely naga chaos.

Aamir had a sword pointed at my mate, the tip directly over Raphael's heart. Nakul was trying to put himself in Aamir's way, but there was nothing to do about the sword without potentially hurting my mate. Dalar was holding both of his children, one under each arm, but I didn't know if he was staring at Aamir or my mate with wide eyes or was just in shock. Each of his children were screaming, faces red. Pavan was holding Roshni close to his chest, glaring in Raphael's direction. Only a second after I arrived, Adhar came from a different direction.

I made eye contact with Raphael. He knew I was there, and he was still in human form, calm in the storm that had erupted all because he was holding their children, letting the babies take a nap next to his warmth. He didn't even try to move from the sword at his chest. It wouldn't be able to kill him, and he trusted me to stop this before it escalated further and made him look like the villain Aamir already wanted to believe he was.

I'm so sorry for this, love. I'll handle it.

"What were you doing with my daughter—"

I moved fast, grabbing Aamir from behind and twisting until I was between him and Raphael, my dagger on the other naga's neck. I held him from behind, ready to kill him if I had to. Adhar rushed in, and everyone was looking at me now. Adhar's expression was one of pleading, his hands up as if he was about to reason with me.

"Kaliya—"

"Threaten my mate again, and I'll end you," I hissed in Aamir's ear. I removed the dagger and shoved him away, letting him stumble. He turned as he came to a stop. I flipped the dagger then threw it, letting it slam into the wall just beyond him, barely missing his head. "I have a lot of patience, Aamir, but I am only willing to tolerate so much. This is the line. Don't cross it again."

"He had my—"

"He had them because *he* was able to get them to take a nap and to give Saranya and Basanti a *break*," I snapped. "Your complaint holds the implication my mate would endanger a *child*!" I was at a roar by the end. I shoved a finger at Aamir as the screams of babies echoed around us. "Have a fucking shred of decency and common fucking sense for a moment, you piece of shit! Those babies were fucking happy, and now they're screaming because you couldn't fucking get your head out of your ass!"

Saranya finally came forward as I screamed. She didn't go to her mate. She went to Pavan and ripped her daughter from his arms, then went to Adhar, trying to bounce her yelling toddler. I saw the stress and the sleepless nights in the bags under her eyes and dropped my hand. The peaceful moment she had was shattered. I looked at Dalar, where Basanti was trying to bounce one of the twins and trying to rock the other. Dalar threw a glance at me, then went back to trying to help his son calm down.

"Damn you," I hissed at Saranya's mate. I rotated enough for Raphael and Aamir to see each other again. "Look at him," I said to my fellow naga in full rant now. "He hasn't shifted. He's not willing to fight you over this because he knows he did nothing fucking wrong. If he wanted, you would be dead right now. If he wanted to kill everyone in this goddamn place, he is powerful enough. All he was doing was letting the babies sleep on him like a goddamn rock, and he was doing a pretty good impression. Saranya knew. Basanti knew. Eshika knew. *Adhar* and I saw it, smiled for a minute, then *moved on*. He's *warm*. You can fucking *see* that, you stupid fucking..." I hissed. Aamir only glared at me. "Damn you. Look at your mate. Look at Dalar and Basanti. Look at how *exhausted* they are. He was *helping*. He's my mate, the mate of a ruler. He rules others. He knew what he was doing, and he..." I shook my head when Aamir's expression remained unchanged.

"You just need someone to hate," I said, sighing. "It doesn't matter what I do, does it? I could bring you the head of our greatest enemy, and you would find some way to cast it aside and lay some sort of blame at my feet. What's funny is I told my mate the only reason he would have a problem here...was me. He's powerful, he's respectful, and he's willing to fight for us, and you'll hate him because he's *mine*. Predictably, here we stand."

I passed Aamir to yank my dagger from the wall. When I headed back to my mate, I reached out too fast for anyone to see and twisted Aamir's wrist, forcing him to drop the damn sword. I didn't miss a step, leaving Aamir hissing as he rubbed his wrist. I stopped by my mate again, letting Raphael stand next to me.

"What's crazy is I've never really understood why you hate me. I wasn't a potential mate for you. You already had Saranya. You just decided I wasn't a good child, I guess, and that's festered all these years. I wasn't a good child, so I could never be a good or productive member of our culture. Even after the meeting we just had." I threw a hand toward the back door, which led to the path we had used. "What is wrong with you?"

"You're poisonous—"

"No," I hissed. "I'm venomous, and I hope you don't make me prove that." I turned to Adhar. "Deal with him, or I will."

I walked out of the room, head high with my mate beside me. The babies were still crying. Raphael and I went into our suite, but the walls weren't thick enough to block the sound of the scared babies. I closed my eyes and put my hands over my face, desperately wishing this wasn't the world I had been born into.

Raphael wrapped his arms around me.

"Dalar thought I was fine," he whispered, his fingers caressing one of my arms. "He grabbed his children after Aamir got the sword out because I asked him to get the little ones out of the way. The poor man was scared and shocked his friend would jump to violence like that. Pavan had already taken Roshni from me on Aamir's orders. They didn't get the jump on me, though. I let it play out. For a second, I thought they would see there was nothing wrong, but Aamir's disgust with me holding his daughter was clear the moment I saw his face."

Behind his whispered explanation of how it happened, the cries of the babies were fading, but not because the children were calm. They were taken to their rooms, so they had some privacy to resolve this.

"I knew better than to fight."

"I know," I whispered. In the place of the babies, I heard arguing. Adhar and Aamir were two I knew for certain, but the others were lost in the mess. "Thank you for waiting for me."

"I kicked over the ottoman out of fake surprise," he continued. "So, you would hear what was happening faster."

"I should have known they would throw a fit," I replied, feeling the guilt of leaving my mate there.

"Adhar didn't even think about it," he pointed out gently, taking that blame off my shoulders. "The babies were sleeping. What sort of father wants to disrupt that? There was nowhere I could go and nothing I could do. I'm still wearing the sling his *mate* put on me. If he couldn't recognize that as a sign, nothing would have stopped him from doing what he just did."

Moving out of his hold, I looked at him and sighed, running my fingers over the swaddle. I helped him out of it, not that it was necessary, and put it on our dresser. I would return it later. Now wasn't the time to see Saranya and Aamir.

"I'm going to read," I declared, looking for one of

Raphael's books. I didn't care which, I just wanted to lose myself in something. Raphael showed me where he stashed them, taking one as well, and we laid together on the bed. I enjoyed the warmth that poured off him as I lost myself in a dry read about demons from around the world.

Time ticked by, and I could see the sun slowly descending, the day continuing as the little world outside our door remained silent.

23

CHAPTER TWENTY-THREE

Raphael and I didn't leave our room until late. We ate quickly from what we found in the kitchen, then went back to our suite, then read until we both passed out. The only reason either of us tried to stay up was to make sure we weren't needed.

The next morning, I had to fulfill a promise I had made only the day before. I had to head alone to the bathhouse and hope any of them showed up. It felt like a walk of shame. An eagle beginning its hunt flew overhead and cried out, giving me that weird instinct to find a place to hide under a rock. It only distracted me for a moment from the impending lonely morning I was about to face.

After yesterday...

Dragging my feet, I walked in and tried not to collapse in shock, but damn near went down and had to lean on the door frame.

They're here. They're all here.

"And I was telling her, you know, she didn't have to do

the dishes," Saranya said to Eshika. Basanti laughed lightly. Eleanor was smiling, away from the group, getting ready just like the others. She was the one who saw me first.

"Good morning," she said, giving me a cautious smile, one that told me she was game for this but was a little uncomfortable.

"Good morning," I greeted, blinking as I watched them undress for a moment longer, then quickly closed the door. My eyes were a little watery as I went to a trunk, pulling off my quickly thrown on tank top and sweatpants. I didn't want them to see me about to damn near cry.

They're here. What...

I was the last to make my way out of the dressing room. The bathhouse was well done. Adhar had tiled the entire room, creating what was essentially a shallow indoor pool with steps and places for people to sit if they wanted. There were shelves with soaps and shampoos, some I realized had always been there, provided for anyone who needed them. The water was room temperature, but that didn't bother me. It was better than the pond, stream, or the tubs we had to fill with buckets of water.

"Thank you for coming to hang out with me," I said a bit lamely as I found a place to sink into the water. Their nudity didn't bother me. We were in the bath, and it seemed like everyone was trying to get comfortable in the water, not rushing to get clean. A quick glance told me everyone was comfortable except Eleanor, who was clearly out of her element. Everyone was silent, looking at me and each other as though we were waiting for something to happen.

"I was afraid...after what ended our day yesterday, none of you would...come here this morning," I admitted. "Um..."

"My mate doesn't get to decide who I spend my time with," Saranya said, her words full of fire I had *not* expected from her. Then I remembered how she took her daughter from Pavan and went to Adhar. "His display yesterday was disgraceful, something Adhar, Mahavir, Dalar, and Nakul all made clear before he came to help me with Roshni. Then *I* made it clear to him. I am so sorry about how he disrespected your mate, Raphael. I hope his shame doesn't tarnish the relationship I believed you and I were building."

"No," I whispered, her words meaning more to me than I could have ever thought they would. It didn't take me long to realize why they were so meaningful. These women, human mates of nagas, were as much my people as the men in the house. I had always known on an intellectual level but had never interacted with the humans among our kind before this trip. "Aamir's decisions are his own, and he has to live with the consequences. You don't have to carry the burden of his dishonor or shame." I cleared my throat. "I'm sorry for threatening him."

"Threaten him all you like," she said, her face going the sort of blank that scared me when other supernaturals did it, especially when it was a woman. A little voice in the back of my often paranoid brain whispered it was something important to remember.

Naga mating doesn't require love.

"He was a fool," Eshika declared. "Maybe fear will teach him to do better."

"Dalar said we're going to let Raphael take the twins whenever he's willing," Basanti added. "It was blissful, and he was so upset our children had to suffer yesterday. They looked so happy with your mate, and we don't get quiet moments nearly often enough."

"Could you have killed him?" Eleanor dared to ask, meeting my eyes with an even stare. The other women looked at her, no judgment on their faces, but maybe a little shock because Eleanor was among them and actually speaking.

"In a heartbeat," I answered in cool confidence. "But only as a last resort."

"What's the story there? Vikrant says it's best to ask you, and clearly, I'm not going to ask Aamir."

I licked my lips, accepting Vikrant's logic to send her to me for that information. If he had tried to answer, he could very well have gotten it wrong or misinterpreted what had happened.

"He and I didn't like each other when I was a child. I broke Adhar's rules a lot, and Adhar tried to be strict with me, but Aamir...He didn't hurt me, none of them did, but there's a cold feeling one can get when they find themselves alone among their own people. He was respected by everyone, and if he didn't like me, obviously he was right, so no one gave me any sort of comfort or love.

"Aamir helped Adhar find me after my parents died, then I was a troublesome, damaged child who was angry at the world, unwilling to bend when they wanted me to. When I didn't end up as a mate for another naga..." I looked uneasily at the women around me. Three of them were mates to men who had been single back then. Fucking uncomfortable. "Well, I was pretty much worthless." I shrugged. "Which was fine because I didn't want to mate with anyone. I wanted someone to find who killed my family, and if they didn't want to do that, I would do it without them. Eventually, I ran. A hundred years later, here we are."

"You made something of yourself!" Eshika snapped. "Don't sell yourself short. Nakul talks all the time about what a warrior you are, how you maintained your honor as well as anyone could while living in the outside world." She stopped and sighed. "You did better than he could, and he plans on making sure no one forgets that."

"I heard about that," Eleanor said. "He—"

"Let's not talk about it right now, please," I pleaded, feeling like my heart was bruised. "Unless someone here doesn't know..." I wished I hadn't promised to do this. Not the bathhouse, but the retelling of that painful portion of my life.

"Adhar had to tell me," Saranya said softly.

"Dalar told me," Basanti said, nodding. "It's a little...uncomfortable."

"Yup." There was no way to avoid that. "Moving on."

"Of course," Eshika agreed. "Was there a reason you wanted to spend time with us this morning?"

"Not really." I hadn't really expected any of them to show up, even before Aamir threatened to kill Raphael and scared the babies. "Um..." I took a deep breath.

There were things I had always wanted to ask, to know about these hidden women. That was a good place to start. "I guess...I wanted to talk about your lives. I want to know more about the day-to-day happenings. I want to know if you're...happy. I want to know who you are, what you want, and if you're satisfied." I had never been so nervous or so unsure. "Maybe...maybe there's something I can do for you, or you might need something I can get for you."

"I'm happy," Basanti declared. "Tired but happy. Dalar and I work together with the twins. We don't have any other option, and his help is...a blessing. I wish we had a third pair of hands...like your mate...." She smiled. "But we'll be fine. Once they learn to sleep a bit more regularly. They just refuse to stay on a schedule."

"Yeah, but that's just your life with the babies," I pointed out.

"I want more books," she admitted softly. "I liked to read before we mated, and getting books is hard."

"I can do that," I said, nodding. "Later, give me a list of what you used to love to read, and I'll try to find books you might like."

"Thank you." Basanti's smile widened and threatened to glow brighter than the sun.

I looked at the other women, wondering who would say something next.

"I want to stop moving so much," Eshika said.

"I can't help with that. In fact, I'm the reason you've moved so much in the last few years," I answered sheepishly. "Sorry."

"Oh, you explain like I didn't already know," she said

with a sharp smile, then burst into laughter. "I'm fine, really, but you mentioned to Mahavir about taking some of my recipes to the cambions and sending back notes. Please do. I'll get several to you, and I expect those reviews in a prompt fashion."

"Done," I promised.

Down to Eleanor and Saranya.

"Vikrant takes care of everything I need," Eleanor said, shrugging. "He's even got a vacuum for me when I had learned what those were. He knows I hate cleaning, so he wanted to make it faster and easier for both of us."

"Oh, one of those would be wonderful," Basanti said, cutting in. "How is it?"

"Oh, it's amazing," Eleanor said, a hopeful smile forming. "He also...um, don't tell Adhar, but he also got an electric mop thing for us. You hit a button, and it squirts out cleaner."

I snorted, covering my face as they all looked at me.

"I'm sorry. I didn't remember that most of you..." I tried so hard not to laugh. "I'll get you all modern cleaning and cooking things. Just make a list of the hardest chores, and I'll get you all upgrades."

"Do I need to replace my vacuum? It's only thirty-something years old. Have they gotten better?"

"Definitely!" Eshika said, laughing. "I'm still using mine from before I mated with Mahavir."

"Much better," I guaranteed, resisting the urge to lose my mind at how ridiculous this moment was. "I'll handle it."

I'm going to need to teach some of them how to use these things.

Part of me was excited about that.

"I feel like we should move off...household items," Saranya said, giving me a sympathetic look. "I like to paint and would love new brushes, canvas, sketchbooks. Get me like a...ten-year supply. I go long periods of time without being able to get more."

I laughed, bowing my head to her. "I can do that," I promised. "Though, it might take me ten years to get you a ten-year supply. Maybe we can set up a steady feed of supplies for you."

"I would also like if you came to visit us more often," she continued, like she was in a conference room, laying out demands to put in a contract.

"I..." I hadn't even considered doing that.

"My daughter will need a feminine influence among the nagas. Aamir and Adhar often forget I have experience with female nagas," she said, giving me a small smile. "I met your mother a handful of times and Vikrant's sister twice. I know there are some things I can't teach my daughter that I would like you to teach her, not her father. Plus, she reaches for you."

"You seemed so demure when you arrived," I said, just an observation I felt the need to point out. "Actually, you're really..." I didn't have the right word.

"He never wanted you near our daughter. Why do you think I brought her to you?" Saranya questioned, tilting her head to the side as she studied me. "Did you think I was the quiet, soft wife who has children and takes care of the house? Aamir would have loved that, and in a compromise, I try to not step on his toes with the nagas... play nice, you can say. He gets a piece of his fantasy.

Eshika and Basanti have seen me do it for years. I'm very good at the act when I need to be. I do a lot of the housework, the cooking and the cleaning, but he's had to make compromises as well, much of it about Roshni. I've called in all the little favors and compromises he owes me." She stretched out her legs, massaging her thighs. "I've been part of this world for too long to believe Aamir's way is always the right one. I play nice, I compromise, I act the way he thinks I should in front of the other nagas."

"Then she strikes," Basanti said with a smile. "When no one is watching, but you can always tell Aamir was outplayed by his mate."

"This is..." I chuckled. "Absolutely fascinating. I had no idea I was getting played."

"Why would you? You probably heard what the men think and figured we were the wives they believed wives should be," Saranya pointed out. "Your mother was a naga and the ruler before you. She didn't need to play the game."

"No, she didn't, did she?" I said, taken with these women.

"Will you teach my daughter?" the mother asked.

"Yeah," I agreed, nodding. "I would like that."

"I want her to be strong," Saranya said, sighing. "No games. Just the ability to choose her own life. Maybe not as extreme as you, but she'll have more space than we do. I have always understood why our lives are the way they are. Seeing the death and pain...I don't disagree with much of it, but she'll have a wider space to roam if I have anything to say about it. She'll be a warrior like the nagini before." Something shone in Saranya's eyes.

"You named her," I whispered, realizing the truth. "I didn't think Aamir would break tradition, even a small one."

"It was the first compromise I forced him to make. Ulupi, nagini warrior princess," Saranya said with a tearful smile. "I hope you don't mind. It has royalty—"

"It's beautiful," Eleanor said suddenly, then flushed. Saranya reached out and touched her knee, pure joy in her eyes.

Yeah, Eleanor would figure out her place with the others.

I pointed at Eleanor.

"She's right, it is. I'm the *last* person you can offend with a naga or nagini name."

"Oh, thank you both," she said. "Do you think she'll be a...warrior?"

"If I have my way, you all will be," I said, crossing my arms. "Did your mates tell you about that?" Based on the four confused looks, that was a resounding no. "I know you're human, and yes, you are physically slower and weaker. You don't have the same arsenal we do, and we protected you because of that for centuries, but there's new information for all the nagas to reckon with. I've finally put my foot down because your safety is too important. You're all going to learn to use a weapon for self-defense. There's just no excuse why the nagas are holding onto the idea you shouldn't, no matter what happens. It's a remnant from ancient times that needs to die. We need to evolve. You deserve the chance to fight for your life instead of being cut down."

"Mahavir has been teaching me since we met," she said softly. "But we've done it in secret, so some wouldn't...condemn us. Nakul likes it."

"Vikrant lets me keep a gun for protection when I stay at home, but other...official training would be nice. We did a little hand to hand training once, but I've never really thought about asking him for more. He's given up a lot for me, and I didn't want to ask too much from him."

"You two get training?" Basanti looked between them. "Really?"

Saranya was silent, but she stared at me.

"Thank you," she mouthed silently, and I could see she had probably asked for it. Maybe more than asked.

We chatted for a little while longer, but it slowly died off.

"I think it's time to get clean," Eshika said, standing.

"Yeah, that's a good idea." I got up and turned away from them.

We washed, respecting each other's privacy, dried off, then got dressed. As we walked out of the bathhouse, it was a different sort of validation I hadn't realized I needed. In this tiny world of women, I saw Eleanor laugh at a tease from Eshika.

However, I saw Adhar standing at the back door, and he wasn't smiling.

"What is it?" I asked him, the ladies moving so I could get to him first.

"I just got word, but two days ago, the rakshasas announced they knew you were in the country and wanted you to face them for the crimes of killing their king, his mate, and his heirs. They've given a location where they wish for you to be handed over. This new king is actually Mehar's cousin, Mahatma. I hadn't received that piece of intel yet. You're still dealing with the same family. Bad blood with that family might make this more…fraught than we might have considered. I thought the new king was someone unrelated to the previous."

"It's fine," I said, patting his shoulder. "I can do this."

"Wait! We're not going to give her to them, are we? Right?" Eshika snapped, coming to my side and glaring at Adhar as if he was going to cut my head off himself.

"I killed their previous king," I explained to her, unsure what she had been told about the situation before looking back at Adhar. "Well, we knew it would happen quickly. It was one of the topics of yesterday's meeting. At least we had time to speak yesterday," I said, reaching out to keep Eshika from getting in Adhar's face. She was a picture of fury.

"I'm not being *given* to them. I'm going to face them, and I'm going to win. That's what I do. I might get the shit kicked out of me, but I'm pretty good at staying alive, which is all that matters at the end of a fight. Do you hear me? That's *all* that matters—I live, and they don't. I've been doing it for over a hundred years. I can do it now."

"Yes, it is," Saranya said, nodding as she moved to pass Adhar, not nearly as distraught as Eshika. She stopped in the doorway to look back at me one last time. "Kaliya…"

"Yes?"

"Please come back. Don't die and leave the burden you carry on my baby's shoulders. *Please*," she whispered, tears filling her eyes before she went inside. The stakes felt much higher than they had been just moments before, the weight on my shoulders heavier. Her face would be burned in my memory, desperate and pleading as she reminded me of the consequences of failure.

My death would be easy on me. I wouldn't be here to deal with it. The people who rely on me are the ones who will suffer.

As that fact settled in and weighed on me, my spine felt stronger. I would not fail these women. I *couldn't* fail these strong, sacrificing women.

I had so many problems with the nagas, even those I liked, but these women were proving to be worth every minute.

24

CHAPTER TWENTY-FOUR

Everything happened quickly. Adhar and I spoke for a moment longer in private, then jumped into planning how it would happen. Three days was fast when so many security precautions had to be followed. Nakul flew us as close as he could safely, and we used bribery to keep our landing from being officially recorded. We traveled by cab with cash if it was necessary, then hitch-hiked and hiked for part of it. Raphael couldn't speak at all for the entire trip because there was no way he could blend in if he did. I didn't speak in English unless I was certain we were alone. We had a duffle bag carrying snacks and weapons I couldn't wear for most of the trip.

It was boring, but we kept moving at a good pace. I was most grateful it was a long trip, but not the longest it could have been. As it was, if Raphael and I had driven by ourselves, it would have been at least a 45-hour trip, and our trail would have been easier to follow home.

Even better, the rakshasas either guessed or learned I had landed in New Delhi when I arrived and picked a village only about fifteen hours from there. They had decided on a place where they could gather without too many humans turning their attention to the activities of those who were not. It was a small village tucked away in the Himalayas, close to where India, Nepal, and Tibet met, where it would be easy to wander off into the vast wilderness and find oneself the hunted instead of the hunter.

Talking to the other nagas before leaving, I discovered the rakshasas had become more nomadic than I had believed. Rakshasas were commonly associated with Sri Lanka, which I should have thought about when I found myself there, chasing after Devika. Time changed people, not just on a micro-scale but a macro one, and culture evolved from the written information we had. The only reason our people knew was from listening to rumors and Adhar's careful spying through the centuries. The nagas had gone through their own changes over the years. At the same time we were changing in India and the surrounding areas, other places in the world had the rise of vampires, werewolves, and more. Even the fae had changed their structure through the years.

I stood inside a small home where we had asked to spend the night, seeing the beautiful world around us here on the edge of the Himalayas, my thoughts spinning back to the same train of thought.

Time changes everyone and everything. Old legends still walk the earth, yet in a new way. Whether it's generational change or change dictated by the rise of humans or a million other possibilities, time brings with it forces that demand those who wish to survive to change. Not even the mightiest of mountains can survive time if it makes no effort.

As I've told so many people time and time again.

"Today's the day, yeah?" Raphael was getting dressed behind me. When I didn't reply, he put his hand on my lower back. "Kaliya?"

"You know...I've been approaching this from the angle that I will probably have to kill some of them." I kept staring out the window, my thoughts changing gear to something I had thought about during the journey. "What if I don't have to?"

Raphael's hand slid up my back, his arm coming over my shoulders as he stepped to my side.

"I think that would be for the best. You're better at politics than me and know more about the people around us, here in India and back home in Arizona. As someone constantly worried about the future of my own, I would think a peaceful solution is the best one. You don't have to be allied with the rakshasas, but neither do you have to be enemies. That's how I treat the vampires in Phoenix. I can't get too close to them, it's too dangerous for both my cambions and the vampires, but I can be honest and polite when I have to be while also keeping my distance. She dislikes you, but Imani and I are polite. If you could get into that position with the rakshasa today or something close to it, you bring more stability to the nagas."

"That's what I was hoping you would say." I smiled as I turned away from the window, letting his arm fall. "You say I'm better at politics, but you're learning. You're getting good at it."

"The thought has crossed my mind that the rakshasas didn't know what Mehar was doing. You can easily angle this to say if their king doesn't answer for his cousin's crimes, there could be war." Raphael smiled, his eyes turning black and red as veins spread. "You can remind them that killing you or me will start a war with not just one but two species. Or you can tell them the truth."

"And what's that?"

"That both species have been manipulated into a situation that pits you against each other." Raphael leaned on the wall, crossing his arms as he watched me arm myself. "Ask them for the truth. Did Mehar work on his own? Did his mate or sons know what he was doing, or did they just think they had to avenge their king and family? Did the rakshasas want war with the nagas all this time and were just too cowardly to declare?"

"Maybe I shouldn't ask them the last one," I said, grinning as I tucked daggers everywhere. "But you're right. There are a lot of ways I can come at this. I thought violence was the answer, and I have to be prepared if it is, but I shouldn't have let that cloud my mind. Playing politics might be safer and more fruitful for me *and* their new king, but I have to give him something since his cousin and predecessor is dead while I'm alive."

"Mehar was directly involved in the murder of your family," Raphael pointed out, moving to help me straighten a belt. Then he threw on a holster and slid his sidearm into it. That was all he wanted to carry, making sure I knew before we left the nagas. "After all the nagas Mehar probably had a hand in killing, do you really think this new king is justified to ask you for anything except his *life*? And that's before we get into the fact his kind assaulted me, the ruler of the cambions. You'll notice I killed one of Mehar's heirs, yet they aren't looking for me. Why do you think that is?"

From peaceful to bloodthirsty and dangerous—Raphael could flip that switch so easily now. He was thinking of things I really should have. I had been so focused on what I had to do for the other nagas, I hadn't considered the implication of the rakshasa only wanting *me*. It was the same reason it took me this long to consider how to talk through this instead of fighting. I had been focused on the worst possible outcomes and hadn't taken the time to really think anything else was a possibility.

This is what I get for trying to solve ten problems at once during the most important trip of my life. The trip, the nagas, their mates, my mating, the cambions, who Mehar and Devika worked for, the new rakshasa, the Tribunal.

I need a real vacation.

"They know I'm your mate," Raphael continued. "If they were connected enough to hear you've arrived in India, they know I was also a target in the events last October, targeted by both Mehar and his family."

"We'll have to see how this plays out," I wanted to talk my way out of this, which would be better in the long run. Raphael's points were valid. "Are you ready? Once we enter the village, one of them, possibly more, will see us."

"I'm ready."

I left first, leaving money for the owner of the home, who had been kind enough to let us stay. The walk into the village wasn't a terribly long one, but it wasn't a simple stroll. Morning had shifted into afternoon when we finally reached the outskirts. We walked side by side until we reached the center of the village. Humans saw us and kept a wide berth. Trading and conversations quieted for a minute, then picked back up. People bartered, trading goods and talking about their days. The longer I stood there with my mate, the more they ignored us, and we didn't feel so out of place.

Catching the rakshasa's scent before I saw him, I turned at a speed that made the rakshasa stop his approach as we stared at each other. He only started walking away after a quiet, drawn-out moment of eye contact, a challenge to the other to try something underhanded. He stopped out of range, motioned for me to follow him, then turned away, walking in the direction he had come from.

We walked out of the village, heading to a farmhouse in the distance, the only structure I could see. Other rakshasas showed themselves, dropping whatever illusions that kept them visually hidden, surrounding us, and closing in. I put my hand on the hilt of my katana, and Raphael's scent changed, causing the rakshasa to look back at us.

He opened the door and gestured for me to enter but put his hand up when Raphael stepped forward to enter before me. That had been his condition, and I had agreed to it after an hour of arguing when we were alone on the trail the day before.

"You aren't welcome," he said in Hindi, thinking my

mate understood him. "We only want the naga called Kaliya Sahni."

"I don't care if he's welcome or not," I snapped in English, so my mate knew what was happening and why. "He's my mate, and his presence is necessary if we're going to talk about the incident that brought us here. If you're not willing to allow him in the proceedings, we'll go home, and you'll never see me again."

The rakshasa growled at me, and Raphael snarled louder, growing taller. In his cambion form, he towered over the rakshasa, as he had Aamir.

"You accuse my mate of murdering your previous king when he maliciously attacked two rulers of other supernatural species. I was the other ruler, and I *will* have the new king answer for the crimes of the previous." Raphael leaned down, getting into the rakshasa's face. I checked behind us, seeing the others still closing in, getting much too close for my comfort. There were six of them around us now, and I had no idea how many were inside. "There doesn't need to be bloodshed, not now, not later, but there can be. The choice is yours. We both go in, we both leave, or you try to kill us right now."

I smiled, fully confident in my mate's intimidation factor. He was just so damn good at scaring everyone.

"Let them in," a rakshasi said from inside. She showed up at the door, looking at both of us with a curl of her lip. "I warned him this could happen." She turned around and walked away. Raphael went inside, and I quickly followed, not liking how we were being closed in and blocked from running back to the village.

At least we're not fighting yet.

The inside of this farmhouse wasn't like the one I had stayed in, thanks to the kindness of a local. They had gutted it, knocking out walls and leaving only support pillars. They hadn't repainted any of the walls, stained the wood, or anything similar. It was still a farmhouse, a temporary situation for the rakshasas. Mahatma, the king of the rakshasas, stood at the far end, the woman who had let us in going to his side.

Raphael slowed just enough for me to take a step that put me next to him, neither of us missing a step, a completely seamless move. We walked into the center of the room and stopped. I kept my hand on the hilt of my katana, staring at the new king of the rakshasas.

"You should bow when you meet a king," someone growled, but it wasn't the king who waited like a statue.

"Really?" I laughed at whoever was speaking but kept my eyes on the king. "Why would I do that? He's not *my* king. He's not the king of anything except his own kind. It's not like he rules India, Sri Lanka, or Nepal." I elbowed my mate. "Do you want to bow, Raphael?"

"Not particularly," Raphael answered, his back straight and shoulders squared. He kept his feet like mine, shoulder-width apart, ready to move at a moment's notice. We probably made a hell of a sight in the middle of the room. "I don't see a reason to bow to a king who wishes to hold everyone but himself accountable for their actions. Doesn't seem like a king I would respect or follow."

That brought the king to life, a snarl filling the room.

"What actions should I be accountable for?" he

demanded. The female reached out and grabbed him, keeping him from charging us.

"As I just told your subject, you're here to hold my mate accountable for killing your predecessor, but you have made no attempt to reach out to my people for your predecessor's attack on me, their ruler," Raphael reminded him. "It just seems...dishonorable."

Letting Raphael throw the rakshasa off balance was a great ice breaker. He'd come prepared for this in ways I hadn't.

"The nagas and the cambions are a packaged deal, King Mahatma. We're willing to come to a peaceful resolution, but if you feel the need to kill me once you hear your brother's crimes, you are not starting a war with the hidden nagas. You are starting a war with two races and potentially upsetting the Tribunal, who guarantees the safety of all those who follow its rule." I smiled. "Are you willing to listen, or are you going to choose the path of glory, which will lead to your death and the deaths of your people if they try to fight with you?"

"You think you can speak to me like that?" He was furious, his face morphing into the rakshasa monster I knew. Fangs grew down, large canines that were probably a solid inch, and his face took on a bestial look.

I wasn't impressed.

"Your predecessor and cousin left a much more lasting impression," I taunted. "Mehar knew how to incite fear. He knew how to *hunt*. You think you set up a trap I can't walk away from without thinking it through."

"We can make you lost in illusions you can never

escape from," he snarled. "You will die living your worst nightmares."

"And you'll pay for it. If not today, then down the road. One day, someone will take up Bhima and come for the rakshasas once again." I folded my arms behind my back, letting the rakshasas consider what I was saying. There was no way they didn't know who Bhima was. He was one of the Pandava brothers, a hero who was well known for many things, including the impressive number of rakshasas he defeated. Funnily enough, he'd also married a rakshasi, who helped him kill her brother and even had a little rakshasa child with her. That child would go on to be one of the few rakshasa heroes in all of our long history.

He was also the only one of their kind to mate a naga. Damn, I actually forgot about that. No one ever really wanted to talk about them when I was being educated.

"Or we can strike a bargain now. You know I could have declared war on your people months ago. I could have sent word to the Tribunal that I had evidence that the rakshasas were enemies of the nagas and called in protections that could see your kind chained and locked away for eternity. I could have done that," I hissed softly, glaring at him. Those threats were possible but highly unlikely. The Tribunal offered nagas ways to skirt the law to protect themselves but would never commit other supernaturals to war for a dying people. The rakshasas, however, weren't a Tribunal species, and I believed their knowledge of those nuances in the Law would be slim. "But I came here, King Mahatma, to speak to you about the crimes of your cousin, so we might have a better understanding for the future."

"Listen to her," the rakshasi snapped from behind the king. "Mahatma, we're not in a place to ignore her."

"Fine. Let's hear it," the king growled.

Well, that gets me out of trial by combat...for now.

25

CHAPTER TWENTY-FIVE

"Mehar attacked my mate and me, intending to kill us. Now, I could put those crimes at your feet, King Mahatma, but I won't do that." I could see that surprised the king, glad to keep him off balance. "I haven't declared war between us *yet* because Mehar wasn't acting with other rakshasas. He wasn't acting alone, mind you. He had several other supernaturals assisting him in his hunt for me and mine." I sighed, thinking about the fates of the other rakshasas. Those had been needless, but they hadn't been all my fault either.

"The deaths of his mate and his heirs were a later incident, as the witch, Devika, involved them to ambush me in revenge for killing Mehar instead of dying to him. She did so for her own reasons, betraying a long friendship I had with her. You know Devika. She often served the rakshasas as well." Mahatma nodded. I lifted my hands in question, ready to continue my point.

"Tell me, King Mahatma, if you were ambushed by predators, would you not fight to defend yourself? Wouldn't anyone? The only reason I'm standing here and you are on the throne is because I fought off unwarranted attacks on me and defeated the enemies before me. If Mehar hadn't attacked me, he could possibly be alive today."

"Possibly?" Mahatma caught that, and I was a little impressed.

"Oh, yes. I said we were going to talk about Mehar's *crimes*. I was looking for Mehar when he attacked me because I discovered he was one of the monsters that murdered my mother, my father, and my brothers." I rested one of my hands on the hilt of my katana. Mahatma couldn't hide his expressions nearly well enough yet to deal with me. It was too early in his rule to learn how to mask. Fury and confusion warred on his face. "He taunted me about it when he came for me. If you didn't know, my mother was the female ruler of the nagas before me. She was one of two, as the Tribunal dictates. She was a leader in our culture. He essentially killed our queen." I tilted my head to the side and hissed, "Then he tried to do it *again* when he came for me."

"Yet you haven't declared war," the rakshasi said, standing slightly behind her king, her fangs now clear.

"I haven't. I also haven't gotten your name yet."

"Maurvi," she said softly, staring me down as her name rang so many bells in my head, there was no avoiding asking some very necessary questions.

"Are you a descendant of Ahilawati and Ghatotkacha? Ahilawati was also known as Maurvi." I was honestly surprised she would have a secondary name for the nagini who mated a rakshasa. I knew her name and the other names given to her through the years from my education growing up, but I had no memories from my previous life I could quickly recall about the couple. There was a chance he had heard rumors, but most nagas like to pretend it didn't happen.

"I am," she confirmed. "And I know."

"I was actually just thinking about those two. Your ancestor was a hero," I reminded her. "Not a villain like so many others, but one of the great warriors who fought as recorded in *Mahabharata*. He mated a nagini, daughter of a king, and had three sons with her. Their sons, for whatever reason, were neither naga or rakshasa. One even became a deity."

"My branch of the bloodline entered the rakshasas again later on," she explained, then lifted her chin, giving me a mean look. Based on that look, I had reason to worry she would attack me if I said the wrong thing. "You don't need to tell me who my ancestors were."

"I mean, Ahilawati was a nagini, so not just *your* ancestor," I pointed out, and it softened her expression just enough not to worry about being attacked. "This has been interesting and brings me to the topic at hand. We're all descended from the legends of those who came before us. Neither of our people are wholly good or wholly evil. You, Maurvi, are descended from a great hero of the rakshasas. I am named for a warrior who Krishna had to kill for his transgressions, one of the few nagas who, in the end, was not the hero of his story.

"Why would I declare war on a group who is just

trying to survive as I am? Especially one who possibly had no indication they knew what was happening. Mehar was the only rakshasa I saw acting against our people." I shrugged. "*Did* you know Mehar was killing my people? Or are we being played by a more cunning force?"

"We did not," Mahatma growled, but his expression was a little more thoughtful, a touch more apprehensive. I had gotten him to think for a minute. "Mehar was always obsessed with the next great hunt. He stopped practicing his magic unless it suited him on this endeavor. I could see him relish hunting down nagas, once some of the most notable and powerful souls of our homeland." He studied me. "You seem certain of all this."

"I am," I said. *Maybe I'll get to walk out of this, and violence won't be necessary. That would be nice.*

"He would often disappear and leave his mate and sons with us," Maurvi said, reminding her husband of history I had no knowledge of. I didn't know much about the rakshasas of the current times. "We would lose track of the time he was gone, and since you were his heir until his sons were men, we had to stay close. We practically raised his sons, helping their mother."

"I remember," Mahatma snapped. "Why do you believe there's another power at work here?"

"Simple. Mehar was going to kill my mate but was disappointed he couldn't kill me. He was going to hand me over to someone else. That might sound unbelievable, but similar happened with Devika. She also gave up her chance to kill us, hoping to turn me over to someone else, someone who she believed could give her more power, possibly immortality. They both made the same fatal mistake."

I let that sink in.

Mahatma started pacing like a tiger in a cage.

"And you would declare war over this if we don't take into consideration what you've brought to us about Mehar's activities against the nagas," he asked, not looking at me.

"I would, and you know what happens if you try to kill me. You also know what happens if you, by chance, succeed." I kept my hands behind my back, watching him carefully.

"A war with the nagas could be devastating for both of us," he said softly, his pacing coming to a slow end. "We are remnants of an old world, looking for a place in a new one."

"Yes."

"We do not know how many nagas even live," he said, looking at his mate. "We don't even have an estimate of that number. Maurvi, do any of our people have any idea of the forces the nagas command?"

"No."

"Then there is your mate." Mahatma pointed at Raphael, still massive in his cambion form. I looked up at my mate, his stoic face giving away nothing about how he felt about the king's sudden attention. "His people, new, young, bold, and from the rumors, unkillable."

A confident and powerful smile formed on my mate's lips, but nothing reached his black-and-red eyes.

"It would go poorly for you," he said, fully believing every word he said. This was a man who looked at Hasan, one of the oldest and most powerful supernaturals on the earth, and said, "I could take him." Raphael could stop a room with his confidence, and it seemed, he rendered a king completely silent.

"My king, do you wish to speak privately about what we should do next?"

"No," Mahatma said, finally tearing his eyes away from Raphael. "There's nothing to discuss. I am willing, Kaliya Sahni, nagini, to absolve you of the crimes brought forth against you. In the effort to keep us from falling to mutually assured destruction—"

"There would be nothing mutual about it," Raphael said, not really speaking to the king but looking around the room at the other rakshasas.

"In the effort of keeping us from going to war, you are found justified in killing Mehar, king of the rakshasas."

"I apologize for killing his mate and his heirs," I said, meaning it. "They walked into a battle I had no choice but to take part in. They were manipulated by someone who is also dead now."

"His mate and sons could be blinded by their devotion to him, even as he ignored their existence," Mahatma said, waving a hand dismissively. "In return for absolving you of their deaths, Mehar's and that of his family, I will need you to formally absolve the rakshasas."

"I find the rakshasas free of the crimes of the late king, Mehar, and the crimes of his mate and heirs. I will even release a statement to that effect, as long as you do. That way, our deal is made public, and the world will know the rakshasas and the nagas do not wish to tear about the subcontinent. The other supernaturals who share space with us can trust we won't accidentally do anything to reveal ourselves to the current world of humans. You may choose the date our statements should go public."

Adhar is going to be so fucking proud of me when we get back.

"I will release a proclamation for both my people and the rest of the subcontinent in seven days' time," Mahatma agreed.

"I will do the same," I promised. "I believe our business is concluded."

"Not yet," Mahatma said. "I actually wished to discuss who has been behind our clash."

"I don't know yet. If I did, I would already be hunting my own prey."

"We shall work on our end to discover this villain. If we discover who it might be or find any information you might use, we will get it to you, so long as you agree to do the same."

"I can do that. We obviously have a shared enemy who was willing to see us destroy each other. I'm glad we could talk this out."

"You may go." Mahatma nodded and waved me away.

"I said our business is concluded." I gestured to Raphael. "His might not be. Raphael?"

Mahatma waited stoically, Maurvi stepping closer to him, protective and wary of my mate and what he might ask of her king.

"We're mostly done," he confirmed. "It was nice to get more experience with another supernatural species who people call demons. I'm satisfied with the conclusion that's been reached here. My people need nothing from the rakshasas other than an apology."

Mahatma seemed a little upset with that. It was one thing he hadn't given me, and I hadn't asked for. A king, especially one still establishing his rule, had to be very careful not to appear weak. Mahatma had a temper, but I had successfully walked him to a conclusion that made him seem wise, that he had the best interest for the rakshasa future in mind and not just petty revenge.

Raphael was pushing it, asking for an apology.

"I, cousin of Mehar, will apologize on behalf of our family," the king replied. "And...I offer a boon you may call upon from my family in the future. If you wish to use it now, do so. If not, please leave."

Raphael nodded politely. We turned together and walked out while my hand shifted back to the hilt of my katana. I ignored the rakshasas as we headed back for the village. An eagle cried overhead, and I hissed at the sky.

"Really?" Raphael asked, clearly amused by my hate for the bird.

"I don't like birds," I muttered. He laughed as we passed through the village and started the journey home. "Especially the ones here." I shook my head in disdain. "Do you know how many birds of prey live on the subcontinent? That was one of the eagles. There are a few eagle species around, including the short-toed snake eagle. If the name doesn't make it obvious, they love eating snakes." I was purposefully ridiculous as I explained that to him, but hearing Raphael laugh and seeing him wipe tears from his eyes was worth acting like a child about the birds.

Aside from my annoyance with the native birds of prey, I was immensely proud of myself. I was walking away from a fraught political situation in the land of my birth.

And no one died.

"It's a fucking miracle," I mumbled to myself.

26

CHAPTER TWENTY-SIX

Getting back to Adhar's home was faster than the trip to the rakshasas since we didn't have to spend an entire day planning it. Raphael and I kept an eye on possible tails, but once we were certain nothing was following us once we met Nakul, we got on the plane. It wasn't where he dropped us off, and there was no way anyone could get official records of this landing and takeoff.

Nakul didn't ask for details of the rakshasas.

"So, it took only one day to figure this out, just as we thought it would," he said lightly. That had been our thought, which was how Nakul knew where to be and when. Raphael and I would have been the late ones if anything had gone wrong.

"Yup. Do you want to know everything now or wait until we're back?"

"From the look of you both, I think I can wait," he said. "I'm dying of curiosity, but the first person you should tell is Adhar. You both need a chance to talk about what whatever happened will mean for the nagas before you present it to the rest of us."

"Maybe we can talk about my mate's sudden frustration with every bird she sees," Raphael teased. From the moment we left the village, Raphael had decided he had a new pastime. Every time we saw a bird out hunting, he threw his hands over my head, trying to protect me from them, sometimes even trying to push me into his jacket if he was wearing one.

"It's very common for young nagas to cry and throw fits when they hear some of our natural predators," Nakul said kindly. "We grow out of it as we get old and realize they can't pick us up anymore. In snake form, we grow more confident with our natural senses to make sure we're not scooped up." Nakul kept his eyes on the sky ahead of us. "If we are, we can just shift back. An eagle can't do much with a fully grown adult naga in our human form."

"See, I told you it was natural," I said, staring intently at my mate.

"No, it's not," Nakul cut in. "You're an adult. You shouldn't be so jumpy. Is something wrong?"

I hissed at my mate, who smiled kindly, having gotten what he wanted. I explained all of this to him while we'd traveled to meet Nakul, and he'd said the same thing. Children were jumpy, but that didn't explain why I was.

"I think it's a remnant issue from my previous life," I explained to my uncle, sighing in defeat. "He didn't desensitize himself to the eagles and other birds. He was watchful. I'd go so far as to call him paranoid. Considering his history with Garuda, it makes sense."

"It does," Nakul agreed. "You got to see his bones. How did it feel?"

"I've seen Garuda's bones a few times in my life, and it felt the same way it always did. Good."

"You know, I've been doing a lot of research about nagas and your stories..." Raphael looked nervous, which made me confused. When he had questions, I tried to teach him but never wanted to force my culture and history on him. He looked up things about me and the nagas, and I was totally okay with it. "There was something about there as an actual species of garudas. I mean, I noticed a lot, but that one stuck out. The whole conflict between nagas and Garuda doesn't make sense. The nagas are rarely evil or bad in their stories except in one case, maybe two, and even your past life was really just a series of mistakes for an otherwise respected naga. The only good rakshasa got to mate a nagini, but if all that is the case, why is Garuda the symbol of justice and great power when he was your worst enemy?"

I opened my mouth and closed it again. The mythology was complex. I looked at Nakul, wondering if he would speak up, but he slowly shook his head. Getting into the little nuances of our history wasn't the warrior's favorite thing, it seemed. This was a sticky topic that touched multiple religions. It was also sticky because it boiled down to family drama.

"Hinduism is one of the oldest religions in the world," I started, still chewing on how to lay it for him. "Scholars of religious history will tell you it has roots in Dravidianism. Dravidianism practicing society has been estimated to predate Sumerian, Egyptian, and

Babylonian." Raphael nodded, which made me feel comfortable continuing.

"Now, Garuda in Hinduism is a single being, a divine eagle, and Hinduism is the *human* religion that got the most right about us. That doesn't mean others are always wrong, but in this case, we got a hit with Hinduism. Garuda was *one* guy, and he was our enemy. We have his bones. After the death of Kaliya, other nagas defeated him, long after the legends you read now stopped being written, and we had already stepped away from interacting with humanity. Wars don't stop because humans stop recording them. Our lives didn't just pause because they stopped remembering that we were real." I pushed a hand through my hair or tried to. We were all wearing the massive headsets common in small planes and helicopters.

"In my life, I've heard references to a bird species that devoured snakes. They were also called garudas and are referenced in some epics and other religions, but..." I looked at Nakul. "I mean, some things never actually existed or were exaggerated. Beyond that, like species of animals and entire cultures of humanity, some supernatural species just didn't make it to modern times. The nagas could join a whole laundry list of others who will only be legend."

"No one has seen anything like Garuda since his death, and we could never confirm there were others like him in our area of the world. There could very well be a bird species of supernaturals somewhere in the world that has nothing to do with Garuda or us," he confirmed. "Also, Garuda was a sunbird," Nakul corrected as I ended my speech. “Eagle-like but not an eagle. You got the rest as right as possible.”

“Look, I’m trying to give him something to visualize. Eagle is easy,” I said, huffing at my uncle, who only made a face. “Moving on. Garuda *wasn’t* evil. The nagas aren’t evil, either. So yeah, it would make sense to ask why, and it boils down to the fact our mothers are sisters. You probably read that. Sometimes, two good forces can be pitted against each other because of things that aren’t good or evil; they just are. Kadru and Vinata were in competition, sharing a husband. Kadru had a thousand naga sons for him. She wanted to give him a thousand powerful sons. Vinata gave him only two sons. She wanted them to be equal in strength to all one thousand nagas. One was Garuda. Through the machinations of our mothers, Garuda was our enemy, and he wanted to see us dead. Kadru enslaved his mom at some point, though some sources say his older brother cursed their mom to be Kadru’s slave. At one point, he was a really important naga and was stopped by Indra...don’t get me started on Indra. No one has seen the gods in literally thousands of years.” I lifted my hands in defeat. “Some nagas were gods in mythology, though they were just ungodly powerful. That’s why it’s a big deal that I got some power *back* thanks to our mating. We’ve grown less powerful over the years. There’s not a naga out there who can even come close to achieving what I can, and there were nagas way more powerful than Kaliya.”

“I’m glad the cambions can create what we are, create who we’ll be,” Raphael said, shaking his head. “I can’t imagine digging into that layer of complexity and trying to make sense of it. We know nearly every religion has met some sort of demon and made their own view on it. Then we move on because that's not us."

"Everything we have from that time are old letters, journals, and the legends passed down. Adhar is three thousand years old, and he's a second-generation naga, but even he's not old enough to know the exact happenings of a lot of the stories. One thing I've learned is when magic is involved, you can't treat something as a straight line anymore. Kadru is the mother of our species. Somehow, she had a thousand snakes as children. The first generation nagas mention her as their mother." I shrugged. "It's impossible to know the truth. Maybe Kadru found a thousand eggs and used magic to turn us into human-like sons for herself. She could have been a powerful witch. Those were pretty common back then. Fuck if I know." And now I was getting a headache.

Nakul noticed and chuckled.

"You know, I'm glad my mate was a nagini and not a human. The hoops that must be jumped through to explain the history of our species are ones I'm not interested in jumping through."

"Right?" I laughed pitifully. "It's awful. You can keep it simple and just talk about the parts you know are true, then someone finds the pieces you have no answers for. Then you get into discussions about how some things are real, but some things might not be." I rolled my eyes. "The worst. Magic makes everything so hard. Humans have it easy. They find and date some bones and probably know a new thing. Even better if they find some other stuff. You know, with all of this mythology, how do we even talk about dinosaurs?" I threw my hands up. "Magic. The bane of history's existence."

Raphael laughed as Nakul grinned.

The rest of the flight, we debated about dinosaurs. Everyone in the plane knew they were real and had existed, but the conundrum of gods, supernatural species, and more made everything complicated. It was a grand thought experiment between three supernaturals, all with different experiences, who were vastly different in age.

It passed the time.

Raphael was the first person who said something that might explore a mystery that was really a fool's errand.

"What if there was no magic at all during the time of the dinosaurs, but something...brought it here or woke it up?" he suggested. "Birthing gods, making witches, and pretty much everything supernatural possible? Then things went from there with the rise of humans following the natural path and us living alongside them as a strange new addition to the world."

"Well, it's the best idea any of us have had," I said, shrugging. "Most supernaturals are based on humanity. Vampires were once humans. Cambions are part human, part demon. The moon cursed. Nagas have a human form...Nakul?"

Nakul mulled it over a few minutes, leaving us waiting for his opinion.

"What if they aren't real?" he proposed. "The dinosaurs. A massive ploy to—"

"Nakul, please," I said, then saw him grin. "Ha-ha."

"He has the best guess I'll probably ever hear, and I

don't plan on looking for answers. There are some things in this world I am comfortable leaving unexplained. This is certainly one of them," he said. "Now, let me land the plane."

We went quiet, making sure our seatbelts were properly tightened as the plane descended. We unloaded and got it put away, heading for the next pick-up. Adhar waited with his truck nearly four miles away. He looked at me, assessing silently.

"You don't seem injured, though..."

"Want to talk about this in the truck or wait until we get back?" I asked, getting into the passenger's seat next to him. Nakul and Raphael got into the back and laid down so no one could see them and recognize my mate.

"Let's talk now so we can have something to tell the others."

I told him about the trip, explaining the conversation I had with the rakshasa once I was before the king and his mate. Adhar listened but was also driving, so in a couple of places, I had to back up and explain something again or more thoroughly. I couldn't hide my pride that I had talked the rakshasas out of war. We'd all expected me to walk into a fight and just accepted that.

"We should have been more open to other options," I said.

"Maybe, maybe not," Adhar said, humming thoughtfully. "We played the odds, and the odds were the rakshasas would choose violence. In fact, it sounds like *they* expected to choose violence. If you had prepared for politics, then faced an execution, you could have been hurt. You and Raphael had time during the trip to consider talking them down without jeopardizing your safety because you had planned for the fight. You were ready for that, which is more important if you wanted to walk away alive."

"Wouldn't you have wanted a chance to school me about how to use politics to...I don't know, just how to do it right?" I frowned at him.

"I wasn't the one negotiating," he reminded me. "Politics, as you well know, isn't just understanding the enemy from research. It's about knowing the other person, understanding the circumstances, feeling the temperature of the room, knowing when to be truthful and when to lie. Training in politics is almost pointless because no one can account for all variables before they walk into the situation. Practice, failing a few times, that's what teaches someone how to work a room, and you've had plenty of experience.

"You verbally dance with other supernatural rulers at a frequency many never will, from local groups around you to the Tribunal. You've handled external politics for our people practically on your own for years. What do you think I could teach you?" Adhar frowned back at me for a second, then focused again on driving.

I didn't know how to reply since I hadn't thought out what he would teach me. Hearing that he had no lesson to teach me was strange for reasons I knew weren't logical.

"As for the statement we need to give and the one they will give, you did well. Forcing the conflict and its resolution to go public is a protective measure. It brings the eyes of the world, especially those here in India, on it.

Imagine if we didn't, then a rakshasa attacked a naga. No one would understand, but now, we have honor at stake and the judgment of the other species at play. Who will want to work with a king who betrays the deals he made faithfully with another ruler?"

"We'll start writing it after Raphael and I get some sleep."

"I'll begin drafting while you rest, and you can scrap anything I've done if it doesn't suit what you spoke to King Mahatma about."

"Sounds like a plan." I leaned back and closed my eyes, relaxing to where I was half-asleep, slightly aware but not capable of doing anything.

"Ah, Kaliya. I am so proud of you," he whispered.

27

CHAPTER TWENTY-SEVEN

I said hello to everyone once we were back, but Raphael and I hurried to our suite and passed out as quickly as we were able. That sleep felt like one of the best of my life, certainly the best I had during this trip. Totally exhausted from travel and stress, my body gave up, and my mind stopped overloading with too many thoughts.

I slept, and it was wonderful.

I wasn't ready to get out of bed when my eyes finally opened, so I reached for my mate, who rolled over, revealing his eyes were open, already aware. I slid my hands over the muscled body he kept in peak condition as I kissed his chest, trailed kisses to his jaw, then pushed him to his back and explored his face. As I reached his mouth, I straddled him. He growled in satisfaction as my lips touched his, and I relaxed, getting comfortable in my position over him.

I wasn't the only one touching. His warm hands moved under my shirt, and after several moments, he pulled my shirt up, asking me a simple question without a single word.

I lifted my arms, letting him get rid of one of the barriers between us. His hands moved back down, and he gently pulled my underwear, still asking a silent question. He slept in the nude, so he never had barriers to stop me from touching his body, and he liked to remind me of that. He enjoyed touch, especially from me, but I had those barriers, especially during times like this trip, a silent reminder I wasn't in the right headspace.

I kissed him in response, not letting myself think about all the reasons I shouldn't. Reaching down, I touched him, smiling as he moaned. Maybe he could see it in my eyes, but this was happening. Right here, right now, the world was only filled with the two of us.

The underwear was ripped off, and he took his time making sure I was prepared. Fingers explored every inch as I kept my eyes on his. Then his head tilted back, exposing his neck, telling me what *he* wanted from this moment.

I sank my fangs into him, faster than I normally struck in bed. I hadn't used them in too long, and his offer was irresistible. He slid into me at the same time, and we reignited the mating between us, finding passion we'd lost when we had come here. It had all been in my head, but he hadn't dismissed me or how I felt.

The urgency rose once I released him. It took no effort for us to keep pace with each other, but he grew tired of being on the bottom. He kissed me and rolled us over, forcing me to sink into the bed.

When I reached the climactic moment, he joined me,

but that wasn't the end. With venom involved, we were at it for a long time. Everything in the world was just him, and I could stay in that paradise for eternity, but nothing lasted forever. Eventually, we were both panting, sweaty, and exhausted, sprawled on the bed and feeling the effects of the heat. The sun had gotten much too warm, and our body heat had made the room unbearable. I couldn't even bear to touch him, it had gotten that hot.

"We need...to convince Adhar...to get air conditioning," he said, pushing damp hair off his forehead.

"Yeah." I weakly laughed. "Let's see if the bathhouse is free and wash off. There's no way we're getting back to sleep in this heat. We need to air the room out and open the windows." I wasn't mentally tired, although my body was sore, but it would have been after a great workout.

"I'll check while you clean up and get ready," he said, rolling off the bed and walking as if we hadn't been physically active for the last three hours. I felt like my legs wouldn't work, and he was strolling around the room, cleaning himself up a little, then getting dressed like it wasn't a problem.

"So unfair," I said as he came over to kiss me. "You can walk."

"I just make it look easy," he said with a chuckle. "If you think my thighs aren't killing me, you have the wrong impression."

He left me to roll myself off the bed and find a towel. Needing to be dressed to reach the bathhouse, I had to wipe off the sweat and anything else. Using the sink to clean up a little, I got dressed in something I wasn't worried about being disgusting and got both of us an extra set for when we were clean. Wearing clothes was nightmarish from the heat in our suite, but I couldn't go without. I checked the time, just past noon, which meant the bathhouse could be open unless another couple was using it.

He came back in and grabbed towels.

"We're clear," he said. I grabbed the clean clothes and followed him to the bathhouse, ignoring the two nagas hanging out in the courtyard. I did my best not to let the rush of embarrassment I felt show on my face.

We didn't get romantic in the bathhouse, taking care of business and moving on. I didn't know if Adhar had rules about it, but I knew I wouldn't want any of the other couples doing it. It would be like sleeping in a bed you knew someone just had sex in.

Feeling refreshed, I went into the courtyard to find that Dalar and Mahavir had been joined by Nakul and Adhar.

"While you slept, I updated everyone on the rakshasas," Adhar explained, coming to my side. He didn't seem fazed in the slightest as Raphael walked past us and found a couch to fall onto. He even started massaging his thighs, my mate not caring at all that the others knew exactly why.

I nodded at Adhar but wasn't really paying attention to him. I was waiting for the inevitable—someone to make a comment, the teasing to start, or even the condemnation I was sleeping with something that was part demon. Adhar kept talking, and I wondered if they were going to wait for Raphael not to be there, or maybe they wanted to mess with him while I wasn't around.

"Kaliya?"

"I'm sorry. Zoned out," I said, turning to Adhar to give him my full attention. "You were saying?"

"I've made two drafts. Each takes a different tone. One is aggressive, while the other is calmer. Both retell the facts as we know them and why you willingly went to meet the rakshasa to find a solution. Then they go over the solution. Would you like to read them?"

"Yeah."

He went to get them, and I waited in the courtyard, looking at the men around me. Eventually, someone spoke, but it wasn't the topic I expected.

"Devesh is complaining you trained him too hard, brother," Mahavir said with a smile at Nakul.

"Is that why he's hiding? I'm not going to go easy on him. The boy is nearly a man. He needs to train. I had a session with the mates, and none of them have been complaining."

Mahavir laughed, and even Raphael chuckled.

"Did you?" I asked, coming closer. "I thought..."

"They approached me," Nakul explained. "While you were gone, I came back for a couple of days between flights, and they asked me to teach them something they can practice on their own or together without supervision. I taught them the first series of forms, corrected their posture to establish good habits early. They're under explicit orders not to swing at each other yet."

"That's...that's great," I said with a grin. "Thanks for doing that for them, Uncle."

"It was my pleasure. I was reminded of your aunt when they asked. She knew how to use a sword and use it well, and we trained together. She had asked me early in our relationship to see her as a sparring partner. Over the years, I trained with her nearly at the level you and I sparred at. Speaking of training, now that we're done with the rakshasa nonsense, you and I should begin lessons in the chakram."

"Really?" Mahavir looked between us. "Kaliya, you don't know how to use them?"

"I know the basics, but Nakul wants to see my proficiency since I'm teaching someone back home. One of the cambions was interested in using them. Training with an expert won't just improve my skill enough to use them regularly but will help me teach her."

"Her?" Mahavir had no condemnation in that simple question, but it was just the wrong word to say, and my hackles raised a little.

"Sammy is a warrior cambion, capable of killing at a level of brutality unlike many others," I said stiffly. "She lacks skills for ranged combat, though."

"If she cuts off her own hand, she can tape it on, and it will heal," Raphael said, now stretching on the ground. He lifted his hand, showing off the scar around his wrist. "Something that's been proven a few times."

"Oh..." Mahavir blinked, looking from me to my mate, then back again. "I hope she enjoys them. Few in the world can use the chakram effectively. It would be nice to see another expert, even if she is—"

"A woman?" I asked.

"Not from here," Mahavir finished. "I fear the skill will die out one day."

"Agreed, my brother," Nakul said, nodding. "So, I will train Kaliya as much as she needs, and she will train this cambion, Sammy. We'll have two experts in the world, ready to pass the skill on. Maybe in the future, we can have a competition, men versus women for fun."

"Fun? We'd destroy you," I said, crossing my arms with confidence. It was a bluff. Right now, Mahavir and Nakul would crush Sammy and me.

"Here they are," Adhar said, walking back into the courtyard. The topic of chakram was dropped when he handed me the two versions he'd drafted. I could see what he meant by 'aggressive' with one of them. It was as if I had written it, pissed off the rakshasas would dare say I murdered their king in cold blood. The other was much more measured, more in Adhar's voice than mine, and more appropriate.

"This one," I said, handing it to him first. "I like it. I was aggressive with the rakshasas while we were there, but there's no reason to be angry now. They know the balance of power and what could happen if they pressed the issue. We don't need to rub it in."

"Then you can throw the other in a fire," he said. "I'll make a few copies of this and drop it off at a couple of places for my contacts to spread. I'll be unavailable for a day—"

"I knew I could hear you," Aamir said, coming in before Adhar could finish. I looked around the old naga to see him staring at me. He walked a little stiffly and stopped beside Adhar, not breaking eye contact with me. "May I cut in for a moment?" he asked with a shred of politeness I never expected from him.

"Go ahead," Adhar said, stepping to the side, giving us space.

"You did a good job with the rakshasas," Aamir said, looking as if the words were difficult to say. He had nerve approaching me and really felt what he was saying. There was also a chance he hated every word that came out of his mouth.

"Thank you." No matter how Aamir felt about what he was saying, hearing it meant the world to me *because* it was from him.

He thrust a hand at me, and for a second, I just stared at it as it waited in the space between us. It took that second to register he was offering a handshake. I put my hand in his as I made eye contact with him again, and we shook.

"I was admittedly worried about what could happen if we sent you to meet with the rakshasas. Of the options I could think of, none of them were brokering peace." He gave me an assessing look as our handshake ended. "You surprised me. When Adhar explained how it went, I was shocked...but I don't think anyone here could have done it better. Certainly, none of us, except for Adhar. How you handled this...and my mate's fondness of you, I wanted to..."

"See if we can restart?" I asked, eyeing him warily.

"I can't change the type of man I am, but I can try to... smooth my edges and jump to fewer conclusions. I could offer you empty apologies about what I've said and how I've acted."

"Apologize and mean it, then I'll ask you about another," I said, crossing my arms. "You can pick what it is you apologize for. If you can suffer this exercise, we can look to the future and try to leave the past behind."

"I was already planning on apologizing to you for the incident. I'm sorry for attacking your mate and insinuating he was a danger to my daughter," he said, lowering his head. "Your words struck me then, but I wasn't willing to listen. I hadn't been thinking about how content my daughter was and giving my mate a moment she deserved to have a cup of tea. I was angry that a man I didn't want to know was holding her. The only reason I didn't want to know him was because I didn't want to know him. I didn't want to know him because he is yours. You were right. From what the others tell me, he's a good man, and I am somehow less for refusing to know him."

"He's a wonderful man. You'll have to deal with him on your own, though."

"Of course. Now you wanted to ask me about one topic?"

"You went to Adhar to have me removed from my position."

"I did," he said, his eyes going wide. He looked at Adhar, who stepped back farther. "I don't have an excuse. I was hotheaded over things I saw, and I…I think I was reacting in my own way to what had happened to your mother and the others. You weren't a child I felt comfortable giving power to, whether or not it was a requirement. That opinion has not changed." Aamir met my gaze. "Judge me as you will for that. I will say, this gathering has already forced me to reevaluate how I see you. You aren't the child you were, and no one wants to be judged for their childhood. Growing up is supposed to give us a chance to move beyond that."

I looked over his shoulder when he stopped talking. Saranya was standing in the shade on the other side of the open space, not quite in the courtyard. He followed my gaze and sighed before he met my eyes again.

"Here's an uncomfortable truth for you, Aamir." I leaned on the closest pillar. "I was furious when Adhar told me about that meeting, which he did after I arrived here. He kept it to himself all these years for the stability of the nagas. I didn't need to know if you weren't still trying." I nodded at Saranya, who nodded back as she slowly walked into the courtyard. "But looking back, Aamir, I can't say I disagree with you. I wasn't a child who needed to have great political power or responsibility. I was heartbroken and spent a century running from all of it. There was no one else, and I had to come to terms with that over the years. So did all of you. But now I'm here, and I'm trying to be a ruler you and the others can respect."

"I will continue to try to see you as the woman you are now and not the child you were," Aamir said as if he was giving me his most solemn vow. "I can't promise I'll always like the woman, but I can work with her."

"And I promise to see you as a man trying to evolve to new, possibly uncomfortable changes and will only bring up the problems of the past if you repeat them."

Aamir actually bowed the way he would if this was a

formal event. He went to his mate, and they left together, Saranya sending a smile back at me before they disappeared.

"He's an honorable man," Mahavir said.

"And she's an honorable woman," Raphael added, smiling at me from his place on the ground.

"I'm going to get to work," Adhar declared. "I'm glad to see two of my strongest nagas find tentative peace, but there are pressing matters." He hurried off. "Dalar! I need your penmanship!"

28

CHAPTER TWENTY-EIGHT

Days passed as Adhar made sure India and the world knew rakshasas and the nagas had come to an agreement. A couple days after, he brought back the rakshasas' statement, which I could only assume Maurvi wrote. It was the same calm language Adhar had used, not giving away the feelings of the writer.

When I wasn't waiting anxiously, I spent time with the other nagas. We ate, shared stories, and I was forced to babysit the twins twice because they asked Raphael. He said okay, and I didn't complain because it was only fair Dalar and Basanti got some alone time, even though everyone knew they were only napping.

I joined the other women at the bathhouse every other day. We laughed and joked around, splashing each other, even sharing beauty tips, something that would have made Sorcha laugh if she saw me. Sorcha, the regal beauty she was, loved that stuff, but I always treated beauty and makeup as a tool, not something I gravitated to regularly. I liked my routine and didn't want to change it all that much, but with the mates, I could tell them about new products. Makeup was a massive industry worldwide with a surprising innovation. For once, I was an almost expert, which was neat. It was certainly the most feminine thing I had claim to among these women.

I have to find a way to introduce them to Sorcha. She'd have so much fun with them.

We also talked about their training with Nakul and how their mates were watching them progress. Every mate promised to follow through with Nakul's training once they returned home. We talked about their babies, their education and development as they got older. As the only naga in the bathhouse, I could answer questions their mates had already answered, or Adhar had already answered for them. Basanti and Saranya weren't stupid, though. They were going to question everyone they could. They wanted every perspective to be ready for their children when they got older.

When we weren't having our girl time in the bathhouse, we watched the daily training for the males. I was invited to join the group, but I wanted my mornings with Eshika, Saranya, Basanti, and Eleanor. I could point out what the men were doing and why. It was another way to further their education, even if they weren't holding the swords themselves. While I wasn't joining the training, Raphael was getting a chance to show off that he was incredibly strong compared to us.

Nagas didn't have super strength. Our human forms had the same strength as any human and required us to build muscle. The only physical advantage we had was our speed, the lightning-fast reflexes gifted to us for being snake people. My mate wasn't the best with the sword, the nagas were better, but at least once, Nakul pointed out Raphael must have learned a lot from me, which was glowing praise for my mate and me.

I wanted the ladies to meet Sorcha, but even if I was beginning to find peace with the nagas, I didn't want them to meet Cassius. Ever. It was hard enough watching Raphael find his footing as part of our culture and keep boundaries with them. There were some he really liked —Dalar was a new friend—but there were personality clashes. Aamir was trying, but the naga hadn't lied when we spoke. He couldn't change who he was overnight. He tried, but he was a harsh, temperamental man. The *only* thing that softened him was being with his mate and daughter. Raphael was also spending more time with Adhar, and they were growing close in a weird way. Not friends, but fellow rulers, a new bond between people who had to make tough decisions. For over a week, I watched it all, finally resting and letting the trip be about my people coming together.

After nine days, I reached out to Sorcha and Cassius to let them know we were having a good time. They had sent daily reports on the cambions, but Raphael hadn't been worried, so neither was I. When he and I finally checked the reports, it sounded like the cambions were on their best behavior, enjoying some extra breathing space with Raphael gone. They didn't abuse the freedom they had, knowing it could end quickly if they did. Some of the cambions even added notes for us to the reports. Mateo told us Sammy had cut herself again. Cole thanked us for the new security room Raphael and I put in the plans for the main house. We'd kept it a secret to surprise him, leaving Cassius and Sorcha to show him when it was complete.

Reading through the messages made me miss home.

"I'm enjoying myself here, but I can't wait to get back to everyone," I said as Raphael leaned over me. We were using Adhar's computer with a VPN in his office, which was next to the archives. I believed the only reason he had a computer was thanks to the Tribunal. He wasn't required to use it, but with proper security measures, he had become proficient. He even had the standard set-up for video calls, with a screen on the wall and a camera above it, which was covered and unplugged when it wasn't being used.

"I miss them, too, but they're fine. You needed this trip and I'm beginning to think *I* needed this trip," he said, kissing the top of my head before sitting across from me. "I know this probably won't make sense to you, but I've never felt more connected to *you* than I have here."

"Yeah?" I tried not to smile. "Why?"

"You have a lot of bad memories of these people and your homeland, but you have a lot of joy and pride, too. The joy and pride are just buried under the pain. I've seen your wistful expressions when you talk about things from home. I've had the pleasure of seeing you decide to cook a dish your mom used to make, and I've seen those same dishes here recreated by Eshika. I've seen the joy that crosses your face while you eat it." He shrugged. "Food can be a powerful thing, but it's not just that.

"I was uncomfortable with you sparring with Nakul, but I saw your fierce pride when you two sparred. You spend a part of the afternoon with him every day, talking about the chakram, how it can be useful and when. I've seen how you hold them and heard you talk about how your people are some of the last to know how to use them with real combat skill. There's a lot of pride there." He smiled as he leaned on the other side of the desk. "Kaliya, why wouldn't I feel connected to you while I watch you reclaim your heritage, and I have the privilege to learn it at the same time?"

"I love you," I said. I felt like a fool for telling Cassius I didn't know if I was happy before we left. I was. As long as Raphael was by my side, happiness wasn't hard to find. I just had to trust that. It brought tears to my eyes because I had never had that before, but sitting here, it was clear I couldn't do forever without him.

"I love you, too. I hope you feel this when you're with the cambions."

"I do," I confirmed. "Maybe not in the same way, but I know they're the people who make you *all* of you, and I love *all* of you. They make you all of you in the same way the nagas make me...all of me."

That was really it. As I settled into this trip and hashed out the problems I'd had for so many years, there was a completeness I had been missing. I had cut off this part of my life for so many good and bad reasons, but now I was strong to address the bad, so I could enjoy the good. Adhar agreed nagas should wait until they were twenty-five to talk about mating. The mates were being trained for their own protection. I watched Adhar slyly force the men to take on some level of burden for the household, not that many of them whispered a complaint.

I had realized I was wrong about some things—like Pavan being unhelpful to the community, still not finding something to do for our people—which that was a bone to swallow, but I did it. He was keeping himself occupied. There had been an entire system for single nagas, and I had never known because of my distance.

After a century, hunting for secrets in the darkest shadows, I learned the world was complicated. I could be friends with a Tribunal member one day, on the same side, and the next, we were cool adversaries in a political shitstorm. I just never turned that knowledge to my people. I never tried to look at their complexities, never tried to see more than my snap judgments.

"Want to go hang out with everyone?" he asked. "Or do you want to keep rereading what they sent because you're that nostalgic about Arizona?"

"Let's go," I declared and stood, chuckling. I took a quick moment to log out of everything before shutting off the computer. Adhar's rule about technology being off as much as possible was not just to conserve energy.

We headed out to find many of the nagas hanging out together, watching the babies roll around, or try to, in the sun at the center. Aamir and Saranya claimed a couch to themselves, Pavan close to them in his own chair. Nakul was telling Devesh something that gave the teen wide, starry eyes and an amazed expression. *Must be an old tale of glory or something.*

Mahavir was next to Basanti and Dalar. Eleanor and Eshika were even sharing a conversation at a small table in the far corner, one that included Adhar, though he looked as if he had given up on adding his own thoughts long beforehand. When Eshika tapped him to say something, he just shook his head, and Eleanor laughed.

I found Vikrant last, hovering in the dark, hiding from the bright sun. He smiled at his mate as she went toe to toe with Eshika. The debate looked like it was good fun, though, when Eshika threw a dismissive hand at Eleanor and grinned.

"You'll learn," Eshika said loud enough to carry over the courtyard. "I promise."

"I love to learn," Eleanor countered.

I found a place to sit with Raphael, joining the circle of people watching the three babies.

"They're all wide awake and not crying," I said with a chuckle. "Did someone make a bargain with a deity I need to know about?"

"Kaliya!" Basanti tried to sound outraged. "You know we wouldn't do that." She covered her mouth and bent over, giggling wildly. When she came up for air, she was still grinning. "I've thought about it, though. Do you know any good deities?"

"Nope."

"I prayed for an entire hour before my boys woke up," Dalar said, looking a little more serious. "Aamir? Saranya?"

"We pray every morning," Saranya answered with an angelic look on her face as she leaned on her mate. "Always for our safety..." She failed to keep the angelic look. "And a good day with her. She's easier to keep up with because we only have one."

"Eshika didn't pray at all with Devesh," Mahavir said, looking over at his son. "She asked for the gods to curse me for daring to give her a troublesome child."

"That's what Kaliya would do," Raphael said. My jaw dropped as I spun to look at him at the other end of the couch.

"Excuse me, I would not." I lost the shocked act and grinned. "I would send Sammy to ruin your day every time I had the chance. I don't need to ask the gods for anything. I already have the power to make you miserable."

"So, you're planning on having children?" Basanti asked.

"Not yet. Not for a long time, but...one day, we'll revisit the idea," I said, shrugging.

"I think you would be a wonderful mother." Saranya sat up and looked at the children, then at me. "And if you're not, *well*, at least naga children love your mate."

"They do, don't they?" I asked, smiling at my mate as he tried to find the most comfortable way to lie on the couch.

"I'm going for a walk," Pavan said softly, then got up and walked out. I watched him go. I still hadn't gotten around to talking to him. He was the last of nagas who purposefully had a less than pleasant time. He was glaring less, but we still hadn't really talked.

I waited twenty minutes, and when he didn't come back, I tapped Raphael's foot, now on my lap.

"I need to do something." He moved his foot, nodding in acknowledgment but kept his eyes on the babies. The man was in love with the babies, and one of the terror twins was staring back at him with a big baby smile.

"Pavan keeps to the main trails," Aamir said softly as I passed him. "He won't have gone far."

"Thanks." He gave me a respectful nod, and I headed out.

29

CHAPTER TWENTY-NINE

As I searched for Pavan, my thoughts were on what Aamir said. He'd recognized what I was planning to do, which showed me just how observant and intelligent he could be when he was thinking. I assume he knew it was the right thing to do. There was unresolved hostility, and part of this trip was addressing the hostility between all of us. It was one of Adhar's objectives, and I was more and more comfortable playing along. I was finally finding a place among the nagas, something I'd lost as a child, something I'd run from as a teen. Pavan was the last naga holding out on giving me a chance. Although I had changed over the last century, I could see my misconceptions about the people I had left behind and that I only knew part of the story. There were things I was right about, but after a century, things changed. We all grew a little wise and saw things a little differently.

After a century, we could finally try to be a community. We didn't have to like each other all the time, but we could try to find understanding and learn to respect each other. I kept coming back to that ideal as I spent time with everyone.

Then there was Pavan. Pavan, who hovered around Aamir when they were in the same room, then just disappeared. Every day, he made fewer attempts to talk to anyone except Aamir. He was closed off, and I wondered what was bothering him. *Is he going through the same transition as the rest of us? Is he trying to wrap his head around the shift in our little community and doesn't know how to land on his feet while we've all figured it out?*

I wanted to talk to him. I walked for ten minutes before I finally caught a soft scent and closed my eyes, focusing on any heat source around me, and found him lying on a low rock in a spot of sun. It was considered rude to talk to someone while in their snake form, but I took my chance. Getting closer to him, I was impressed by his stunning patterned scales every shade of green.

"Pavan, I've been hoping to talk to you," I said, talking with my hands and feeling a little nervous. "I'd like to hash out some of our issues and see how you feel. I'll be in the meeting room, and you can meet me there, okay?"

I took a step toward the meeting room as Pavan slid off the rock in the same direction. I had no problem with him traveling in snake form, maybe not yet ready to talk, so I kept walking as he followed. I only stopped to get the door, holding it open for him. As I closed it, I addressed the first problem.

"We can't talk while—"

A sharp pain hit my calf as if I'd been poked with something. I didn't understand for a minute, looking down in confusion. It took too long for me to process what was happening, long enough for Pavan to let go of me. I watched him lift, opening his cobra hood, and try to strike me a second time. I moved out of the way, hitting a bench, and tried to think about what I needed to do about the bite.

We're not immune to each other.

I knew there was a slim chance I could survive. There was a chance. I kept my distance from Pavan, tearing off a piece of my shirt, and used it to tourniquet my thigh, hissing in pain as I made sure it was tighter than it had to be. I knew it was just a temporary measure. The venom was spreading through my bloodstream, and my heart was racing, making it even more likely this wouldn't help, but I still tried. I went to one knee, trying to slow my heart and assess how I could get out and find help. With one hand, I felt for my dagger of the day, glad I wasn't comfortable enough to leave my suite without a weapon. Pavan was in the way of the door, though.

"Pavan, you need to think carefully if you want to do this," I said, watching him move to block the door and shift into his human form. He pulled a dagger from a hidden sheath and started walking across the room.

"I have."

I stayed low, but my head was spinning. Our venom worked quickly. Depending on the type of venom he had, I could be paralyzed in minutes or bleed out even faster. The bite wound could necrotize, and I'd lose my leg or cause my blood to coagulate. Organ failure was in my future. A naga's venom was on steroids and so monstrous, it almost couldn't be compared to a normal snake. Mine destroyed tissue and burst blood vessels and caused people to bleed out from pretty much everywhere. Internally, externally, including from their eyes, nose, and ears. I had no fucking idea what Pavan's could do.

I grabbed my dagger and tried to stand as he grabbed my shoulder and shoved me back. I allowed him to move me, needing to conserve my energy.

"Long live Roshni," he hissed.

In a moment that felt like an eternity, those three words ringing in my ears.

Long live Roshni.

Roshni.

Something snapped. Fury flooded me, and power followed. I grabbed his wrist as he tried to sink the dagger into my chest. I didn't hiss. I roared in rage as I broke his wrist, forcing him to drop the dagger. Without missing a beat, I slammed a fist into his face hard enough to break bone, forgetting I was holding a dagger in the same hand. I kicked him back, hearing the crack of ribs breaking. I was moving faster than he could recover.

He wants to be an assassin?

Grabbing his shirt, I threw him into a wall, roaring again. The sound I made reminded me more of Raphael than any naga I'd ever met. Pavan was dazed as I pulled him back to his feet, finally remembering the dagger in my hand, a good nine inches long—long enough. I slammed it into his chest, aiming for the spot that would give me the ability to force it all the way through him and into the wall. I kept pushing it until he was completely pinned, then punched him again.

I hit him again as I heard people yelling. Raphael

burst into the room, grabbed me, and pulled me away. Pavan was still alive, but I wasn't done with him. I screamed at his still body, but he only whimpered from his pain.

"Kaliya, calm down," Raphael ordered, pulling me to the other side of the room as other nagas ran in. Adhar was first, a sword in hand. He dropped it as he saw me, then Pavan.

"What happened?" he asked. "Kaliya! I need an explanation!"

I kept trying to fight my mate, so I could kill the son of a bitch, waiting there to die, but each moment I fought, I grew weaker.

"Kaliya?" Raphael's voice was clear in my ear. "We need to know what's going on. You are *glowing* with demonic magic. *I* need to know what's happening."

I felt the terrible shake in my hands as I looked down at them. I hadn't realized my vision was blurring. The venom was doing its job. I could feel it tearing something apart inside me as the magic tried to heal it.

"He bit me," I tried to say. "Left calf..."

"I'll get a sample of Pavan's blood," someone said. "We need to get her to the house."

As others started talking, I focused on my hands, watching the red demonic magic swirl, flare-up, fade, then flare again. Eventually, I figured out I could keep it from fading if I just focused on the painful battle it was fighting for my body.

"Why?" Adhar demanded. "Kaliya, I need you to talk to me. Please. Do you know why he would bite you?"

"Long...live...Roshni," I said, groaning as I lost my

focus, and pain wracked my body, causing me to tense and lose the ability to stand. Raphael kept me from hitting the floor.

"This will help, hopefully," Nakul said, rushing close. He grabbed my arm and cut a line, but the magic healed it too quickly for him to introduce Pavan's blood to mine. "Damn it. Ingesting doesn't work as fast; you're not a vampire. It could take time you don't have." He forced my mouth open and poured Pavan's blood into my mouth, anyway. I tried to swallow as it felt like my body went to war with itself.

"What the hell does 'long live Roshni' mean?" Aamir demanded. "What does my daughter have to do with any of this?"

I couldn't bring myself to say any more.

Raphael lifted me, and I focused on my shaking hands, and the magic flared again. I had no better idea, so I kept staring as Raphael got me back to the main house. He went directly to our suite and put me on the bed.

"Kaliya?" he whispered, pushing hair out of my face, but I didn't respond. I had to focus. If I didn't, the magic would fade, and I would die. That much I knew for certain. I fought to keep my eyes open, but there was no way I could spare the mental strength to reply to him.

"Is she still alive?" Mahavir asked as he entered the room. I could hear them, which gave some solace as the loudest thing in the room was the pounding of my heart.

"Yeah," Raphael answered.

"What is that?" the other naga asked, coming closer until I could see him out of the corner of my eye.

"Demonic magic. Not every cambion can do it, but

Kaliya got it from our mating. I think it's helping her heal, but we're not really sure what she can do with it." Raphael sounded stressed, and just realizing that made me lose focus for a second. Biting my tongue, I focused again, turning all my attention inward, listening only to my heartbeat, my only solace in the world of pain. I kept my eyes open, afraid to lose consciousness and stop fighting.

The world only became me and the body I was fighting for but didn't need to focus as hard, my mind strangely quiet. The pain was intense, but it was only pain, and I could survive pain. I had been trained to survive pain.

I wanted to tell them I was in so much pain, I could scream. I wanted to tell them I had to fight this, or I would die. I wanted to tell them exactly what I had meant.

I kept my focus, knowing if I fought long enough, I could survive this. I was in a fight Raphael and I had talked about. Could the fast healing of the cambions beat the venom of a naga?

We were all about to find out.

As time passed, words drifted over my ears, overcoming the crashing of my heartbeat.

"Meditative..."

"Focused..."

"Will power..."

Oddly, I was at peace and wasn't scared. This was a battle of will. I knew I could snap out of this and defend myself from someone, but what I needed most was to defend myself from the enemy in my body.

Different people came in and out of my suite and entered my view. I didn't understand the passage of time, so I had no idea how long each person sat there, but in the back of my mind, I knew they were there. Mahavir, Eshika, and Devesh. Saranya and Roshni. Vikrant and Eleanor. Dalar and Basanti. Adhar.

So it went, almost as though people were keeping watch, a vigil over me.

I kept my trance-like state. I didn't know if Pavan's blood made any difference. If it could have been injected straight into my veins, it would have worked to neutralize Pavan's venom, but ingesting it wasn't as effective unless the person drinking it was a vampire.

I knew the moment the venom was eradicated from my system. Taking a deep breath, I finally looked up to *see* the person in the room with me. Others had been in my vision, but I hadn't really *seen* them.

I looked at Aamir's face as he grew shocked, realizing I could finally see him.

"Raphael!" he called out, rushing closer. Raphael came in and grabbed me, but I was already falling back, ready to sleep and let my body finish healing.

30

CHAPTER THIRTY

Trying to get out of bed, I nearly fell as I put weight on my legs. Since I was still clothed, I didn't let my legs stop until I reached the door and tried to open it. Someone wrapped their arms around me from behind.

"Are you sure you want to go out there right now?"

I leaned back into the warmth.

"Yes," I whispered.

"You don't know what you look like," he whispered desperately. "Kaliya..."

"I need to...I don't know. I just need to."

"Okay," he murmured, kissing my neck softly and opening the door for me.

While cambion healing had kept my body alive, the damage the venom had done was severe. Each step, I felt stronger as I got used to my legs being under me and moving again. My chest felt tight as we reached the edge of the courtyard. I wasn't sure if it was nerves or the venom, but I rubbed my chest uncomfortably.

Everyone was there except Pavan, all getting to their

feet at my arrival. I looked for Adhar first, who approached before any of the others, who stood like statues. Adhar was a little pale as he stopped in front of me.

"Pavan?" I asked softly.

"In holding, still alive," Adhar answered. "While you were...unavailable, we held a vote on his fate, depending on your vote."

"Did you question him yet?" I asked, reaching to hold on to a pillar.

"Yes. I'm certain you know what we've learned."

"Kill me. Roshni is the ruler." Adhar nodded at my words. "Why? She's a baby."

"That's why. He truly believed you were a poison to our culture, forcing us to change to suit your whims. He'd hoped the rakshasas would kill you. When they didn't, he believed it was time for him to take matters into his own hands." Adhar looked down.

"Tell her the rest," Saranya said clearly over the thick tension of the courtyard. It was the crack of a whip, a condemnation, and full of righteous fury.

And a little bit of fear.

"He believed Roshni would be his mate when she was old enough," Adhar continued. "He would then be mated to a ruler, the perfect position to make sure someone like you never came to power again. He was planning on kidnapping her and molding her into what he felt she needed to be."

I hissed, the fury coming back. Looking past Adhar to Saranya, the passionate fury in her eyes was like looking into a mirror. Aamir leaned over and put his head in his hands, not sitting next to his mate but alone. He didn't even have his daughter.

"And what fate have the people voted for him?" I asked.

"We've voted on execution," Adhar explained. "He threatened both you and Roshni."

"You have my vote for execution."

He and I stared at each other for a moment, a respectful nod the only thing that passed between us.

"Come sit down," Saranya said, marching across the courtyard, her hand outstretched. "Come sit with me. Please."

I took her hand and let her lead me. Raphael hovered behind me, his hands close but not touching me. *He's waiting to catch me if I fall...He won't force me off my feet, but he'll be there to catch me.*

I sat down slowly, looking at my thighs. They looked smaller than normal. I touched them and saw my hands were bony. Saranya wrapped an arm around me, holding me as though I was her most precious sister and friend.

"I've lost weight," I pointed out.

"Yes. Probably twenty pounds of both fat and muscle." Raphael knelt in front of me and covered my hands with his own. Twenty pounds was a lot—too much. "I try my best not to order you around, but I want you to eat everything you can and rest. Build some of it back the easy way. Then I'll get you back into a gym and see what you're capable of."

"I ate my body to heal..." I looked at my thin forearm. It could have been thinner. I wasn't completely emaciated, but I was certainly the smallest I'd been since I left Hisao's training.

"We believe so. These things can take a toll on the body," Adhar confirmed. "You needed to eat more than the average naga and needed to burn a lot of energy."

"Scared me," Raphael whispered, lowering his head until his forehead was on my knees. "Scared me to fucking death, Kaliya."

"Well, now we know it's possible for a cambion to heal through naga venom," I pointed out. He growled. I took my hand out of his and touched his hair. "I'll heal. Give me a couple of days to rest, and I bet recovery will be easy—"

I went silent when he looked up, his eyes black and red.

"The magic got you this far. I don't think it's going to take you any further," he growled.

"We'll see. Part of this weakness is probably from exhaustion and recovery," I countered. I leaned my head back, letting the sun pour over my face. It was warm and wonderful until I saw a stupid bird fly overhead too distant for me to identify. "How long was I…fighting?"

"We think you went into a meditative state." Adhar sat on the other side. Raphael rubbed my calves, keeping his head on my knees. "You were fighting, as you call it, for six hours. If you hadn't, you should have been dead in less than thirty minutes. We watched you slowly grow smaller and didn't know if you could hear or see us. You were barely breathing, but we had to trust you. Thankfully, our trust was well placed."

"How long was I asleep?"

"Close to eighteen hours," Adhar answered. Raphael's hands rubbed my calves a little harder.

I nodded, then yawned. I had just woken up, but I was tired. Then my stomach growled.

"Can I get something to eat?" I asked softly.

Eshika was in front of me faster than she should have been capable of. She put a plate in my lap, then gave me a spoon.

"You should all eat, too," I said, waving the spoon around. "It's weird to eat by myself with everyone staring."

It was as though something opened the dam, and the flood washed away the tension. Most of the crowd started moving around, getting plates of food for themselves, and some quiet conversations started.

No one mentioned that Pavan was waiting to die wherever they were keeping him. I emptied my plate and had more. Only three people didn't eat, and they surrounded me—Adhar, Raphael, and Saranya. When I finished my second plate, I looked at the woman beside me.

"How do you want him to die?" I asked plainly. Her eyes went wide as she realized I was addressing her. "They all voted for execution, but Roshni is your daughter."

"Cut his head off."

"I might not be able to right now," I said, moving my legs as a warning to Raphael that I wanted to stand up and see how I was feeling.

"I'll do it," Aamir growled.

"No," Adhar said softly as Raphael moved out of my

way and stood. Adhar rose when I stood, looking at me with soulful eyes that held too much. "If one ruler cannot perform the execution, then the other should. I have taken life before, and I can do so again."

"We're doing it now. He doesn't get to see another sunrise, and…I don't want to go back into that room, close my eyes, and sleep knowing he's still alive. Saranya deserves to know her daughter will be safe tonight."

"Nakul, Mahavir, get the prisoner," Adhar ordered, looking at the brothers. "Clear the food, everyone."

Eshika rushed around with Basanti and Eleanor, grabbing plates and running them into the kitchen. Devesh went to Dalar, giving the other naga a nervous look. Dalar patted his shoulder, offering silent comfort.

"Devesh, did you vote?" I asked, walking slowly to him. A little food was already helping. It would take time to get back to prime physical condition, but I wouldn't collapse any time soon. I focused on the young man instead of my weakness. He was only seventeen. Seventeen was a hard age.

"I did," he confirmed with only the slightest waver. He was trying to be calm like the others, all experienced with death in a variety of forms. I waved him over, positioning him to stand next to me. He kept eye contact, understanding the severity of what was happening. He was young, but not too young. He stood on the edge as I had once, like everyone here had.

It was one thing to tell him I had killed a lot of people and would keep doing so. It was another to watch a man die on his knees. Part of me wanted to protect his innocence, but I knew better than to try. He wouldn't appreciate it. I wouldn't have.

"I know the first time you have a hand in someone dying can weigh on the soul. Your father or uncle would have said this already, but it bears repeating. Pavan did this to himself. He made the decisions that brought us to this point. His death is on his shoulders and no one else's. Remember that."

"I will," Devesh said, nodding.

"This will stay with you, even if you remember and take everything I just said to heart. If you need to talk, you can talk to me, your father, your uncle, or Adhar. Hell, talk to your mother. Talk to someone. I don't care who you pick, but don't suffer in silence, okay?"

"I will," he whispered. "Thank you." He bowed his head.

I sent him back to Dalar, whose respectful nod told me I made the right decision.

Mahavir and Nakul brought a box with breathing holes too small for a snake to squeeze through. It was just enough space to fit a grown man, and I knew Pavan was inside. The fact that Adhar even kept one of these was surprising.

Dalar stepped forward, taking over for Nakul, who looked uncomfortable taking part. Dalar helped Mahavir open the box and pull out Pavan, who looked drugged out of his mind. He was weak, unable to stay on his feet. If he'd gotten any other sentence than execution, his treatment would have been different, but I knew they had done this to him so he wouldn't try to escape. He wouldn't be able to think clearly enough to change into a snake.

Adhar walked back into the courtyard, a talwar in his hands. Mahavir and Dalar let Pavan fall to his knees. Adhar struck quickly in one clean cut, not giving anyone a sign it was time. Pavan's head fell, then his body slumped and tipped over.

No one spoke as Adhar wiped his blade with a small handkerchief, bowed to the crowd in the courtyard, then walked out.

I didn't move, watching the blood spread over the ground. Saranya came up beside me, also quiet. We watched as Aamir stepped forward and looked at Pavan's head before joining the clean-up duty. He grabbed the head as Raphael took the body from Mahavir and Dalar. He carried it with ease, following Aamir out of the courtyard. Devesh scrubbed the ground with Dalar while Mahavir and Nakul took the box away. None of the women jumped in to help.

Eventually, the evidence of what had happened was gone.

"What happens next?" I asked Saranya, who had stayed at my side.

"Tomorrow, Adhar is having a meeting with Aamir and me about signs Pavan might have been plotting against us. We're also going to talk about our family's protection." She took a deep breath. "And we'll talk about if I feel comfortable living with my mate. Aamir knows about that one, but he won't be involved."

"Saranya—"

"Pavan was his friend," she snapped. "How can I...

They were both part of the group that wanted you out of power. Pavan thought Aamir would understand when we first got here. He only planned to kidnap Roshni after he saw Aamir make amends with you." She shook her head, and I reached out, wrapping an arm around her. "For most of the time you were unconscious, I left Roshni with Raphael. Aamir hasn't held her since it happened. He claims he had nothing to do with it, and there's no evidence he did. He said he told you how to find Pavan because he believed you and Pavan needed to talk."

"We did," I said gently. "I looked for him so we could put the past to rest or try to."

"Still. We kept a monster in our home, who was looking at our daughter like..." She wiped her eyes. "I don't know. I just don't know the truth, and he...She's our *daughter*."

"You have time. Even if it takes years, you'll know the truth. You protect Roshni better than anyone. And Saranya? I only fought Pavan so hard because he made me realize what was at risk, why he was doing it. He said, 'long live Roshni,' and I wanted to tear him to pieces. You aren't in this alone."

"I know," she whispered. "Thank you for...for fighting so hard for her."

"And you," I said into her hair. She wrapped her arms around me, and I held her until Raphael and Aamir returned. Aamir looked at us, and I saw the haunted pain in his face, but he didn't reach for his wife. There was no anger.

You had no part in it, did you? Oh, Aamir, the decisions we make sometimes come back for us, and they take their payment. Sometimes, the cost is so much more than we bargained for.

Good luck. You'll need it if you want your family back.

He was a broken man, and the only thing that could fix him was Saranya. He turned away and walked through the courtyard, heading not to his suite but to a staircase, heading upstairs, banished to the singles rooms without a fight or a single word.

I released Saranya, kissing her forehead.

"Get some rest," she ordered me.

"I plan on sleeping for at least twenty-four hours," I said, knowing it was coming. I was exhausted. I wasn't shaking anymore, but I was so tired. "Kiss Roshni for me."

Her smile was weak but real as she headed to the suite she once shared with her mate.

Raphael and I went into our suite, where he helped me clean up and change into something more comfortable, soft sweats and a comfortable tank.

"If you wake up before me, don't feel the need to hold a bedside vigil, okay?" I said as I got into bed. He fell face-first on the other side, his head in his pillow. "Go out there and help with the babies. Help Saranya if you see her. Talk to them. Keep yourself busy. I'm just sleeping. I'll be fine."

"Fine," he mumbled, the word muffled. "Go to sleep."

I closed my eyes and fell asleep.

31

CHAPTER THIRTY-ONE

I woke to banging on the door, then someone barging in. I struggled to sit up as Mahavir ran in.

"Kaliya, we have multiple unknowns testing the borders," he said quickly as I blinked, trying to figure out what time it was.

His words sank in quickly, though. We were in the worst possible territory scenario now.

"What?" I said, trying to jump off the bed. He reached out, grabbing me as I struggled with my legs for a moment, then found my balance. "How long ago?"

"It just happened, and I ran here to get you up," he explained.

We both heard a distant crash.

"It's a breach!" Nakul yelled, his voice echoing through the house. "They've broken through the border wall!"

We were on the clock.

"Where is everyone?" I demanded as I threw on better

pants. I couldn't fight in baggy sweatpants. The tank was fine, so I left it and grabbed my weapon bag.

"Devesh is getting Basanti and the twins into the safe room in the basement. Eshika is making sure Eleanor goes there as well. Aamir is looking for Saranya and Adhar, who went for a walk while they talked. They should be on their way back by now, even if Aamir can't find them. They wouldn't miss the warning signs. We can't send the women and children to escape because we don't know how many are out there. It would be an easy trap." Mahavir looked back through my open door as I nodded at the judgment of their decision. "Do you know where Raphael might be right now? I haven't seen him."

My weapons belts were too big, so I had to tighten everything. Raphael was the *last* person I was worried about. He wasn't fragile like the rest of us, and he thrived in a fight against multiple opponents in open space. I focused on our mate bond, letting it point me. He was close enough, I knew he was already on guard, waiting for the enemy to show. He'd put himself between the house and the sound of the breach, probably not even taking time to grab any weapon. He didn't need weapons. He was ready the moment this had started and put his body on the line before anyone else was able. Out there, he could go into his demon form and be the weapon of mass destruction we might need.

"He's ready," I answered. "He's just outside the house on the western side. He doesn't need anything. He'll buy us time, then probably fall back. Or he'll go full demon and make whoever is here regret their life choices." I was finally finished when I secured my talwar at my waist and my katana at my back. The entire thing only lasted two minutes. Mahavir and I ran out of the suite, finding Nakul, Dalar, and Vikrant in the center of the courtyard. None of us were wearing any sort of armor, there wasn't time for that, but we all had our weapons.

"Our emergency plans say women have to go into the safe room, but I won't ask that of you," Nakul said, looking at me. "Your mate?"

"He'll be fine," I promised as Devesh ran toward the basement door carrying a diaper bag and a hundred other things. If the women and babies were stuck down there for long, they would need it all. "He's going to stay in the safe room, right?"

"Yes. He's the last line of defense." Mahavir looked at the basement for a minute. "He's too untrained to be out here. He'll be in the way, and he knows it. He also knows what to do if the basement is breached."

Die for the others. Devesh would throw his life between the enemy and the women and babies that needed him—one of those women his own mother. Devesh would do it, and his father knew it. By the look on his face, Mahavir also knew he would be dead by the time his son had to make that sacrifice.

"Who else is down there, Nakul?" I asked, knowing he had probably been here the entire time.

"Eleanor and Esh—"

I heard Raphael's roar and started running through the closest door to him and rounded the house at the top speed I could muster. He was in his cambion form. I stopped next to him, looking for what he saw. Walking through the thick jungle, the rakshasas were coming, and they outnumbered us.

Damn you, Mahatma. How did you even find us?

I drew my talwar and hissed. The questions could wait. The first thing we had to do was fight to survive.

They kept walking but slowed. I could see King Mahatma moving toward the front of the group.

"King Mahatma, you have one chance to turn around," I called out. "I don't know why you've tried to attack us, but it won't end well for you."

"We're finally going to become the dominant species of the subcontinent, and your dying people won't be able to stop us." Mahatma laughed. "You had a good bluff, Kaliya Sahni, but why should I fear ten nagas and a single demon? We have the power to defeat you, and we will. No one will ever know what happened except us, for the victor is the one who writes history, as it should be. I shall be a legend, the one who finally wiped the snakes off the face of the earth."

How did you know how many of us were here? Not exactly right, but way too close.

"Raphael, let's show him how bad a mistake he's made."

Raphael started shifting, his growl shaking me to my bone. He rose, a massive demon who could scale the house with ease, with large teeth, larger horns, and spikes shooting from the thick fur that covered him. I saw Mahatma's fear as he realized we had a supernatural WMD.

That wasn't all we had. I was weaker and slower than normal, but that didn't mean my magic was unavailable. I jumped, grabbing fur on my mate's side, and pulled myself up, shifting from human to monster. With a long snake body forming at my hips and replacing my legs, armor replaced my modern clothes, taking me to a more traditional look. I used my new size to help push me up Raphael's back, then pushed myself higher, using the snake half of my form to hold on to him. We were the perfect proportions for this. He roared as I drew my sword.

"Leave here!" I yelled, using my mate as a mount.

Raphael, my beautiful demonic mate, rose onto his back feet, and I moved a hand to his shoulder, holding myself up. I could only imagine the sight we made—monstrous, beautiful, powerful, horrifying.

"Or face the consequences!" I roared.

Mahatma was scared, but he looked up as if he could find answers in the sky, written in the clouds.

Something blocked the sun, and I followed his gaze up, confused.

With a cry sounding too close to that of an eagle, the massive bird started its dive.

I was caught in both reality and memories as I watched the golden bird of prey make its descent, disbelief paralyzing me as the horror of what I saw sank in.

No. This can't be.

Raphael made a move before I could. He grabbed my tail and pulled, taking me off my perch on his back. As the bird came close, he reached up and took a swipe. I heard his roar as black tar-like blood hit the ground next to me.

"Charge!" Mahatma roared.

"We need cover!" I yelled to Raphael as I got up. I couldn't fight in the open if that bird was who I thought he was.

It's not possible. Garuda is dead. *We have his bones.*

Raphael didn't reply, putting himself between me and the small army of rakshasa running for us. He kicked me with a back foot and growled back at me.

He wanted me to go, and I could figure out why. With the number of rakshasa coming, he wouldn't be able to kill all of them. Some would make their way inside. I could help protect the safe room, which was the most important thing.

I raced for the door, getting inside before the golden bird could attack again. I slammed into furniture as I entered the courtyard. Nakul, Mahavir, Dalar, and Vikrant were waiting, weapons drawn. When Dalar saw me, he dropped his sword.

"Pick it up," I ordered, trying to get my roughly thirty-foot length into the courtyard. "Damn this body," I hissed, slamming furniture with my tail to make more space.

"You're..." Dalar was retrieving his sword as Nakul talked quietly and quickly to his brother.

"Yes, Dalar. I have the power to use our legendary form. I know. Get ready. There's a fucking bird in the sky and at least sixty rakshasa outside."

"We saw the bird," Vikrant said. "It flew over us. It... Kaliya, it *blocked the sun*."

"I know," I said solemnly. That should have been enough evidence of not just the what but the *who*. I couldn't let myself think about that yet. First, we had to survive.

"Raphael is going to do everything he can to keep them from getting in here, but they will break through. There are too many of them. He can't come in here at his size. He would bring the building down on us. He's more effective on an open field." I looked around. "Have you blocked entrances yet?"

"The one you left through and came back is the only one left open," Mahavir said, pointing. We all paused as Raphael roared again, and the screams of his victims were heard.

"Then we'll prepare for them to come from there," I said, using my tail to slam the discarded couches in that direction to slow down the path of the rakshasa.

"Keep an eye for the sky," Nakul ordered as he took a better position in the courtyard. "Not just for the bird but for rakshasa trying to climb and use it as an entrance. This is the best place we have to fight. Today, we will fight because we must. Today, we will die if we must. The naga must persevere." Nakul lifted his sword. "For our people."

"For our people," Mahavir, Dalar, and Vikrant repeated, lifting their weapons, loyal warriors, righteous warriors.

Nakul looked at me.

"For our future," he said softly.

I lifted my sword.

"For our future," I agreed.

Above us, an angry cry came from the bird. Outside the walls of our home, screams of the dead and dying filled the air. All too soon, there was banging at the doors.

I couldn't get back into the hallway where the rakshasa would come in. I couldn't stop them at the door, but I wasn't the only one who had the idea to do that. Nakul and Mahavir, the most experienced warriors, took the position to be the first nagas the rakshasa met. I took the center of the courtyard, pushing Vikrant and Dalar closer to the safe room. They had to defend that door. We didn't have the time to send the women and children away, and I was grateful we hadn't gone that route. The bird would have been a fast end to it.

"Where's Aamir?" I asked quickly. "Saranya and Adhar?"

"None of them made it back," Vikrant explained. "They had baby Roshni with them. We locked the safe room when we saw the bird."

It was too late to find them. I could only hope Adhar had other ways to keep them safe. This was his home, and he knew all of its secrets. He had plans for plans, just like me.

"Get ready!" Nakul roared. "The door is going!"

I coiled, ready to strike, sword in my hand.

I wasn't trained for war, but I was damn ready to fight one.

32

CHAPTER THIRTY-TWO

The rakshasas came with weapons of all types, ready to draw blood and to wipe an entire people off the face of the earth. Nakul and Mahavir were a deadly duo. They started with chakram, throwing them down the hall and killing one with every strike. Once they were out of those, they met the next with swords. The first four dropped in the initial clash. The next group did better, able to tie up the brothers in duels in the confined space.

While the brothers were distracted, other rakshasas made their way around them, and I met them. I was faster than the rakshasas, cutting them down, slamming them away with my tail. While pushing them around would not kill them, it gave me a chance to focus on one or two at a time.

One tried to strike my long, snake body, but it healed as I drove my sword into his chest. I swirled and coiled around the courtyard, keeping them focused on me. I was the biggest monster in the room. It was probably self-deprecating to think of myself as a monster, but I had to believe it if I was going to keep the attention of the rakshasas. They needed to kill me if they wanted to win today and claim the precious lives we protected.

Outside, Raphael roared, and his stomps shook the earth. The cry of the mythical bird sent shivers up my spine. One sound was reassuring while the other was far from it.

I felt something heavy land on my back, sending my upper body down to the ground. I wasn't entirely helpless, though. I was thinner, frailer, but in this form, I had a thirty-foot body to throw around, giving me the momentum and power to shake off the attacker. When I was up again, I saw the one I knocked away, a rakshasa. Before I had the chance to attack, another three jumped in from the open space of the courtyard, having scaled our home.

I cut them down as they landed, knocking them away if I couldn't, and let Vikrant and Dalar do some of the work. There were so many of them, all with a singular focus—to kill us—at the order of their king.

That gave me a goal, an objective. The moment I saw Mahatma, I would aim for him.

I'm going to rip his damn heart out and feast on it.

Bloodthirsty, I screamed a battle cry and kept fighting.

I lost track of the death around me. It was relentless. I could feel the beginnings of exhaustion, my stamina running out. It was a reminder of two things. I wasn't trained for war, assassins not being built to do these long, drawn-out fights with so many enemies, and I was still recovering from Pavan's attempt on my life.

My swings were growing slower, and my hits were growing weaker. Pain lanced my tail, and I turned to see a few rakshasas attacking my body instead of facing me with my sword. I tried to wipe them away, able to shake them off for a moment, but I was healing slower as well. I ripped one of the swords out of my tail, another talwar like my own, and started using both. I wasn't trained in dual-wielding, but with so many enemies, I had to try.

While I was fighting, so were those around me. Dalar and Vikrant had a growing wall of bodies to contend with. The bodies were hindering them, getting in the way. The rakshasa couldn't know where our safe room was, but that didn't matter. If they defeated those two, they would hunt for others in the house, and those below would be found. I went over to them and knocked away rakshasas with a powerful swing of my tail, freeing the space of enemies, both dead and alive. In the moment I had stolen for them, with our enemies pushed back and recovering from my hit, I looked them over. Each was bleeding from a handful of places, but there was no way to check if they were fatal.

Vikrant gave his own battle cry and continued to fight while Dalar took a second to touch the black scales of my form. He nodded to me, then jumped back into the fray. I jumped back into the middle of the courtyard, knocking down a handful of rakshasas.

That's it. I can run them in circles and take them out as I move.

I had spent the fight coiling in one place, but I launched into a devastating attack. I was powerful, cutting through them with two swords, and they couldn't stop me. So long as I defended my human upper body, the soft bits so easy to hit, I could keep cutting them down. Mahavir gave a powerful and joyous scream in solidarity as I passed him and Nakul. I was practically riding the walls, spilling blood at a rate beyond anything I had ever done.

I'm not trained for war, but apparently, this body is made for it.

Feeling vicious and victorious, I dove back into the center of the room, taking on the rakshasa there, then I heard the scream of a man that echoed in my ears like nothing else could. I looked over the heads of my enemies to see Mahavir fighting, but his attention wasn't on his fight. He kicked his enemy away, and I tried to find what he was looking at.

Nakul's back was to me. His arms hung limply at his side, and his sword was gone. The only sword I could see was the one coming out of his back. Then it was gone, and my uncle—a man I had such a complicated relationship with—fell, and I knew he wouldn't be getting back up. I didn't know how to feel about that, and there was no time for me to process that.

The rakshasa who had gotten the fatal blow died quickly to Mahavir's rage.

Then I saw *him*.

Mahatma was inside. He'd made it past Raphael, whose fight was still raging outside, the sounds of which were a constant backdrop to our fighting.

"King Mahatma!" I roared. "Face me!"

He growled and ran through the crowd. I met his swords, our steel sliding. We locked hilts for a second, then he shoved off me, going for a downward slash from above. It was a long, slow arc, an attack only useful if you knew you could either overpower the enemy or they were nearly defeated. It was a foolhardy attack.

Sliding to the side, I cut a line through his armor and exposed ribs, then slammed him with my tail in a spin, sending him flying. I ignored the other rakshasas, who were trying to take down Vikrant, Dalar, and Mahavir, leaving their king and me in this dance.

I heard something slam into the house, a thud that made me look up.

The bird had landed. As I looked, it shifted, a magical moment from one form to another. Dressed in traditional armor, holding weapons that looked ancient, stood a man. He had a hawkish face, his hair the same rich dark brown or black many of us had. He looked like the perfect Hindi man, and women would kill to have him. He was beautiful, regal, and oh so deadly.

He jumped down into the fray.

"No introductions are needed," he said softly, lifting his sword.

No...anyone but you. A son, maybe, a descendant. It has to be because he can't be...

"Face me, Kaliya." He lifted his sword and pointed it at my heart. "And die to my blade as you should have centuries ago."

He charged, the path clear for him. I caught his attack. He was fast, as fast as when Nakul and I had sparred, pushing me to my limits. As I fought him, I knew Mahatma would come back, hoping to claim the glory of killing me himself. I was in for the fight of my life, desperately trying to survive. I wasn't in shape to take on this warrior. There weren't many naga in history who had ever achieved the peak physical condition needed to take him on.

He pushed me back, forcing me against a wall. Desperate, I shoved him back with my body. Before he could come back for me, Mahatma was in front of me, ready to claim the kill. I dueled with him until I could force him back as well, only to quickly turn and have to fend off my oldest of enemies.

Something cut across my back, and I hissed in pain, turning to kill the king, then took another injury from the fucking birdman. I couldn't allow myself a single moment to see how my people were doing. I couldn't hear anything except my heartbeat, using it as the beating, breakneck pace of this fight.

Growing weaker, my ability to block and hold the attacks back was growing ineffective. I could only be grateful everything was superficial, and my demon healing was able to keep up. Not well, but it was trying. It was the only thing keeping me from dying of a thousand cuts.

I lost the sword in my left hand, and my armor was being torn up.

A single roar broke through my concentration on trying to survive. I was looking at Mahatma when it rang through the space, then Mahatma was thrown out of my view. It was only a split second, a blur of gray, followed by screams.

I didn't question it or look for answers to what had just happened. I turned on my other foe and felt renewed, able to focus entirely on him. I was still tired, still weaker, but fiercer all the same, and that drove me.

As I dueled, Mahavir launched his own attack on this challenger. For the first time since he'd landed, I saw a small seed of doubt in him. Then Raphael came in, which forced the man to jump but not to dodge. He entered the air, his arms now wings, and went to the top of the building, staring down in disgust and fury.

"I should have known the rakshasas would be useless," he said. "This isn't over, Kaliya. This will *never* be over."

"Yeah?" I dropped my sword and lifted my hands. "You know where to find me. You've always known! Get your cowardly ass back down here, and let's finish it!"

"You snakes baited me with that once before. It won't happen again," he said, hatred coming through every word, lining every angle of his hawkish face. "I've worked too hard this lifetime to throw it away now. Your kind will meet your end. If not today or tomorrow, then someday, and I will kill you...personally." He pointed at me. "Kaliya, the renowned warrior, or as I like to call you, the *coward* who ran."

As he spoke, I was also surveying what was in my field of view. Embedded in the body of a rakshasa was a single chakram, one of Nakul's. It was so close. I just needed to keep him distracted.

He's a warrior with a grudge. Keep him talking, stroke the ego a little.

"You talk as if you know me."

"I do. We've played these games now for two lifetimes. I know you better than you know yourself," he sneered.

"Imagine my surprise when I heard you ran away in this life just as you did in the previous."

"So, this is it, huh? You kill us, we kill you, we're all reborn, and we do it again."

"That's right, and thank you for keeping my bones from my previous life. They're now in the hands where they should be," he said. "Until I wipe you out, I'll keep coming back. No matter what life I'm on, the only goal I'll ever have is to wipe out the naga, as I was *born* to do. No one will help you except these demons you keep finding."

"To think you're so petty you couldn't even enjoy just being fucking *alive*. No, you decided you wanted to continue the fight that two petty, competitive sisters started," I hissed, making known my disgust for him and his fucking vendetta. "None of us were there!"

New lives were supposed to be free of the past, learn from it, and not be condemned for it. Wars we fought and died in weren't supposed to be repeated in our new lives. In my heart, I believed without a doubt, it was *wrong* to continue fighting a battle from a previous life—nothing learned, nothing gained. Reincarnation was supposed to be a new chance at everything. That was what I was taught, and every moment I lived with the memories of my previous life, the more I truly believed it.

"You are nothing but a grown child, trying to fight the petty squabbles we should have left behind thousands of years ago," I snapped, wanting to cut him deep enough that he'd drop his guard enough for me to end this. "A mama's boy who thinks anyone still cares about any of this. You are nothing but an egotistical man-child who refuses to move on!"

"I will destroy you! It is my destiny!" he roared. I took my chance and dove for the chakram and threw it, memories flashing through my mind of how in my past life I was a natural with them.

Right as I expected it to carve into his chest, it flew through empty space. The cry, so much like an eagle, as I had mistaken it for so many times, was the last evidence he had ever been there as he disappeared from the sky.

I turned to my people and found them looking at me. At some point, those below had crept out of the safe room. They all saw me for everything I was, laid bare to them in a way I had never been before. All my secrets were out now, but it wasn't only that.

All the secrets were out now, even the ones I had been hunting for my entire life.

Mahavir slowly walked past me and picked up a single object, holding it out.

A feather.

Garuda's feather.

33

CHAPTER THIRTY-THREE

"We need to leave," I said, not taking the feather from Mahavir. I had so many problems to fix, and thinking about Garuda wasn't one of them. He was gone...for now. "Start loading essentials into Adhar's vehicles. We're taking both." I ran a hand through my hair. "I'm going to go find them. I have to. I'll be back."

"We'll be here," Raphael promised. "Be safe out there. I killed everything I could see until I ran out of things to kill and came in here, but you never know."

I nodded and worked through the bodies and broken furniture until I got out of the house. For safety, I stayed in my third form, twisting through the trees, searching every structure Adhar had on his property, wondering if they had found a place to bunker down. The bathhouse was empty, as were the work sheds and the small places Adhar built to pray in. Reaching the one furthest from the main house, I entered the meeting building, and the first thing that drew my eyes was the place where Garuda's bones had once been placed. He'd taken them, probably for his own fascination. Maybe it was to stop me from using them for magic to track him. Either way, they were gone.

I looked down and saw the evidence something was wrong here. I put my hands on the ground and started searching for a discrepancy, able to taste blood in the air and smell it. Finally, I felt a tiny draft between the boards and got my fingers into them. My arms screamed as I pulled, revealing a hidden hatch. Adhar had never told me, or possibly anyone else, about this.

The smells that hit me as I looked down made me want to puke, but I didn't let that stop me from heading down. I saw the bodies of three rakshasas upon entering the hidden basement. Then I saw Aamir, his eyes blank. He'd fought, and he'd lost.

I saw more bodies in the dark space. It was so dark, but I could see enough. I could also hear the softest of breathing. I found evidence of blood trails and followed them through the space until I reached the very thing I had been afraid of.

Adhar was against the wall, holding Saranya to his chest as though he was cradling a little girl. Tears flooded my eyes.

"Adhar? Saranya?" I whispered, reaching out to touch her neck first. There was no pulse. Saranya, the beautiful, cunning Saranya who played the game, was lost, and I couldn't do anything. I was powerless here.

My hand was shaking as I reached to touch Adhar's neck. The moment I made contact, he took a hard breath, his eyes flying open, surprised by my touch.

"Oh god, Adhar." I reached to move Saranya off him.

"No," he hissed, a weak whisper. Pain flashed in his face, but his eyes were blank as if he was fading fast. "Don't. You can't...save me."

From the smell of the blood, the obvious devastation in the room, I knew he was right. There were no healers and no hospitals even remotely close enough for us to reach. Humans would ask questions, and supernaturals might not be trustworthy.

"Adhar..." I sounded like a little girl now, pleading against the inevitable.

"Look..." he whispered, "at the...daughter of...my heart. My...cunning...snake."

I watched as he moved slowly to push Saranya's hair from her face. My jaw was shaking. Coming from Adhar, it was the highest praise, the most passionate declaration of love. Of course, he adored Saranya. She was a snake in human form, able to wait so patiently, then strike when she needed to. She was beautiful and smart. There was nothing more naga than that.

"She's *beautiful*," I whispered, tears pouring down my cheeks. I had faced death time and time again, but this one...I expected Adhar to live centuries longer than I ever would. I had expected him to always be here. "Adhar, I...I can't do this without you. Please. We were just starting to...finally figure this out. I'm not a good ruler. There's still so much..."

He had been my crutch for a hundred years. We'd fought so hard against each other, between the past and the future, but he'd always been my crutch. He did the things for our people I was too unemotionally unavailable to do. We had finally started listening to each other, to see each other, to heal. We could have done amazing things together.

I was losing him.

I'm not ready.

"I...am honored," he said, looking at me again, his eyes still blank, fading so fast. His hand tried to reach for me, and I picked it up. He curled his fingers weakly to cup my cheek. His hand was so cold. He was fading too fast, and I wasn't ready. "To see...one more...*Nagaraja*."

I sobbed as I felt life escape him and the last breathing body in this awful place stopped moving. I fell to the ground, slamming my hands on the earth, crying and screaming in fury and pain. I hit my fist against the dirt, my screams trying to let out the pain, and nothing worked.

The price to have answers was high. The price was always too high.

I was fucking tired of paying it.

Something touched my hand, and I opened my eyes. I was ready to fight, but there was no enemy there. A tiny snake, probably no more than five or six inches long, was trying to coil around my hand and wrist.

Seeing Aamir, Saranya, and Adhar dead, I hadn't even considered that one tiny heartbeat could have survived this.

I was barely breathing as I shifted into my human body, getting my normal clothing back. I didn't move my hand, letting the little snake explore. I didn't want to frighten her any more than she probably already was. Now wasn't the time to get bitten by a baby running completely on instinct.

I had to move, eventually, so I slowly lifted my hand, letting her get comfortable on my fingers like a natural snake would. She was a little chubby, which was a good sign.

Being a snake, though, wasn't a good sign at all.

A miracle wrapped in a problem of its own.

Slowly standing, I let this precious life give me the strength to stay on my feet. I knew I had to get us out of here, had to get away from the dead and the words Adhar had whispered with his dying breath. I lifted the little snake to my chest and covered it with my other hand, sheltering her.

I'll protect you. I failed them, but I'll protect you.

I headed for the ladder to get out of this place that would haunt my nightmares, turning back once.

She's safe with me, Saranya. I promise.

I climbed the ladder with one hand, then covered the little snake again and walked out of the building without looking back again. Mahavir and Raphael were standing outside, waiting for me. Raphael looked up, his eyes pleading.

"Thank you for not coming in," I said, my voice stronger. "Adhar, Saranya, and Aamir have fallen. We need to build a funeral pyre, and quickly, so we can put them to rest without poachers finding them. The poachers have the rakshasa. Let their corpses be butchered for the betrayal they've given us."

"Dalar and Vikrant have started building one for Nakul," Mahavir said, nodding. "And...what about..."

I stepped closer, letting him peek at the miracle I was

holding, and saw desperation and pain, but also joy on his face.

"I see," he whispered.

He also understood, as I did, we were not out of the woods yet, not even close.

"Continue preparations to leave while they build. Someone will have to go down and get the bodies. Aamir is near the ladder. Adhar and Saranya are in the back of the room."

"I'll do it now," Raphael said softly, walking past me. "Head back to the main house."

I nodded and started walking, my legs shaky, but I kept moving. Mahavir stood close, doing the same thing Raphael had done before. He was there to catch me if I needed it. Before we went inside, he sighed.

"About—"

"I'm sorry for Nakul," I said, trying to sound gentle, but it just sounded empty.

"Don't be." His eyes were pools of dark brown sorrow. "I am not sad he fell in battle. It was the way he always wanted to go, and we saved many in our part of the battle. I am sad...he will never know if it was *enough*."

"Mahavir..." I shook my head, not sure how to say the complicated thing that needed to be said.

"Speak freely, please."

"It wasn't and would *never* be enough for what he had done," I said, looking up at my uncle's brother. Nakul had been my uncle through marriage. He was the only thing that tied Mahavir and me into even remotely the same family. "He committed crimes that will haunt me and so many others for the rest of our lives. He'd been a broken man in all ways. There wasn't a sane thing about your brother during that. He knew that." I took a deep breath. "He *wanted* to die, Mahavir. You and I know that more than anyone. He was your brother, and I was his jailor. If I had executed him when he practically asked me to, I would have been giving him a peace he didn't deserve." I had no tears for my uncle. I couldn't and would never be able to summon them. I continued as my dry eyes met his tearful ones.

"What happened to him and his family was *evil*, what he did to others was *evil*, and the life he tried to live after was complicated and stained by *all* of it. He was both the victim and the villain, and one didn't get to excuse the other. There was *no* redemption for him in this life. He got to give his life and face that, though. He didn't run from death, didn't abandon his people. For that, he can be cremated with the others, and we'll let the gods sort out his complicated life. Only they know the true weight of who he was to judge the evil done to him and the evil he did. That's not for me to decide, and I'm *tired* of trying to reconcile the two halves of my uncle—the one who could make me smile and the one I couldn't look at. I'm tired, Mahavir."

I took a deep breath, trying to find my calm again. I had precious cargo, and she was moving around.

"I'm sorry," I whispered to her. "It's okay. Nothing is wrong."

"*I'm* sorry," Mahavir said, putting a hand over his heart. "I am, Kaliya. You're so young to be faced with these things, and...it all would have been easier if Adhar had allowed Nakul to be executed all those years ago."

"Would you have ever forgiven me for killing your brother?" I asked him honestly.

"I don't know," he said, giving me the truth.

"Don't...don't go back in time and say what if. We don't know anything, Mahavir. Maybe today, we would have lost if not for Nakul, and the gods kept him here until this very moment so he could fall in battle for us. Maybe *this* was his destiny. Apparently, we still have those types of things, destiny and all that. I don't know. You don't know. Adhar couldn't have known." I looked at the little snake in my hands. "We can only hope it's all worth it in the end, the hard choices and the mistakes. We can only hope any of this is worth it when we close our eyes for the final time."

I walked into the building without his assistance because there was no door anymore. Inside, Eshika and Basanti were talking over a couple of bags as though they were running through a mental list.

"Make sure you pack enough baby stuff for three," I said.

Eshika turned to me with wide eyes.

"And her parents? Adhar?"

I shook my head and saw Eshika's fire grow softer for a moment, then it roared back to life, and she nodded.

"I'll take care of everything she needs," the fierce woman promised, then ran for the suite where Saranya and Aamir had stayed.

Devesh ran past me, heading outside.

"I'm going to help with the funeral pyre," he called back to me. As everyone rushed around, I knew what I needed to do. I went to Adhar's office, which was untouched by the chaos. Struggling to control myself, I turned on his computer and connected to the internet, then plugged in the camera and made the hardest call of my life. There was only one person I could trust with this phone call. One person who always had a place for me to fall.

Cassius answered, clearly using his cellphone.

"Hello?"

"Hey, Cassius," I said, my voice shaking.

"Kaliya?" He blinked, wiping his eyes before narrowing them at the screen. "Kaliya, what's wrong? What happened?"

"We need your help. The nagas are leaving India."

34

CHAPTER THIRTY-FOUR

When I finished explaining, Cassius was already starting his plans to get us to Arizona and more, so much more. My people weren't safe staying here. I had to get them out before Garuda thought he could come back to pick us off. We were weak, our resources depleted, and our protections were destroyed. We didn't have time to pick Adhar's replacement. Until we were safe, I had to lead on my own.

My first act as the sole ruler of the nagas would be ripping them from the land of their ancestors. I would always be known as the one who lost India, but I didn't let the potential shame stop me from making the call.

When I walked back out and entered the courtyard, only Eleanor was waiting there.

"You were in there for a long time," she said, pale and strained. "We've loaded up essentials. Some men will have to ride in the back of the truck on top of stuff. The babies won't get car seats, either, but we'll make it work."

I did a mental count of everyone. I had just done it for Cassius, but I was fried.

Mahavir, Eshika, and Devesh. Dalar, Basanti, and the twins. Vikrant and Eleanor. Me, Raphael, and...

I looked down at the tiny snake, my chest growing tight.

Roshni.

"Twelve, three able to sit in laps, so nine," I said, nodding, trying to chase away the thoughts of the problem I couldn't and might never be able to solve.

"Mahavir told us...about..." She trailed off, looking at my closed hands. "It's true, then."

"Roshni is alive," I confirmed, finally allowing myself to say her name. "But I don't know for how long. We need to get her back into her human form, but there's really no way to convince her to do that. She was trapped in a room while the adults she relied on and trusted were killed. I think all we can do is make her feel safe and secure...and pray."

"I'll pray," she promised, her blue eyes shiny with tears I knew everyone wanted to shed. "If you need anything..."

"I need to get you all to safety," I said, starting the long walk outside. Rakshasa bodies were left behind among the furniture. In the mad rush, the people who betrayed us could rot in the sun. None of us would give them any respect.

Cassius said he would deal with it. He said he would deal with a lot for me. Thank the gods for good friends.

Eleanor walked beside me, showing me where the funeral pyre was ready, and the bodies of our loved ones waited. It was a necessity to burn them before we left, so they wouldn't be butchered later. The surrounding area was cleared to at least ten feet to keep the fire from spreading. What I didn't expect was pieces of the crate among the kindling.

Sitting between our fallen were the very reasons we were doing this. Adhar and I had never gotten around to dealing with that, saving for a later meeting to tell the other nagas once the immediate needs were addressed. I stared at a snakeskin purse, a lump in my throat as Mahavir waited to light the pyre on my order.

"I knew we had to handle it," Raphael whispered, coming to my side. "Is this..."

"Perfect," I said, nodding. "You did good. Thank you." I looked at Mahavir. "Light it."

He shoved the torch under one side of the pyre, then walked to grab a second from his son. He used it to light the other side, making sure it was burning as evenly as possible.

"I wish we could stay," I said, turning my back on the fire as Mahavir and Devesh joined the others. I stared at my people who needed me to make those fucking hard decisions now. When we were safe, I would get help, but not a moment before. We didn't have time. It was a whole event, and there were some traditions I wanted to keep now that Adhar was gone. For him.

"Do you know which home you want us to move to?" Mahavir asked, the oldest left.

"We're not staying here," I said, preparing myself. "I don't mean Adhar's home. I mean, we're not staying in India. We're not staying on the subcontinent we've called our home since the first nagas were born of Kadru. We're going to Arizona...America. There, I can better keep you all safe." I glanced at Raphael. I wished I could have talked to him about this, but he didn't seem surprised.

"We'll do it," he whispered, knowing my intention. "The cambions will keep the nagas safe, as one naga worked so hard to free us. I am more than willing to bring them to my home."

Aside from the fire growing behind us, it was silent, and his whisper carried to the others.

"With the cambions, you'll be safe. They're strong but small in number like us. They don't have a large community. They're a young, passionate species who's known great hardship, just like we have. Once I know it is safe to return to India, I will let you come home, but not a moment before. I can't let any of you stay. Maybe if our enemies had been only the rakshasas, but..." I closed my eyes, thinking of the hawkish man. He was more attractive in this life than he had been in the last. He could have been a beautiful warrior, fighting for good, but we were still doing the petty eye for an eye started by our mothers. That was one of the saddest parts.

Garuda was family. Our cousin.

"Garuda hunts in the skies over India," I said, opening my eyes to see them. "I won't let him take another naga. I hope you all understand."

"Then we should get on the road," Dalar said, looking at the others. Vikrant and Mahavir nodded at the same time. They were my hopefuls to replace Adhar.

"What about...the archives and everything here?"

Eshika asked. "I agree with you, I'm just...Adhar kept all of our history."

"I contacted a friend back home and gave him our exact coordinates. You don't know him, but you will. His name is Cassius. He's a prince of the fae and my longtime friend and ally. He's sending the most powerful members of their staff to collect anything and everything of value left behind, hopefully safely. They're all trustworthy. They'll be on a plane within the hour. We'll be taking that plane back to the United States without them. Unless this place is looted in the next few days, they'll save it all and bring it to us."

"And our homes?" Basanti asked in a small voice.

"As long as they stay secret, they're safe. You all have homes all over the subcontinent you rotate between. This is just...a new rotation. I'll bring you back, and if you don't want to come back, I'll get everything you want and bring it to you." I was asking so much from them, and none of them were arguing per se. These were legitimate concerns. After losing so much today, I was asking them to give away this one last thing, and it was so big.

"I'm ready," Mahavir said. "We'll follow you to America."

Others chimed in as we left the pyre to burn on its own.

We headed for the garage, where we struggled to load everyone into the cars.

"We're driving to Bangladesh to use the airport in Dhaka," I explained before giving Mahavir the keys to the pickup. Raphael and I would drive the SUV while Mahavir and Vikrant drove the truck. "Follow us. If I look back and don't see you, we'll pull over. Keep Devesh *in* the truck. Dalar, you, or Vikrant can ride in the back with the bags."

With no disagreement, he got in the truck, and I got into the SUV, unable to start the trip as the driver, thanks to Roshni. She refused to move to anyone else. Crammed in the back of my SUV were Eshika, Basanti, and Eleanor, with the terror twins taking two laps and a diaper bag taking the last one. We buckled in and started the drive.

It was a long drive, and no one talked more than a few minutes unless it was to a crying baby. I kept an eye on the sky for any sign of Garuda, hoping he'd headed back to wherever the fuck he'd come from.

The things I screamed at Garuda in my head during the drive weren't things I would ever repeat, even to my mate or our closest friends.

I bribed the patrol at the border with more money than needed to get my people into Bangladesh. We entered Dhaka six hours later, and I felt a little more comfortable, knowing it would be harder to find or follow us in the massive crowd.

Not for Garuda. He had to have been the...the eagle I heard when Raphael and I landed.

We were allowed into the airport and pointed to a hangar for private planes. Inside, I let everyone get out as I dealt with the guilt I was trying not to face.

He'd been right there the entire time. I knew what he sounded like. I must have recognized him and not even realized it. I could have known we were in danger, and I...

When the plane with Cassius' team landed, I shook

their hands, thanking them for their help. They were all so respectful.

Then I saw Leith. He said nothing as he wrapped his arms around me.

"You..." I let him hug me for a long time. "You're too proper for hugs."

"No, I'm not," he said gently. "I'll be flying back with you, helping everyone get comfortable for the flight. Injuries?"

I looked back. Dalar had a bad cut we didn't want to look at. Vikrant was going to keep a scar over his cheek and lips for the rest of his life.

"Yeah, we have a few, nothing fatal, but a lot of it should be cleaned as soon as possible."

"We'll handle it on the plane. They'll let us load for safety before they refuel and prep to leave," Leith said.

I led my people onto the airplane. For some of them, it was the first time they would ever fly, not yet having the chance to take the bush plane Adhar and Nakul had bought, and this wasn't a bush plane. None of them had been on a modern passenger flight. Cassius had to have spent a lot of money I didn't want to think about, to get us this one, this fast.

He told me not to worry about it. There's so much other stuff I have to worry about.

"The entire staff is supernatural," Leith explained to me. I hadn't been paying attention. "Fae, werewolves, and a witch."

"Whose...plane is this?" I asked.

"Alvina's or rather the Tribunal's. Cassius called them to say one of their own, an executioner and ruler, needed an immediate evacuation for a small group. They let him take this plane. They knew who he needed it for but don't know anything else, only that you came to India, and now you need to get out quickly with others."

I sat down, breathing hard. It weighed on me, not having Adhar to play politics. The Tribunal just existing…I hadn't even considered them yet.

"Great. I need to speak to Cassius as soon as we get in the air. I need to push that meeting with them to the first moment after we land. The nagas have had a change in leadership, and the Tribunal has to be notified," I whispered. "You can go help everyone else. Everyone speaks English, so don't worry about a language barrier."

Leith nodded and went to meet the other nagas and their mates, shaking hands and taking drink orders. He comforted Basanti, who looked as if she was about to cry at his kind professionalism.

When the plane took off, I had two thoughts on my mind.

First, my people were refugees.

Second, this had all been my fault.

Roshni curled around my fingers, and my chest tightened painfully.

All my fault.

35

CHAPTER THIRTY-FIVE

Arizona was blissfully hot, and my people didn't know how to feel about it. There were things I would have to teach them about dealing with this level of dry heat, lotions, hydration, and all of that. It would keep their feet from drying and cracking if they stuck with it.

It was a stupid, mundane thing to worry about, but their care was my responsibility. I told them that as we landed, and at least the women listened to me. This was important to the health and comfort of their children.

I didn't speak again until we stopped our caravan of SUVs at the cambion compound. Raphael greeted Sammy, then Mateo. Gabi ran forward, asking Raphael a thousand questions. He pointed out our injured, then I saw him point to me. Gabi came to me, and I was glad someone told her to keep the wings hidden, which would have scared the shit out of my people.

"Kaliya," she cried, throwing her arms around me. Raphael had sent word once we were in American airspace. I let her hug me, even attempted to return it. A few of my naga and humans hovered, watching the exchange. When Gabi pulled back, she left her hands on my bare arms, looking me over with a frown. "I...he said you had gone through something, explained it to me while you were on the plane, I promised I would see if I could do anything...Kaliya..."

"Tell me what you see...or feel, whatever it is you do. I'm strong, Gabi."

"The venom and the healing? It's left major scarring." She closed her eyes. "You protected your brain and your heart the most, with minimal damage. Lungs have some, but you can get back to what you were. The damage isn't too severe to hinder you. Your liver, kidneys, and others? Lots of scar tissue. I can't heal scars. You'll need to see someone else. I'm sorry."

"It's okay," I murmured. "Gabi, I survived. That's all I needed. I'm immortal. Scars fade. Eventually. The body will continue to repair itself over time, cells replacing themselves."

"Okay. Also, cute baby snake in your pocket."

Taking my chance, I called Vikrant and Dalar, then took Roshni out of my pocket. She had slithered in there on the drive from the airport, but I was more comfortable with her in my hands.

"Leave mine," Vikrant ordered. "I want to keep the scar."

"I can leave the scar and just heal it faster," Gabi said. "Please?"

"What is she?" Dalar asked me, licking his lips. I was grateful one of them noticed her uniqueness.

"Nephilim," I answered. On cue, Gabi revealed her

stunning wings. I didn't react, but some of my people took a step back as well. Fear and instinct were powerful things. "Not a bird. An angel. More accurately, the angel equivalent to a cambion. She's under their protection."

"They're my family," she countered.

"That too."

I stepped back and withdrew, closing in on myself as I watched Gabi heal. Raphael started introducing his people to mine. Two worlds clashed, looking at each other with curiosity and caution. Two sets of refugees, each at different stages.

Cassius and Sorcha were around, but I didn't see them. Instead of finding either of my friends, I was suddenly faced with a whole lot of Sammy.

"Yes?" I asked her, rubbing my temple as she stared at me, slowly drawing closer.

"Are you okay?" She crossed her arms, wanting to know, one warrior to another.

"There's no being okay. Not for me. Not anymore."

"Yeah? You sure?" She came a little closer and stopped directly in front of me. She was full-blown attitude, a mix of tough, condescending, petty, and bitchy. She was fucking Sammy.

My temper snapped.

"What do you want, Sammy? We don't talk. We haven't in five and a half months, close to six. I understand why, but if you're going to cut me out, please don't come and harass me when I'm in a terrible fucking mood. It's only fucking fair, and I need a shred of fair right now." I glared at her, poking her in the chest. "So, you can fucking get lost!" I thrust my finger to the desert, telling her exactly where I thought she could take her shit attitude. Roshni curled around the fingers of my other hand, not liking when I lost my temper.

Sammy didn't move and smiled.

"There's Kaliya."

I dropped my hand and stared at her, wondering when the fuck she had grown a second head. Just because I couldn't see it didn't mean it wasn't there.

"You lied to me, but you and Raphael have been gone. I…figured I was going to forgive you when you got back. I wasn't expecting you to come back like this."

"Why?"

"Because you let me be mad at you. You took it all that time. So yeah, I was planning on seeing if you wanted to try friends again. But then you get here, and you all look like you've been running through a jungle for weeks."

"We kind of were," I muttered, shaking my head.

"I've seen you get through a lot of things and do it with your head held high. You always fight your hardest, yet you look so…defeated."

"I lost people I wasn't prepared to lose," I whispered, lowering my head. "I took my people out of their home…"

"Did you fight your hardest?"

"I did. I really did."

"Then you did literally everything you could," Sammy said, throwing her hands up. "You don't need me to tell you this."

"It was my fault."

She slammed a hand against the back of my head and had me staggering before I went down to my knees. She had enough control not to crack my skull open now. In fact, she had too much control because she hit me literally as hard as she could without causing permanent damage.

"Say something stupid again, I dare you," she growled.

She wasn't the only growl. Raphael's rumbled over the space, a clear warning he was not in the mood for our bullshit.

"She said this was all her fault!" Sammy yelled. "Your mate is a fucking idiot!"

"I heard him," I whispered. I repositioned and sat on my ass, staring at the baby snake in my hands. "Garuda was spying on us from the sky, and I should have known. I should have—"

"Sure, because just *anyone* would think, 'Oh, that *bird* is totally our arch-enemy reborn and has his memories just like me, even though I got mine back through some fucked-up magic my mom did on me.' Come on. Seriously?" Sammy put her hands on her knees, coming down to my level. I knew Raphael had relayed the story, including that little detail, because I told him to. I had to own my failure. "Think about that for a fucking minute. If you didn't consider it, no one would have. You *literally* overthink everything."

Now, Sammy was making me regret that.

"Sammy, I have it from here," Sorcha said. I closed my eyes, so grateful to hear her voice.

"Good. She's not a fucking idiot, and she shouldn't fucking act like one," Sammy snapped, stomping off.

"Thank you," I whispered, standing up with Sorcha's help, her hand gentle but firm on my elbow. We hugged in a tight embrace once I was steady on my feet, and I carefully kept my little snake away from her.

"Sadly, we can't talk right now," she said, rubbing my upper arms. "Cassius got the meeting rescheduled, and they're going to convene for you in one hour. They have to if there's a change in leadership for one of their species. He asked me to come get you so you can get cleaned up and ready."

"Thank you."

I waved at Mahavir, telling him quickly where I was going and why. He nodded and passed it along before turning back to me.

"We'll stay close to Raphael. He's already talking about finding us places to sleep. You have a good mate with him."

"I know." I patted his shoulder and left.

I showered, with Roshni still hanging onto me, then let Sorcha help with the mess of my hair. She didn't ask why my face was bony or why my body was model-thin instead of athletic. She didn't ask about why my clothing wasn't charmed like most supernaturals' clothing, so it was loose on me now.

I got ready. I had to keep moving, dealing with the mess left behind. I couldn't go forward until I dealt with the problems facing me now.

"Okay, one more thing," she said, shoving me out of the house. "They wanted to see you before you went to the Tribunal. Since they're your people, I said yes."

I stared at my people, wondering what they needed. She must have talked to them while I was showering, the only time she wasn't in the bathroom with me.

"Do you want to name someone as the male representative now?" I asked. "I recommend Mahavir, with Vikrant as a second option."

"We would like to beseech you to take the role only you can," Mahavir said, going to one knee in front of the rest of them. "Practical reasons are easy to find. You have allies and political experience. You have been a ruler since you were a child—"

"I'm not good at it," I said, cutting him off. "Mahavir—"

"You *are* good at it, and you grow better at it every day," he countered. He looked over his shoulder and nodded to the others. They all went to one knee, giving me hopeful looks. "You are our power, the most powerful of us, reclaiming things from our past. You...you are Kaliya, the Demon Serpent, just as you were in your last life. Am I wrong?"

"No," I whispered. Of course, one of them would have put the pieces together and figured it out. "You're not wrong."

"So, you know..."

"So did Adhar and Nakul," I explained.

"Even better," he said, lowering his head. "We have spoken in whispers. The idea came to me when you spoke to me about my brother. Dalar, Vikrant, and Devesh agreed. Our mates agreed. You don't need a man of our people to stand beside you. You have a strong man already there, your partner, your mate. He is the Warlord of the cambions, sole ruler of his people... We would like to declare you the *Nagaraja*."

I put my hand over my heart, wondering if I could

breathe. As Adhar had said, that word came back for me. I wasn't ready.

"Mahavir, I knew the bird—"

"I heard you whisper to yourself during the flight. You also spoke in your sleep. No one here blames you, but if it rides you so hard, then go kill him...as the *Nagaraja*."

"What does that mean?" Sorcha asked softly over my shoulder. I looked over the nagas and saw my mate standing behind them, hands in his pockets. He nodded, understanding what was happening. Someone had told *him*.

"It means...king of the nagas," I answered. "Though, in English, I'd go by queen." I bowed as deeply as I could. "I accept this honor with all of its responsibilities. I will be the *Nagaraja*. I will fight for you, and I will rule with care and, hopefully, wisdom. I'll reclaim our homelands. I'll do it all." I came up from the bow. "Get up. Would you like to sit in for the Tribunal meeting?"

"I would," Mahavir said.

"Anyone else?" I asked, looking at them. They all took one step forward. I looked back at my best friend. "Can we get them all in?"

"Of course. You're declaring a change in leadership for your people. Having them there looks better for you, especially with *this* change." Sorcha looked a touch concerned. "They don't like changes like this."

"We were ruled by the *Nagaraja* long before we had two representatives to the Tribunal," I countered. "They'll suffer the decision of my people. They allow Raphael to rule alone. They'll allow me."

Sorcha nodded, then led us to the door into the

Tribunal chambers. Raphael came to my side, taking my hand.

"It was between you and them," he whispered as Sorcha opened the door. "But I agreed with them and told them not to let you say no."

I looked at him as we walked in. Sorcha pointed out places for the naga and their mates to sit. Roshni was curling around my left hand and its fingers. My right hand was in Raphael's. He let go of my hand, sitting at the closest spot he could, as I went before the Tribunal.

"Kaliya, you have important news for us about the status of the nagas," Hasan said, looking like a worried father.

"I do. Adhar is dead, murdered by enemies of my people, the rakshasas. They betrayed a peace treaty we made, allied themselves with Garuda, and attacked us. Behind me..." I waved to my people with my free hand. "Is all that remains of my people."

"Our condolences," Alvina said, leaning forward, clearly troubled by the news. Others nodded. Adhar was reclusive, like all of my people, but he was well liked when he showed his face. They had all known him since the founding of the Tribunal itself. "It is early. You don't have to name a replacement for Adhar."

"There won't be a replacement for Adhar. My people made their decision and have asked me to pass it to you."

"Are you leaving the Tribunal's oversight?" She seemed surprised. "We can and will help you. You've done so much for the supernatural community during your tenure with us."

"No, we're not leaving. However, we are *telling* you, not

requesting, that we have a single ruler, declared the *Nagaraja* by the entirety of our people."

"With so few nagas remaining, I'm certain we can allow it without complaint..." Corissa seemed confused, looking up and down the long table where the others sat on either side of her. Alvina was the first to nod, and the others all followed, not a single complaint being brought.

"Let the king of the nagas step forward," Hasan said, intrigued. "And tell us his name."

"You may call me Kaliya Sahni, the Demon Serpent, Queen of the Nagas," I declared, raising my chin, daring any of them to question the judgment of my wonderful, powerful people.

My first act will be to hunt down Garuda and end his reign of terror once and for all.

EPILOGUE

ONE LITTLE LIFE

I was running out of ideas for the little snake sleeping on my fingers. Raphael paced as I sat in bed and stared at her. He looked pretty funny in plaid pajamas, but I had asked him to wear some.

After three days in Arizona, there wasn't a single person on the compound who didn't know about little Roshni. Explaining to the cambions was difficult for my people, but everyone knew the problem now.

"Why can't she stay like that for a little while? Why are we trying to rush her?" he asked again. For the hundredth time, he needed to hear it.

"She'll either starve or go wild if she doesn't return to her human form. I don't want a baby to starve, and we... we can't let her go wild, Raphael. We absolutely can't allow that." As much as it broke my heart, there were strict rules about nagas going wild, for everyone's safety.

"We can go to...the pet store..." He ran a hand through his hair, giving me a desperate look. He wanted to save her just as badly as I did.

"And get her baby mice to eat?" I asked. "Feeding her like a pet snake and basically telling her we're fine she doesn't want to be a baby? Raphael, it's way too early in her life to let her think more like a snake than a human. Her snake will always be fully developed and ready to go, as it is right now. We can't let her skip learning to be... human, for lack of a better word, or she will be a *wild snake*. So, she either starves, goes wild, or comes back to us. Two of those involve dying." I ran a finger over her little head. She was a beautiful sunset of colors, all the reds, oranges, and yellows I could think of. Fire.

"We're lucky she's not dead yet, a healthy baby instead of a sick one. Sick babies will turn into snakes, a natural defense mechanism, but they don't know what to fight, and they...they normally die in a couple of hours. It's only happened a few times in our history. Roshni is the first healthy baby who has gone into snake form and refused to come back that any of us has heard about. Adhar probably would have all the answers, but...he's not here."

That still killed me inside to think about.

"So, you're going to put her back into the terrarium for the night?" His shoulders were slumped. My powerful, confident mate faced a challenge neither of us knew how to face.

"No, tonight, I'm going to try something else. I'm her queen, so I have to try everything before I give up. I need to help her, or I will never forgive myself," I whispered. "She's going to stay with us."

"What?"

"You heard me." I wiggled enough to get my legs

under the covers. "I was asking Eshika and Basanti, and they all co-sleep. Saranya and Aamir did, too. She's used to sleeping with her parents. We're going to..."

"She knows we're not her parents," Raphael said softly.

"But maybe we're safe. We're going to do it, anyway."

I laid back, putting Roshni on my chest, letting her feel me breathe, my heartbeat, my warmth. Raphael looked uncomfortable as he got into bed.

"This is why you wanted me to find pajamas, huh?"

"Yeah," I whispered.

I couldn't sleep. Staring at the ceiling, I felt her scales over my skin as she curled up between my collar bones.

Saranya, I'm trying. I'm trying so fucking hard. Please be right about her and me, about our bond as naginis. I just want to help her. I'm not a mother, not her mother. I can't replace you, but please be right about us. Let her see me as safe enough.

Eventually, the stress and exhaustion caught up with me, and my eyes drifted closed. Raphael's soft snore was one of the last things I was aware of.

I dreamed, just flashes of things I would forget when I woke up.

"Kaliya," Raphael's voice cut through those watercolor dreams.

I opened my eyes, groaning.

There was a baby between us, sleeping peacefully between my shoulder and Raphael's chest.

"I...I was going to roll over, and something woke me up," he whispered.

I closed my eyes and fought tears as I touched her

chubby cheek. She didn't stir. I lowered my head to the pillow and cried, muffling it in the pillow while Raphael rubbed my back.

When I was done crying, I sat up and pulled her to my chest, letting her snuggle into me. I played with her thick hair as Raphael got up to quietly spread the word. This was too important.

"I'll protect you," I whispered, my solemn promise. "And I'll tell you all about your mom and dad. I'll tell you about Adhar and so many others." I kissed her head and held her until the sun came up.

Then I went to show her the new world she was going to live in, one where she could be who she wanted to be, do what she wanted to do, and there would be no limits. I wouldn't let a single person put walls around this little survivor, this tiny warrior. Not now. Not ever.

Her little life meant too much to me.

She had been the last battle we had to fight, our little Roshni. The last battle, for one little life, but it was a victory I needed. It was a victory my people needed. Everyone else could rest easier knowing our little Roshni was going to be okay.

Now I just needed to win the war.

DEAR READER,

Here we are, at the end of Kaliya Sahni's penultimate book. Only one more and what a journey this woman has been on. I almost gave her goodness and happiness in this book. She's finally matured enough to talk about things instead of arguing about them. Because she can do that, she was finally repairing relationships that have been broken for a century.

Oh, and uh... sorry for killing so many people. You know, I genuinely fell in love with Saranya. I wasn't expecting to. Her, Adhar, and all the women of this story. Introducing her to the story and finding this gloriously beautiful woman of a character only to know her fate was really hard.

That's all. I hope you'll all stay with me to see these characters to their finale.

DESTINY
KALIYA SAHNI BOOK 6
COMING IN MAY 2022

Dear Reader,

If I still have you head over to my website to get the latest updates on the next book in the series. Head over to my website and sign up for my mailing list! There are exclusive teasers and shorts for those who are signed up:

knbanet.com/newsletter

And remember,

Reviews are always welcome, whether you loved or hated the book. Please consider taking a few moments to leave one and know I appreciate every second of your time and I'm thankful.

THE TRIBUNAL ARCHIVES

Kaliya Sahni is a series set in the world of The Tribunal. Every series is written so it can be read alone. For more information about The Tribunal Archives and the different series in it, you can go here:

https://knbanet.com/worlds/tribunalarchives/

ACKNOWLEDGMENTS

I'm very bad at giving really public praise. I shower people in praise in private. But that's not everyone's love language and that's okay.

So this little page shall now be dedicated to everyone who helps me get these books from the concept to the release and beyond. From my PA, to my editor and my proofreader, to my wonderful friends helping me through the hardest moments. To my husband, who doesn't read my books, but loves that I write them and is willing to listen to me talk about them for hours.

And to you, the reader, for without you, I wouldn't have anyone to share these stories with. I'm a storyteller at heart and you have given me the greatest gift of listening.

I love all of you. Thank you for continuing to go on this journey with me.

ABOUT THE AUTHOR

KNBANET.COM

Living in Arizona with her husband and 5 pets (2 dogs and 3 cats), K.N. Banet is a voracious... video game player. Actually, she spends most of her time writing, and when she's not writing she's either gaming or reading.

She enjoys writing about the complexities of relationships, no matter the type. Familial, romantic, or even political. The connections between characters is what draws her into writing all of her work. The ideas of responsibility, passion, and forging one's own path all make appearances.

facebook.com/KNBanet
instagram.com/Knbanetauthor
bookbub.com/authors/k-n-banet
amazon.com/K.N.-Banet/e/B08412L9VV

ALSO BY K.N. BANET

The Jacky Leon Series

Oath Sworn

Family and Honor

Broken Loyalty

Echoed Defiance

Shades of Hate

Royal Pawn

Rogue Alpha

Volume One: Books 1-3

The Kaliya Sahni Series

Bounty

Snared

Monsters

Reborn

Legends

Destiny

Volume One: Books 1-3

The Everly Abbott Series

Servant of the Blood

Blood of the Wicked

Tribunal Archives Stories

Ancient and Immortal (Call of Magic Anthology)

Hearts at War

Full Moon Magic (Rituals and Runes Anthology)

Made in the USA
Middletown, DE
03 May 2025